DARKENED HOPE

World of Nälu

The Short Stories

The Hidden Dagger Trilogy

THE HIDDEN DAGGER TRILOGY
BOOK TWO

DARKENED HOPE

J. L. MBEWE

BROKENSEED
BOOKS

Darkened Hope
The Hidden Dagger Trilogy
Book Two
First Edition:
10 Year Anniversary

Published by BrokenSeed Books
San Antonio, Texas

ISBN-13: 978-0692637333
ISBN-10: 0692637338

DEDICATION

To Mom
Who foresaw the future of computers
and made me take keyboarding.

To Dad
Who loaned me *The Sword of Shannara,*
and I've been hooked on epic fantasy ever since.

Thank you!

Secrets Kept

Semine

To some, she is the sorceress. To others, she is the high priestess of Raezana, a glorious being trapped in the Underworld. To the guardians, she was once a promising student until she turned against them. With a curse, she builds her army as she prepares to release Raezana, but first she must find the corrupted dagger and the prince whose blood will open the portal to the Underworld.

Derk

"Want to be king?" Semine had asked. They had once been friends, but Raezana had destroyed that. Derk had lived as an exile among thieves and murderers until Semine had sent for him. She needed someone to hold the power of the curse, and she had chosen him. Now, he plays king and waits for Semine's plan to unfold.

Ayianna

After the enemy killed her father and kidnapped her mother, Ayianna joined Kael, Desmond, and Vian on a journey across the shifting sands to discover a tonic that will free the plains people from the sorceress's curse. At Bonzapur, Desmond pushes her to finalize their betrothal with the promise of returning home to rescue her mother, and she gives in. After all, who would want a bride marred by harpy venom? Except Desmond didn't return as promised, and now she must head farther west in search of the ingredients for the tonic.

Liam

Ayianna's constant companion. The wolf was a gift from her brother when they had first moved from Zurial to live among her mother's people in the plains.

Kael

The son of an elven lord, Kael was determined to follow in the footsteps of his father until tragedy struck—not once, but twice—losing all he held dear. When Dagmar was destroyed, his plan to join the guardians was strengthened, his vow to never love again resolute. Except he hadn't expected his journey to become so entangled with his best friend's sister, Ayianna. After escaping the harpies in Nganjo, he set out to find the tonic that would set the plains people free from the sorceress's curse. Unfortunately, the High Guardian wouldn't let him go alone.

Desmond

Desmond is a draper of the finest silks and weaves and a dashing young man with an eye for the royal courts of Badara. He is as shrewd as he is handsome and wants nothing more than to be Prince Vian's right-hand man. To fulfil the position, he needs a wife, so he chose Ayianna.

Prince Vian

Son of King Valdamar of Badara, Prince Vian lived a sheltered life of ease, but his father was distant, and the servants whispered behind his back. When his father's kingdom was overthrown, he escaped with the aid of his friend, Desmond. He sought answers from the Guardian Circle, but much to his dismay, he was sent west to help Kael find the cure that would release his people from the curse, instead of storming the castle and rescuing his father.

Tariq

A feline-shapeshifter and the nephew of Queen Emani of Bonzapur, Tariq traveled through the jungles, dealt with the natives, and accompanied his uncle on business trips to Ganya. He is the perfect guide for the quest. But he isn't worried about getting them to where they need to go, it's the creatures they will encounter on the way that has him concerned. He has prepared them for the worst, but will it be enough?

Captain Eloith

Captain Eloith once served under Queen Leora when the fairies once ruled. After the Great Fairy Rebellion, Eloith and a handful of other fairies were imprisoned and forgotten until Ayianna and her companions stumbled upon them within the Forest of Inganna. He has joined the quest to save Nälu.

The Guardian Circle

Saeed

High Guardian and Headmaster of the Kayulm'sa Nutraadzi. The oldest living elf among the nations, he saw the last sacrifice performed and was one of the first to volunteer to become a guardian, even if he was only five years old at the time. But he'd rather forget those memories. Unfortunately, Semine is dragging them back as she seeks to undo that last sacrifice and release Raezana from the Underworld.

Nerissa

She is a merwoman from Ganya, and an ambassador to her people, the Kaleki. She aims to convince the merking to join the Alliance and bring with him the aid of the dragons.

Darin

He is a half-giant from Moruya Island and an ambassador to the Pauden, who hopes to restore the relationship between the giants and the rest of Nälu.

Hadrian

An Igazin dwarf with a questionable past. He is an ambassador to all the dwarven clans except the Stozic, where he is no longer welcomed. He will rally whom he can to aid in the fight against Semine.

Leora

A fairy, thought to be the last of her kind until Ayianna released them from the dungeons of Mandar.

Unai

The only human among the guardians. He is the ambassador to the people of the plains and the coastal city, Praetan. He is Saeed's closest friend and the most likely choice to become the next High Guardian.

Lazar

A Haruzo from Arashel, feline shapeshifters of the north, and the youngest guardian. He seeks to bring Arashel's power to aid the Alliance, but he is not hopeful.

Raezana

The glorious being bound in the Underworld. The guardians call her Taethza and believe her to be the queen of the Underworld. Sometimes she is referred to as the goddess.

Vituko

The Shadow God of the guardians. Also known as One-With-Many-Names, Dreyu Osaryn, Kvamiig, Parzan, Parzanah, Akonamalihi. The giver of the Yenzo Tanil and eternal ruler of Zohar.

The Nuja

The divine quartet embraced by the humans and protector of the seasons.

The Sacred Pearl

Karasi is a spirit from Zohar imprisoned in a large pearl. She once guided the guardians but hasn't spoken in centuries. She was stolen away during the attack on Dagmar.

Across the shifting sands, you will find
A release from that which binds
These ingredients you seek
Among the sea and mountain peaks

The Dwalu Tonic

Silver pure
Mind secure
Into the belly of the earth
Grows a tree of hailed worth
Through a maze of dark and stone
Hangs the silver pinecone

Water Pure
Wound's cure
Upon earth's end
Gathering rivers bend
To the sacred waters beneath the land
Drawn only by virgin hand

Roots pure
Strength's endure
In a land giant's roam
A cave fills with foam
Where healing streams flow
The deepest roots do grow

PART ONE

1

THE HUGE SWATH of downed trees crushed Ayianna's hope of passing through the mountains alive. A stench of wet metal and rancid fish clung to the underbrush and burned her throat. Underlying decay triggered a ripple of needles down her spine. She should know that scent, but it fled beyond her recall. Deep grooves scarred the earth, and several mangled trees blocked their path. A beast or two had been there, perhaps fought or bedded down at one point. But where was it now?

To the left and the right, prickly ash boxed them in, except where their thorny limbs had been crushed. The pines and oaks that hadn't been destroyed towered above them. Their boughs twisted in odd, distended shapes, perhaps harboring dead or deformed limbs. If she squinted, she might have imagined eyes glaring at her, the spindly branches reaching toward her as if to snatch her away, their shadows creeping over the destruction in the waning sun. The caw of a crow broke the silence and sent another wave of needles down her back.

Her companions sheathed their weapons and fanned out, exploring the damage. They would have to climb over the fallen trees if they wanted to continue on the trail and find shelter before evening descended upon them like thieves.

Ayianna stepped over the churned dirt and branches, but her foot caught, and she pitched forward. She grabbed at the brush, its thorns digging into her palms. Pain shot up her hand and into her arm. She recoiled and regained her balance, her movement awkward in the stiff leather cuirass the queen had outfitted for her. The extra layers didn't help, but at least she was warm against the increasing cold. And not wearing a dress.

Kael glanced back at her, and his dark gaze held hers for a moment. The scar across his right eyebrow bulged as his frown deepened. His long, black hair hung loose past his shoulders, the gold earring in his curved ear glinted through the strands. He turned to survey the damage. He was ever difficult and colder than winter. Surely, with as much elf blood as he had burning in his veins, he could have been more cordial.

No. Ayianna rubbed her stinging palm on her pants. It was her fault he was like this. If she hadn't been so rash and signed Desmond's betrothal contract, he wouldn't be avoiding her. But why did it bother him? It wasn't as if he had given her a real reason to defy Desmond and her duty to her family. His care for her was nothing more than a vow to her brother. The sooner she accepted that, the better she would be able to embrace her decision. Didn't he understand that she did what she had to do?

Liam's wet nose pushed into her palm. She sat, subdued, without her usual crooked, wolfish smile. Burs collected in her gray fur, around her legs, and along her tail. Ayianna groaned. She'd have to cut the burs out when they made camp.

She rubbed Liam's ears. "Has the danger passed, girl?"

Maybe the damage had nothing to do with them or their quest. It could have been animals fighting, like bears. Mountain bears were big. Except they would have been hibernating already. Could they have caused this much damage?

A dozen or so pine trees and three broad oak trees had been knocked over and the soil pulverized. The branches of the remaining trees drooped as if mourning the loss of their fallen companions. No doubt the dryads were in mourning.

Ayianna straightened. The dryads! They would know what happened.

She dug out her small wooden flute and blew on it, but only silence answered her back. Couldn't the dryads see she was a friend? Or did such devastation quell their little souls? The shadows darkened between the prickly underbrush and evergreens. Perhaps the threat was still near, hiding, waiting to pounce. Like the cat-beast of the Inganno Forest. Ayianna's breath caught. No. She couldn't—*wouldn't*—think about such things or her fear would destroy her.

Besides, she was armed now. She had a sword and the noqui stones that could turn anything to salt. She would fight her fear and win. Maybe not with the sword, but she would try. A week's worth of lessons had to count for something, right? She returned the flute to the pouch at her hip.

Liam yawned, stretched out her paws in front of her, and stood. She shook her silvery fur and picked her way around the broken branches. If the wolf was fine, then she was fine.

Ayianna grasped the nearest limb for balance and tried to step over the shredded remains of another tree, but something tumbled down from above. She threw her arms up to block it, but the heavy object smashed into them and clipped the left side of her face. She crashed into the ground, the heavy weight on top of her.

She shoved it away and scrambled out from underneath it—a half-eaten animal's head with large spiraling horns. The head and horns were nearly as wide as she was tall. Hollowed sockets stared back at her where its eyes had once been.

"Are you all right?" Kael pulled her to her feet. "Your face is bleeding."

So now he was talking to her. Did it take almost killing herself to get his attention? She brushed his hands away, despite her desire to grasp them in hers and never let go. To see the warmth of his smile again. She shook her cloak out a little harder than necessary. Maybe it was better when he ignored her.

"I'm fine." Aside from the throbbing of her face and arms, the humiliation hurt worse. "What is it? And why was it in the tree?"

"Looks like a head of one of the greater wild sheep of Kha Vaaro. You're lucky it only clipped you." Kael lifted his gaze. "And there's more."

She followed his gaze to the other trees. The odd-shaped bulges were not deformities of the trees or dead branches as she had first thought. Instead, numerous bloody sheep heads with huge curving horns hung at odd angles high in the limbs of the remaining trees. "What did this?"

"I do not know." Eloith dropped from the sky, his wings a blur. His bald head gleamed in the afternoon sun, but neither heat nor cold affected him. The size of a cat, he could have perched on Kael's shoulder, but that would have gone against the fairy captain's honor. Instead, he hovered alongside him. "There is no sign of any living creature for miles."

"What kind of beasts do these mountains harbor?" Kael asked.

Eloith darted to the left of Kael and continued to hover. "There is no beast among the highlands to cause this kind of damage. Maybe in the jungles, but not here."

"Kael." Prince Vian stood at the base of a large, shattered tree with Tariq and Liam. His bright red curls hung to his shoulders, and a film of coppery bristles covered his lower face. He had readily replaced his finery with proper traveling clothes fit for the mountains of Kha Vaaro. Such a contrast from when Ayianna had first met him.

Tariq, the nephew of Queen Emani of Bonzapur, squatted next to Vian and ran his hand along the deep trenches in the earth. His black curls edged his bronze face and blended into his sideburns and cropped beard. He scooped up a handful of dirt and rubbed it between his fingers.

Vian yanked back some of the roots. "You have to come see this."

Kael strode over to him, and Ayianna followed.

The fractured trunk tilted to the right. Its tangled roots lay partially exposed, its fibers shivering in the breeze. At the base of the tree, a hideous form with a face like a man was squashed into the dirt—an imp. Blood and mud caked its coarse, wiry fur.

Its entrails, or what was left of them, oozed from a split in its overextended stomach.

Ayianna looked away. Bile seared her throat, but she swallowed it back. The stench of decay was unmistakable now. "Imps, here? How?"

Their twisted bodies among the carnage at Dagmar had not faded from her mind, nor had the images of her father's murder and her brother's headless body. Could the enemy be hunting them so soon? She tugged Liam closer, lest her knees gave out. "We've not seen imps since we crossed the desert."

"The tracks are days old." Tariq wiped his hands on his pants. "I've only ever read about them. They've never been this far west."

"Imps—are you serious?" Desmond jerked at the branches on the far end of the tree. A jerkin of bright scarlet and deep purple covered his black shirt. Practical clothes, albeit flashy, replaced his fancy attire. Except his hat. Somehow, he had acquired one with a large feathery plume. He even bought a copper razor to keep his face clean-shaven and his blond hair at the proper length. If appearances were so important to him, why didn't he care that she was a cursed half-elf? Surely, a human merchant with a desire for the courts of Badara would have put an end to their betrothal.

He stomped toward them but halted when his gaze fell on Ayianna. "What in the name of the Abyss happened to your face?"

"One of the sheep heads fell out of the tree."

His eyes narrowed. "Well, don't you have that vial of healing water? Shouldn't you be tending to your cuts? The last thing we need is for you to get sick on us."

Ayianna gritted her teeth and turned her back on him. As if he cared. What a contrast from the Desmond the village girls had dreamed about. He could be so charming when he wanted to be, but lately he seemed to have lost his desire.

She dug into the pouch hanging from her belt, pulled out a velvet bag, and slid the vial of kulin from it. The healing water from Nerissa was already half gone. Would it be enough for them to reach the underwater city? Not if she kept injuring herself. She dribbled it as best she could along her face. She had to be more careful. She could not risk the safety of her companions if her curse should awaken.

"Imps could not have done this much damage." Kael plucked a broken branch from the ground. "I think . . . " He eyed the crushed underbrush. "It was a dragon."

"Impossible." Vian's head snapped up, his flaming red curls bouncing around his face. "I should know, my father's jurisdiction includes all of the Northern Province. We would know if the sorceress had dragons there."

"When Dagmar was destroyed, the enemy employed the use of imps and a troll, but the thief who stole the Sacred Pearl escaped on a dragon." Kael reached over his shoulder and fingered the feathered arrows, probably counting them. As if arrows were any match for a dragon. "Three days from Bonzapur, and the sorceress is already tracking us? How does she even know we survived the massacre at Zajur?"

"It doesn't make sense." Vian released the roots and brushed his hands on his pants. "If she was trying to stop us from finding out about the Dwalu Tonic, why didn't she send the dragon in the first place? If this is even a dragon."

"Surrendering her best weapon would be imprudent." Eloith hung in the air next to Vian, his voice small, but firm. "A dragon gives her an advantage over the plains people, that is, until the merfolk join the Alliance." He crossed his arms. "Perhaps she thought the sand leeches in Zajur would have been enough to stop us. She would not lose her advantage for something as trivial as a quest that may or may not succeed."

"What?" Vian straightened. "Then why are we so concerned about it?"

Kael kicked dirt over the imp's body. "Have you forgotten the souls of your people so quickly?"

Ayianna cringed. Who could forget the ghostly images that lined the tunnels beneath the Forest of Inganno? The kulin slid down her neck. Using her scarf, she dabbed at the water and rubbed it into the puncture wounds. Spasms of pain shot through her. Cursed. The sensitive flesh would never heal. She'd have to keep track of the time, otherwise the harpy venom would grow stronger.

"Of course, I've not forgotten." Vian planted his hands on his hips. "They'll be fine once they receive the tonic. But I don't see what's so pressing that the guardians would have me traipsing out here in the middle of nowhere when the world is on the brink of a war. My father, if he knew." He shook his head and dropped his arms at his side. "Desmond was right. We should have parted company back in the desert."

Eloith settled on a twisted branch. "Do you know what the Twammurt Curse does to the inflicted?"

Vian shrugged. "It makes them do the bidding of the one who placed them under the curse."

"It destroys them." Eloith lifted his chin. "People are not designed to be forced to do another's will. Many will try to fight it, few will succeed. The internal turmoil is too much for them. Their minds turn inward and deteriorate. Then they begin to harm themselves. There is no release, except in death."

Ayianna returned the vial to her pouch. The image of her mother, pleading and weeping, plagued her. Would her mother fight the curse and be destroyed? Or would she succumb? "What happens if they don't fight it?"

Eloith's eyes saddened. "They become pawns to another's whim and slowly die within."

"So . . . " Vian hesitated. "How long until a person . . . how long do we have?"

"A year, maybe."

"That does put things into perspective," Vian replied. "Still, if we succeed in retrieving the ingredients for the tonic, she will lose her army. I'd be concerned, if I were her."

"If all she wanted was to conquer the plains, yes." Eloith folded his arms across his chest. "But that is not why the guardians are rallying the nations. Do you think the nations care what happens in the plains?"

"Excuse me."

"Oh, hush." Kael scraped his boot along the edge of the tree. "The sorceress plans to release Taethza, the queen of the Underworld, and to do that she needs the Dagger of Raemoja."

"Yes." Eloith stalked down the branch toward Vian. "All her plans will be for naught if she does not have that dagger. If she thinks Ayianna has it, she will not stop until she finds it. She is impatient to succeed."

His gaze slid to hers. With his bright pale eyes, he could peer inside her soul, peeling away the layers and barriers, and expose the remaining secrets she clung to, but he didn't. Still, he had to know of the curse running through her veins yet said nothing about it.

Eloith's gaze lingered. Was he expecting a response from her?

"But I don't have it."

Or did she? Surely, her brother's simple dagger was not the blade the Sorceress sought. Her father's final words about the Morning Star and Trygg being locked in battle had to be a clue to the dagger's hiding place. Why else would he have told her? But what if Saeed was wrong? That could explain the sorceress's dragon hunting them, instead of preparing for battle in the plains.

"Either she does not know that, or we have something else she wants."

"What else could the Sorceress be after?" Ayianna quickly rewrapped the scarf around her neck.

Eloith hovered closer. "What else does one do with a corrupted dagger? It is not a fierce weapon to behold—what dagger is? No. This dagger is a tool to sever the very fabric of our world and release the greatest evil that has ever treaded upon this land."

"Of course, it would be." Vian groaned and paced the length of the fallen tree. "But what has that to do with us?"

"The Sorceress needs a sacrifice." Eloith settled on a bough, and his eyes clouded. "It was how Lord Stygian became immortal and reigned as a god for centuries, unstoppable and growing more wicked with each passing year. The sorceress is

Taethza's high priestess, and Taethza would like nothing better than to resurrect her lover and reinstate their unholy dominion."

"Are you saying that she wants to sacrifice one of us?" Vian asked. "Out of all the people in Nälu, she would go after us? Why?"

"I am merely stating a fact." Eloith fluttered back into the air. "Those are the things the Sorceress is after, how we figure into all of that, I do not know."

"And perhaps, one of those reasons is enough to send her dragon." Kael stepped away from the group and scanned the trees again.

"Lovely story, fairy." Desmond smirked. "But shouldn't you be looking for whatever beast made this mess?"

"Perhaps you know." Eloith raised his brows and glared at Desmond until Desmond averted his eyes.

What did he mean by that? Ayianna tugged her cloak's edges together and tucked her fingers under her arms. As the day faded, so did its warmth, and the cold drained whatever heat it could from her face and hands.

Desmond shrugged. "You know more than I." He opened his arms and swept them out to the side. "But from the looks of it, whatever made this mess, we don't want to meet them in our sleep or otherwise. I suggest we put as much distance as we can between us and this place."

Kael adjusted his pack. "Eloith, take to the sky. We need to know where the imps are, who they are with, and if this beast is indeed a dragon. We camp at sunset. Once the imps start hunting, we won't stand a chance."

Eloith shot into the air and disappeared.

Kael faced Tariq. "Do you think you can find us shelter before then?"

Tariq glanced at the sky, and Ayianna followed his gaze. The sun slid behind a cloud, casting a shadow across the shattered trees and scarred land. The half-eaten sheep heads glared down on them as if warning them to flee while they still had the chance to escape the nightmare to come.

"There is a cave not far from here." Tariq's voice sliced through Ayianna's thoughts. "But we won't make it before sunset."

"We must try." Kael scanned the area. "Until we hear from Eloith, we run. No rest."

Tariq unbuckled his machete and slashed at the branches impeding their progress. A tool they hadn't planned on using until they reached the jungles.

A crow's guttural cry shrieked nearby, and Ayianna jumped.

"It's only a stupid bird." Desmond rolled his eyes and flung the trimmings aside.

A large black crow flapped into the trees, joining others who feasted on the sheep's remains. Where had they all come from? Hadn't Eloith said there was nothing living for miles around? Of course, he hadn't been looking for birds.

Once Tariq had cleared a path, Desmond scrambled over first.

Ayianna followed, but before she dropped to the other side, she glanced back at the trees. A crow, bigger than the rest, perched atop one of the sheep heads. Its beady eyes glared at her as if it was watching her. Her gaze shifted to the other birds. Their dark eyes met hers, and the air grew colder.

Liam growled.

They were birds. Just birds. But her hand went to the pouch of noqui stones.

"We haven't all day, you know," Desmond hollered from below.

"Are you all right?" Kael leapt up next to her and scanned the area. "What is it?"

An urge to embrace him and bury her face in his shoulder, to hide from the journey to come slammed into her. Ayianna shook herself. "Nothing. It's nothing."

2

AYIANNA HID HER hands beneath the folds of her heavy cloak and rushed up the worn path. Her leather armor hugged her body over the layers of the dress-like tunic and pants and kept the chill from seeping into her bones.

An icy breeze swept down the mountain pass and rustled through the evergreens and bare trees. Mountains loomed above the uneven ground, shadowing them in the sun's descent. She almost welcomed the change from the heat and the sea of sand back in Bonzapur. Almost.

Liam scampered along the trail, sniffing around. She dashed off into the trees, then loping back, never venturing beyond eyesight. For that, Ayianna was grateful.

Vian jogged in front of her. He carried considerably less belongings than when he first joined them. Had that been only a month ago? The crown prince of Badara, except Badara now hailed another man as king. But Vian would fix that. They all would. As soon as they retrieved the ingredients for the tonic.

The Dwalu Tonic. How could a silver pinecone, tree roots, and the merfolk's healing waters free the plains people from the curse? Did a silver pinecone really exist? Perhaps they were risking their lives for nothing.

No. Saeed and the guardians were relying on them to return with the ingredients. They wouldn't risk the future of Nälu on false riddles.

Ayianna glanced over her shoulder. Desmond trudged behind them, bringing up the rear. A frown creased his forehead, his mood worsening the higher they hiked. Was he upset that Prince Vian wouldn't accompany him back to Badara? Or was he still upset that she refused to consummate their betrothal? He would bide his time, he had said, but for how long?

She looked away. Farther up the path, Kael caught up to Tariq. He kept his distance from her. She knew why, but it didn't lessen the ache in her heart. She turned the silver ring on her finger. If things had been different, if her brother had returned with his future wife and Kael in tow, would her parents have reconsidered the betrothal to Desmond? Would Kael have seen her differently? But none of that mattered. She had signed the contract. She belonged to Desmond now.

How could she? Duty to her family? What did duty have to do with it all the way out here? No. She had signed out of fear. Fear of the future, fear of the truth. And she had hoped to leave the quest behind and rescue her mother. But instead, she embarked on another journey where her presence was not welcomed.

She straightened her shoulders and sucked in a lungful of cold air. She may be unwelcomed, but she would not be a burden. She would put aside any thoughts of the betrothal until the quest was finished. She would think only of the now. And right now, they were hiking up into the mountains of Kha Vaaro on the eve of winter, with a possible dragon and an army of imps hunting them. This couldn't bode well for them.

How do you even fight a dragon?

She fingered the sling at her hip. Maybe an arrow was no match for such a beast, but what of the noqui stones? Tariq had claimed they would turn their target to salt, but she had yet to test them. Shadows shifted to her right, and Ayianna flinched. Nothing. She chastised herself. What she feared stalked them from the sky, not the ground.

Tariq led their mismatched band along the ever-narrowing path up the mountain. His travels had taken him beyond the desert to the jungles and to the city of the merfolk, making him the perfect guide—he had claimed. Although, his concerns were the places not found on a map and the creatures that dwelt there.

He paused near a grove of evergreens, their spindly branches scratching at the sun. He glanced back, scanning the area. His amber eyes glimmered in the shadows, reminding her he was neither human nor elf. His skin, lighter than the other Haruzos, suggested mixed blood. If so, could he still transform from man to cat?

He didn't wear a leather cuirass as the others did. A simple jerkin covered his brown tunic, even that was more than what his kinsmen preferred. But then, how many of them entered the mountains bare-chested and leading a group to the icy peaks of Kha Vaaro?

No. If the Haruzo of Bonzapur had their way, they'd remain in the desert or reclaim the jungle. Their white cousins could have the mountains, the bitter winters, and the highland dwarves. Ayianna couldn't blame them.

The wind nipped at her skin, and a spasm of pain shot through her neck. She tightened the scarf. The heightened sensitivity to the change in temperature and every shift of fabric was a constant reminder of the harpy lord's poison burning in her veins, threatening to consume her. She adjusted the strap across her chest. As long as she had the merwoman's vial of healing water, she'd manage.

Her scabbard slapped her legs as she sprinted, and Ayianna rested her hand on its hilt, angling it away from her body. The blade felt good on her hip, even if she didn't know much about fighting with it. She'd learn eventually, and in the meantime she had the noqui stones and sling. She could best even Desmond— at a distance.

Captain Eloith blurred into view overhead and landed on an overarching tree limb. He folded his wings tight against his back. His thin eyebrows pinched together. Once they had all reached him, he said, "Two dragons and a horde of imps—too many to count. One group is bedded down to the far east, the other south of us."

Vian gasped. "Enemy dragons?"

"Of course, we're too far from the Kaleki for them to be friendly dragons." Tariq leapt atop a boulder and sniffed the air. "How close are they?

"That can't be right." Desmond crossed his arms and a wave of his pungent cologne washed over Ayianna.

She rubbed her nose and stepped back. "How did they find us?"

Eloith's eyes narrowed. "The sorceress knew the guardians would try to thwart her curse with the tonic, and the whereabouts of its ingredients are not a secret to her. If she knows we survived Zajur, then the next logical step would be the mountains of Kha Vaaro. The dragons and imps were already here, waiting for us."

Just like Zajur. Images of hot sand and Aberim's eyeless face flooded Ayianna's memories. Her heart ached for his pregnant wife and kids. By now, Niyah would have given birth. Alone. They had to know something went wrong. Kael's letter should have reached the guardians by now. Saeed would make sure Aberim's family knew what happened. Her throat tightened. How quickly life could be snuffed out!

Kael glanced at her, his eyes questioning. Had he sensed her grief? She looked away and rubbed her arms. The evening had grown colder.

"The dragons will be waking soon, and they'll be hungry." Kael unhooked his bow and restrung it, turning his attention back to the fairy captain. "Eloith, keep watch. We need to know how they hunt, how fast they move, and which direction they'll go. If we can reach the heart of Kha Vaaro, the dragons will not be able to follow us."

Ayianna glanced up at the failing light. "Perhaps, they've already passed through here."

"I would not count on that. I will find you." Eloith flew up and disappeared in the dimming light.

Desmond guffawed. "You think you'll take down a dragon with your puny bow?"

"I use what I have." Kael lowered his bow. "A carefully aimed arrow can take down almost anything. You just need to know where to hit it. And unlike you and your sword, I won't be in range of its claws or flame."

"And we have the imps to think about," Vian added. "Now if you two don't mind, I think we should be putting some distance between the dragons and us. Don't you agree?"

Kael turned and dashed up the trail, his stride long and effortless, almost matching Tariq's. But who could outrun a Haruzo? They were born to run. The others weren't so graceful.

Ayianna jogged after them. Her pack slipped and jerked, throwing her rhythm off. But even with her bulky burden, she found her stride and managed to outpace Desmond and Vian. After all, she was part elf. A sense of pride warmed her insides, and she quickened her pace.

Tariq dodged off the path and wove between the prickly ash and evergreens. "The cave is not far." He shouted back to them. "We'll reach it by nightfall."

The sun faded from the late afternoon sky and the shadows lengthened. Dusk would be there before they knew it. Ayianna stumbled as she zigzagged between branches and pine needles. Any trace of pride had long since disappeared. Her legs burned and her lungs cried for relief, but she pushed forward.

Liam loped on ahead, keeping pace with Tariq. Did she suspect the danger that hunted them? Or was she enjoying a romp through the trees? If they could call it that. Branches leapt at them. Thorns smacked their faces, arms, and legs, tearing cloth and skin alike.

"Hold up." Tariq halted, and Kael nearly ran into him. "There's a dwelling through the trees." He pointed to the left. "Over there, nestled beneath that outcropping of stone."

Ayianna peered closer. The shadows shifted, and an outline of a small hut emerged.

"Who . . . out here?" Vian panted as he and Desmond caught up. He bent over and placed his hands on his knees. "Friend or foe?"

Tariq shrugged. "It wasn't here the last time I had passed through here, but that was about fifteen years ago."

"Dwarves?" Ayianna asked, her voice dry and scratchy, her chest heaving. She unstopped her waterskin and took a drink.

"I don't think so." Tariq strode toward it. "But I could be wrong."

"Wait." Vian grabbed his arm. "What if—"

"The only living soul out here would either be a dwarf or a Haruzo. I don't think we will find the sorceress or her cohorts." Tariq pulled his arm free. "I say we investigate."

Desmond leaned forward. "But the question is, who would? Someone living out here alone would not want to be disturbed. And the last I heard, the highlanders are not the friendliest of sorts. Mark my words, he will be an ornery, old hermit who would rather relieve us of our heads than aid us."

Vian nodded. "He might not be alone. We can't go charging in there without some reconnaissance."

"We don't have time for this." Kael pushed past the prince toward Tariq. "Either we take our chance here, or we make for the cave instead. You're our guide. What do you suggest?"

Tariq scanned their faces. "We take our chance. But ready your weapons just in case." He withdrew his sword and crept toward the hut.

Ayianna unsheathed her blade and weighed it in her hands. Her fingers trembled, but she stepped forward, determined to be an asset instead of a hindrance. A branch crunched under her foot, the sound blasting in her ears.

Desmond snorted. "You think you can help us? They'd hear you coming before you got there." He swept his cloak aside, hoisted his sword, and followed the others.

"Well, at least they wouldn't smell me coming." Ayianna clenched her jaw and sprinted after him. Just maybe he'd stop abruptly, and she'd run him through with her blade. Ack! How could she think like that? She shoved those thoughts aside and tried to focus on her surroundings.

Tariq and Kael reached the hut first and stopped outside the door. Desmond and Vian quickly flanked them, but Ayianna picked her way to the edge of the clearing. Away from the hut and their intentions.

A small fire pit blackened the forest's floor, its ashes long since cold and scattered about. Bound logs leaned upright against the outcropping, forming a wall twice the length of a normal hut. A small panel of bearskin and wood hung as a door.

Something scratched and shuffled inside the long hut. The noise seemed to come from the right, so Ayianna inched closer to the end of the logs. The scratching grew louder, and new sounds joined it. Chirping and clicking.

Ayianna's pulse quickened. Could the imps have found them already? No, their stench would have given them away. Instead, the odor stirred memories, taking her back to her family's stable and goat pen. Was it the gathering of shadows that drove fear through her heart like a dagger? Surely, any number of natural, native animals could be on the other side of that wall. A squirrel even.

But she knew better. Creatures that should have only existed in her worst nightmares roamed freely in the dark places of Nälu. The Forest of Inganno had taught her that.

She reached the edge of the hut, but her feet would go no farther. She craned her neck to the right. Was the darkness a wall or an opening?

"*Zabbi!*"

Tariq's voice punctured the air like a trumpet, and Ayianna started. Her heart thudded against her ribcage. She took a deep breath and blew it out slowly. What was he thinking?

"*Zabbi, haru pa rza zahal!*" Tariq said, louder.

Kael touched the Haruzo's shoulder. "What if he is a dwarf?"

Tariq nodded. "*Glaaka, dazi na kha tuhokvic.*"

Silence settled upon the hut again, except for the scratching and clicking. Ayianna drew closer and peered around the edge. The darkness gave way to a wooden fence. Huddled shapes scurried about the interior, clucking and scratching.

Chickens.

She sighed. A branch hung suspended between the fence and another, larger branch. A few scrawny hens already roosted there. The others soon joined them, hopping upward and flapping their wings, stirring the dust.

It could hardly be called flight. Their erratic wing beats summoned her brother's falcon to mind. He had flapped around on the bush not unlike these flightless birds. And there he had perched, with his broken wing and a soiled cloth in his talons. That morning, everything had changed.

And here she was, a world away from her home.

She shook off the encroaching emotions and backed away from the hut. The chickens settling in for the night meant one thing. Evening was upon them. What was taking Tariq and the others so long to figure out what to do? If no one was home, they should leave. It would be foolish to risk the anger of a stranger. The hermit could return any moment, and he would not be pleased to find trespassers. The consequences could be deadly.

Liam poked her nose between the wooden slats of the fence and scratched at the dirt.

"Oh no, you don't. Don't you get any ideas." Ayianna tugged on Liam's neck, dragging her back to the edge of the woods. "No chicken supper for you. Stay here."

Ayianna turned toward her companions, but they were no longer standing outside. The bear-hide door had been flipped aside. Fools! If the hermit returned now, they'd be dead for certain. She slammed her sword into its sheath and rushed after them.

"What are you thinking?" she asked, her voice higher than normal. Her eyes adjusted to the fading light, and her companions emerged from the shadows.

Kael held up the small orb from the guardians. "*Yetakoith taheza.*" It flared to life, casting a faint glow around the room.

It was big enough for a family of four to call home, but considering the sparseness of furniture, only one, maybe two lived there. The stone of the outcropping formed two of the walls. A cot stretched along the back one and a rough-cut table sat to the left. To the right, a thatched wall separated the chicken pen from the living area.

Desmond shrugged. "No one is here."

"You can't just walk into someone's home."

"We just did." He lifted a stack of dishes from the table and pushed them aside. A plate, a knife, and a kettle. "I'd say he lives alone."

"But is he dwarf or Haruzo?" Kael held up his small, glowing sphere.

"Haruzo." Tariq pulled a white fur hide from the cot. "Dwarves don't bother with the great white bear of the north. Only a Haruzo out to prove himself."

"Which means this hermit will not only be ornery, but a skilled warrior too." Vian grabbed Tariq's arm. "Ayianna's right. We shouldn't be here. What if he comes back?"

"What?" Desmond shoved the prince's shoulder. "You're not afraid, are you?"

"Only a fool would deny his fear." Vian scowled at him and rubbed his shoulder. "But caution in light of our circumstances would be better than roaming about like sheep too stupid to know fear."

Desmond's eyes narrowed. "Are you calling me stupid?"

"Enough." Kael stepped between them. "We have to decide if we leave now or stay here and risk an encounter with the owner." He glanced out the doorway. "Night is upon us. And we have yet to hear from Eloith. Perhaps there is hope the dragons went elsewhere."

Desmond swiped his hat off and stretched his arms. "I say we should stay."

A horse neighed outside, and Ayianna spun toward the door.

"Wrong answer, boys." A harsh voice cried above them.

A shadow dropped from the ceiling. Two blades glinted in the orb's light. Kael recoiled, but the orb was knocked from his hand, the light spinning. Tariq and Desmond fell away, but Vian dove for the door, grabbing Ayianna as he went, thrusting her outside.

Ayianna's hip slammed into the ground. The pain shot through her leg and back. "Vian!"

"Hey, I just saved your life."

She shoved him off of her. "Not if I can't walk."

"Ungrateful, aren't you?" He stood, grasped her hand, and hauled her to her feet. "Stay here." He unsheathed his sword but hesitated at the entrance. "Two against one—not much room for another."

Ayianna rubbed her backside and peered through the doorway. Elongated shadows pulsed on the walls as Tariq and Kael engaged the attacker. The clanging of blades rang out and feet pounded the floor. The orb lay against the far wall. Its glow barely bright enough to light the area. Where was Desmond? What could she do?

"We need more light—a fire." She pulled her pack off. Would she be able to find enough kindling to get it started?

The clanging of blades grew louder and the scuffle spilled outside.

Vian yanked Ayianna out of the way. "We don't have time for that."

"Well, what do you suggest?" She pressed her back into the log wall and fumbled with the straps of her pack. Any light in the evening sky had fled. Tariq and the other Haruzo could see well enough. Kael, on the other hand, was at a disadvantage. They needed a light brighter than Kael's orb.

"Distract him." Vian grabbed her shoulder. "You go talk to him."

"Why me?"

"Because you are a woman, and women distract men."

"Then you start a fire." Ayianna shoved her pack into Vian's chest.

What was she going to say? A sword slammed into the hut and clattered to the ground. A blur of movement rolled into her, knocking her forward. She caught a flash of long hair and glint of an earring before the person crashed into her.

"Ayianna!" Kael's face was inches from hers. He heaved her aside. "What are you doing?"

"You were the one who hit me." Ayianna scrambled away and stood. She inched toward the struggle.

Blades hissed and clanked through the air as Tariq engaged the man with double blades. Liam paced wide circles around them, dodging them if they got too close and slinking back toward the trees. The horse whinnied and pawed the dirt. He jerked against the rope anchoring him to the edge of the chicken pen.

"Stop this!" Her voice sounded small in her ears. She moved closer and tried again, but louder. "Haruzo, we don't want trouble. We're sor—"

Kael seized her around the waist and yanked her away from the tumult of blades. "Are you crazy? Go hide in the trees."

A glance at the shadowy forest banished those thoughts. A light flared behind her, and Ayianna blinked, her eyes readjusting again. Not as bright as she had hoped, but it was enough.

Prince Vian passed the torch to her and held out a sword to Kael. "Drop something?"

Kael snatched the blade from Vian and charged toward Tariq and the stranger.

"Not even a thank you. What an ungrateful lot you all are." Vian grabbed his sword and joined the others.

Finally, three against one, they managed to knock the blades from the stranger's hands. Tariq and Vian subdued his arms while Kael leveled a sword at his throat.

Ayianna inched closer with the torch. The flickering light fell across the hardened face of a woman. Black and white spiky hair crowned her head, her almond-shaped eyes otherworldly— like Tariq's, but silver and cold instead of his amber glow. She dressed like a man in leather pants and a tunic, but her slight feminine curves and slender jawline were evident.

Kael lowered his blade. "We didn't know."

"Trespassers!" The woman growled. She struggled against Tariq and Vian, but they held her tight. "Didn't know what? That you were trespassing, or that I was a woman? Does it change anything?"

"I didn't—no—we're sorry." Kael stepped back and raised his other hand. "We came upon your home, seeking refuge. We hollered—no one answered."

"So you decided to help yourself to my hospitality." Her silver eyes smoldered. "Release me."

"Will you promise to remain calm and not do something foolish?" Kael asked.

She snorted. "Why should my word mean anything to you? You don't know me."

"Any person as good as you with a blade knows discipline. People of discipline know their word is all they have."

She straightened and lifted her chin. "If you will leave and never return, I will not harm you."

"Let her go."

"No." Desmond burst from shadows.

"Where've you been, coward?" Kael sheathed his sword.

Desmond pushed past him. "There was hardly any room for me."

Kael shook his head and turned back to the woman. "Tariq, Vian, let's go."

"Not yet." Desmond snatched the torch away from Ayianna and angled it toward the woman's face. "Who are you and what are you doing out here in the middle of nowhere?"

The woman shied away from the flames. "My name is Jathil. You may consider this nowhere, but this is my home."

"A little far from Arashel, aren't you?"

"Arashel is no longer my home." She continued glaring at Desmond as if daring him to challenge her.

"You are a Haruzo, are you not?" Desmond's gaze didn't falter.

Ayianna leaned forward. Jathil was nothing like the Haruzo in Bonzapur, for one she lacked the dark skin and curly black hair. The woman's eyes flicked in her direction, and Ayianna held her breath.

"Enough of this." Kael placed his hand on Desmond's chest. "I said, let her go."

38

"Why?" Desmond's eyes narrowed. "We could seize this place, and she'd be safer for it."

Jathil grunted.

"That is not how we operate." Kael's other hand slid to his hunting knife. Would he fight Desmond over a stranger? "Now, let her go."

"But what about the dragons?" Vian asked.

Kael raised his brows, and they obeyed.

Jathil rubbed her arms. "Dragons don't come this far north—too cold."

"These two do not belong to the Kaleki." Tariq picked up his sword and sheathed it. "They are hunting us, thus our desperation in finding a place to hide."

"And you think my place will do the trick? Wood? Dried herbs and grain? What chance would you have against a dragon?"

"More than you think. Dragons hunt at night by sight. If they can't see us, they will pass us by."

She eyed them. "Lies. I want all of you out of here now and never come back."

"But the dragons?" Vian asked.

"Your problem, not mine."

Desmond spun on Kael. "You have wasted our time."

Kael shoved him aside. He disappeared into the hunt and returned with his orb.

"I'm sorry we didn't meet on more pleasant terms." Tariq dipped his head toward her. "Will you reconsider?"

Jathil shook her head.

"Kael!" Eloith dropped from the sky. His gaze darted to Jathil before focusing his attention on Kael and Tariq. "The dragons. They are on the move, and one is headed this way."

3

SEVERAL HOURS LATER, Ayianna and the others huddled in a cave. She and Vian had done their best to inspect it and clean out the old, moldy leaves while the others cut and gathered a few branches to cover the opening.

And now they waited. Vian's torch had long since been snuffed out, and Kael refused to light the small orb from the guardians. Patches of a star-speckled sky glittered beyond the pine boughs. Would they be enough?

Ayianna shuddered at the small, closed space. It reeked of decay and mold. Perfect for spiders and bugs. Did they have scorpions in the mountains? Her skin crawled at the thought. No, she had to think of something else.

She curled against the wall and wrapped her blanket around her tightly. Liam lay next to her. Her musty smell nearly overpowered the cave's odor, but not quite.

She lay quietly, waiting for the sound of wings. Silence shrouded the mountainside, except for the short breaths of her companions. Did they sleep when she could not? Doubtful. She hugged Liam closer and stroked her fur until a bur bit her finger. She gently tugged the fur around the bur, loosening it bit by bit.

Her restless thoughts wandered like chickens pecking at scattered grain, but always returning to Jathil—alone, defying society's rules. What kind of woman lived alone in the wilderness? Was she an outcast? Maybe a criminal? Or were the Haruzos of the highlands different than the other races?

Ayianna placed the fragments of the bur against the wall and began working on another one. Why couldn't she be more like Jathil? Just ride away from duty and be a free person. But then that would leave her mother alone. The image of her mother's anguished face stared back at her, pleading for help from some unseen foe. Guilt slammed into her. How could she do this to her mother? Wishing against Desmond, longing for someone, something else. Her parents had meant well— under the circumstances. Why couldn't Ayianna just accept her fate in life?

Women of the plains mattered little to the world unless they were married or under their father's authority. Her father was only trying to protect her and her mother. He knew his days were numbered. He knew it was only a matter of time before the sorceress would find him. Desmond had been the most logical choice.

The queen of Bonzapur said she had to be willing. And hadn't Ayianna tried that? She had signed the contract. She could make her heart obey, right?

Still, Kael's touch lingered. No matter how hard she tried to forget the dance they had shared. Her hand in his, his gray eyes shining. They had glided to the rhythmic song, the drums matching her heart. For one moment, Ayianna had felt alive, free, and then the iron bars of reality closed in on her. Shame and guilt threatened to drown her. She had disgraced her family.

Ayianna turned over, trying to shut out the warring feelings. Deep inside a tiny flame had ignited and warmed her soul, beckoning her. Like a butterfly seeking light, she had fluttered toward it, only to have her wings charred. She closed her eyes and buried her face into Liam's fur, willing sleep to come.

But it evaded her.

Why is it so hard to do the right thing? Ayianna looked beyond the cave's opening. The pine needles and tree limbs sliced the evening into glittery shards. *Osaryn, are you really there? Why is everything so confusing?*

So many questions, so many secrets—secrets her father harbored had destroyed their family. A new feeling emerged. Anger.

Liam's head jerked up. Ayianna held her breath, listening. The night's silence pressed against her ears. Then she heard it.

The rhythmic swoosh and snap of large wings.

Like a hundred enemy standards heralding their charge, it grew louder with each stroke until it filled the mountainside. Gusts of air tore through the treetops and ripped away the branches covering the cave's entrance.

Ayianna scrambled backward, pressing her back against the stone's cold surface.

A black shadow slid through the sky and blotted out the stars. For a moment, darkness swallowed her up. A roar shook the forest, and a blast of orange lit the sky. How could they even hope to escape notice in a small cave guarded by dead tree limbs?

The beating of the wings faded. Had the dragon passed them by? Or was it circling them? A faint orange glow illuminated the pines beyond the cave's entrance.

"Are you sure we're safe?" Ayianna tried to keep the tremor out of her voice.

"Yes but be quiet." Eloith settled onto her shoulder and touched her temple, his palm cold. "They will not see us in here, but they could hear us."

Could they smell them? Ayianna slowly let out her breath.

A scream shattered the silence.

Eloith took to the air, and Ayianna scrambled out from her blanket. She bumped into Kael, who was strapping on his quiver. Behind her, Desmond cursed.

"Come on!" Tariq bounded into the darkness.

Vian and Kael ran after him, but Desmond lingered in the opening of the cave. "It serves her right. I don't see why we need to rescue her when she didn't listen to us in the first place."

Ayianna ignored him as she belted on her sword.

"Where do you think you're going? You think you can take down a dragon?" He laughed.

"It's our fault the dragon is here." Ayianna shoved past him and rushed after the others.

In the distance, trees burned bright against the darkness. Orange haze hid the stars and clung to the trees. A serpentine head rose above the trees. Black scales glinted. The dragon's roar shook the mountainside, rattling her soul. She collapsed against a boulder. *Maybe Desmond is right, maybe I need to just stay put. As if I can kill a dragon.*

Shouts erupted. A horse's sharp neighs pierced the night. Ayianna flinched. She pressed her face against the boulder's cold surface. Nausea twisted her stomach. If she could only wake from this nightmare and it be all over. Liam pressed her wet nose on her cheek. Ayianna took a deep breath and gripped her sword, but the hilt slipped through her clammy hands. She wiped her hands on her pants and glanced down at her knapsack—the noqui stones.

No, she would not cower.

She crept out from her hiding spot and made her way toward the clamor of battle. A stench hung in the air, placing her back in Dagmar. Imps.

A furry creature burst from the underbrush. Its human-like face split into a hideous grin and charged her. Liam lunged. The imp shrieked and clawed at the wolf.

Ayianna fumbled with her sword, her fingers trembling. She ripped it free of its sheath and swung, but the stroke was awkward and bounced off the imp's back. Tightening her grip, she raised it and plunged it into the imp's chest. The imp went slack, and she shook her blade free.

The dragon smashed a group of pines with its tail. It ducked and snapped its jaws. When it straightened, a dark form hung limp in its mouth, too large to be a person. Then the dragon shook its head and flung the object skyward.

She rushed toward the dragon and burning trees, but Liam slammed into her, knocking her against a tree. Moments later a horse's body, broken and half-eaten, crashed through the underbrush and landed next to her.

Ayianna fought the urge to vomit. She crawled to the other side of the tree and froze. The dragon reared its head and stretched its leathery wings above the trees. Its dark scales flashed in the fiery light. A large imp sat astride the dragon's neck and held a chain connected to a large iron ring hanging from the dragon's nose. The imp jerked the chain, and the dragon swerved to the left. Its great tail bashed the trees in its path. It folded its wings and pulverized the soil with its claws.

Behind the shimmering waves of heat, Ayianna glimpsed Jathil's home. Her heart caught in her throat. The bound logs had been crushed. Flames engulfed the other end. It wouldn't be long before the entire hut burned. A handful of imps huddled near the chicken pen, chattering and shrieking. Blood and feathers clung to their fur and lined their mouth. One plunged its teeth into the breast of a chicken, ripping meat and feathers away.

Where was Jathil? Had they eaten her? Was she still inside?

Ayianna darted toward the hut, ducking behind the trees as she went.

"Take care of the dragon!" Jathil's harsh voice sliced through the clamor. "I can handle these filthy creatures."

Ayianna spun. On the far side of the clearing, the woman brandished a wood staff and plowed into a trio of imps like a farmer wielding a scythe.

The dragon lumbered toward them, its body nearly filling the clearing. No matter which way it turned, it either trampled trees with its feet or knocked them over with its tail.

"Apparently not." Vian slashed through an imp, who had dodged Jathil's staff.

Tariq lunged to the other side of her and caught another one in the chin. "Kael needs an opening. We must get this beast to turn around."

To her right, Kael mounted a boulder on the edge of the clearing. He knelt and leveled an arrow, but the dragon's tail hammered against the rock, throwing him from her sight.

Ayianna sprang from her hiding place. The dragon's tail sliced through the air, and she ducked. She leapt to her feet, but now the dragon had completed its turn and faced her.

Eloith sped along the dragon's spines and spun across its vision, the fairy captain a mere gnat to such an imposing beast. Fiery breath spewed from the dragon's snout, but Eloith dodged it. He hoisted his sword and somersaulted over the dragon's head. He struck the dragon's eye, but its scaly eyelid flashed and blocked his assault. The dragon swung its head around and snapped at Eloith, but the fairy shot skyward.

Ayianna darted toward the boulder, but Kael wasn't there. She yanked the sling from her belt. She tried to balance the bloody sword in the crook of her arm while she dug in the pouch for a noqui stone.

Several imps rammed into her, knocking the sling and sword from her hands. Liam snarled and ripped into them. Ayianna scrambled after her sword, but an imp seized her cloak, yanking her backward and slamming her head into the ground. It pounced atop her and slashed her cheek with its claws. Ayianna shoved the imp's grasping hands away.

Its hideous face hung over hers. Its putrid breath assailed her lungs and burned her eyes.

She turned away and locked her arms, keeping the imp's claws and teeth from her face. If she let go, it would slice her open, but she couldn't thrust it from her. She tried to kick it off, but she couldn't get her knees under it. Instead, she rolled toward the boulder and smashed the imp against it.

The imp jerked. It gnashed its teeth and tried to wrestle free from her grasp. She slammed it into the boulder again. Its grip loosened and it shook its head.

Liam's heavy weight dropped on top of Ayianna. Claws shredded flesh, and jaws snapped above her. Ayianna blocked the assault with her arms. Liam buried her teeth in the imp's neck and shook it. The imp screamed and flailed, trying to reach Liam's throat. Ayianna spun free. She jerked her brother's dagger from her boot and buried it in the imp's distended stomach.

Ayianna knelt, running her hands along the forest floor. She had to find the sling. Without it, she wouldn't be able to throw the noqui stone hard enough or far enough, and she had no intentions of getting any closer to the dragon.

The earth shook, and she spun around. The dragon lurched forward and snapped at the air.

Eloith corkscrewed through the air just out of reach of the dragon's teeth. If he could just keep the dragon's attention a little longer, she could find her sling.

But then the beast craned its neck, its marbled eye glaring at her.

Forget the sling. Ayianna fumbled for another stone. The dragon swiped, but she leapt out of the way as its claws shredded the nearby trees. What was she thinking? She could have, should have remained hidden in the cave. That's what Desmond wanted. Kael would have too. What could she do against such a formidable foe?

No. She couldn't doubt herself now. Later, maybe.

Ayianna took hold of a noqui stone. She planted her feet and lifted her chin. She would meet death head on.

The dragon's mouth descended on her like a snake with a mouth full of fire. Ayianna threw the stone into its throat and then rolled away, expecting the crushing pain of teeth and fire. But none came. She sprang from the ground, ready to flee.

The dragon coughed and shuddered. It shrieked. The scales on its head and neck crystallized and turned white. The magic of the noqui swept over it like a wave washing over sand until it stood immobile, its wings outstretched, its eyes fierce, but forever sealed in salt.

Its shriek still echoed in Ayianna's ears.

Silence settled over the mountainside. It was over. The nightmare had been defeated.

Ayianna's knees buckled. She leaned against the boulder, her whole body trembling, and slid to the ground. Her chest heaved as she gulped the cold air. Smoke burned her lungs, and a fit of coughs tore through her body. She covered her mouth with her cloak.

Liam's wet nose nuzzled her forehead, and Ayianna raised her head. The wolf held the sling in her mouth. Her bushy gray tail swished back and forth, waiting for approval.

"Well done, Liam." Ayianna wrapped her arms around her and hid her face in the filthy, matted fur.

"Ayianna!" Tariq shouted.

She glanced up, her face wet with tears. The scratches on her cheek burned. Why was she crying?

Tariq dropped beside her, a big grin split his curly beard, and he engulfed her in a hug. "You did it!"

Then Vian and Kael came around the other side of the dragon, shouting for joy. Vian pushed Tariq aside and grasped Ayianna's hand. "Well done! We might have been roasted dinner tonight if it weren't for you."

Kael nudged Vian aside and squatted down next to her. A smile cracked his somber mask, and his eyes had never been brighter. "Are you hurt? Aside from those scratches on your face, I mean." He touched her face, inspecting her injuries.

The rush of emotions swallowed her words, so she shook her head. More tears sprang to her eyes, but he wiped them away. His touch sent a wave of warmth over her soul and through her body. She would face the dragon all over again to just to see the tenderness in his eyes and smile.

"We need to put some of the kulin on those scratches."

"No, I can't waste it. There's only a half of a bottle left."

His brows furrowed. "You call protecting your health a waste? Those claws were by no means clean. You could get an infection and be worse off than a reopening wound on your neck. It's not like you will die without it."

But you could. Ayianna stiffened. She'd turn into a monster, instead, and then they would have to kill her. Should she tell him? He had a right to know. But as long as she had the vial of kulin, she would be fine. No one else needed to know, right? Well, except Desmond. He knew.

"It'll be fine." Concern washed over his eyes. "I'll help you, so you don't waste any."

She pulled out the vial and handed it to him. He dabbed the water into her scratches. His nearness made her head spin and her pulse race. Or was that from holding her breath?

He sat back on his heels and dropped the vial into her hand. Would he go back to being distant and cold again?

"Thanks." She returned the vial back to its pouch and glanced at Liam. Blood soaked her fur in great splotches across her shoulders and rump. "Oh, Liam!" She dug her fingers into the filthy fur, looking for wounds. More tears burned her eyes and choked her words. She would use the entire bottle of kulin to heal her if need be.

Kael ran his hands along Liam's muzzle, back, and legs. "No wounds, she seems fine."

Ayianna nodded. She brushed away the tears and straightened. Liam put her paw on Ayianna's leg and cocked her head as if reassuring her.

Tariq hovered over them. "We need to move out, in case that other dragon is nearby, or the surviving imps change their mind and return."

"What happened to the others?" Kael asked.

"There was just a handful remaining, but they fled." Tariq stepped back and cleaned his sword on an imp's carcass.

Kael's hand slid under Ayianna's elbow and helped her stand. "You did great."

"Thanks." The warmth of his presence flowed over her. Standing next to him, she could believe the world would be set right again. She wanted desperately to lean into his embrace, for his reassuring touch and smile to linger, but the moment ended too soon as he pulled away.

Eloith landed on the boulder and saluted her. "Well done, mighty dragon-slayer!"

Victory. Warmth blossomed in her chest, and she smiled. *I did it . . . I killed a dragon.*

Desmond strode toward her. Sweat pasted his golden locks against his head, and his jerkin hung in strips from his shoulders. "You just got lucky." His scowl deepened. "I doubt you will be so fortunate next time."

His words smothered the afterglow flooding her soul. Not even a *thank you* or a *well done*. But it didn't matter. She had killed the dragon; she had saved them. Nothing could steal her victory away, except maybe the second dragon.

"And you think you could have done better, coward?" Kael's harsh mask slid back over his face.

"Those are fighting words." Desmond's hand hovered over the hilt of his sword.

"Save it for another time." Vian smacked Desmond's shoulder. "Unless you want to be fighting that other dragon and a bunch more imps tonight."

"Where is Jathil?" Tariq scanned the destruction.

Ayianna knew. If she were Jathil, she would have been trying to save what she could of her home. She broke into a run.

The logs, half-eaten by the fire, had fallen away to leave a gaping, splintered maw. Jathil scurried about the flickering darkness. She flung a bundle and a pack out and disappeared inside.

"The smoke won't be good for her." Tariq passed Ayianna and sprang over the smoldering logs. "Get out of there!"

Ayianna reached Jathil's pile of belongings. Double blades in their sheaths sat atop packs filled with food and supplies. She hauled them away from the heat and returned to pick her way through the debris and glowing embers. There was a loud crack, and a fiery log from one of the rafters crashed into the ground.

"Let go of me." Jathil yanked her arm from Tariq's grasp and lunged for the cot, grabbing the bearskin.

"Leave it, foolish woman!" Tariq pursued her. "You need to get out of here, or you'll die."

Kael leapt over the wreckage. He and Tariq grabbed Jathil's arms and dragged her away from the smoke and flames.

Jathil dropped to the ground and jerked her arms free, knocking Kael and Tariq off balance. "I don't need your help." She flipped backward and scooped up the bearskin. The thatched wall of the chicken hut collapsed, sending an explosion of sparks into the air. She swerved toward the entrance but tripped.

Kael and Tariq seized her arms and propelled her forward, flinging her out of her home. They leapt after her just as the entire roof came crashing down.

She collapsed next to the trees, clinging to the bearskin and coughing.

"Foolishness." Tariq shook his head. "What were you thinking?"

"You wouldn't understand." Her voice cracked. She shifted to her knees and stared at the destruction, the flames reflecting in her watery eyes.

Ayianna picked up the staff and a few more pouches she found near the hut and plopped them down next to her, but Jathil didn't flinch. Didn't even acknowledge Desmond and Vian when they came scurrying over to them.

"We need to go." Kael glanced up at the sky. "The other dragon is still out there, and the remaining imps might come back."

"Will we return to the cave and wait until dawn?" Vian asked.

Kael shook his head. "The imps will smell us out."

"True, but are we not a match for them?" Eloith perched on a spindly limb above them. He jumped to the end, closer to them, the branch jostling with his movement. "If we hike through the night, it will expose us to the other dragon, and we will be weary." He glanced at Kael and then Tariq. "We should return to the cave."

"Don't you think these flames," Tariq swept his hand toward the destruction, "would act like a beacon for the second dragon?"

Jathil turned her glare on him. "Who are you and why are the dragons after you?"

"We'll explain later," Tariq said. "Right now, we need—"

"No." She sprang to her feet, the staff in her hand. "Look at my home! The chickens, my food! My horse! All destroyed. Winter is nearly here. I have nothing—all because of you!"

Desmond rubbed his shoulder. "We tried to warn you, but you wouldn't listen."

She swung her staff, but Tariq parried her blow with his sword.

"What? You think you can take on all of us?" Desmond snorted. He raised his sword and stepped forward.

Vian grasped his shoulder. "What do you think you'll accomplish by engaging her like this? She has lost everything, and we're to blame."

"Ridiculous." Desmond shoved Vian's hand away.

The woman held her staff ready, but she didn't attack again. "Compensation." She pushed the words out through gritted teeth. "Have you no honor?"

Tariq lowered his blade. "We do not have enough gold to replace what you have lost, and we have just enough supplies for our journey, nothing more."

"Come with us until we can make reparations," Vian said. "I am Prince Vian of Badara, and I will personally see to it."

"Oh no, you won't!" Desmond slammed his sword into its sheath. "We saved her life. We could've just as well let the dragon eat her. But we didn't. She is indebted to us."

Jathil shook her head. "I can't possibly go—"

"You can't stay here, either," Tariq said. "Where else will you go? As Vian has spoken, we must make amends. We can't in good conscience leave you here."

"What? Are you going to force me to go with you?" She glared at the blackened hull of her home and the flames beyond the splintered remains.

Ayianna's chest constricted. Jathil had nothing left, just like her.

Tariq stepped even with her. "Time is against us. We need to go. The other dragon is still out there, and the imps might return. But unless you wish to meet this dragon on your own, I suggest you come with us. If not, go your way and keep yourself hidden in the evenings until the danger has passed, but forfeit any possible reparations, because there is no way we will be able to seek you out later."

She tightened her jaw and rolled the staff between her palms. "Where are you headed?"

"Stark's Peak." Tariq replied. "Then to Ganya and the Island of Moruya."

"Not Arashel?"

Tariq shook his head.

Jathil's brow furrowed. She dug at the earth with her staff before raising her gaze to meet Tariq's. "Perhaps I might be able to repay my debt as the blond brute so kindly pointed out." She smiled. "You know my name, but I don't know yours."

"Let's save the introductions for later, shall we, cat?" Desmond said. "We are wasting precious time." With that, he turned away and started back to the cave.

"We can at least exchange names," Tariq said. "The blond brute, as you called him, is Desmond. The elf is Kael. The fairy is Captain Eloith. She is Ayianna, and I'm Tariq."

"Queen Emani's nephew?" Jathil cocked her head, and her gaze slid to Eloith. "And a Naajiso?"

Tariq's eyes narrowed. "How do you know me?"

Jathil shook her head and turned her silvery eyes to her home. Tongues of flames flickered along its edges while deeper inside the splintered wood burned hot. There would be nothing left in the morning. She lifted her chin and turned away. "I'll gather my belongings."

"We'll help." Vian held out her double blades and trappings.

"I don't need your help." She seized them, flung them over her shoulders, and secured the straps. Then she scooped up the packs and the bearskin. She halted. "I—you must forgive my rudeness. I have not needed anyone for a long time."

"I understand," Vian said.

"Do you?" She raised her eyebrows.

"I mean—the rudeness. It's all right. No harm done." Vian rubbed his hands through his hair. "We better get going."

Tariq nodded. "Eloith, locate the second dragon. If it's far enough away, we'll stay in the cave tonight."

The fairy put his right fist over his heart and darted into the night.

Tariq sprinted up the trail while the others fell in line behind him. Jathil strode after them, bearing her awkward bundle much like Vian did so long ago with his attempt to carry all his princely robes and such. Something that had once brought a smile to Ayianna's face, but this time, there was nothing funny about it.

Ayianna brought up the rear. A small flame burned deep inside her. Something had happened, something had changed within, but what, she could not say. And how quickly their journey could have ended! If she hadn't killed the dragon, all would have been lost, but now they continued with another member added to their quest.

Unlike her, Jathil would be an asset to the group. Her skill with weapons was undeniable. Perhaps someone Kael would want on the quest, not a fumbling girl that he had to rescue every time he turned around.

But not tonight. Maybe he would think differently of her now.

Maybe Jathil would teach her, and she wouldn't have to marry Desmond. She could take care of her mother on her own. She would not be a woman of the plains, mere servants to their men. She would be able to embrace her elven heritage once more. She could live where she wanted. Like Jathil.

The northern Haruzo rushed after Tariq, her step agile despite the awkward bundle. Who was she? Why was she living in the wilderness, alone? Would she really travel the entire journey with them? But the real question weighing on Ayianna's heart—she was almost too afraid to ask it.

What would Jathil think of her?

4

AYIANNA EMERGED FROM the cave into the early morning cold, and a sharp odor assaulted her lungs. She covered her face with her blanket. The others staggered ahead of her, gagging. Desmond took off up the mountainside and didn't look back. Black and yellow dragon dung clung to the nearby pine trees and splattered the dying grass.

A shadow of fear slid over her, and she could not shake the feeling of being watched. She scanned the sky and trees and then lowered her gaze to Kael's, but his somber face revealed nothing. Wouldn't he be able to seek the dragon's presence? Liam prowled the area, sniffing at the dung as if she did this all the time. She gave no sign of danger. There was nothing to fear, right?

A harsh caw shattered the stillness, and Ayianna bolted after Desmond, her companions close behind. A bird, it was only a bird. She kept telling herself that, but she didn't stop until she had caught up to him.

Once they had put enough distance between them and the stench, Tariq signaled a rest. He dumped his pack and sat cross-legged on a bed of pine needles. His dark brow shone with sweat despite the cold air. He wiped it away and scrubbed his face. His black beard made him appear older than the rest, but there were no wrinkles or other telltale sign of age. Still, to travel as much as he said he did, he would have to be older.

Kael, on the other hand, with his scar and stern expression, seemed to be the oldest. He balanced atop an outcropping, his bow in his hands, and scanned the sky, perhaps looking for a sign of Eloith or the other dragon. Strands of his long hair had slipped from his messy braid, and the wind flicked it across his face. What stories hid behind his eyes? Eyes that had seen much. Was he always so somber? From his demeanor at the king's wedding feast, she doubted it. He had laughed, they had danced. He had won her brother's confidence, Teron even dying to protect his sister. They would have been family. Kael hid more than a death of a sister or friend. His sorrow ran deeper, older. She averted her eyes before the rush of emotion overwhelmed her.

On the other side of the outcropping, Desmond and Vian dug out the jerked meat and corn biscuits and settled their belongings at the base of a gnarled, old oak tree, one of few among the evergreens. Desmond shoved his plumed hat back and tore into a piece of the meat. The prince, on the other hand, nibbled on the biscuit. Either out of habit or enjoyment, Ayianna couldn't tell.

The thought of food turned her stomach. Instead, she ran her fingers through Liam's fur, working out the burs. Remnants of dried blood matted the gray coat. Ayianna had tried to wipe off what she could, but dry leaves could hardly replace a bath. And how she longed for one! The thought made her skin crawl and her head itch, intensifying the ache in her body even more.

The night before was a haze in her memory, but not the burn in her muscles or the scratches on her cheek. Once they had reached the cave, they had collapsed. Eloith had reassured them the second dragon was far to the east. It appeared to be heading south rather than north. Perhaps they'd get lucky.

She wouldn't count on it.

But then which dragon had left the dung behind? Ayianna glanced up at the sky. Nothing but white wispy clouds against a pale blue. The sun glared down upon them, but she felt no heat from it.

Her gaze wandered over to Jathil.

She perched on a log, away from everyone else. Her gear clung to her back and hung from her belt. She neither ate nor drank like the others but set her staff at her feet and crossed her arms. Her black and white spiky hair was wilder than before. Her almond eyes were cold and wary.

"What I'd like to know . . . " Desmond wiped his mouth with the back of his sleeve and corked his waterskin. "Is why you are living way out here in the middle of nowhere?"

Jathil lifted her gaze and smirked. "Why do you live where you live?"

"Not to intrude." Tariq glanced at Desmond, before turning his attention to Jathil. "But you are a mystery."

"Not more than you, I'm sure." She drew her knees up and rested her arms across them. "What do you want to know? But let's not get too personal, okay? Any question beginning with why—too personal. My reasons are my own."

"Fair enough." Vian stretched his legs in front of him, leaned against the tree trunk, and crossed his ankles. "But I can't think of any questions that don't start with why."

"I can." The words were out of Ayianna's mouth before she realized she had said them. She swallowed as everyone's attention turned toward her. "How long have you lived out here?"

"Maybe seven years. I've lost track." Jathil shrugged. "Nature has a way of making you forget."

"Are you trying to forget something?" Tariq wrapped his food in a cloth and replaced it in his pack.

"Aren't we all?" Jathil smiled, but there was no warmth in it. "But what are you all doing out here? Not everyone has dragons hunting them. Trouble with the Kaleki?"

"No." Vian plucked a dead leaf from the ground and rubbed it between his fingers. "Have you heard of the guardians?"

"Those troublemakers?" Jathil snorted and shook her head. "What are they up to now?"

Tariq cocked his head. "Why do you say that?"

"They are always digging around in people's lives, pushing their agendas, trying to run kingdoms." She glanced away. "Most times causing trouble."

Ayianna shifted to her knees and focused on pulling a stubborn bur from Liam's fur. How could Jathil say that? Saeed sought peace and unity among the nations. Was that so bad? He would never force his agenda on anyone. If he had, the king of Badara would not have been locked away in his own dungeon. Perhaps Jathil wasn't someone they could trust. If she had a quarrel with the guardians, wouldn't they be at odds?

"Well, I happen to agree with you. Imagine that." Desmond slapped his feather-plumed hat back on his head.

His admission did not ease the growing tension in her soul. A bur stung her finger, and she bit back a yelp. She needed a comb. She opened her bag and rummaged through it. Her fingers brushed over the hairpin her father had given her. A dark sapphire glared at her from its nest of bronze-webbed petals. Silver and copper twisted around its base and down the center prong—her mother's workmanship. Her father's last gift to her—a betrothal pin. Precious—yet not. How could something bring both pain and comfort? She slid the prong behind the bur and pried on it, tugging it free from Liam's fur. At least it would be useful.

Tariq stood and brushed the pine needles off his cloak. "Being that Arashel no longer embraces them, I can understand why you might say that."

"Not all of Arashel."

"And you think Arashel is better off because of it?" he asked.

"Well, for starters, we don't get involved in your messes." Jathil pushed to her feet and cradled the staff in her arms. "So why did the guardians send you and this mismatched group all the way out here?"

"How much do you know about the sorceress?" Vian asked, still reclining against the tree.

Jathil frowned. "You mean the guardian who defected about forty some years ago?"

"She was an apprentice." Kael lifted his bow and dropped from the outcropping. "She is responsible for the dragons. There is war brewing on the plains, and we're trying to stop her."

"Out here?" Jathil leaned on her staff. "Looks to me like you're the defectors."

"Now see here." Vian leapt to his feet and shoved his face into hers. "We were sent on this mission by the High Guardian Saeed himself. The sorceress placed a curse on *my* people, binding them to do her will. With them, she is building a massive army to conquer the plains. Do you think she will stop there? Oh no. She will march west and conquer it all if she is not stopped."

"Watch it, Vian. She doesn't need to know everything." Desmond knocked his knuckles into the prince's chest. "We don't know who she is. She could be a spy for all we know."

Jathil raised her hands. "Ah, yes, a likely story—a lone woman wandering around in the mountains, and now homeless and horseless, thanks to you. You're brilliant, you know." She shifted the belt across her waist. "But a better assumption would be that you and your companions are the spies. We don't see many humans out here, much less a fairy and an elf."

"Believe what you want to believe, madam." Vian picked up his pack. "Your beliefs don't negate the facts. If Nälu has any chance against the sorceress, it lies with us and our mission."

"And what exactly is that?"

"We must gather the ingredients for the Dwalu Tonic." Vian squared his shoulders and lifted his chin. "It will set my people free, and the Sorceress will no longer have an army. But if we don't hurry, the curse will destroy them."

"I see." Jathil shook her head. "Well, what a lovely mess I've found myself in."

"You don't have to go all the way with us." Kael stepped closer. "We could leave you at a village on the outskirts of Arashel."

Jathil snorted. "I will never return to Arashel." Her eyes shifted to Ayianna. "And what are you doing here, *Dragonslayer*?"

Jathil's tone of voice squashed the thrill attempting to course through her. Ayianna tucked her hairpin back into her bag. She pushed up from the ground and placed her hand on Liam's head, the fur comforting against her palm. She lifted her gaze to meet Jathil's. "What do you mean?"

"This isn't exactly a mission for girls, is it?" Jathil rested her staff in the crook of her arm. "Most unattached girls in such company are here for other reasons."

Desmond burst into laughter, but Vian punched his shoulder.

Heat flooded Ayianna's face. She wanted to disappear, to take off up the mountain. They should be hiking, not digging into each other's private matters. Hadn't she respected Jathil's request not to ask personal questions? She shifted her feet and bumped into Liam, her presence calming and reassuring. Jathil's almond eyes bore into her. What did she see? Pity? Disdain? Ayianna pushed the words past her knotted throat. "I am betrothed."

"Betrothed . . . yes, that's seems right. You don't seem the type." Jathil dropped one end of her staff to the ground and leaned closer to Ayianna. "A word of advice, girl, marriage isn't worth it."

"How would you know, traipsing around here with not a care in the world?"

"You think I started out like this?" Jathil's lips twisted into a lopsided smirk. She stepped away and shook her head. "I have enough cares on my shoulders, I don't need the world's too. Men are hungry creatures, always looking for their next meal. Their hunger is never satiated. Eventually, he will trample you under his feet for a younger, more vibrant lover." She slammed the staff in the dirt. "Trust me. It's not worth it."

Ayianna crossed her arms and lifted her chin. "You must be a lonely woman."

"No—I don't need a man."

"Sometimes," Kael interjected, "you don't know what you need, much less want."

Jathil turned her silvery eyes on him. "Are you her betrothed?"

"No." He spat the word out a little too quickly.

"But you're a male . . . you should know all about these things. What I say is true, isn't it?"

"Elves hold themselves to a higher standard."

"Still a male." Jathil cocked her head. "Selfishness and disloyalty invade all races."

"And genders." Kael swung his bow over his shoulder. "If one finds a wife, she is a treasure and finds favor with Osaryn, why would he treat her thus?"

"The Thar'ryn Drayue. How quaint." Jathil leaned forward on her staff. "Tell me, does the great One-With-Many-Names still speak from Zohar? What do the guardians call him . . . Vituko? The great Shadow God? The Sacred Pearl has been silent for centuries. Arashel has moved beyond its influence despite Nevin Lazar's insistence to return."

"You know a lot for a common wanderer." Tariq's eyes narrowed.

Ayianna thought she saw Jathil stiffen at his words, but the Haruzo shifted her feet and shrugged.

"You'd be surprised how much drunk merchants talk," she said.

Desmond shot Jathil a glance Ayianna couldn't quite read. Did he take it as an insult? Or was he worried he might have crossed paths with her before? Being a merchant and all, had he spent evenings at a tavern before, drunk and talking to anyone who would listen? She wouldn't put it past him.

Tariq slung his bag over his shoulder. "Time to pack up. I'd like to make it to Gruben Pass before nightfall."

Ayianna quickly stepped into line behind Tariq. The farther she was from Jathil, the better. Maybe it wasn't such a good idea to have her along after all.

"Try to keep the talking to a minimum. We want to be able to hear our enemies before they hear us," Tariq said over his shoulder.

"True, but we'd smell them first," Vian said.

Tariq glanced back at the way they had come, before he drew his gaze to Vian. "The imps aren't the ones I'm worried about."

5

TWO DAYS LATER, low hanging clouds encompassed the mountains like a thick, wet blanket, and they still hadn't reached Gruben Pass. Kael scanned the pocked mountainside and quiet evergreens. The normal chatter of squirrels and birds had hushed. Even Jathil had ceased her questioning and opinionated comments.

He shivered. The moist air dampened his face and clothes. He would have given anything for a roaring fire, but Tariq insisted they keep moving. He stretched his stiff arms over his head and rolled his shoulders. Evening would be upon them soon, and they had yet to find a suitable campsite.

Tariq pressed forward and Kael continued after him.

"With this kind of cloud cover we could travel day and night," Vian said.

Kael arched a brow, but the others glared at them.

"Or not," Vian quickly added.

"Isn't it about time we rested?" Desmond asked.

Kael paused. He hated agreeing with Desmond, but . . . "We could use the rest."

Tariq scratched his thick sideburns and glanced around. He returned his attention to Kael. "We'll rest for a moment, but we need to reach Gruben Pass before nightfall."

"You've said that twice already, and we've not reached it yet. Are we lost?" Vian plopped down on the ground, not bothering to remove his gear.

Desmond reclined against a boulder. He took off his hat and ran his fingers through his oily hair. He plopped it back on, the scrawny feather drooping more than before. A film of beard and dirt covered the bottom half of his face. He had yet to use his copper razor. Early mornings didn't allow for such vanity. Why was he even here? He didn't care about the quest or the future of Nälu. It wasn't for the prince, as much as he would have liked them to believe. No, he was concerned only with himself and his rank within the courts of Badara. But how did the betrothal to Ayianna figure into this? He didn't love her, but what human from the plains loved their wives? Even if Desmond had good intentions, he did not deserve her.

Ayianna settled down with Liam away from everyone else and leaned her forehead into the wolf's neck. She seemed even more distant since Jathil joined them. The ache in his heart deepened. If anyone should have been ostracized, it should have been Jathil.

But then, he hadn't spoken with Ayianna since Bonzapur. Since the night before she had signed the contract. Why hadn't she listened to him? How could she agree to marry Desmond? He clenched his teeth. What was Desmond telling her? Surely, she could see the emptiness of his words.

He removed his bow and pack, pushing the anger away. It distorted his thinking, and he didn't have time or energy to waste. She had made the decision, and he would respect it.

"What's the hurry? Aside from the dragon, the curse, and running into a patrol of dwarves?" Jathil sat on the ground and placed her staff across her knees. Two nights ago, she had wielded it like a weapon, but today she used it as a walking stick. Who was this strange woman? She could hold her own against him and Tariq. And, as Tariq pointed out, she knew too much to be a simple commoner. "Are we not making good time?"

"The dithza-mielis." Tariq squatted and opened his bag. "It's too warm for this time of the year in the mountains. No doubt, they are near."

"You call this warm?" Vian crossed his legs and pulled his cloak over them. He tucked his chin beneath his scarf.

"Those old hags?" Jathil shrugged. "Haruzos have nothing to fear from them."

"But we have more than just Haruzos here." Tariq dug in his bag and pulled out a wooden crescent. "And I am responsible for their safety."

"Wait, what hags?" Vian straightened.

"He mentioned them back in Bonzapur." Kael hoisted his long bow and pulled back the sinew, testing it. Perhaps he'd have enough time to apply another coat of wax to the strings. He sat down and dug in his bag for the wax.

"Bows and arrows, daggers, or swords." Tariq shook his head. "Those weapons do not stand a chance against them."

"But you have prepared us for them, have you not?" Kael lifted his gaze to meet Tariq's.

"Of course." Tariq's smile didn't reach his eyes. He held up the crescent moon. "As well as I could. The wooden moons have been reinforced by the dwarves and their giftings. It will disperse them, but don't get too close to them." He stuck the moon in his belt then dumped his pack out and rummaged through his belongings. "You wouldn't happen to have a map on you, would you?"

"I thought you had the map, being the guide and all." Desmond propped his elbows on his knees. "Some guide you turned out to be."

"That's what you said about Kael, remember?" Vian lifted his chin, his gaze cut to Ayianna. "But if we had listened to him, things would have gone a whole lot smoother. Some things wouldn't have happened. Remember Nganjo?"

Vian's words shot daggers though his soul. Kael didn't need to be reminded of his mistakes. He shoved his pack closed and stood. "Perhaps we should move out."

"I can't find the map." Tariq tossed the empty bag down and pulled at his curls. Concern flashed in his eyes. Or was it fear?

"Maybe you forgot it." Vian stretched his arms over his head and slowly stood.

"What kind of guide forgets to pack a map?" Tariq shoved his things back in his bag and glanced up at Kael. "Do you have one?"

Kael shook his head. "Either you've lost it, or someone took it."

Tariq was not careless. But to think otherwise implied a thief or a traitor among them, and neither thought bode well with him. If only Saeed had not insisted on taking their mismatched group across deserts and mountains, he wouldn't have been dealing with this mess. He could have been farther ahead. But he wasn't being fair to Eloith or even Vian. He had a problem with only one of his companions.

"Who would have taken it?" Vian adjusted his pack and belt, ready to trek on as much as a tender-footed prince could. If the king of Badara could see his son now, he'd be proud.

"This is ridiculous." Desmond stood and shook out his cloak. "How will we find our way now?"

"How about asking the dryads?" Ayianna stroked Liam's nose. "I still have my wooden flute. I could summon one."

Tariq grunted. "The dryads of these mountains are old and bitter. I doubt they would be much help. Besides, this close to winter, they would have already entered their dormant state— like their trees." He flipped the bag over his shoulder and secured it around his waist. "I'm familiar enough with the terrain, and we have Jathil. I had wanted to recheck the distance and make sure we chose the correct pass, or we'll be heading south instead of north."

Jathil stood, her movements graceful and purposeful, like a cat's. "The farther you travel west, the less accurate the maps are. I'm sure, with both of us working together, we'll find the right path. This is, after all, my homeland we're talking about."

"Tariq, Kael!" Eloith's voice trumpeted above them before he appeared next to them. "The second dragon is heading north. I was wrong to think otherwise. It has been flying along this side of the mountains in great sweeps, running southeast to northwest and back again. I do believe it is headed our way."

Not again. Not here. Kael scanned the darkening, gloomy skies. The cloud cover would help, wouldn't it? The scant trees and solid rock to the left would do little to hide them. "How soon will it reach us?"

"The dragon and the imps could be here by tomorrow night, or sooner."

Kael faced Tariq. "There's no shelter here, and we don't know how long it will take to get to Gruben Pass. We could leave the trail, look for cover, and wait for the beast to pass us by, or we find a defensible position and take it down." He glanced at Ayianna. Her eyes widened as if reading his thoughts. Did she doubt herself? But she wouldn't have to do it alone this time. They could all be armed with the noqui stones—except Desmond. He returned his gaze to Tariq. "What do you think?"

"If we enter the pass, the dragon will not be able to fly into it."

"We make for the pass." Jathil twisted the staff in her hands. "Then we won't have to worry about the hags complicating things."

Kael eyed her harsh face. Her wild black and white hair overshadowed her silvery eyes, making her seem older. But behind the hardened exterior, he sensed hurt. Like his own. Did his face reflect hers? What did Ayianna see when she looked at him? The same bitter expression? He touched his brow along the skin's uneven edge—a reminder of an older, deeper hurt.

"Kael?" Tariq touched his shoulder.

He averted his gaze and nodded. "We make for the pass."

Evening descended quicker than Kael anticipated, and with it came the rain. As if they weren't wet enough. The cold drops hit his face and slid down his neck. He flipped the cloak's hood over his head, but the day's dampness had already penetrated his clothes, chilling him even more. They'd have to make camp soon.

He perched on the stone ledge, scanning for disturbances in nature. Low clouds swallowed the mountain peaks and pressed down on them. Wisps of fog slithered through the few trees dotting the rocky terrain and veiled the slopes in a gauzy mist. The heavy air should have been colder. For that, he was grateful. Where was Eloith? He should have returned at dusk.

Tariq and Jathil hiked farther up the trail; the rest fell in behind them. Ayianna and Liam brought up the rear. Her eyes studied the trail before her, and her forehead creased as if she warred with her own thoughts. A pain of regret slashed through him. He needed to make amends.

Kael stepped off the ledge as she trudged past. "Holding up all right?"

"I . . . ah . . ."Ayianna glanced at the others.

Kael followed her gaze. Beyond Vian's red mess of curls, Desmond's plume of feathers limped with each footfall. Was she afraid he would notice? Farther ahead, Tariq and Jathil were nearly eaten by the shadows and fog. He and Ayianna would have to quicken their pace, or they'd lose sight of their companions. Maybe he wanted to.

"I'm fine, thanks." She grasped the edges of her cloak and wrapped them tighter around her small frame. "Do you think we'll come across any dwarves?"

She *would* change the subject, but at least they were talking. He matched her stride. "I don't know. They once claimed most of the northern mountains and burrowed through them, mining all sorts of metals and gems, but that was before the clan wars. They probably still patrol Gruben Pass, but they have long since abandoned those mines. Let's hope we don't encounter them." Kael buried his hands beneath his cloak. The cold, wet air had sucked the warmth from them and his face, his pointy ears already numb. Elves were not made for the cold.

"I've heard that nobody has seen Ta'vazi and lived to tell of it," Ayianna said, her voice low. "Is that true?"

"Ah, yes, the great hidden city." Kael shifted his pack, the straps digging into his shoulders no matter where he placed them. He sidestepped a ridge of dirt and stone. "Strangers haven't been welcomed within their gates since the end of the war. Now all we have are stories of its magnificence. Who's to say if they are true or not?"

Ayianna clasped her hands in front her, a gold bangle flashed between the folds of her cloak. Desmond's token of marriage—more like bondage. How could she wear that thing? Couldn't she see he was a filthy, no good, arrogant dog? She wouldn't choose money over truth, over love, would she? Was that why she signed the contract? Surely, her parents held great sway in her choice—family duty and all—a grand thing to a point. But now her family was gone.

Like his.

Except her mother still lived, and the Sorceress was probably torturing her to reveal the whereabouts of the dagger. Was she strong like Ayianna? Would she resist the enemy? From the glimpse of her ghostly image in the tunnels, she fought the bindings of the curse, but for how long? He had vowed to help find her. Hadn't Ayianna believed him?

She hiked next to him, shoulders straight, chin lifted, and stubbornness written all over her face. A rare star of hope in the growing darkness. Would she survive it? Eloith's words returned to him as if spoken only last night. *"Her essence dims."* What did he mean by that?

"I bet it's amazing." Ayianna's voice cut into his thoughts and yanked him back to the present. "A city carved right out of the mountainside. Probably the perfect place to study the stars." A smile brightened her face and warmed his heart.

"I think Zurial is by far the best location for studying the stars if you were still interested in pursuing the study."

"Only pureblood elves can do that. Besides, I doubt Desmond would consider it."

There she went again. He bit back his snide comment. "You don't—"

"Don't what?" She clenched her jaw. "What do you know about what I can and can't do? You are an elf and a male. You can be or do anything you want."

"That's not what I—"

"My mother is human, and we are now living among her kind. Without Desmond, we will starve to death. We will be nothing, have nothing, and be trampled by the humans and their demeaning laws."

Kael pushed the pent-up frustration through his nose. Was she that blind? Or was he? He had lived among the humans for six years, but it had been in the north with the guardians. Ethnic prejudice was expected no matter where he traveled, but learning the laws and the ways of the host nation was important.

Leena had voiced her disgust at the social nuances of the plains people plenty of times, but he had been too busy studying to care. Besides, most of the rules hadn't applied to him. He had been oblivious. Guilt rippled through him. The memory of Leena's broken body slammed into him. His sister had helped him in so many ways, and he didn't even realize how much she had sacrificed to do it. How could he have been that blind?

Ayianna faced him, her dark eyes imploring. "Don't you understand? My parents betrothed me to him. And now my home is destroyed. My father is gone. My mother and I . . ." She turned away. "We would become scavengers and risk being exiled to Durqa. Or we would have to sell ourselves to the lords. I can't do that to her when I can save her."

He had to bring his thoughts back to Ayianna. Revisiting the death of his family and friends was the last thing he needed, and it wouldn't do her any good. Still, the echoes of his failure surrounded both Ayianna's future and his past compounded into a thunderous windstorm of voices in his head. It was his fault she bore the harpy's curse. If he had been able to save Teron, she wouldn't have to be considering Desmond's worthless proposal.

His chest tightened and guilt's abyss threatened to devour him. How could he answer her? He couldn't. He sidestepped her and started after the others.

"Wait—look!" Ayianna pointed up the mountainside where a thick fog oozed in and out of the crevices, clinging to the earth.

A shiver raced down his back. Shadows shifted in the mist as an eerie presence chilled his thoughts. The shadows grew darker and closer until figures emerged. Nine, no, *ten* wraiths hovered above the ground.

"Do you see what I see?" Ayianna whispered.

"Tariq!" Kael lifted his bow and nocked an arrow. The arrow sailed through the advancing figures as if they were an illusion.

"Dithza-mielis." Tariq jogged toward them. He reached for the crescent moon tucked into his belt.

They glided closer. Kael could just make out their wrinkly skin hanging from their bones like old hags long dead. White eyes peered out from under their heavy eyelids. Their blackened lips curled into sneers, revealing crooked, rotting teeth. A few strands of greasy hair draped the back of their bald heads and wiggled down their back like worms. Their shabby robes swirled about them as they swarmed upon the travelers, the air growing warmer. They hummed a discordant tune and gnashed their rotting teeth.

Kael unsheathed his sword and charged them. He would not fail this time. The hags encircled him, arms raised. Skeletal fingers slashed the air, their long nails like daggers. They reached for him. Kael swung, but the blade hissed through the hags without injury. They shrieked with laughter.

"The klhoddas, Kael!" Tariq launched a moon into the throng of hags. "The wooden moons."

Kael fumbled for the klhodda at his side, but one of the hags seized his head. Pain exploded across his skin as if the hag would crack his skull open. The sharp nails dug deeper, piercing his mind and soul. He doubled over, trying to shove against the intrusion. The hags had no substance. This could not be happening. But the hag's fiery touch plunged deeper, sending waves of shock and agony through him. Darkness swallowed him, heavy, like water at the bottom of the sea. He thrashed upward; he needed to breathe.

Rysa's anguished face flashed before him. Her words burned in his head. *Save Braedon, don't worry about me!* Her gurgled screams pierced his soul. He sought her, but did not find her. His memories lashed him like a whip, their barbs tearing his soul. He fought them, but still they came. Ayianna's limp body in his arms, the festering wound at her neck. Teron's headless body, Leena's blood pooling at his feet. Braedon—*no, not my son!* He would not, could not. *Osaryn, I can't do this!*

Death. Let it take him. He strained for it. If only to peel away his skin, his flesh, and be set free. Ice stabbed his head, and the chill trickled down his neck and eased through his body, reaching for his heart.

Ayianna stumbled to Kael's side. His still frame drove fear into her heart like a dagger. Her knees buckled. He couldn't be . . .

The hag descended upon him. Ayianna jerked the moon from his belt and chucked it at the hag, but the tip of the crescent snagged her cloak. It wobbled and fell to the earth. She scrambled to retrieve it.

The hag continued to dig her nails into Kael's head. She opened her mouth as if she would consume him whole. Would she? Ayianna flung the moon hard, and it clipped the hag's throat. The hag dissolved.

"Use your klhoddas!" Tariq's shout rang out as Ayianna dropped to her knees next to Kael.

"Kael?" She shook him. His skin was cold and clammy. She leaned over his head. His breath brushed her skin. *He's alive!* Relief flooded her and tears stung her eyes. She fumbled for the vial of kulin.

"What are you doing?" Tariq darted to her side. He flung a wooden moon. It whistled through the air in an arc toward an oncoming dithza-mieli. The moon sliced through her and returned to Tariq.

"Kael needs help."

"There's no time for that now." Tariq yanked Ayianna to her feet. "We must eliminate them first."

Ayianna searched the ground for Kael's moon but couldn't find it. She reached for her bag and dug out hers. For the next several minutes, she attempted to master the art of throwing the klhodda. Soon, the number of hags began to dwindle, and Ayianna grew in confidence.

One with a bulbous nose hurtled toward her. Ayianna threw the moon, but it sailed past her. Before the moon could return, the hag grasped her head.

Ayianna screamed as the nails pierced her head and reached into the very fiber of her soul. Pain exploded throughout her body. Horrible memories flooded her mind: her brother's headless body, her mother's sunken eyes, the sword protruding from her father's dead body.

Osaryn, help me . . .

The long fingernails dug deeper, ripping open Ayianna's deepest fears and secrets. A hideous creature rose in her mind's eye, his human face smudged with blood and bat-like wings stretched about him. The harpy lord. He was the one who had cursed her forever. She struggled against the invasion of hopelessness as icy venom seeped into her soul, numbing her senses.

But the agony disappeared, and the images faded. Ayianna crumbled to the ground and curled inward, rocking against the pain and cold.

"Ayianna?" Tariq asked.

Her limbs continued to shake as the aftershocks of the hag's intrusion died away. The rain sharpened, lashing her face with tiny blades of ice. Her teeth chattered.

Tariq lifted her cloak, wrapped a blanket around her shoulders, and replaced her cloak. "Can you stand?"

Ayianna nodded but didn't move. Her gaze fell on Kael. He lay motionless beneath several layers of blankets. Vian spread his cloak over him and knelt by his side. Ayianna looked up at Tariq. His amber eyes seemed to glow.

"The kulin can help, right?" She pushed herself to her knees but couldn't find the strength to stand. Not yet. "The merfolk's healing waters, it can help?"

"I'm afraid not," Tariq replied. "The kulin can only heal real wounds."

"But this feels real!"

"Yes," Tariq replied. "Stand, we need to move quickly."

"Kael is still alive." Vian lowered Kael's arm and placed it under the blanket. "But he is not responding."

"We need some *maezam aenlu*," Eloith said as Desmond joined them, out of breath.

"Where can we find that?" Vian asked.

"In Vadazi's Gorge," Eloith replied. "It is not too far for one such as myself."

"Go, Eloith," Tariq said.

Eloith leapt into the air and disappeared into the fog.

"We need shelter." Tariq grabbed his pack and swung it over his shoulder. "How close are we to the pass?"

Jathil scanned the terrain and sniffed the air. "We should be close."

"There are abandoned mines there—we can seek shelter within them." Tariq scooped up Kael, and Vian grabbed his gear. "Let's go."

Desmond stomped past where Ayianna knelt. "We should leave the half-breed behind. He might not even—"

"You will not use that term." Tariq's voice held a steely edge. "We will do whatever is in our powers to save him. If we cannot . . . we will worry about that later."

No. They would find a way to save him. They had to. Ayianna staggered to her feet, her vision swimming. A hand clutched her elbow and steadied her.

"Easy there, Dragonslayer." Jathil wrapped her arm around Ayianna, and together, they followed Tariq.

6

"I BET YOUR little heart is breaking." Desmond's breath hissed near Ayianna's ear.

"And you are gloating." Ayianna jerked her cloak tighter and refused to look at Kael's bundled form lying next to Vian.

The mine's cold, damp walls were worn and most of the timber had splintered. Were they safe? Perhaps from the dragon, but what about the imps? Or other natural disasters, like tunnels caving in or stumbling upon wild beasts? Of course, Liam would have alerted them already if that was the case.

"You should have seen the look on your face."

Ayianna clenched her teeth, and a spasm shot through her skull. "You've won. I've already signed the contract, or did you forget that?"

"I did win, didn't I?" He leaned back and smirked. "And you've forgotten that so quickly. Contracts mean nothing when your heart belongs to someone else—unless, of course, he dies."

"He won't." He couldn't. She wouldn't allow herself to think otherwise, or she'd lose whatever composure she had.

Desmond's presence and the dark of the narrow tunnel threatened to suffocate her. She took a deep breath, hoping the spinning would not start again. She pushed past the ache in her body and stood. The pressure in her head mounted, but she stumbled toward the old mine's gaping mouth where Jathil and Liam watched for Eloith's return. Or for the hags or the imps—whichever came first.

The clouds slowly shifted and revealed glimpses of the moon's pale face. Its dim light bathed the pass in silver. The recent glaze of ice glinted, daring them to venture beyond. Dark holes like vacant eyes pitted the mountainside and glared down on them.

Jathil shifted her feet and pressed a hand against the other side of the stone wall. Her only response to Ayianna's presence. Fierce, independent, and alone.

Ayianna folded her arms across her waist. Did Jathil hold the betrothal against her? She wouldn't have signed the contract. She would have seen Desmond for what he was. And what was he? A typical human from the plains. If Ayianna hadn't grown up among the elves, she wouldn't have known any difference. She would have rejoiced with her mother and eagerly waited for their day of union. But, surely, not all men of the plains were like him. Vian wasn't.

Jathil uncorked her waterskin and took a drink, her movements graceful and measured. Were all the northern Haruzo recluses like her? No, or none of them would marry and have children. They would have all died off.

Her bitter words from earlier slammed into her. *It's not worth it.* Why did she hate marriage? Had she been hurt? If Ayianna could deny the desire for such, she would. But could she bind herself to Desmond? She glanced over her shoulder.

Desmond reclined against the stone; eyes closed. His usual handsome face was drawn and clouded. His charm had all but disappeared. The discord between him and Vian had grown. Would their friendship survive the quest? If not, then what? A man like Desmond wouldn't walk away from a future of wealth and nobility. Unless, of course, he had something grander than the courts of Badara. And if that was the case, why would he even want her?

The wound in her neck throbbed as if agreeing with her.

Ayianna gritted her teeth. A sharp pain blossomed in the back of her head and tears stung her eyes. She had to stop doing that. And stop worrying over her decision. What was done was done. But the hag had dredged up her memories, awakening the raw pain and grief. It burned sharp in her chest as if it had all happened yesterday.

She glared at the scarred mountainside, willing Eloith to appear. Tariq had slipped out as soon as they had settled to scout the area and to watch for Eloith. How long would it take them? Would Kael's condition worsen? Would Eloith be able to heal him? The questions drowned her, but she couldn't stop. If she did, she'd have to face her deepest fear. What if Kael never woke up?

She gasped, taking in a lungful of cold, bitter air.

"Are you all right?" Jathil's eyes glimmered in the moon's pale light.

"Yes." Ayianna turned her face away, brushing at the tears. "What—why do your eyes glow?"

"I am Haruzo, and we are cat, even when we walk like a human." Jathil's gaze returned to the dark paths below. "In my true form, I can see in the night as if it were day, but here in human flesh, I see better than you, but not quite as good as when I'm a cat."

Ayianna's vision blurred. The world started tilting again. She leaned against the mine's wall and slid to the ground. If only the dizziness and the pain would go away. She hugged her knees to her chest.

Liam pressed her wet nose against Ayianna's cheek as if to say all would be well. Ayianna stroked Liam's damp neck, but a bur bit into her skin. Again. Ayianna sighed. Would she ever get all the burs out of her fur? She tugged the strands free of the prickly spines, her mind returning to the churning of her heart.

No. She had to focus on something else or she would suffocate. She pried the burs from Liam's fur, forcing her thoughts anywhere but the dark form bundled next to Vian. Still, the tears slid down her face, and the ache in her head grew.

Jathil lowered into a crouch and placed her staff on the ground. She tugged at a bur along Liam's tail. "There is nothing wrong with crying."

Flames engulfed Ayianna's cheeks. She wiped away the tears with the edge of her cloak, the rough material scratching her eyes. Her grief sought release like an air bubble rising through watery depths, but Ayianna fought it. She rubbed her face harder. "It's weakness."

"It's a part of life, the healing process. If you don't let go of the tears, they will swell and drown you."

She clenched her jaw, and the pounding in her head increased. "Now is neither the time nor the place to be blubbering with tears."

"Who determines the right time and place? You? Me? The world? In that case, is it ever the right time and place?" Jathil shook her head. She placed her palm on Ayianna's head, and the coolness of her skin calmed the ache throbbing behind her eyes. "We aren't guaranteed tomorrow, and you don't want to waste your life waiting on some supposedly right time that might never happen."

"Is that why you are living out here alone?"

"No." Jathil removed her hand. She plucked her staff from the ground and straightened. She stared out into the darkness as silence settled between them. After a while, she lifted her chin. "Tariq comes, and he does not bring good news."

Moments later, a black panther slunk into the entrance, but before Ayianna could react, the large feline had flickered into Tariq. She blinked. Had she really seen him as a cat?

"The dragon is here." Tariq rubbed the sweat from his forehead and shook ice crystals from his curls. "It's perched on one of the higher cliffs, but it can't come this far down. The pass is too narrow and steep. The imps, on the other hand, can."

Ayianna staggered to her feet. "What should we do?"

"I say we attack." Vian stepped up next to her and unsheathed his sword. "It might give us the advantage."

"But what about Kael?" Ayianna glanced at his still form, his somber face forlorn. "We can't leave him."

"Yes, we could." Desmond pressed his shoulder into the wall near Ayianna, his gaze mocking her. "He's nearly dead already."

Jathil shook her head. "We can stay here and defend our position."

"It's a dead end." Vian raised his eyebrows. "And what do you know about war strategies?"

"The narrow entrance would hinder an outright charge, and we wouldn't have to worry about our backs."

"Okay, so maybe you know a little."

"We could retreat?" The last thing Ayianna wanted was to go deeper into the mines, but it couldn't be worse than the ravine they had fallen into back in Inganno.

"We wouldn't be able to fight well in such cramped conditions." Vian rolled his shoulders. "We should take the offensive and fall back if need be."

"But the imps could circle behind us and block our exit." Tariq stepped out of the entrance and into the moonlight. He nosed the air like a cat.

Liam brushed against Ayianna and growled. Ayianna could smell it too. The horrible smell of something long dead drifted on the air. She was back in Dagmar again.

Tariq hoisted his blade. "We don't have time. They're here."

Ayianna steadied herself and pulled out her sling. Her fingers trembled as she fitted a stone. Fear riddled her body like holes in a sieve. Whispers of footsteps padded the ground. Claws scratched against stone and ice, growing louder, quicker as they neared.

A horde of imps materialized out of the shadows, pouring into the pass. Tariq and the others grabbed their swords and bounded forward. Jathil unsheathed her two short blades and joined them. A bow and arrow would have been most useful.

Somewhere above them a dragon roared, belching flames into the night sky. The blast of light cast the sheer walls of the narrow pass in severe jagged lines. Hundreds of yellow eyes shimmered in its wake.

J. L. MBEWE

Ayianna's breath caught. *Osaryn, help us.*

She whirled the sling above her head, snapped her wrist, and the noqui sailed through the air. It struck an imp, turning it into a stark white statue. The other imps rammed into it and shattered it beneath their feet. Gaining strength, Ayianna flung stone after stone into the charging imps.

They surged closer, and Vian, Tariq, and Jathil leapt to meet them. Her hand fumbled with her pouch; the stones nearly half gone. She couldn't grab a stone quick enough.

An imp slammed into her, and she drew her sword.

The imps washed over the weary travelers like a tsunami wave. Ayianna charged, but dizziness threatened her balance. Her foot slipped on an icy patch, and she fell to her knees. A sharp spasm shot through her legs. Throbbing pain split her skull. If relief didn't come soon, her head would explode.

She scrambled up and swung her sword at the advancing fiends, plowing through them like a drunken farmer. Again and again. Hot, rancid blood sprayed her face, mixing with her tears, and gushed over her hands. The sword's hilt slipped in her fingers, but she tightened her grip, her strength waning. How much more could they take?

Against the darkened sky, fiery torches bobbed from the other side of the pass. Metal from armor and weapons glinted in the light. Shrieks rose from the imps. Full-bearded men no taller than children crashed through the melee, their battle-axes swinging. The dreaded highland dwarves.

The remaining imps fled before them and scrambled back to the dragon perched above the pass. Relief flooded Ayianna. They were coming to their aid—or were they?

Ten burly dwarves marched toward them, their chainmail clinking with each step. They wore thick pants and long-sleeved tunics, and their faces were as stony as the mountains they called home. Their hair and beards were shades of blond, except one. His was red, and his gaze flicked from Ayianna and her companions to the other dwarves until they had surrounded them with their axes raised.

Ayianna stepped back and bumped into Tariq and Vian. Jathil stood to her right. Her hood hid her face, but her shoulders were squared, her body tense, her double blades at the ready.

"This can't be good." Vian lifted his shield.

A dwarf with white-blond hair and beard lunged. "*Vosrra!*"

But the redhead leapt forward and brought his axe up. The clang of axes reverberated in the mountain pass. The two exploded in an exchange of harsh words that Ayianna could not understand.

Jathil pressed into her and whispered. "They want to kill us, but the redhead refuses."

"Can we take them?" Vian slowly brought his sword up, but Jathil pushed his hand down.

"There are too many. It won't end well."

"I will not go down without a fight."

"Of course not, you fool." Jathil cocked her head, but her eyes never left the arguing dwarves. "Just don't be stupid about it."

Vian grunted. "I am not—"

"No." Tariq elbowed Vian. "We will not fight."

"*Vosrra kruskavim!*" The white-blond bellowed, gesturing at them.

"Well, unless they try to kill us." Vian squared his shoulders and kept his sword at the ready.

"*Zi. Khadu zakkad khan klehvr ona* Nälu." The redhead stepped between them and the other dwarf.

"He won't kill us." Jathil's gaze slid to Vian. "Because we bear the shield of Nälu. Perhaps the guardians hold more sway over Ta'vazi than I thought."

Ayianna lowered her sword. "So, they will let us go?"

"No." Jathil snorted. "They are taking us prisoner."

7

THE SALTY AIR misted Saeed's face as he gripped the balcony's railing, forcing the tremor in his hands to calm. His long white beard whipped in the wind rolling off the glittering sea below. To the east, the blue-tinged mountains of Zurial hugged the coast and disappeared into the Kadrokar Swamps to the north. Behind him, Praetan, the golden city of the south, sprawled across the heights at the edge of the plains—so close to the elves, yet separated by more than just mountains and rivers.

Saeed shook his head. The elves cared not for the ways of man and who could blame them. The race of man had given the Guardian Circle the most trouble since the dissolution of the old Alliance.

"*Nawaeliha,* Headmaster."

Saeed turned.

Nevin Nerissa stood beneath the arched doorway. The wind tugged at her gray robe. Her long white braids swirled around her angled forehead. The sun glinted off her opalescent skin, making her almost glow.

He pressed his fingertips to his lips and bowed slightly. "*Nawaeliha*, Nerissa. How was your visit home?"

"Home . . ." The merwoman sighed, and her gaze shifted to the sea. "It was good to be home. Each year I am away, the older I feel and the slower my body transitions between land and sea."

"Perhaps next year you could oversee the observation phase in Ganya."

"If we live to see next year."

"We will." Saeed gazed across the rippling waters. He refused to think otherwise.

"You are optimistic in the face of such adversity."

"Doubt breeds fear, and fear only paralyzes the thinker. We must not fail, or the consequences will be disastrous."

"But of course, Headmaster. Forgive me."

"You have done nothing in need of forgiveness."

Nerissa bowed her head and stared into the sea below. They stood quietly while the sea roared beneath them. The crashing waves filled Saeed's ears, and for a moment he was lost in their lilting song as they lulled him to a distant place far from the ominous times at hand.

He ran his fingers over the braids in his beard. Each passing year, the tremor in his hands grew worse. He was older than anyone ever should be. He had seen more than anyone should have. The sands of time buried him; death reached for him like ice on the edge of winter. Why him? He was not fit to lead the Alliance to victory.

For such a time as this.

Vituko's words covered him like a healing balm. Of course, he would serve until his time came. But would he live to see the end of the curse and the plains people set free? If not, who would lead them? Perhaps Vituko would give him grace to see this through.

He lifted his chin. "I know you didn't come out here just to stare longingly into the sea."

A faint smile brushed Nerissa's lips. "What you say is true, but I would find any excuse to visit the sea, even if it is just to stare longingly and feel its fresh, salty breath on my skin." She gathered her wayward hair and pushed it back from her face.

"Unai and the others are here, except Hadrian of course—running late as usual."

"Well, let's not keep them waiting, shall we?" Saeed held out his arm and escorted Nerissa back into the king's council room.

"Why Praetan, Saeed?" Unai asked after the guardians had sat down around the large round table. Slender, stained-glass windows splintered the afternoon sun across the spacious room. Bright tapestries and banners adorned the walls, boasting of Praetan's strength in battle.

Saeed frowned as Unai reclined in his chair and drummed the polished marble with his fingers. "King Teman has allowed us to use his private hall for the time being. I find it rather convenient since Darin arrived by ship, and time seems to escape us. Besides, it keeps the enemy guessing our whereabouts."

Unai nodded and continued drumming.

Across from Unai sat Eldwyn with his back straight and his shoulders squared. His long black hair complemented the gray of his embroidered tunic and contained not a single silver strand. Like most sea elves, his posture and behavior conveyed excellence and grace to a degree of coldness, which balanced Saeed's demeanor quite well. Desert elves were passionate to a fault and had no time for proper decorum, or perhaps he'd become too old for such nonsense. Eldwyn lifted his gaze to Saeed. "What news does Runako's servant bring of the quest?"

"They started out from Bonzapur several weeks ago," Saeed said. "But they have had trouble in the desert."

"What sort of trouble?" Nerissa's smooth face showed no expression—typical for the merfolk, but concern swirled in her pale eyes.

"They found the people of Zajur dead. All of them destroyed by yellow creatures with large blue eyes and a mouthful of teeth."

Unai ceased his drumming and straightened. "What?"

"Kael thinks the creatures were waiting for them." Saeed folded his arms and leaned on the table. He skimmed the guardians' faces. What was he looking for? A spark of hope? But what he found was a quiet desperation against formidable odds. Was that not hope enough?

"Why would he think that?" Unai asked.

"Because the creatures were chanting *quatat, quatat* when they attacked."

"*Kill, kill* . . . that must have been awful." Leora twirled her golden ringlets around her finger—a nervous habit she'd had since Saeed had known her. The cat-sized fairy sat atop the table on an upside-down mug. Her iridescent wings folded against her back. Even in her simple tunic and pants, she emanated royalty. Queen of the fairies, and, until recently, last of her kind. She turned her violet eyes to Saeed. "What kind of animal would do such a thing?"

"Even if Kael possessed the gift to speak to animals, he would not have heard the words in Táchil." Darin scrubbed his bristly face. He had arrived only that morning and had skipped a bath and a shave at Saeed's request. "I would not consider these animals, but creatures of the Abyss. Animals don't kill for killing's sake."

"A pack of wild dogs will." Unai flicked his hand up as if to brush Darin's comments aside. "If they were from the Abyss, how would they have crossed the Perimeter, and why would they have killed everyone in Zajur? And why Zajur?"

Eldwyn cleared his throat. "Did the quest suffer any casualties?"

"One."

The room succumbed to silence as they waited for Saeed to continue. He glanced around. He hated being the bringer of bad news. As the High Guardian and Headmaster, he'd had more than his fair share of tragic tidings. He took a breath and glanced at Darin.

The half-giant reclined in his chair; his long legs stretched out beneath the table. A dark leather patch covered one eye, but his remaining one pierced Saeed's heart. Perhaps he already knew. Darin straightened under Saeed's gaze and crossed his bare arms.

"I am sorry, Darin," Saeed said. "Aberim didn't make it."

Darin's jaw tightened as he closed his eye, the lines in his face deepening. Saeed reached over and squeezed the half-giant's hand. Keeping his composure, Darin glanced at him. "I will speak with Aberim's family."

Saeed nodded.

"So according to Kael," Unai began, "these creatures had been sent to Zajur to kill them. Any leads on who might have sent them?"

"Who do you think?" Darin rubbed his bald scalp and readjusted his eye patch.

"Of course, the Sorceress Semine, but how would she have known?" Unai pressed on. "Everyone knows it is safer and quicker to send them through Mútni. Who would have known they would be in Zajur?"

Darin stiffened. "I knew, because I told them to go there."

"Why?"

"Are you suggesting that I told her?" The wooden chair scratched against the stone floor as Darin stood. The half-giant towered over Unai's squat form.

"Calm down." Saeed grabbed Darin's arm. "Nobody is accusing you of this dreadful deed."

Darin shook his arm free and sat back down. He continued glaring at Unai, but remained quiet.

"Darin, I know you didn't tell Semine our plans." Lazar leaned forward and rested his crossed arms atop the table. The highlander was the youngest of them all, despite the white streaking his black hair, but his recent trip to Arashel had depleted the sparkle from his pale eyes. Saeed didn't have to ask. The Haruzo of Arashel would not be joining them. Lazar tilted his head and continued. "But I am curious why you sent them to Zajur instead of Mútni?"

"Because Mútni would've taken them too close to Durqa. Do you know how Semine suddenly has an army? The exiled criminals. Lord Derk has rallied the support of the Durquians and has overthrown the guards. But not everyone has joined his cause. There's no telling how many thieves and murderers have escaped. The northern desert is treacherous." Darin clasped his hands over his bald head and leaned back. "Besides, if everyone knew it was safer and quicker, wouldn't you think the enemy would have thought of that?"

"Well, obviously not." Across the table, Nerissa tucked a white braid behind her ear. "But she has other ways of finding out information."

"Were there any others who might've known? Did you tell anybody?" Unai asked.

Darin leaned forward and folded his arms. "Any one of you could have known."

Saeed stroked his beard and glanced around the table. Could there be another defector? Someone so deep in the Guardian Circle he hadn't noticed? He still hadn't figured out how the apprentice, Imaran, had learned of the hidden vaults and the secret chants to open them.

"Look, we were in Raemoja, I was telling Kael to go to Zajur, and then . . ." Darin paused. "Hadrian handed Kael a bundle of rope. He disagreed with me; he seemed to think that Mútni was better."

"Hadrian?" Leora's head snapped up. "Could it be?"

"Enough." Saeed stood. "Let's not be quick to jump to conclusions and accuse each other of betrayal."

"But he said—"

"Have you forgotten the enemy has eyes and ears all over the place? Anyone could have eavesdropped on that conversation." Saeed tugged on his braided beard and eyed each and every one of the guardians. "We must all be more careful."

"It has happened before," Nerissa said. Everyone turned to look at her. "Betrayal has shaken the Guardian Circle before."

"Hadrian doesn't exactly have a clean past," Lazar said quietly, keeping his eyes down.

"He is a dwarf," Eldwyn said. "Dwarves aren't noted for their trustworthiness beyond their own clans."

Saeed rubbed his face. He dropped his hands and brushed the table with his fingers. "Might I remind you that neither Semine, nor Derk, nor Ronan were dwarves. In fact, Ronan was an elf."

"A Wofsamor elf," Eldwyn said, but quickly added, "But you are right; we must not allow our prejudices to run ahead of us."

"Well, at least question him." Leora's voice was higher than usual.

"Would you like to do the honors, Leora?" Unai asked. "How do you think it would sound? My dear, old friend, have you betrayed us?"

Saeed raised his hand and waited for their undivided attention. With age came wisdom, but also forgetfulness, and sometimes Saeed had to remind them to use their wisdom. "There is no evidence of a traitor in our midst, and until such a time there is, I say we speak naught of this again."

Just then a door creaked, and Hadrian shuffled in. A dark scowl etched his jagged face. Thin streams of silver swam through his brown hair and beard, and bags hung under his eyes. He looked as if he hadn't slept in a week. The door clicked shut behind him. The sound was magnified in the quiet room as everyone stared at him.

"So . . . I'm a bit late!" Hadrian growled. He unbuckled the belt across his chest and slid his double-headed axe from his back. "Did I miss anything?"

"Not at all, we were just getting started," Unai said rather too quickly. He leaned back in his chair and feigned a smile. He motioned toward the empty seat next to him. "Care to join us, so we may continue?"

Hadrian grunted. He limped to the offered chair and sat down with a huff.

"We have some news about the quest." Leora's eyes narrowed.

"Oh?" Hadrian dropped his axe on the table. It clattered against the stone and echoed off the walls. "Have they failed already?"

"They had some trouble at Zajur," Darin said.

All eyes were on the dwarf as the guardians waited with bated breath. Saeed shook his head. He held Hadrian in the highest regard; the dwarf wouldn't have betrayed them—but then, Saeed held all of them in high regard. It was what made a guardian a guardian.

Hadrian raised an eyebrow and glanced around the table. He shrugged. "Well, I told you you should've sent them to Mútni."

Leora's eyes flicked to the others and then returned to the dwarf. "Somehow Semine knew they would be in Zajur and sent creatures to kill them."

"Really?" Hadrian's brows jumped. "What happened? Did they make it to Bonzapur all right?"

"They made it." Unai shifted his weight, and the chair creaked beneath him. "Do you happen to have any ideas on how Semine would have known they would be in Zajur?"

"No." Hadrian readjusted the leather vest over his dingy tunic. "Why do you ask? You think I told her?"

"Of course not." Unai smirked and exchanged glances with Leora.

Saeed cleared his throat. "Since Hadrian is here, let us begin." He turned to the dwarf. "What news do you bring from the dwarven clans?"

"Aye! The Igazin and Klovan will provide the Alliance with a combined force of two thousand and fifty warriors."

"What about the Stozic clan?"

"We haven't associated with them since the clan wars."

But Hadrian had and had failed. The prince's wedding hadn't been that long ago according to elf years, or dwarf years for that matter. Did he still blame himself for Ta'vazi's refusal to join the Council of Nations? Saeed leaned forward and touched Hadrian's arm. "It is never too late."

Hadrian batted Saeed's hand aside. "Kvazkhun and Stratuvec are as good as you will ever get from the dwarves."

Saeed grunted. Dwarves could be so thick-headed. "Lazar, what news do you bring from the highlands?"

Lazar's shoulders slumped. "King Nagid has refused."

"Then he has sided with the enemy!" growled Hadrian.

"You seem quick to judge." Leora's thin eyebrows arched, and her wings trembled. "All things considered."

Hadrian hit the table with his fist. "You're either for us or against us. There is no neutral ground in the battle against evil."

"We will not yet judge those whose allegiance remains questionable." Saeed's gaze shifted from Hadrian to the others. "There is still time." He turned to Eldwyn. "What about the elves?"

"Indeed, King Vuryn is readying his army as we speak. He has nearly a thousand archers and five hundred swordsmen at the Alliance's disposal."

"That could be doubled if the Wofsamor elves joined us."

Eldwyn shook his head. "I would not place my hopes, as slim as they are, on them. They hide deep in the enchanted forest of Striisa Vaar and bar any attempt on our part to communicate with them."

"Perhaps they've all died out by now." Hadrian flipped the leather belt to one side.

"Good riddance, if that is the case." Eldwyn frowned. "No race has turned out as many pirates as the Wofsamor elves."

"Gentlemen," Saeed said. "We need all the numbers we can get. Semine's army is nearly ten thousand strong and continues to grow. Not to mention, she is reinforcing it with the curse."

"Why don't we add a little power to ours?" Lazar asked. "Even out the odds a bit."

Saeed shook his head. "That would be an abuse of the Yenzo Tanil, and we'd be stripped of it."

"Forgive me for sounding childish." Lazar scratched the thick sideburns stretching along the sides of his face. "But that seems unfair. Semine can do it, but we can't?"

"Semine has pledged herself to Taethza, the queen of the Underworld. This gives her access to the Tóas Dikon, but doing so comes at a great price. Semine has traded her soul for temporary glory. If Semine is successful in releasing Taethza from the Underworld, she will no longer be needed."

"What will happen to Semine?"

Saeed's shoulders slumped. How had Semine—the little babe left on his doorstep—become this formidable sorceress? She had held such potential. Granted, he knew nothing of raising babies, but he hadn't done it alone. The whole of Dagmar had taken her in and reared her as if she had been their own. What had caused her to forsake the Shadow God and everything they had taught her? Not even her mentor knew, although he had blamed Derk. Saeed sought Lazar's youthful face again. "Taethza does not share her glory with anyone. She will destroy her."

"We don't know that for certain." Unai folded his arms across his belly.

"Nothing is certain until you are dead." Saeed leaned back. "Let us hope we can stop her."

"So where does that leave us numerically speaking?" Darin asked.

"At the most . . ." Saeed tugged on his braided beard. "I would say around six thousand, including Bonzapur and Praetan."

Darin whistled. "Not quite as many as we had hoped."

"What about the Giants? Who have they sided with?" Unai asked.

"They, too, have refused to join the Alliance," Darin replied.

Hadrian's chair creaked as he tried to get comfortable, his stubby legs swinging inches from the ground. "I don't blame them."

"And the Kaleki?" Saeed turned his gaze to the merwoman.

"The king will uphold his commitment to Nälu." Nerissa pulled a crystal vial from her satchel and poured several drops of its clear liquid into her palm. She rubbed it over her face and neck. "He has promised ten dragons of his Royal Aviation Force, two hundred foot soldiers, and a special surprise for the lake and rivers."

"I can imagine this surprise," Saeed said. "Let us hope it is easy to clean out of the lakes and rivers once the battle is over."

"What's the strategy then?" Eldwyn asked. "Do we attack them or wait for them to make the first move?"

Saeed frowned. "We must gather the Alliance and confer with the generals, but I wish to remain on the offensive. If all goes well, I want to march on Badara by spring."

"Will the plains people be able to fight?" Eldwyn asked.

"They are worthless to us." Unai scratched the tuffs of hair behind his ears. His polished pate gleamed in the ray of sun streaming through a nearby window. "Once they've fully surrendered to the curse, they will do Semine's bidding as their own. Lucky for us, she did not take into the consideration that the more they fight the curse, the more debilitated they will become."

"The quest is our hope." Doubt flitted at the edges of Saeed's words. He touched his balding scalp and breathed a plea to Vituko.

Unai frowned. "A fool's hope, you mean."

Nerissa returned the vial to her bag and lifted her gaze to Unai. "Without the Dwalu Tonic, the people of the plains have no hope."

"Guardians." Saeed placed his hands on the table. "This brings us to our next topic. Semine's curse will destroy the plains people. Even now, we see them struggling against it, and it drives them to hurt themselves and others. We must gather them to safety to protect themselves and where we can administer the tonic."

"They will not go willingly." Darin shifted his long legs, his knees bumping the table. "What do you suggest? Throwing them all in the dungeons? There are not enough cells in all of eastern Nälu to hold them. You would do it appropriately, right?"

"Of course, and I believe Leora might have a solution." Saeed nodded toward the fairy.

Leora stood and strolled around the tabletop, glancing at each guardian as she went. "The fairies know a sleeping charm. We could assist you in gathering as many of the cursed as we can and putting them to sleep, provided we have a place to keep them safe."

"Magic." Lazar's pale eyes widened. "How?"

"No." Leora faced him and folded her arms against her chest. "We do not have time to go into detail, but we are not like the created races of Nälu. We have different gifts and purposes, and we are held to a greater standard. With knowledge comes power, but also accountability. The fairies will answer to Vituko on how they have used their giftings as you all will too." Her gaze shifted to Hadrian. Then she pivoted on her right foot and strode back to the overturned mug.

"Where could we house so many people?" asked Unai.

Saeed clasped his hands together and rubbed one thumb over the other. "I think the logical choice would be Kvazkhun. The great city of the Igazin dwarves, once grand enough to house two dwarven clans with room to spare."

"What?" Hadrian sprung from his chair like a rattlesnake ready to strike. "The dwarves are proud warriors. And you lessen them to mere nursemaids?"

"Come now, Hadrian. They will have their taste of war. It will only be until we have the tonic."

Hadrian crossed his arms and glared back. His brow furrowed deeper. He blew a puff of air through his moustache. "Fine, but Kael better hurry."

"The Dwalu Tonic alone will not be enough," Unai said. "The source must be destroyed, and we don't even know who or what the source is."

"Oh, I think we do." Saeed stood, signaling the end of the meeting. "I will speak with King Teman and secure troops to aid us with the plains people. We will meet in Talem when finished."

"Wait." Unai clasped the edge of the table and leaned forward. "What about the dagger?"

"What about it?"

"Shouldn't we try to find it? It's what Semine wants. If we get it before she does, we will have the victory."

"I do not—"

"The prophecy commands us to guard it."

"If it is hidden from us as much as it is from her, does that not make it safer?"

"I would call that a gamble." Unai stood and adjusted the robe over his rotund belly. "Let us hope she does not find it. The consequences would be more devastating than losing all the plains people to a curse."

Saeed gripped the chair's back. "Would you sacrifice innocent people?"

"If it meant saving the world."

"I see." Saeed pushed the chair under the table. Maybe Unai was right. Perhaps finding the dagger before Semine would be better. "And do you have an inkling where to start?"

Unai's shoulders sagged, and he slowly shook his head.

Neither did Saeed. Well, except what he had gleaned from Ayianna. Her father's final message to her brother had to have hinted at the dagger's location, but he had no luck in figuring it out.

The Morning Star forever locked in stone. Every prominent building displayed some sort of depiction of that great battle and final sacrifice. Perhaps he should tell Unai. Maybe together they would have better luck at figuring out the riddle.

Yet Saeed could not.

"We must address the immediate concerns." Saeed clasped his hands in front of him. "I know you mean well, but I think it is divine wisdom we were not allowed to guard the dagger, despite what the prophecy says." He turned to the others. "We are finished here."

As the rest of the guardians filed out of the room, Saeed stopped Hadrian, Nerissa, and Darin. "Hadrian, if you could get the approval for us to keep the plains people in Kvazkhun as soon as possible, we will begin gathering them while the Alliance prepares for war."

Hadrian nodded.

Saeed glanced at the doorway. The others had already disappeared down the corridor, their footsteps echoing off the walls, slowly fading. He turned back to them. "You three I will entrust with this mission. Do not speak of it to anyone. After Kvazkhun, you must go to Badara and free King Valdamar. I believe that Semine has chosen her first sacrifice."

"King Valdamar?" asked Hadrian.

"Yes."

"Valdamar is the chosen one?" Hadrian's bushy eyebrows leapt to his hairline. "You must be jesting."

"You misunderstand me." Saeed leaned closer. "The Nu'mrarym of Zurial foretold the birth of the chosen one thirty some years ago, Valdamar is much older than that—no—it is Valdamar's son who is the chosen one."

"Prince Vian?" Hadrian couldn't raise his brows any higher. "That hot-headed, gangly youth you sent on the quest?"

"No, not Vian." Saeed glanced around the vacant room.

"But Valdamar has no other son." Darin sat atop the table and crossed his arms. "Not publicly anyways."

"Valdamar had one other son. The mother . . . she died giving birth. The child was marked as cursed, rejected by the Nuja priests. His birth was never recorded, so naturally Semine thinks Vian is the chosen one. She has the books, the records . . ."

"Wait, the king has had only one wife." Darin straightened. "And she gave birth to only one child, Vian."

Saeed nodded. "There was another woman."

"What?" Darin stood. "Who?"

Saeed held up his hand. "Our time is limited."

"But why kill Valdamar?" Nerissa asked.

"Who knows why Semine does what she does?" Saeed shrugged. "I can only assume she hopes that by killing Valdamar, she might lure his son out into the open. I doubt she knows he is on the other side of world retrieving ingredients for the tonic."

"So who is he?" Nerissa asked.

"Saeed?" Unai's voice drifted down the hallway.

Saeed hesitated. Now was not the time for disclosure. He looked at the three of them. The king's life rested in the hands of a merwoman, a half-giant, and a dwarf, but he was confident in their abilities and their loyalties. "We must attend to the matters at hand."

8

DAMPNESS CLUNG TO the dungeon's walls and floor like sweat. Carved out of stone, the cell gave no respite from the cold or potential escape routes for Ayianna and her companions. She gazed through the iron bars at the small fire pit on the other side of the room, longing to feel its heat. If she could just get warm enough, maybe the haze consuming her mind would burn away and the resurgence of old wounds and sorrows would fade.

Behind her, Kael remained lifeless atop the only bench. His skin had turned ashy and his lips blue. She refused to look at him. She would not give Desmond the satisfaction of seeing her wrestle with fear. Kael would pull through. He had to. He was stubborn enough.

She pulled her cloak tighter and stomped her feet, trying to ease away the ache in her legs as a chill seeped through her body and up her spine. At least the dizziness had subsided, now if only her headache would disappear.

The others huddled together, muttering about which was worse: dwarves or imps. At least they had a fighting chance with the imps. But if the dwarves hadn't shown up, would they have been able to defeat the imps on their own?

And where was Liam? Was she safe? In all the commotion Ayianna had lost track of her. And what about Eloith? Had he made it to the gorge? How would they ever be reunited?

Osaryn, how could you let this happen?

"*Tlaka!*" A dwarf captain stormed into the dungeons flanked by several dwarves. The captain, a head taller than the others, marched over to the cell, muttering under his breath. Medals of honor and various chains rattled against his fur-lined jerkin. His disheveled blond hair and waist-length beard gave him the appearance of a crazed bear. His beady eyes, almost hidden by his huge knobby nose, bore into the prisoners.

"Jaeger!" The captain spat and dug his fingers into the belt around his waist.

The young dwarf with red-blond hair pulled back into a tail stepped beside him. He had been the leader of the patrol and had given the order to bring them back to Ta'vazi—alive.

A full beard brushed his chest, still short compared to the captain's. He wore no chains or medals. Just a simple fur-lined jerkin, tunic, and pants. From his belt hung an axe, a leather pouch, and a band of braided hair.

Braided hair? Was that normal? Did the dwarves remove their captives' scalps in some gruesome ritual? Ayianna glanced at the other dwarves but saw nothing that resembled braided hair.

"*Kloc zit kavoc zarkomic!*" The captain stomped his foot. "*Tladu zit sraka khan idaros tamoc khada? Klont ka bracht truhodsrun ka* Ta'vazi?"

Ayianna looked to Tariq for translation.

"He isn't happy," Tariq whispered.

Desmond grunted. "I could have told you that. Must not have learned dwarvish on your adventures out west—eh?"

Tariq frowned. "For your information, the language is called Tarôc, and he is wondering why the patrol didn't just kill us."

"*Doka zarkahm, khadu zakkad khan klehvr ona* Nälu." Jaeger motioned for one of the dwarves, and he returned carrying Tariq's shield. Ayianna could barely see the dwarf's stocky boots much less his head.

The captain glanced at it and shoved it aside. He moved closer to the cell, pulling at his long blond beard.

Ayianna stepped back.

"Vhat do ve have here? Four men, an elf, and a voman . . ." he said in a thick dwarvish accent.

Puzzled, Ayianna glanced back at Jathil. The northern Haruzo had withdrawn behind the others, her cloak's hood hiding her face.

"Vhat is your name, dark-bearded one?" The captain glared at Tariq.

"*Dadu zidac ikv* Tariq."

"You speak Tarôc?"

"Enough," Tariq said.

"I see the *daziklaa*, vhat do you call them—dithza-mielis— they have made good vork of your companion, no? Vhy have you come to Ta'vazi?"

"Our intentions were not to come here, my *srard*. We have no quarrel with Krihn Varick."

"They know the old krihn—they are spies!" The captain snarled and whacked Jaeger on the back of his head.

Jaeger rubbed his head, scowling at the captain.

"We are not spies." Vian stepped up to the iron bars.

The captain planted his thick fists on his hips and lifted his chin. "And who might be young-no-beard?"

Vian squared his shoulders. "I am Prince Vian of Badara."

"Eu! A prince!" The captain laughed and slapped his thigh.

Tariq placed his hand on Vian's arm. Maybe to show moral support or to stop him from saying anything more that could get them killed. "Does your krihn respect the Guardian Circle? You must know Hadrian."

The captain grunted and pulled at his jerkin, rattling the chains. "We do not speak his name here. He is an Igazin d'arf, ve are not."

"You once were, until Krihn Pruvac split the clan and brought about the Highland Civil War."

"Krihn Pruvac vas a great leader. The Stozic clan has nothing more to do with the other clans, the Guardian Circle, nor the rest of Nälu." He turned to leave. "Kill them."

"*Dac Eyezakvec*." Jathil stepped forward.

Desmond's eyes widened. "You speak dwarvish, too?"

"Tarôc." Jathil pushed him aside and grabbed the iron bars. "The Stozic Clan has a *krizac* with Arashel."

The captain halted and faced her. "Who are you?"

Jathil removed her hood and straightened her shoulders. "I am Tirza Jathil of Arashel. If you kill us, you will break the *Krizac na Dakad* between your people and mine, and you know the consequences of such."

He smiled, his eyes glimmering in recognition. "Tirza Jathil of Arashel, you are not in a position to be discussing politics vith us. I say you are all trespassers. And you are avare of the consequences of trespassing, no?"

"We were not trespassing."

"That can be debated."

"King Nagid will have your head."

"Vhat the King of Arashel knows not, vill not concern him. I am sure."

"Are you willing to take that chance?"

The captain looked around at the other dwarves. "Good riddance, Jaeger, I vill have no more of this nonsense."

"But captain." Jaeger leaned forward. "There is a revard for her return. Fifty yettus."

That was more gold than a commoner would see in a lifetime! Either Jathil would be their deliverance, or she just killed them.

The captain glanced back at Jathil and shrugged. "Dead or alive shouldn't make a difference to King Nagid, no?"

"Preferably alive." Jathil crossed her arms.

Ayianna shifted her feet and eyed the Northern Haruzo. Who was she, really? The dwarf captain recognized her, and the king of Arashel offered a reward for her. What crime had she committed?

"Perhaps ve arrived too late, the imps, you know, and she vas already dead."

Jathil's eyes narrowed. "A hundred yettus—alive."

The old dwarf shrugged, his thick lips splitting into a menacing grin. He started up the stairs. "Jaeger, you may turn the Haruzo over for the revard. I vill take eighty yettus of the revard; you can keep the rest. The others—kill them."

"But—"

"If you cannot fulfill your duties, I vill find someone who can, and then it vill be the shavers for you."

"No, *srard*, I vill personally see to it." Jaeger patted his beard.

The captain dismissed the others and stomped up the stairs.

"We are doomed!" Vian exclaimed. "I'd kick something right now, if everything wasn't stone."

"Maybe we can overpower him." Desmond paced the length of the cell. "There are three of us and one of him."

"Five of us." Ayianna glanced at Kael—six, if he would wake up. A wave of grief and nausea washed over her. Where had that come from? Ugh, the instability of her emotions! They roiled within her, uncontrollably. She rubbed her temples, trying to push away the remnants of the hag's attack. Memories haunted her. Her father's death, her brother's broken body, the hideous creature that had cursed her—all clung to her thoughts like cobwebs.

"I can hear you." Jaeger strutted toward them. He pulled and twisted the small locks of his beard. His brows knitted together as he eyed the condemned prisoners. "Vhat brings you to the highlands?"

"Why should we tell you?" Desmond asked.

"Because I am to kill you. Now if you have a good reason to live, I suggest you speak up."

"Why would you help us?" asked Tariq

"Depends on who is helping who and to vhat end. Tell me, vhy do you carry the shield of Nälu and how do you know Hadrian?"

Vian perked up and sidled up to the bars, pressing his face against them. "Hadrian? Why, he's an old friend of ours. We go way back."

"Not according to d'arf years."

Vian pushed away from the bars and started pacing again. "Hadrian sent us here. Well, not here, specifically. We have your patrol to thank for that."

"Vhy?"

"Why do you want to know?" asked Tariq.

"I am not the enemy, if that is vhat you are insinuating."

Desmond folded his arms. "You look like it from this side of the bars."

"I mean to say I am not one of the Sorceress's allies."

"You know about the Sorceress?" Ayianna pushed through her sluggish thoughts. "Doesn't your king—er chief, I mean, krihn know about her too, and the destruction of Dagmar, and the kidnapping of the Sacred Pearl?"

"You could say that."

She balled her hands into a fist inside her cloak. "Then why doesn't he do something?"

"Ve live apart and, like Arashel," Jaeger looked at Jathil, "ve do not concern ourselves vith the trouble that plagues the rest of the nations."

"What affects us, will one day affect you."

The dwarf turned his attention back to Ayianna. "I know this."

"Then you will help us?" Ayianna stared into Jaeger's hazel eyes, willing him to go against orders. *Please, Osaryn!*

Jaeger smiled. "You haven't told me vhy I should and vhy you are in the highlands."

"Listen," Vian said. "The guardians—Hadrian—has sent us on a mission to combat the Sorceress's attempt to gain control over the Prathae Plains."

"So she is a little power hungry. That didn't stop Badara and Praetan in their conquest of the plains from the giants."

"That was different."

Jaeger raised his eyebrows.

"Well, maybe Badara and Praetan could have done some things different back then. But the Sorceress won't stop at the plains. She wants to release the Tóas Dikon and bring back Stygian from the Abyss."

Jaeger smoothed his moustache as Vian tried to talk his way out of death. Ayianna remained hopeful. The dwarf obviously cared enough to give them a chance to plead for their lives. The captain wouldn't have done that, or any other highland dwarf for that matter.

Jaeger held up his hand, silencing Vian. Rats squeaked and water dripped somewhere in the dungeons. "How does this mission have anything to do with the highlands? The Sorceress is in the plains."

"The Sorceress has placed a curse on the plains people, binding them to her will." Vian crossed his arms. "The only way to free those people is with the Dwalu Tonic. The first ingredient is some silver pinecone, supposedly hidden away in the Kha Vaaro Mountains—I think."

"You think?" Jaeger shook his head. "You risk death because you think your destination is here."

"The riddle wasn't exactly clear." Vian shrugged. "It said we had to climb the highest to reach the lowest and something about becoming low—I don't know." Vian threw his hands up. "Who speaks in riddles anymore?"

"So you seek Stark's Peak?"

Vian nodded.

"I vill help you, but you must trust me and take me vith you."

Tariq stepped forward. "Not to discourage you, but why would you help us?"

Jaeger fingered the strip of braided hair at his waist. "Vell, you see, Hadrian is my father."

9

THE DUNGEON'S DOOR groaned against the rock floor, wrenching Ayianna from her sleep. She lurched up from the warmth of a white and black fur blanket curled around her. Her vision swam, and she blinked away the dizziness. How long had she been sleeping? Her headache had faded to a dull throb, but the grief was still raw, as if her father had died yesterday. The cold, damp dungeons didn't help.

She rubbed her face and glanced around. Tariq and Vian stood near the iron bars, conversing. Desmond paced the other end of the cell, away from everyone. Where was Jathil? Had they taken her?

Before Ayianna could ask, the blanket shifted and rolled over. Two silver eyes blinked back at her. The large snow leopard swiveled her ears and yawned, stretching her paws in front of her, her claws scratching across the stone.

Ayianna scrambled to her feet, her heart hammering in her ears.

It's just me. Jathil's voice pressed into her head. The large leopard bowed and hunched her shoulders, the fur receding.

"I . . . um . . ." Ayianna closed her mouth. What would she say anyway?

"You were cold." Jathil straightened, now in human form once more.

Shivering, she rubbed her arms. "Thank you. I—"

"Did you rest vell?" Jaeger strode toward their cell, carrying a clay jar and a bulging wool sack bigger than him. He dumped the sack on the floor and proceeded to the cell.

"As well as anyone could in a dungeon." Vian blew on his hands and stamped his feet. "You could have at least given us some blankets or something."

"Eh, quit your bellyaching, *zi-dahlt*. I cannot have the captain think I have grown soft, now can I?"

"What did you call me?" Vian cocked his head.

"No-beard. You are like a boy to the dwarves. Ve take pride in our long beards."

"So I see." Vian ran his fingers over his chin, the red-blond stubble barely noticeable.

"I have *kvazi kah*." Jaeger unlocked the barred door and slid the clay jar through to Tariq. "It vill varm your insides."

Tariq nodded, took a drink, and handed the jar to Ayianna.

Ayianna sniffed the amber liquid. The aroma of cinnamon and oranges filled her nose. She sipped it. The *kvazi kah* swelled in her mouth, its flavor bittersweet. As she swallowed, the warmth trailed into her stomach and blossomed. The heat expanded to her face, arms, and legs, chasing away the achy chill in her body. She gave the jar to Jathil who gulped some down while Desmond and Vian waited their turn.

Jaeger removed a small tin from a pocket in his fur-lined jerkin and handed it to Ayianna. "It is vhat you call *maezam aenlu*, rub this on your friend's forehead. It vill help." He nodded; his hazel eyes twinkled with a half-smile as if to reassure her. He turned and strode into the adjoining room.

Ayianna took the tin, not daring to glance at Desmond. Would he interfere? Would he berate her later? Did it matter? She clenched her teeth and knelt where Kael lay. She dipped her fingers into the jar. The red substance felt warm and gritty as she smoothed it over his forehead. It grew warmer the longer she worked it into his skin. What had Kael seen? Why didn't he wake as she had?

Tariq knelt beside her. "The *maezam aenlu* can only do so much. A person touched by the hags must want to live, must fight the desire to surrender." Tariq placed his hand over Kael's heart. "We must pray that he will find a reason to live, or he won't return to us." He peeled back the blanket, undid Kael's leather cuirass and tunic, and lifted them away. He scooped some of the red dirt and applied it over his chest.

Ayianna averted her eyes, her face burning. Pray? What would she say? Her gaze returned to Kael's still form. Would he give up on life? Her throat knotted. No, he couldn't. His sense of duty would be enough to make him pull through.

Osaryn? He believed in you, please . . .

No. She couldn't pray. How could she? She wasn't even sure if Osaryn was there anymore. Did he even hear her? Tears blurred her vision, but she blinked them away. She leaned forward and grabbed Kael's forearm, his skin cold to her touch. She squeezed harder.

Please, live!

Tariq returned Kael's tunic, cuirass, and blankets, and then glanced at Ayianna. "How are you feeling?"

Ayianna shrugged. She didn't trust her voice yet.

"It wouldn't hurt to apply some of the *maezam aenlu*." He touched her forehead and rubbed the gritty texture into her skin.

The warmth grew hot and seeped into her soul like liquid fire. The haze dissolved and clarity returned like the sun burning away the fog. Even in the dungeon's murkiness, hope emerged. They would escape. They would succeed.

"Don't want to break up your little dirt party, but Jaeger is back." Desmond bent near Tariq and lowered his voice. "Why are we even trusting him? He's a dwarf."

Tariq's amber eyes narrowed. "And you're a human. Your point?"

"How do we know we can trust him? Dwarf or not. How can he be telling the truth? Hadrian is a guardian. They don't marry and have kids."

"We don't have a choice." Tariq stood and strode toward the cell's door.

Desmond hovered over Ayianna. "You look ridiculous."

"I'd like to see how you'd handle a hag." His words pierced her, despite her quick retort. She brushed the rest of the dirt from her hands. If only she could brush him off just as easily.

"You wouldn't have seen me running at them with a sword. And I don't hang on to my past like Kael does. The hags would have nothing on me."

Ayianna pushed him aside. Kael didn't need Desmond's verbal assault, much less his demeaning presence. It would make anyone surrender what little hope they had. Like she had. Hadn't she? The bitter edge in her soul had grown, deepened. Even with the lingering effects of the warming dirt on her forehead, the expanse of hopelessness yawned before her like the abyss ready to devour her.

"Excuse me?" Desmond straightened. His eyes flashed a warning and sent a shiver racing up her spine. He tightened his fists. "Don't you ever push me aside again."

Dread seized her. Would he hurt her? No—not in front of the others, he wouldn't. She quickly turned away and joined Tariq and Vian. Why did she do that? The look in his eyes! Fear surged through her again, and her breath caught. She had to be careful, more respectful like a plains woman should be, and for now, avoid being alone with him.

Jaeger leaned against a wagon he had pulled from the adjoining room. "I must blindfold you and bind your limbs on our journey to the *vosrricht*, the killing stone."

"Blindfolds?" Desmond stomped forward from the back of the cell. "You're not going to blindfold me, much less tie me up."

"Fine vith me. You can stay here."

"Hold on." Tariq crossed his arms. "Why would you take us to the killing stone, if you were going to help us?"

"There are only two vays out of here. The front gate or the *Rokhava*," Jaeger said. "The Path of the Dead."

"If you would pardon our fear, being held captive and all." Vian placed his fists on his hips. "But that doesn't exactly sound promising. You expect us to trust you when you are taking us exactly where the big dwarf wants us. Is this your idea of a joke?"

Jaeger cocked his head. "No, but vould you like to hear one?"

"This is not a laughing matter." Vian gripped the iron bars. "What is your plan?"

"The plan." Jaeger pulled a smaller sack from the larger one, but this one writhed and shook.

Vian stepped back and held up his hands as if he could ward off whatever the dwarf had pulled out. "What is that?"

"Rabbits. They vere my mother's." Jaeger's voice caught, but he dumped the sack into the wagon. "I vill kill them, instead of you. Fresh blood for evidence. The captain vill be satisfied for a time. I vill pretend to follow orders to gain access to the *vosrricht*. Then ve vill escape through the *Rokhava*. It is vhere the accused are discarded. The captain vill think I have returned the Haruzo for the revard. No one vill know any different until ve are long gone."

Jaeger picked up the large sack and placed it in the wagon. "I have provided furs to keep us varm. This Gefährlich Pass you spoke about—I vill take you there." His gaze swept over them.

Ayianna glanced at her companions. Their faces were hard as they eyed the dwarf, their suspicions obvious, but none more so than Desmond.

"I vill see my father one vay or the other. I do not have to take you vith me." Jaeger dropped his hands at his side. "You know vhat vill happen if you remain here. Vill you trust me?"

"We will." Tariq touched his heart and extended his hand through the iron bars.

Jaeger did the same and placed his thick, callused fingers against Tariq's. "Ve have a deal."

"Wait a minute." Desmond grabbed Tariq and spun him around. "You have no right to make such a decision for all of us."

Tariq raised his brows. "And you don't have to come with us."

"Enough already." Vian stepped between them. "We will go with him. If there is a hint of betrayal, we have two Haruzos who could gut him quicker than a stuck pig."

Jathil snorted but didn't refute his claim.

"Vell, then, vhat are ve vaiting for?" Jaeger dropped one of the wagon's sides down with a bang. "Time to go."

Ayianna glanced at the half-open door, expecting the captain or the patrol to burst through and apprehend them at any moment. At least, they would appear to be following orders. Would the captain believe Jaeger would kill them?

Jaeger strode toward them and unlocked their cell door. "Climb inside. I vill only bind you for appearance's sake."

"How are we all going to fit inside this little box of wood?" Vian crossed his arms. "Why don't we walk?"

"Vhat kind of prisoner valks to his own execution?" Jaeger yanked a handful of woven sacks from one of the bigger ones. "You are not allowed to see the inside of Ta'vazi. Nor the vay to the *vosrricht*."

"Come on." Tariq grabbed Vian's arm. "Help me with Kael."

Jathil climbed into the wagon and sat at the front. Her back against the other side, she drew her knees up and rested her arms atop them.

"Your name is Tirza?" Ayianna settled herself next to her, careful not to touch her.

"I go by Jathil now."

Ayianna hugged her knees. "What did you do?"

"Do?"

"Why does the king offer a reward for you?"

"Ah, that." Jathil leaned her head back. "Why else do kings offer rewards? To entice people to bring criminals to justice."

"Are you a criminal?"

Jathil closed her eyes. "You ask a lot of questions."

Ayianna gritted her teeth. She wouldn't have to ask, if Jathil wasn't hiding something. A lot of something. Enough for the king of Arashel to place a reward on her head, dead or alive. Jathil was keeping secrets, just like her. Hadn't her father placed their family at risk with his secrets? Someone had wanted her dead, her father alive, except they had made a mistake. Ayianna wrapped her arms around her waist and glared at her boot where she had hidden her brother's dagger.

"Living with secrets makes for a lonely existence." She glanced at Jathil out of the corner of her eye. "No one wants to be alone."

Jathil rubbed her hands through her spiky black and white hair. "That is where you are wrong. To assume what others want or don't want based on what? Your own experience?" She shook her head.

Vian jumped into the wagon and hauled Kael up with Tariq's assistance. Vian dropped next to Ayianna and situated Kael between him and Tariq. The pallor had faded from his face, but his head fell against Vian's shoulder. Lifeless.

"Closer." Jaeger hoisted a box of shackles and dumped them into the wagon.

"You've got to be kidding." Desmond huffed and slumped next to Tariq.

They squeezed together until Ayianna's shoulders were shoved into Jathil's and Vian's. Anxiety twisted her gut. She sucked in a deep gulp of air and blew it out slowly through her nose. She would not let the panic set in. If she could survive the tunnels beneath Inganno, she could at least manage being squished in a cramped wagon in the dungeons of Ta'vazi.

Jaeger began clasping the shackles around their ankles and wrists and blindfolding them. By the time he reached Ayianna, beads of sweat dribbled off his brow. He snapped the heavy, cold iron shut around her wrists and then pulled the hood over her head, plunging her into darkness, except for a few sparks of light filtering through the weavings.

Fear twisted like a spider inside Ayianna's stomach and wiggled its way through her body up to her throat. The wagon lurched forward and so did her stomach. She tried to listen and pay attention to the direction they were going, but it was no use. The path wound one way and then another. At times, the walls hovered so near, their clammy presence breathed down her neck.

Thoughts of the stone crushing her raced through her mind and stole away her breath. She gulped the stale air to silence the screams lodged in her chest. Other times, the presence of the walls fell away to a hollow darkness, the creaks and thumps echoing beyond them. Never once did the wheels leave the clop of wood on stone.

"Jaeger!"

The wagon halted. A rushed conversation ensued and ended with laughter. Jaeger had joined in. Ayianna tensed. Why was he laughing? If only she could understand Tarôc. Jathil or Tariq hadn't reacted to the dwarves' exchange. Perhaps everything was going as planned.

Footsteps clipped toward them. Something bumped Ayianna's head, and Jathil stiffened.

"*Tlad va duho* Tirza?" the other dwarf asked, his voice stern, his words clipped. "*Zit du-klont kha gaklolt?*"

Jaeger replied, his words rushing together and harsh. What was going on? Had Jaeger's plan been found out?

Something hit the side of the wagon, and Ayianna flinched. After a few more terse words, footfalls slapped the stone and faded.

The wagon started forward again, but slower this time. They didn't turn down any passages, but steadily descended until the air grew colder.

Then she heard it. The shrill sound of rock against blade rang off the stone walls. They had to be near the killing stone. Ayianna shuddered.

The wagon rumbled to a halt, and a loud crack reverberated around her. Vibrations trembled up her spine, and the room succumbed to silence.

Where was Jaeger? Had they been foolish to trust him? The silence strained on, except for her pulse in her ears and her ragged breath. Shouldn't they do something? But no one moved.

Sharp words punctured the air. Questions were asked, and Jaeger replied, the exchange almost business-like. The business of the condemned.

More grinding and grating, and then the wagon jerked forward again. The voices faded, and the clop of wood on stone returned.

How long would this take? Ayianna shifted her knees up. The shackle on her ankles cracked open and slid to the wagon with a thunk. Her heart hammered. Should she run? No. He hadn't locked them. Jaeger was surely on their side. But what if they encountered another patrol? They might see through his lies.

The wagon creaked to a stop. Nothing. What if he was found out now? Would they be able to escape?

Hands touched her back, and she recoiled.

"Easy there," Jaeger whispered. "It is me."

He pulled off her hood and shackles, and moved on to Vian. The stench of wet metal and old feces hung in the air. She tried to rub the chill from her arms. The room was even colder than the dungeons. Three torches lined the stone walls to her left and right. A large flat boulder lay in the center of the room. A few shackles hung from the back wall, and several axes gleamed in the torchlight. Dark stains marred the walls and floor.

Jathil leapt out of the wagon and dumped one of the bags on the floor, spilling the fur coats and hats. Jaeger worked on Tariq's bindings now, leaving Kael to Vian.

Ayianna scrambled to her knees and aided Vian as he slid the shackles from Kael's hands. Kael jerked back at her touch. He moved! Ayianna tore the hood off.

"Kael!" She grabbed his face. His skin was warm again. His color had returned. She could almost kiss him. Tears stung her eyes, but she quickly blinked them back. "You're all right." Her voice cracked.

Confusion clouded his face, and his stony mask returned. "What's going on?"

She dropped her hands and scrambled back, her face and ears burning. Had she lost her mind? She wrapped her arms around her waist and avoided Desmond's icy glare.

"That's what I would like to know." Desmond rubbed his wrists as Jaeger undid the shackles at his feet.

Kael tried to stand but pitched forward. Vian grabbed him before he could crash into Ayianna. Tariq leapt atop the wagon and helped Vian stabilize Kael, then Vian stepped down.

The desire to reach out and help him nearly overwhelmed her. Instead, Ayianna withdrew and joined Jathil by the sack of furs and weapons. What was wrong with her? Her thoughts, feelings, actions—they were all a tangled mess. The hags were responsible. If it hadn't been for them, she'd have been able to keep her feelings in check. She wouldn't have been reliving her grief—nor would she have almost lost Kael.

But she couldn't think like that now. Kael was fine. Their quest would continue, and everything would work out all right. She'd worry about Desmond later.

Desmond stepped off the wagon and stretched his arms over his head. "What was going on back there, dwarf?"

"The guard asked vhy I had brought Tirza. The captain vould vant his revard, he says." Jaeger unloaded the large sack. "But the captain did not find her, did he—I say."

"What?" Vian smacked Jaeger's shoulder. "Do we need to worry about a dwarf patrol, too?"

Jaeger grinned. "No, I told him after I killed you all, I vould take her to Arashel."

"And you all are okay with this?" Kael's eyes were wide. He leaned against Tariq and glanced at the others. "Where are we? Where's my bow, my sword?"

"We're in the dungeons of Ta'vazi—thanks to our new friend, Jaeger." Vian lifted his hand. "Can you walk?"

"Friend?" Kael grabbed Vian's hand and climbed down from the wagon. He wobbled. "Is it really so cold? How did we get here?" His eyes flicked to the Jaeger. "Who is the dwarf?"

"One question at a time." Vian handed Kael one of the fur coats. "Well, first there were the hags—"

"Hush, Vian." Desmond tugged on his coat. The sleeves were a bit short, but the dwarven-made gloves made up for the lack. "We don't have time for explanations."

"This vay." Jaeger grabbed the sacks and strode to the right corner of the stone room. He stuck his fingers into the corner and heaved. The wall ground to the right, exposing a thick wooden door on the other side. He unlocked it and tugged. The door creaked open, its hinges screeching and echoing in the silence. A tunnel lay beyond and disappeared into nothingness.

Rokhava, the Path of the Dead.

A blast of putrid, dank air slammed into Ayianna. She covered her nose and stumbled back. Had the imps found them? The black hole in the wall remained still, the echoes fading. Numerous skulls and bones littered the entrance as if they had died pounding and scratching against the door.

"They are just bones." Jaeger touched her elbow. "Their spirits have long since flown beyond the Abyss. Kvamiig—vhat do you call him—Vituko, Osaryn—he goes before you. No need to fear." He glanced at the others and lifted his chin. "Vait for me vhere the tunnels cross. I must kill the rabbits. All of your personal items are in these sacks." He dumped the contents at their feet.

Jathil scooped up her things and disappeared into the dark tunnel, not once looking back. Would she abandon them to the dead?

Ayianna's heart sank. Why would she not? She had a reward on her head. A hundred yettus—thanks to her bargain with the dwarf captain. She risked Arashel's wrath, if she was discovered. And even if Jaeger chose not to turn her in, how many other dwarves knew of the reward? Would they try to recapture her for themselves? She couldn't blame Jathil for leaving them. The quest was not hers to bear.

Ayianna buckled her sword belt around her waist and hung her father's bag across her back. She wrapped the fur coat tighter around her shoulders. She eyed the black abyss before her. Jathil didn't seem to have a problem with the tunnel, why should she? Maybe she had been there before. Or maybe she trusted Jaeger.

"Wait—we are just going to do as this dwarf says?" Kael swung his quiver of arrows and bow over his shoulder. His movements jerked, and his fingers trembled as he belted on his sword.

"For once we agree on something." Desmond adjusted his plumed hat and rested his hand on the hilt of his sword. "One wrong move, dwarf, and I will run you though."

Jaeger snorted but turned away and lugged the bag of squirming rabbits toward the flat stone.

Kael lifted his gaze. "If Desmond distrusts him, then I have full faith in Jaeger."

Desmond shot him a hateful glare and buttoned his coat. The tension between the two had intensified. Instead of dying like Desmond had hoped, Kael lived and was crosser than ever. No doubt the effects of the hags still lingered. How long had it taken Ayianna to overcome? A day or two? And she had the dwarven drink to thank for the clarity she experienced now. But Kael had almost succumbed to the hag's destructive touch.

Kael took out his sphere from the guardians. "*Yetakoith taheza.*"

The orb flared to life. Its glow drove the darkness back and revealed more gleaming white bones along the edges of the tunnel. Skulls littered the ground here and there. Their blackened eyes sockets scowled at her, reprimanding her for disturbing them. No peace in life, nor death. Did the dwarves just dump the bodies at the entrance? How could they not give them some kind of proper burial? One skull tilted on its side; its jaw cracked in a scornful laugh. Tooth marks and scratches crisscrossed its forehead, and its laughter became silent screams instead. Had something eaten the dead?

Ayianna swallowed. It might have been better not to know what lay along their path. The path of the dead. Made sense. She should have known. But seeing it . . . her stomach twisted.

Kael handed the orb to Tariq. "Here, lead. I've not the strength yet."

Tariq nodded and stepped into the old tunnel, his boots crunching on the layer of old gravel. Kael, Vian, and Desmond followed closely behind.

She shuddered. Refusing to look left or right, she kept her eyes on their backs as they inched forward in the dark.

10

AYIANNA TREKKED ALONG the tunnel, hoping the orb's glow would fall upon a crossing any moment. Or an opening to the outside world. The stench of death had faded, or she had gotten used to it. Could one ever get used to the smell of decay?

A harsh grinding reverberated through the tunnel and ended with a clang that rocked Ayianna's insides and stung her ears. She covered her head, but the jarring sound continued to ring off the walls.

Tariq glanced back at the way they had come. "Jaeger." But his voice lacked conviction.

They pressed forward, their pace quickening and growing louder with each step. They had no need for caution. Who would hear them?

Vian halted, and the others slammed into him. "Something's there!" His voice echoed around them and unleashed a torrent of fear in Ayianna's soul.

"Hush, you fool." Desmond shoved the prince forward.

Vian spun at him, his fist ready to strike. "How dare you! What if you had shoved me into something dreadful and-and deadly?"

"Are you trying to get us killed?" Desmond raised his hands as if he was calming a wild horse. "I thought for sure you'd have a better grip on yourself. You screaming like a girl probably already scared it away."

Vian drew in a deep breath and squared his shoulders. "I was not screaming like a girl."

Tariq lifted the orb, and the light arched across the walls of the tunnel. Ahead, the darkness swallowed it and gave way to the black abyss stretching forever before them and behind them.

No end. No way out. She gulped in the cold, bitter air, but her throat closed even more. Peace evaded her. She clutched her waist and withdrew from the men until her back hit the wall. She needed more air and the wide expanse of sky above her. A hand gripped her elbow. Her gaze flew up to meet Kael's.

"*Zjótharyn*, Ayianna. We will get out."

Peace flooded her soul just like it had when she had been trapped underground. Did he think she would panic again? She had her fear under control. Mostly.

His harsh countenance faded into weariness as if he was too tired to frown, too tired to live. But he had. Something had pulled him from the grip of death. His faith? His sense of purpose? Sorrow clouded his eyes, no doubt reliving old hurts dredged up by the hags. Oh, how she ached to comfort him! But how?

"It'll pass." She pushed the words out. "The pain, the grief . . . the hag's effects. It'll pass. Mine did."

"The hags got you too?" He rubbed his temple as if the effort to carry on a conversation was too much.

She nodded and glanced at the others huddled together discussing something. Maybe they had decided to wait for Jaeger. She turned her attention back to Kael. "But I'm fine now."

"What happened?"

"After the hags, we took refuge in a cave. Then the imps came and the dragon, and we fought the best we could, but we were losing. Then the dwarves came, dispatched the imps, and captured us for trespassing."

"I missed a lot, didn't I?" He shook his head and folded his arms across his chest. "What about Liam and Eloith?"

"Eloith had left to find the warming dirt for you. Liam . . ." Her voice cracked, and she averted her eyes. She would not cry. Liam was fine. She had to be. No matter how many times she told herself that, she doubted it. "I-I don't know."

"Hey." He directed her chin back toward him. "I am sure she is all right."

She studied him. How was it that she had wanted to comfort him, but he was comforting her instead? "How will I ever find her again?"

"I don't know." He squeezed her shoulder. "But I don't doubt she will find you."

He pulled away too soon and joined the others.

Desmond lifted his face. His eyes burned with hatred, but Ayianna didn't care. She remained at the edge of the orb's glow, relishing the moment—Kael's words, his attention. His touch.

"We really need to keep moving." Tariq paced in front of Vian and Desmond.

"I'm telling you; I saw something. It had glowing eyes—or something." Vian's voice was a harsh whisper. "I think we should wait for Jaeger."

"Well, there's nothing there now," Desmond replied. "Let's go. Maybe we'll find the exit before the dwarf finds us, and we can leave him behind."

Ayianna stepped toward them. "What about Jathil? Maybe Vian saw her."

"Why would she be hiding from us?" Tariq shook his head.

Desmond took off his hat and tugged his fingers through his matted curls. "She probably left us here to rot. Can't trust those—"

"Enough." Tariq strode past Desmond and Vian. "Keep watch. You never know what else might roam these tunnels, especially considering the dwarves dump the remains of the condemned here."

Tariq led them forward at a cautious pace and held the orb out to give the most light to their path.

Ayianna hiked closer, scanning the ground and walls for movement. It could have been anything. A rat even. They probably had nothing to worry about.

Hissing and scurrying echoed off the tunnel's wall. Ayianna darted behind Tariq as he raised the orb higher. The others drew their swords. Imps?

Two large eyes reflected in the orb's light. It lowered its head to the ground and sped toward them, hissing.

Ayianna retreated as everyone scattered. The orb's glow bounced around the tunnel.

The creature halted and lifted its nose in the air. It was almost as big as Liam, but fat with short stubby legs. It dipped its triangular head and revealed strips of white fur framing its muzzle.

Kael lunged, but his movements were clumsy. The creature hissed and dodged the blade. Its fur rippled as it bounced forward, and Kael jumped out of the way.

Ayianna pressed her back into the wall, but the animal nosed the air, swinging its head back and forth.

"Ah, a badger." A voice echoed from behind. "I had forgotten about them." Jaeger appeared and rushed the animal. He waved his axe to the left and then the right. The badger hissed, bobbing and darting from the blade.

Something in her pack poked Ayianna—had to be her hairpin, since her brother's dagger was in her boot. If she pressed back against the wall any farther, she'd risk stabbing herself with her own betrothal pin. How ironic. But Ayianna refused to move or pull her gaze away from Jaeger and the badger. What was the crazy dwarf doing?

"Don't just stand there." Jaeger stepped back but continued to distract the badger with his axe. "Go!"

"Why don't you just kill it?" Desmond stood against the opposite wall, fear and anger twisted his face.

"Vhy? He only vants to eat, and you all are standing in his vay."

"Excuse me?" Desmond cocked his head and hoisted his sword.

"Come on." Vian grabbed his arm, but Desmond shoved the prince aside and stormed off. Vian sheathed his sword and followed, glancing back.

Tariq tilted the orb toward the dwarf. "Are there more of them?"

"Most likely." Jaeger reached into a sack at his waist, pulled out a dead rabbit, and slowly backed down the tunnel away from the orb's glow. "The sound of the door closing calls to them. Fresh meat, it says. *Dukv*, ve can't have decaying corpses lying around, can ve? Go on ahead, I vill meet you at the crossing. It's not far now."

Tariq nodded and took off after Desmond and Vian.

Kael sheathed his sword, his hands trembling, but his eyes remained on Jaeger and the badger. He sank against the wall.

Ayianna lingered. "Are you all right?"

"Yes," he snapped. He rubbed his face and sighed. "Sorry. It's not your fault. I'm disoriented."

"It will take a while for the effects to fade." She stepped closer. "I still feel some of it."

He groaned and grabbed his head. "I don't have time for this."

She glanced down the tunnel. Jaeger managed to turn the badger around. He flung the rabbit at it and wiped his hands on his pants.

"We should go." Her attention turned to Kael.

He leaned his head against the stone, his eyes closed, his breathing slow and labored. He had to be struggling with nausea and headaches, just like she had. She wanted to embrace him, make the pain go away, but her arms hung numb at her side. "Can I help you?"

No." His face hardened, and he pushed away from the wall. "I wouldn't want you to get into trouble."

The words stung. He must have noticed Desmond's glare. Still, she couldn't let him suffer alone. He was grieving all over again for his sister and her brother. He'd have to sort through it all just like she had.

Kael trudged after the others. Maybe he needed to be alone. The last thing she wanted to do was cause him any more pain.

Jaeger stepped beside her. "All right, there?"

Her voice wouldn't work, so she nodded.

"Vell, then ve best be going before any more of those badgers show up for dinner."

Together, she and Jaeger strode toward the orb's fading glow, and, for once that night, Ayianna felt perfectly safe.

Hours later, the small band of travelers resurfaced outside of Ta'vazi. Ayianna pulled the fur-lined hood over her head and took a deep breath. The pale sky above was a welcome sight. She would not let Kael's attitude ruin the moment. Nor the fact that Jathil was nowhere in sight.

The crisp mountain air stung her lungs and face, but she remained warm beneath the layers of fur. Turning around, Ayianna could barely see the magnificent city carved into the mountainside. The morning sun splashed across the cold mountains, giving the walls of the city a rosy hue.

"Gefährlich Pass is beyond that ridge," Jaeger said.

Ayianna looked where he pointed. A gray slab of stone jutted up from the ground. Behind it, white-capped mountains rose into the sky. "Ve shall reach the pass by nightfall and camp there before ve attempt to scale the summit. Stark's Peak vill be three day's hike. Ve must hurry. The Captain vill be expecting his share of the gold in two veek's time."

They spent their first night at the mouth of Gefährlich Pass. The early gray of dawn found the tent put away and Ayianna and her companions climbing a narrow, slippery ledge. She struggled to steady herself in the snow and ice. Spasms shot through her neck wound at the slightest draft. She inhaled against the pain, but the icy air burned her nose and lungs. Would her curse be the death of her? She tugged the fur hood tightly over her head and readjusted her gloves.

The others seemed to fare little better. Each were bundled so alike she almost couldn't tell them apart. Except Jaeger. He was half their size and pulled a simple sled with their tent and supplies. Tariq and Kael kept together, keeping pace just behind Jaeger. Kael seemed to be recovering from the hag's attack, at least from her vantage point. He hadn't needed a break all morning. Vian hiked just in front of her. He wore his fur cap nearly pulled down over his nose, his red curls sticking out where the cap met his scarf. Desmond was somewhere behind her, but she refused to check on him and risk losing her footing.

By evening, the wind had picked up, flinging ice and snow into the air. Jaeger found a ledge where their tent could be safely pitched, and the men began setting it up. Ayianna stomped her feet to stay warm as she waited. She exhaled and watched her breath crystallize and disappear into the wind.

She squinted her watery eyes to get a better view of the gorge beneath her. Far below, fog cloaked the valley, except where ominous stone spikes pierced the misty shroud. She inched closer to the edge.

Vadazi's Gorge. Jaeger had called it the Devil's Mouth. It split the Kha Vaaro Mountains in half. According to Jaeger, deep in its throat mud boiled and the earth birthed miracles. It was down there that the best warming dirt could be found. Perhaps Eloith had returned to Gruben Pass looking for them only to find rotting imp carcasses. Where was he now?

Ayianna looked to the north. White icy peaks jabbed the moonlit sky, casting much of the mountainside into obscurity. Somewhere beyond lay Arashel, and Jathil was nowhere to be seen. She strained to catch a glimpse of a snowy cat leaping among the shadows. An ache cramped her heart. Why did Jathil's absence bother her so? It wasn't as if the Haruzo was her friend.

Tirza Jathil of Arashel. Did her name carry importance? She obviously thought so, but not enough to change the dwarf captain's mind. Although, he did for gold. If Jaeger didn't return with the gold, would the captain come after them? Nobody saw a hundred yettus in their lifetime, except kings, nobles, and the stewards counting it.

Laughter erupted in the cold night, its echo bouncing off the mountainside. Ayianna turned to see who had made so much noise.

"Desmond, you must be quiet or you vill bring danger to us." Jaeger glanced up higher into the mountains and then returned his gaze to him.

"What is so funny?" Kael held the tent's wooden pole up as Tariq slid a ring over its bottom.

"Wouldn't you like to know?" Desmond snorted. He pulled on the opposite pole while the prince copied Tariq. "The prince thinks he can change my mind about a certain—"

"Enough already." Vian straightened and jerked Desmond to the back of the tent. "We need to get this tent finished."

Jaeger shook his head. "Too much talking." He glanced back at the mountain peaks, glowing white in the moonlight.

Ayianna followed his gaze, taking a step back as she did. The gray clouds from earlier had dissolved into a crisp, black sky. Stars sparkled like diamonds embedded in endless velvet, disappearing periodically where the mountains hid them. The moon was so close she could almost reach out and touch it.

"Ayianna." Jaeger's voice brought her back to the frozen earth. "Come avay from the edge. It is too dangerous. It could be only hardened snow, and you vould plummet to your death. Besides the tent is ready, and it is varm inside."

Ayianna turned, but the edge gave way. Down the ice, snow, and rock fell, taking her with it. Her stomach rammed her throat and snatched her breath away. She scrambled for traction, but the snow and rocks tore the gloves from her hands and ripped into her skin. Fire shot through her. Was this it? What this how she would die?

Osaryn, no!

Her body slammed against the mountainside. She tried to brace herself, to catch something, but her arms flailed at empty snow. She slid until a protruding ledge of stone broke her descent. She gasped. Her lungs fought for air, but each breath sent fire through her chest. She lay still, too afraid to move and risk plunging farther into the gorge.

She heard crashing above and the swish of snow as a shadow raced toward her. Ayianna closed her eyes and braced for impact, but the noise shushed. She glanced up.

Kael. Her heart swelled. Everything would be all right.

He eased down onto the ledge next to her and placed his hand on her shoulder. The touch, though separated by layers of fur and clothes, sent comfort through her, and longing. Longing for home and a family that was no more.

With Kael, she was home.

The moon glared down at her, admonishing her. She was betrothed to Desmond. She should not be contemplating such delusions with another male. Yet where was her betrothed? Why hadn't Desmond come? If he really wanted to marry her, wouldn't he have been the first to dive after her?

Kael tugged his glove off and pressed his fingers along her temple and jawline. "Are you all right?"

No. How could she be? The man she was supposed to marry didn't care enough to rescue her, and the one who did only did so because of his vow to her brother. Her chest constricted, and pain rippled through her body. She wanted to brush Kael's hand aside, but her limbs refused to move.

"I'll be fine," she managed to say. Her bottom lip felt thick. She touched it with her tongue and tasted blood.

"No broken bones, I hope." Kael checked her legs and arms.

Ayianna was about to shake her head, but searing pain gripped her neck and shoulders. She gasped. Only pain. Nothing more.

Kael held out his hand. "Can you walk? We need to get off this ledge."

Ayianna grasped his hand as he helped her to her feet. "How did you get down here?"

"I slid." Kael picked up his shield and slung it across his back.

She inhaled against the pain and glanced over the ledge. The moon immersed the mountainside in an icy glow that disappeared into a valley of shadows and mist. A cloud of snow crystals had billowed up from her descent and now drifted across the ravine.

"Did you bring a rope?" she asked.

Kael clenched his jaw and looked away. "No."

"You didn't think to—"

"Stop—okay?" He rubbed his head. "I . . . I didn't. I saw you fall and dove after you. If you hadn't been—"

"I know. It's my fault. You don't need to remind me." Anger intensified her aches, and tears stung her eyes. Couldn't she do anything right? She glanced up, blinking away the tears. The swirling snow and ice hid the others from view. How far had she fallen? She buried her cold, raw hands beneath her cloak. "How are we going to get back up to the others?"

"We can't. It's too far, too dangerous to climb. We must go down into the gorge."

11

HUNGRY AND SORE, Ayianna shuffled after Kael along the bottom of the gorge. Its steep, jagged sides disappeared into a ceiling of fog. No snow found its way in. Scraggly trees dotted a small stream winding its way through stone and gravel. The farther they hiked, the more the mist increased until it swathed the land like a shroud. Trees and rocky formations became only ominous shadows towering above them like silent accusers, condemning them for trespassing.

She paused, her ribs burning with each breath. They would have to rest soon. She checked the bindings on her hands. The blood had dried, but their wrappings had loosened. She removed her fur-lined hood, wincing as she did. At least it was warmer. She tried to look up, but a sharp pain shot through her neck and into her back. Instead, she kept her gaze on the broken terrain before her.

"Come on," Kael said.

He stood deeper in the chasm. Stone spikes towered above him and lined the stream like sharp fangs, as if the very mouth of the Underworld had opened to swallow him. The heavy mist hung like veils, blurring him from view. Its wispy breath seemed to rise from the very stone itself.

Ayianna limped to catch up, her strides shortened and pained. "How are we going to find the others?"

"Good question." Kael uncorked his waterskin and stooped to fill it from the creek. "Eh—this water is warm." He stuck his hand into the stream again.

Ayianna stripped off the bloodied cloth binding her hands and knelt. She dipped her hand into the water, the bruises and scratches stinging from its warmth. She bit her tongue as she rubbed the dried blood from her skin.

"Do you think it is safe to drink?" she asked.

"Not after you washed your dirty hands in it."

Ayianna gaped at him.

"I'm joking." Kael smiled, but his smile faded into concern as he touched her cheeks. "How does your face feel? It looks a little pale. You might have some frostbite."

"I'm fine," Ayianna replied quickly. Her face burned, but not because of frostbite.

"Well, I'm not sure if the water is safe to drink." Kael stood and brushed the gravel from his knees.

"What makes the water warm?" she asked.

"Perhaps the answer lies upstream."

Deeper into the gorge, something moaned like an old man with a belly ache. White steam billowed from the ground. Moving closer, she saw a frothing mud pit. The greenish slime groaned as several large bubbles formed on its surface. One popped, splattering the surrounding stone with mud. She tried to rub the acrid smell from her nose.

"Wait, could this be the warming dirt that Eloith was after?" She inched closer. If she could just reach it, it could help them cleanse any lingering ache or dullness from the hag's touch. But hadn't Jaeger's warming dirt been red?

"Careful." Kael placed his hand on Ayianna's shoulder. "The ground might be soft. We will make camp where the stream is deeper. Maybe we can wash up a bit and find some food."

Ayianna nodded, her stomach growling

The going was slow as they picked their way through the large boulders and sharp ridges. Soon, the rocky terrain sank into a deep valley, its jagged edges softening into grassy slopes. Dark evergreen trees stretched toward the gray sky. Velvety moss blanketed the boulders and climbed the tree trunks. Steam swelled from a small waterfall splashing down from the mountainside, spilling water into a pool below.

"I'll bet those waters have healing properties." Kael dropped his knapsack and slid off his longbow and shield.

"Yes." Ayianna plopped down her knapsack and fur-lined coat, gritting her teeth against the searing pain shooting through her ribs. She loosened her sword belt, dropping it next to her knapsack.

"You should bathe, it will help."

"Bathe!"

"There is no one around for miles." Kael piled his belongings into a mound.

Ayianna raised her eyebrows.

Kael glanced up. "I won't look."

"Right—of course you wouldn't."

"Well, if you won't, then I will." Kael pulled his tunic off.

"Ah . . ." Heat flooded her face, leaving her ears tingling. It wasn't as if she hadn't seen him without his shirt before. "I will . . . ah . . . go find some firewood." Ayianna whirled around, pausing for a second. The temptation to peek flitted across her mind. Horrified at the thought, she ducked into the trees and fled.

When Ayianna returned, Kael had finished bathing and had gathered some wood. His dark hair had been braided and hung wet against his gray tunic. Cleaned and refreshed, and without all the layers of fur, he looked as if he had just stepped from the king's wedding feast back in Bonzapur. That night, she had learned his sister had been betrothed to her brother. They had danced, and for a moment she had felt free.

Why did she torment herself? His vow to Teron had influenced his behavior toward her. It had nothing to do with who she was, and it definitely didn't take into account her harpy curse.

She averted her eyes and joined him. She dumped her bundle of sticks and dead logs next to his.

"Are you going to bathe?" He knelt and arranged some branches. "It will help soothe your aches."

"I think it would be good."

"Good. Although don't go too close to the falls. The waters are cold." Kael picked up his quiver and bow. "I will go look for some food while we can still see."

"Kael . . ." Ayianna glanced at the lengthening shadows. "Don't go too far."

"I will stay within hearing distance." Then he turned and disappeared into the woods.

Ayianna looked around at the trees and then at the pool of water. The rumble of the waterfall drummed in her ears, its spray wetting the trees around it. Steam mushroomed from the pool and obscured the rest of the valley from sight.

She dug out the second outfit from Queen Emani and grabbed her hairpin. She removed her leather armor, peeled off her damp clothes, and stepped into the pool. The warm water lapped at her shins. She piled her braid on the top of her head and secured it with the pin. The last thing she needed was to mess with wet, tangled hair. She sank into the warmth of the pool and sighed. The hot waves pounded her aching body. Her skin burned from the multitudes of scratches and bruises.

By the time Kael returned, Ayianna had dressed and hung her other clothes on a tree to dry. Would they dry with such moist air? Perhaps a fire would help, if Kael could get one to light. She took out her small bottle of kulin and applied it to her scratches and her neck wound. For a moment, the horrible image the dithza-mielis had summoned sprang to her mind—the pale man's face with a forked tongue. She shuddered.

"Feel better?" Kael set his bow and quiver on his cloak.

"Yes, thank you." The ache had faded, and she could move without her body protesting. With the kulin, she'd be good as new tomorrow.

Ayianna slid the kulin back into its velvet bag. She'd have to be more careful with it, or she'd risk running out before they reached the merpeople. And at the pace they were going, it would be months before they reached Ganya. She glanced at his empty arms. "No meat tonight?"

"None." Kael knelt and pulled out the firesteel from a pouch at his waist. "At least we can have a fire."

"Oh, well, I have some nuts and dried fruit." Ayianna picked up her knapsack and rummaged around for food, dumping what she found in a pile. She untied her blanket from the pack and unrolled it on the ground. She pulled the fur-lined coat around her shoulders, warding off the chill evening brought.

Ayianna munched on the nuts, watching Kael strike the flint and rock together. Soon, the sparks gave way to small flames, and he fed it more wood till the blaze was roaring. Strands of hair had worked free from his braid and slipped over his furrowed brow. He was brooding again, but about what? Was he upset that she had gotten them into this mess?

"Kael?" Ayianna broke the silence. He looked up from the fire. "Thank you for saving my life again."

He shrugged. "That's what friends do."

He had called her that before. Was that all he saw in her? Then the firelight glinted off her bracelet from Desmond, warning her as if it had been reading her mind. Ayianna drew the fur coat around her more closely. "Do you think the fire is safe?"

"I doubt the dragon could fly into this narrow valley." He added a log to the flames and sparks scattered into the air.

"What about the imps? Or the dwarves?"

He sat back on his heels and poked at the blaze with a long spindly stick. "The imps have probably lost our scent, and I wouldn't worry about the dwarves. They aren't the best trackers, and with Jaeger's plan, I doubt they suspect anything—yet."

Ayianna glanced at the shroud of darkness above. Were the others all right? Did they know she and Kael were fine?

Kael. He dove off the mountainside to rescue her. A thrill tickled her spine, but her thoughts warred with her heart. Friend. Almost family. No matter what he called her, she was safe with him. And right now, he was the only familiarity in a world of chaos and pain.

Yet something awkward and ugly hung in the air between them. She was betrothed to Desmond. A choice she had confirmed back in Bonzapur. How could she have been such a fool? He never intended to help her find her mother. He didn't even risk his life to save her.

The night seemed to grow darker and colder. She inched closer to the fire.

"Do you think the others will be able to see the fire from up there?"

"Maybe. Worried about Desmond?"

"No, not like that . . ." Ayianna paused, realizing she had been rubbing the bracelet around her wrist.

He shifted from his knees and sat cross-legged. "How well do you know him?"

Ayianna hesitated. Desmond was a merchant and a nephew of Lord Ramiro, but even Kael knew that. Her stomach sank. She should have more to say, shouldn't she?

He twisted a stick between his fingers. "I think a person should know who they're making a lifelong commitment to, especially those with elven blood."

"And this is a concern of yours?" She dug in the cold dirt. "The plains people live differently than the elves. I don't expect you to—"

"You don't love him."

Ayianna stared. She had to deny it, but when she opened her mouth to do so, no words formed on her tongue. Hadn't she decided to trust him? Why couldn't she make her head and heart agree? Her mother thought she could. The queen thought she could. She frowned. "Some people do not marry for love. Apparently, my mother didn't think it did her any good."

"Even so, he is not a good man."

Deep down his words rang true, but what could she do?

Kael fed another broken limb into the fire.

Ayianna turned away. She ached to embrace the concern she saw in his eyes—to trust him. But she couldn't break the betrothal with Desmond. Such acts were condemned among the plains people. Did he not understand what he was asking her to do? She could not blindly rebel against her family and society without a plan or a promise of something different. Her mother was counting on her. She looked out into the dark. Loneliness swooped in like a vulture ready to feast on her dying heart.

Kael sighed. "I'm not your family. I'm not your brother." He cracked a twig and threw it into the fire. "But I knew your brother. He wouldn't want you marrying Desmond."

Ayianna twisted her brother's ring on her finger as grief washed over her. She blinked away the tears. The truth burned.

"Why do you keep going on with it? Why didn't you refuse him back in Bonzapur?"

She faltered. The sorrow and confusion suffocated her. She wanted to run, flee from his eyes and probing questions. She stood and rubbed her arms. "I don't know. Why do you care? I'm not your responsibility."

Kael jumped to his feet, his eyes blazing. "It doesn't matter whether I care or not. You're the one who will have to live with this decision. Why didn't you tell him no?"

Why didn't she? Because of her parents? Because she was cursed? Fear. It all came back to fear. How paralyzing it could be! She glared at Kael through her tears. "You wouldn't understand."

He clenched and unclenched his jaw. "Do you want to marry him?"

"No." The word was out before she knew it.

"Then don't."

She stared at him through watery eyes. "You think I can just walk away?" Her voice cracked, but she pushed her words out. "If I say no, do you know what will happen to me—to my mother? I see no other way."

Kael shook his head. "Then you have no faith." He turned away and stalked off into the darkness.

The tears spilled down her cheeks unchecked. Ayianna sank to the ground and buried her face in her cloak.

Osaryn, help my unbelief!

12

AYIANNA RECLINED AGAINST a moss-covered tree next to the small lake, the falls droning in her ears. The rush of icy waters from above poured into the warmth of the pool, propelling wave after wave to break along its rocky shore. Her thoughts drifted like the steam billowing from the falls. The constant downward pull of the water tugged at her eyelids, imploring her to sleep.

And maybe she would. The valley was a dead end. The only way out was up or back, but neither option bode well for them, so instead, they waited. Perhaps the others would discover the riddle's meaning. *Climb the highest to reach the lowest.* Couldn't get much lower than a valley, could they?

A branch snapped. She glanced up as Kael made his way toward her. He had spent much of the morning exploring one end of the valley, and she the other, hardly exchanging a word except short snippets here and there.

The ache from last night had faded into a bitter emptiness. No faith, he had said. Faith in what? Society? Osaryn? Her mother's Nuja? Vituko, the Shadow God of the guardians? Did it matter? Nothing could change the facts. *Osaryn, what other way is there? What does Kael see that I don't?*

"Enjoying the falls?" He sat down next to her. Dark circles rimmed his weary eyes. Had he not slept at all?

The bitterness in her soul melted. He had his own struggles and decisions to make. What had she expected—for him to sweep her into his arms, to make it all disappear, and take away her difficult choice? How could she be so foolish?

Her gaze returned to the falls. "Beautiful, isn't it? Reminds me of the falls at Mladam Rysum. My brother and I would hunt for dove eggs there."

"Yes, I have been there. Dove eggs, quite a delicacy in Zurial. You know the elven lords are building the new *nu'mraryzi* there."

"A good place to study the stars. The way the cliffs stretch above the Dzitaryn Sea, nothing would block the sky from its view." Ayianna sighed. It had been years since she had lived among the elves, the cliffs and glittering sea such a distant memory. Never once had she suspected her family had been keeping secrets, living in fear while she enjoyed a happy, carefree childhood—until they had moved to the plains.

"Have you always wanted to become a *nu'mrarym*?"

"No, my first choice would have been a *niyadzifen*, but girls aren't allowed to be sailors."

"The Dzjorym Council has been discussing that for the past century, but I don't think they are about to change their minds any time soon. Not that I blame them. The sea is no place for a lady."

Ayianna opened her mouth to object, but the distant look in his eyes and the harsh set of his jaw changed her mind. "How do you know so much about everything?"

"I wouldn't say everything."

"Well, you know more than a simple guard would know."

Kael didn't deny it, but he didn't reply either. Instead, he picked up a stone and flung it into the pool. "My father was a lord of the Dzjorym Council in Zurial."

"Oh." Ayianna drew her knees up and hugged them. An elf in high standing and moral obligation—no wonder he wasn't interested in her. "What were you doing at Dagmar?"

132

"As my father's son, I had to fulfill my *rydazi*—my duty to nation and family—so I served as a guard and received training to one day take my place among the lords."

She plucked at the moss covering the tree's root. "So when this is all over, are you going to return to Zurial and become a lord of the council?"

He crossed his legs and leaned forward, resting his elbows on his knees. "Nevin Saeed has asked me to join the Guardian Circle."

Ayianna looked away. "Guardians don't have families, do they?"

He shook his head.

"So . . ." Her heart sank. "Will you?"

"There is nothing left for me in Zurial."

The truth was jaded and sharp like a dagger, ripping through her heart. He shifted. Did he sense her emotions? If only she had learned how to shield them. She tried to envision a shield to hide her crashing hope. What had she expected? He'd only cared because of his vow to her brother. Hadn't he said as much back in Bonzapur? He could never love her, especially if he knew about her curse. Her heart sank deeper.

"We need to get out of this place." He stood, picked up another stone, and rubbed it between his fingers. "This is nothing but a dead end."

"How?"

He flung the stone, and it skipped across the surface of the pool before sinking beneath the ripples. "We'll have to look for a place where the sides aren't as steep and climb out. Maybe go back—"

A howl shattered the stillness. Kael dropped next to her, and Ayianna scrambled to her knees, her stiff muscles protesting the rash movement. The valley remained calm. Nothing stirred but the mists from the waterfall. They had yet to see wildlife in the valley.

The howl came again, but closer. A gray blur burst through the far entrance and streaked across the valley like a falcon in flight. Liam. Ayianna's sprang to her feet and raced toward her.

Kael's words were lost behind her. Liam leapt and bowled Ayianna over.

Ayianna clung to her. *How is this possible? Oh, thank you, Osaryn! Thank you!* She pulled away and wiped the tears from her eyes. Liam licked her face. She sat on her haunches with a crooked grin on her muzzle and nuzzled Ayianna's shoulder.

Kael hovered above them, a smile softening his face. He rubbed Liam's head and ears. "Welcome back, friend."

Liam panted. She shook her head and swiped her tail back and forth.

The air swished like wings beating upon it. Another blur sped toward them, breaking branches and scattering leaves as it went. A shout of glee reached their ears.

"Kael! Ayianna!" Eloith plunged downward and lighted on Ayianna's shoulder, grasping her head in a hug. "I knew it! When Liam bounded over the side of the mountain, I knew it was you!" He shot into the air and saluted Kael. "You have no idea how glad I am to see you two."

"Likewise." Kael touched his fingertips together and dipped his head.

"How did you—what happened?" Ayianna draped her arm around Liam's neck and tugged her closer.

Eloith crossed his arms and hovered in the air. "When I had returned with the *maezam aenlu* and saw the imp carcasses in the pass, I feared the worse. I scouted the area for hours and then caught sight of Liam tracking you. We followed your scent until we reached Ta'vazi the next morning, but before I could figure out how to sneak in and rescue you, Liam took off again." He flitted to the other side of them and scanned the mountains. "What happened after I left you?"

Ayianna told him of the imps, the dwarves, and their escape from Ta'vazi, and how they ended up in the gorge.

"This isn't the gorge," Eloith said when she had finished explaining. "You two have passed through the gorge and are now in Grozac Valley."

"Grozac Valley?" asked Ayianna.

"Yes, it is also known as Prowil Valley." Eloith paused, trying to catch his breath. "The Valley of Grace. And to fall like you did and survive—Vituko must be watching out for you."

"Hold on," Kael said. "If Stark's Peak is the highest, then Grozac Valley must be the lowest."

"Yes, I was just thinking that." Ayianna shifted to her knees. "But then, why did we have to climb the mountain if the pinecone is here in the valley?"

Eloith settled on the ground. "The valley is surrounded by steep mountains, and you have the gorge on one side, the waterfall on the other. There is no way in unless you have wings or burrow through stone like the dwarves. Unless of course you fall in, which is generally a less advisable means of arriving here."

"The riddle said to climb the highest to reach the lowest, so there's got to be a way of getting into the valley from up there." Kael turned and scanned the valley. "Have you seen the others?"

"We ran into Jathil, and together, we began tracking them, but when Liam picked up your scent, I went after her, and Jathil continued on up the mountain."

Ayianna could not deny the hope stirring in her soul, but she cautioned it. Jathil was still a wanted criminal, and her loyalty was not to them.

"Well, this valley must be what the riddle is referring to." Eloith flew up into the air. "Let us find the pinecone."

"We've searched this entire valley." Kael raised his hands and gestured at the steep slopes towering above them. "Unless you know something more about it than we do."

"Kael, I think there is one place we've forgotten to check." Ayianna stood and adjusted her tunic over her pants. "What is the lowest point in a valley?"

"A river, but we have followed the river into here. We didn't see anything that looked like a silver pinecone tree."

Ayianna glanced at the waterfall and smiled. "That's it!"

"What?"

"It has to be in the pool or behind the falls." Ayianna took off her outer garments and walked into the water, feeling with her feet until it got too deep.

Kael frowned. "Pine trees don't grow at bottom of lakes or in dark caverns." His voice had grown harsh as if he blamed her for the confusing riddle. He tugged his shirt off and stepped into the pool. "Be careful, Ayianna!"

"Do you think a silver pinecone would be found on a natural tree?" Eloith placed his hands on his hips and paced the water's edge. "I apologize, but I cannot go in."

"Don't worry about it. Just keep an eye out for the others, in case they should find their way into the valley." Kael disappeared under the water.

Ayianna swam along the edge, running her hand across the smooth stones. The warmth of the water eased away the remaining ache from her unfortunate plunge down the mountainside. The ripples from the falls rocked her back and forth. She pulled herself along the stone embankment, determined to find the silver pinecone. If she did, she could redeem herself for all the times Kael had to rescue her.

As Ayianna neared the falls, the water became colder and more forceful. She clung to the wet stones as she inched behind the falls. Her grip slid off the polished stones, and she banged her knee into the wall of rock and bit her tongue. But she continued to feel along its slimy surface with her free hand. Then, she slipped.

The force of the falls shoved her deeper and deeper. The waves pummeled her against the stones. She struggled, clawing at the rock, but she couldn't reach the surface. Fear taunted her. She couldn't go two days without needing rescuing. No. Not this time. She fought against the current, kicking and flailing. Her lungs screamed for air.

Her arm brushed across an opening in the rock and a current sucked her into the hole. The water seemed warmer. She kicked her legs and propelled herself in a direction she could only assume was up. Suddenly, she broke the surface of the water and gasped. She needed to find the water's edge, before her limbs gave out. She grabbed out at the darkness. Nothing.

She continued treading water and trying to see what sort of cavern hid behind the falls. Could this be the meaning of the riddle? But what kind of pine tree didn't need light to grow?

"Kael? Eloith?" Could they hear her on the other side? "I think I found something! Kael, Eloith!"

The silence swallowed her words. She took a deep breath and dove back under. Where was the hole? If she could find it, she could swim back through.

But fear slowed her. The last thing she needed was to slam her head into stone. Her lungs demanded air before she found the wall, so she resurfaced and treaded water. She had to find the hole, but her strength was waning fast. She needed to rest and soon.

Glimpses of gray light sifted through a crevice above her—an opening she assumed was the direction of the falls. As her eyes adjusted, the rocks and water shifted from each other, taking on different forms. She paddled toward the rocks.

Her muscles burned, but she pushed on. She had to find a way out. Ahead the rock surface disappeared into blackness. Perhaps there was a break in the stone, and she could pull herself up. Ayianna paddled toward it.

A ledge loomed before her. If she could just reach it, she could rest. A severe cramp seized her legs. Her body arched. She flailed her arms, trying to keep her head above the water. She gasped and then went under.

13

DESMOND GLARED AT his shivering companions climbing the narrow trail in front of him. It was their fault. He could have been done with the quest. He didn't have to suffer like this. He clenched his jaw against the cold, daring his teeth to chatter. He blinked away his blurry vision. Ice crystals had formed on his lashes and nose hairs. His feet numbed; his legs tingled. He fumed at the Sorceress, Ayianna, and the world.

His mission seemed pointless now. Ayianna was gone. If she knew anything of the dagger, the knowledge had gone over the mountain with her. Desmond tightened his grip around the dragon pendant, tempted to remove himself from the hostile conditions. At least one thing made him happy—Kael's absence. Well, almost . . . *Why do I even care if Ayianna likes him? I have Semine.* He balled his fists. *I hate it. I just do.*

Reaching the peak, Desmond waited as Tariq and Jaeger poked the snow for clues. Jathil and Vian huddled together against the driving wind. Desmond refused to join them. It played into their thoughts about his loss. Poor Desmond had lost his betrothed. He must be devastated. He would have grinned, but his face couldn't move. Once they got off the mountain, he could really take advantage of their sympathies, but right now it was just too cold.

"Vhat are ve looking for?" asked Jaeger.

"I don't know. The riddle said climb to the highest to reach the lowest!" Tariq shouted over the wind.

"There is nothing here," Jaeger said.

Desmond closed his eyes. The warmth of the Sorceress's bed beckoned him. He longed to be in Gwydion, finished with everything. Wait, what was stopping him? Why was he waiting? He could throw everyone off the mountain, except Vian, of course, and call the dragon. Sure, he had lost Ayianna. Semine would have to understand. Or would she want him to investigate? Could the harpy's curse continue to work even after Ayianna's death? Doubtful. Besides, it wasn't like Semine needed a harpy. Just the dagger. And what if Ayianna had it? No, Desmond could not return until he knew for certain.

"Ve must go," Jaeger hollered. "The air is too thin up here."

"Wait. I think I found something," Tariq shouted. "Vian, Jathil, come here. You too, Desmond."

Desmond wanted to open his eyes, but he was warm, floating on his way to Gwydion.

"Desmond!"

Something hit him.

Desmond jerked his eyes open, furious. The wind flung snow and ice into his face. He brushed it away with his fur-wrapped hand and glanced around. His heart pounded. He was alone. For the first time, he noticed the wispy clouds hanging in the blue sky and the smaller white-capped peaks littering the mountain range beneath him.

Everywhere he looked he saw nothing but snow and ice, and the cold mountains below. He rushed around, looking for footprints.

A great screech shook the mountains. Desmond dropped to all fours.

Then he saw it—a black gaping hole in the side of the mountain. The mountain screeched again, and a stone slab appeared, closing the hole.

Desmond scrambled to the edge. The others had to have gone this way. But what if he was wrong? It had to better than freezing to death. He slid inside just as the stone door thundered to a close. He braced himself for impact, but it never came. He kept falling. And falling.

14

KAEL RESURFACED AND climbed out of the pool. Frustration ate away at his newfound hope. The valley was a dead end. He wrung out his hair and retied it.

"Nothing?" Eloith sat, petting Liam. The wolf lay stretched out on the ground; her eyes closed.

"I don't understand this riddle," Kael said.

Liam jumped up, knocking Eloith over as she charged toward the pool.

"What is bothering Liam?" Eloith stood and brushed himself off.

Kael's stomach sank. Where was Ayianna? He scanned the pool. She had been making her way along the shore to the back of the falls, but she wasn't there. Liam whined and leapt at the mountainside, scratching with her paws.

Why did it have to be water? Did Osaryn like to mock him? Kael dove into the water and screams pierced him. Were they Ayianna's? No, only memories drudged up. Rysa's horror-stricken face flashed in his mind's eye. The hag's intrusion was still too fresh. He fought the undercurrent and the flood of memories tormenting him.

He slid behind the rushing water but found only solid rock. He ducked under the falls, and felt along the rocks, the force of the water pushing him deeper. His lungs ached for air. Was this how Rysa felt before she drowned? His hand found an opening in the rocks. He kicked hard, pushing himself through the hole.

Ayianna's panic slammed into him. He swam toward her. Her fear grew in intensity, but he didn't dare block her feelings. He surfaced and saw nothing but darkness. Where was she? Water splashed, and he lunged toward the sound.

Ayianna thrashed just ahead of him, and her head went under again. He grabbed her around the waist and yanked her up. Her elbow hit him in the jaw, sending sparks across his vision. He lifted her head above the water, and she gasped. She thrashed about, nearly kicking him in the stomach.

"Calm down." He struggled to keep her from kicking him while he towed her to the rocks nearby. "I've got you. Calm down."

Ayianna gasped. "My legs!"

Kael tugged her the rest of the way and shoved her onto the ledge. He hoisted himself up and began massaging her legs. He pushed against her toes, stretching the cramped muscles. She groaned as they contracted.

"Relax into it." Kael continued working in silence. Rysa's death burned fresh in his heart. He had sacrificed her life to save Braedon, only to lose him too. What would she think now? He clenched his teeth. How could Osaryn spare Ayianna, but not his wife?

He gripped Ayianna's ankle, bending her foot back, then forward. Why did he mourn now? It had been years since the accident. Blast those hags! Would he ever regain control of his mind again?

He picked up her other foot and repeated the stretching. He pushed her wet pants up to her knees and rubbed the length of her calves, her skin cold, the muscles still taut. He returned to stretching her feet. His pulse slowed and the fear and anger faded. Warmth blossomed in his chest. He had done something right for once. He eased her foot down.

Embarrassment surged from her, and she quickly pulled away. "I'm fine now, thanks."

Heat flooded his face. What was he thinking? He sat back on the ledge and heaved a sigh.

"I'm sorry." Ayianna pulled the loose pants back over her legs. "I keep messing up. First, I fall off the mountain, and now I almost drown."

"You're safe, that's all that matters." He looked away. "When you're feeling better, we'll look around. Maybe you've solved the riddle."

He scanned the area. Mostly rock and water to the right, but to the left a faint light sifted through cracks in the stone. "Maybe we can get out that way."

Screams and shouts erupted above them and echoed in the cave. Kael grabbed for his sword, but he had left it on the other side of the falls. Ayianna scrambled back. Kael halted her retreat and pulled her close. Flying lumps of fur dropped from the ceiling and splashed into the water. The quiet cavern burst into chaos and noise.

"Ah! These waters are hot!" A woman's voice echoed off the walls. Could it be Jathil?

"Now, that was a ride." A voice much like Tariq's bounced around the cavern.

"I think I lost my stomach back at the peak."

Kael smiled. Who would've thought he would have been so happy to hear the prince's voice again?

"Quit your bellyaching." Jaeger's thick voice carried above the others.

"These furs are impossible to swim in." Vian and his complaining. Kael shook his head.

"Over here!" Ayianna grabbed Kael's arm. A grin broke across her face like sunlight bursting through storm clouds. "They've found us!"

Jaeger swam into view. "Ayianna? Kael?"

"Yes, yes!" Ayianna laughed. "Where—how did you—what happened?"

"Ayianna, we thought we lost you." Tariq appeared and swam to the edge. He glanced up at Kael and shook his head.

"You scoundrel! I can't believe you did that. Leave it to an elf to do something insane and live to tell about it."

"Give me your hand, I'll pull you out." Kael hauled Tariq out of the water, but Jaeger didn't wait for assistance as he scrambled up the side of the rock without difficulty. Vian came next, paddling like a dog, his curls plastered to his face. He grabbed the prince's hand and pulled him up.

"Some old codger had a horrible sense of humor when he wrote that riddle." Vian dumped his soaked fur coat onto the rocks and stamped out the water.

"And where do you find humor in this?" Jathil's eyes shimmered white in the dim cavern. She grasped Kael's outstretched hand and hoisted herself onto the rock ledge. Once on land, she grabbed Ayianna's shoulders. "Look at you. I can't believe you survived!"

Ayianna's face hardened. "Why did you—"

A shriek of terror filled the tavern and echoed off the walls.

Kael frowned. "You could've left him behind."

"Kael!" Tariq punched his shoulder.

From out of the darkness, Desmond plunged into the waters. He resurfaced, coughing and spitting out water.

"Nice of you to finally join us." Vian laughed, wiping the water from his face.

"Thanks for leaving me behind." Desmond grunted as he swam to the edge.

"It's not my fault you ignored us."

Desmond held onto the stone outcropping and paused. His glare settled on Kael. "You're alive."

"That's a nice way to say thanks to someone who has saved your betrothed's life—again." Kael held his hand out to Desmond, but Desmond brushed it aside and hauled himself out.

Desmond faced Ayianna. He grinned, but his smile didn't reach his eyes. He draped his arm around her in a sloppy hug. "How did you survive?"

A chill snaked down Kael's spine. His stomach clenched. He grabbed some of the fur coats and threw them into a pile. They smelled like wet dogs—like Desmond. He stomped the water from them, forcing his thoughts away from Ayianna wrapped in Desmond's wretched arms.

The ground trembled and he froze.

"What is that?" Ayianna asked.

Everyone hushed and looked around. The air chilled and Kael shivered. The waters gurgled and the smooth surface rippled. He peered closer. Down in the depths of the pool, a golden light seeped through a crack in the stone.

"Do you think this is it?" Vian's voice was barely audible. "The riddle—the highest to the lowest. The silver pinecone could be hidden down there.

"It has to be," Jaeger whispered.

"How do we reach it?" Vian asked.

Kael stepped to the edge of the pool. "We go for a swim."

"I'm already wet." Vian shrugged. "Let's go."

"No," Desmond said. "I don't think we should all go. What if something goes wrong?"

"What could go wrong?" Vian asked. "We're just going to look. Besides, someone lived to write a riddle about it."

"What about your father?" Desmond asked. "Shouldn't you be thinking about him? You're the future king of Badara. I'd think you'd take a little more precaution."

Vian frowned. He glanced at Kael, then back at Desmond. "You do have a point."

"I have nothing to lose." Jaeger kicked off his boots. "I vill go." He peeled off his tunic and started to remove his belt.

"Hey!" Desmond twisted Ayianna to the side. "We have a lady here."

Jaeger frowned. "I am not blind." He removed his belt, wrapped it around his sheathed sword, and placed it on the furs. "Veapons vill only veigh me down.

"I'll go too," Tariq said. "The rest of you can look for a way out of this cave."

"That suits me fine." Jathil shook out her hair. "Blasted water."

Kael glanced back at Ayianna. Desmond's arm had shifted to her waist. The urge to break that arm swept over him, instead he faced the golden pool. At least she'd have Jathil and Vian. She'd be all right. Then he dove into the water, Jaeger and Tariq close behind.

15

KAEL SWAM TOWARD the light filtering through the crack. He ran his hand along the top of the hole, the upper part smooth and warm to the touch. He shoved through. Once on the other side, he kicked to the surface. He wiped the water from his face and climbed out of the water onto a polished marble floor.

The golden glow illuminated a dome-shaped cavern. Marble pillars carved right out of the mountainside spiraled up to the center of the room. The polished floor gleamed gold, except where he had crawled out of the water. The half-moon pool was black against the brightness. How did the water not flood the room?

Tariq and Jaeger broke the surface of the pool. They pulled themselves out of the water and looked around.

Jaeger's eyes widened. "Vhat is this?"

Tariq climbed to his feet and helped the dwarf up. His gaze drifted. "This is a sacred place." He circled the room.

Sacred indeed. Were they not in the belly of Vadazi's Gorge? What good could come out of this? Kael shuddered. A presence of times past, older than any tree or rock overwhelmed the cavern. It clung to him like a shroud of spider webs. He pressed through, but it remained before him and behind him. He withdrew his mind lest it smother him and blocked its presence.

"There are runes carved into the stone." He slid his hand up the wall. "The whole wall is covered in them."

"Vhat do they say?"

"I've never seen them before." Tariq shrugged. He scanned the walls and ceiling. "Where is the light coming from?"

Kael glanced up at the dome. There were no torches or any other visible means for the light. There were no shadows here as if the very rock glowed. The otherworldly presence grew heavier, or was the air growing thinner? His vision spun and he blinked his eyes. The weight of the mountain pressed in on him, threatening to collapse and block his watery exit. His breath caught. Was this what Ayianna felt in closed spaces? He shoved the feelings aside. "Let's go."

"Vhat is your hurry?" Jaeger asked.

"We don't want to spend all day down here." He started for the other side of the dome. "We might run out of air."

"I vill not argue that." Jaeger strode along the base of the dome. "Vhat are ve we looking for? I see no tree down here."

Kael shrugged. "Maybe we'll recognize it when we see it. The riddle said, silver pure." He faced the others. "I don't see any silver down here, do you?"

Tariq shook his head. "Nor do we see a maze of dark and stone. I don't like the sound of that."

"So no silver, no tree, no maze." Jaeger put his hands on his hips. "And vhy do you think ve are in the right place then?"

"Because," Kael said. "I can feel it."

"Well . . . " Vian looked around. "Where should we start?"

"Don't you think one of us should stay by the water, in case they need help?" Ayianna eyed the golden depths where Kael and the others had disappeared.

"You can stay if you like," Jathil said. "We'll need to dry off before we venture outside this mountain, or we'll freeze." She sniffed the air and turned to look down a dark corridor. "I think I'll check out this direction. If I don't come back, don't worry about me."

"Are you going to run off again?" Ayianna asked.

Jathil shrugged. "I can take care of myself. I'll let you know if I find anything."

She dropped to the ground as her body blurred white. In her place sat a large white cat with black spots. A deep purr rumbled in her throat. She flicked her tail and bounded off into the darkness.

Vian cleared his throat. "Remind me never to cross her."

Ayianna shook her head. Always coming and going, keeping her distance—Jathil was a difficult one to understand. Half the time she didn't seem to care, and the other half her heart managed to leak through her constant barricade. She knew too much to be a commoner, too skilled to be a noble. Perhaps she was an assassin. It made sense. Maybe that was why the king of Arashel offered a reward for her return.

No matter what crime she had committed, Jathil had proven herself an ally thus far. But would she really join them for the rest of the journey? Who would risk life and death on a journey that didn't pertain to them? Someone who had nothing to lose.

The weight of Desmond's arm grew heavier. Ayianna cringed. She'd never be like Jathil—free, skilled with a sword, able to defend herself and her mother. But if she had freedom without a home or skills without a job, Ayianna would not be able to provide for their future.

"Well, since she's gone in that direction, I shall . . ." Vian scanned the cavern, then faced Ayianna and Desmond. "I'm not venturing in the dark, alone. And since we can't see without light it would be pointless to go beyond this cavern." He looked up. "Why don't we try to loosen the stones over there?" He pointed at the gray light sifting through the rocks.

Ayianna peeled Desmond's hand off her waist and walked around the pool. The light in the water bathed the cavern in gold. Stalactites glittered amidst the shadows. It might have been romantic under different circumstances.

She glanced back at Desmond, who followed her. A frown cramped his face, and his blue eyes were harsh in the soft glow. Repulsion hit her hard. She faced forward and followed Vian. She couldn't go through with the betrothal.

She halted.

Rocks and boulders created a jagged wall. Above, faint light streamed through the crevices. The waterfall hummed on the other side like the blood roaring in her ears.

"We could probably move those stones." Vian stuck his foot into a hole and hoisted himself up.

Ayianna shifted her weight, placing her arm on the rocks. "Be careful."

"Careful never won a victory, did it?" Vian continued climbing. "But Desmond will catch me if I fall."

"If the rocks don't catch you first," Desmond said. "Pay attention to what you're doing. I'm certain your father wouldn't want me carrying your broken body back to him."

"Ah, you were ever the optimist, weren't you?" Vian reached the light. He removed the loose stones and dropped them into the pool behind him. The crevice widened, spilling more light into the cavern. The roar of the falls filled the cavern. He pushed on the bigger stones.

"Hey!" Vian cried.

Liam's furry white face broke through the rocks. The wolf whined and scratched the rocks with her claws.

"Liam!" Ayianna clambered up the rocks, but Desmond grabbed her around the waist.

"Don't be stupid. I'll not have you fall and break your neck. We'll get through to your mutt soon enough."

Ayianna frowned. "I'm not stupid."

"Well, your behavior tells me otherwise."

She looked away. Maybe he was right, but still. He didn't have to call her that.

Liam's face disappeared, and Vian knocked a large stone free.

"Watch it!" Desmond stepped out of the way as the stone tumbled past.

"Sorry about that," Vian said. "I think we can squeeze through. Let me—"

A blur of gray fur lunged through the opening. Vian struggled for purchase but fell backward. Desmond lunged to catch the prince as Liam plunged into the pool below.

"Cur of a beast!" Desmond collapsed beneath the weight of the prince, and they both toppled into the water.

Liam paddled straight for Ayianna. She reached the side and scrambled out of the pool, her nails clicking and scratching on the rock. Ayianna grasped her around the neck and pulled her the rest of the way. Liam licked her face, and Ayianna laughed.

Ayianna looked for Desmond and Vian. To her relief, they were unharmed, sitting on the edge of the rocks. "Sorry, Vian."

"For what? I told you Desmond would catch me." He shook the water from his curls and stood, eyeing the opening. "What's on the other side?"

"A dead end." Ayianna covered her face with her arms as Liam shook her wet fur, sending a spray of smelly water everywhere. "But Eloith is there, and so are our supplies."

"I'll go take a look around then," Vian said. "We'll need to get a fire going so we can all dry off."

"We'll just stay here." Desmond squeezed the water out of his hair. "Just in case they need us."

Ayianna quailed. No. She couldn't remain alone with Desmond. She had to protest, to volunteer to join Vian, but her jaw wouldn't unclench. Liam pressed against her leg, and the terror melted. She'd be all right.

Vian lingered, his eyes on her for a moment before nodding. He scaled the stones and disappeared through the opening.

"Well, well, well." Desmond turned to Ayianna. His face darkened. "What providence. The goddess must be pleased with me."

16

KAEL CIRCLED THE room again. The nameless presence continued to hang over him like a shroud. Or was it his imagination? What was he missing? The cavern was empty. From the polished floors to the chiseled walls to the dome-shaped ceiling. There were no trees, no mazes, no silver anything. Maybe this wasn't the place. Maybe they were wrong. *Osaryn, are we in the right place? Or have I failed again?*

He rubbed his face and retraced his steps.

Could it be a tomb? He had heard of legends of kings buried in magnificent tombs, but that was before the days of Stygian. Before they had been plundered.

Tariq studied the runes engraved on the walls. Kael looked closer but didn't recognize them. Jaeger slumped in the middle of the floor, staring up at the ceiling.

Kael cocked his head. "What are you doing Jaeger?"

"I am thinking."

"How is that helping us?"

"Vell, ve have not figured out vhere the light is coming from. Maybe ve have died and slipped into some after life."

"Not likely." Kael paced the room. The gold just seemed to glow. Was it some kind of magic? He halted. The room glowed like the orb the guardians had given him.

"*Taheza* . . ." Kael hesitated. What if the light didn't appear again? He inhaled and pushed the command out. "*Uzath taheza.*"

Darkness swept down upon them, swallowing them whole.

"What did you do?" Tariq asked.

"*Yetakoith taheza.*"

The gold walls glowed again, first soft, then gradually brighter until they resumed their former brilliance. Were the walls created like the guardians' orb? Or did the presence respond to him? A wave of unease shivered across his skin.

"I spoke to the light," he said.

Jaeger sat up. "You speak Táchil?"

"Nevin Saeed is teaching me."

"The language of Zohar." Tariq scanned the room. "The runes must be Táchil. Can you read it?"

"A little," Kael said. "But these runes look different."

Jaeger climbed to his feet and stuck his thumbs in his belt. "Say some more words. Maybe you vill find the right ones."

"We can't just throw out words," Tariq said. "We need to think about this."

Kael crossed his arms. "What do you think I should say?"

"I don't know. Maybe ask it to show you the silver pinecone?"

"Okay." Kael took a deep breath and let it out slowly. Why should he be nervous? Maybe because there was a veiled presence overwhelming the room. What if it didn't like being told what to do? Maybe he should ask nicely. Or should he just command it like he did with the lights?

"Vhat are you vaiting for?" Jaeger motioned with his hands. "Speak! Ve do not vant to spend all day down here."

Kael frowned. "*Praeza elel, viko a ith lu dwo eni matatud kojlu njasi shogo murth lu thitachin dilwilel.*"

The light blinked out, and wind tore through the cavern. Did he hear voices screaming? Or was that the wind? Stone ground against stone, the floor trembled. A dim light blossomed beyond the limits of the cavern. The glow parted the shadows and blurred into a slender tree. Its boughs and branches, nude and delicate, stretched out into a gossamer web of silver. The tree of hailed worth.

Kael refocused his eyes. Orbs of shallow light hung in the air. The cavern still surrounded him. Its walls like gauzy veils separated him from the tree. The runes remained, glowing. Then they shifted, lining up to reveal countless doors. When his gaze settled on one, they'd disappear, yet there they were, between him and the tree. Three doors stood more vibrant than the rest. He eyed them, but they didn't alter.

He swallowed. "Tariq, Jaeger, are you seeing what I'm seeing?"

"The doors?" Tariq asked.

Kael nodded.

"This must be the maze." Tariq stepped closer to Kael.

"And we must choose one of the doors." Kael looked at the three. But which one? The riddle only mentioned a maze, not a door. Did it matter which one?

"There are three doors and three of us." Jaeger placed his hands on his hips again. "Maybe ve are to all try our luck at this maze."

Kael shivered. "I don't know if that is a good idea." He glanced around. What other option did they have?

"Vhy not ask?" Jaeger strode closer to the doors. He cocked his head one way, then the other.

"Ask what?"

"Anything," Jaeger said. "Ask the door to be opened. Ask if ve can all go or ask vhat ve should do."

Kael glanced at Tariq. Tariq shrugged. Kael looked at the doors again. One door was made of gold, another of silver, the other of wood. Above the doors, runes glared brighter than the others. Runes he recognized.

"There's an inscription above the doors." Kael stepped closer. "Highest to lowest, you have come," he translated. "Lowest to highest, you may enter. Only he worthy to enter will find what he seeks, but woe to him who is found lacking."

"On second thought." Jaeger stepped back. "I vill vait here."

Kael studied the doors. Gold, silver, and wood. Which one should he choose? Was it even a choice? The pinecone was silver. The obvious answer would be the silver door. But what if he were wrong? What if he were found lacking?

Osaryn, which door? Perhaps the three were all needed. One to go, one to return, one to get out of this place. His eyes landed on the silver door. It had to be that one.

"I think it's only one door we are to choose." He paused. "And one of us to enter."

"I don't speak Táchil." Tariq placed his hand on Kael's shoulder. "You are just as worthy as the rest of us. Why not give it a try?"

Kael's stomach knotted. How could he be worthy? *Osaryn, help me.* He stepped toward the silver door. "*Edile.*"

17

AYIANNA FROWNED. SHE should've known he served the Nuja, just like her mother, but then her mother never referred to one deity apart from the others, had she?

"I thought I had lost you." Desmond moved closer. "But here you are."

She leaned back and tried not to breathe in the pine-infused, rancid odor wafting over her. His blue eyes were cold and hard, unforgiving like the icy mountain slopes. She needed to stand up for herself, but the words wouldn't come. Her mouth refused to open.

"Aren't you glad to see me?" He propped his right foot on a rock and leaned against the stone wall, ever nearer. His breath brushed across her forehead, and she nearly gagged.

"I'm . . . yes . . . of course." The words tumbled out. How long was she going to live a lie?

He smiled. He grasped her hand and drew her closer. "I've been thinking. About you, me. Us."

"Me too." Ayianna forced the words out. "We need to talk."

"Ever wonder if what we've believed all along might be a lie? That maybe what we thought was a lie, really was the truth?"

Of course, he'd change subject. She glared at the blond stumble on his chin. She would not be dissuaded. "What do you mean?"

He shrugged. "Take the Guardian Circle, the Nuja rubbish. The Shadow God. What if it is all a lie?" He ran his fingers over hers. "What if there really is a goddess unjustly bound in the Underworld?"

"What are you saying? That you believe the Sorceress?" Ayianna attempted to pull away.

He tightened his grip. "I'm just saying what if. I'm not saying I actually believe all this stuff, but what if?" His blue eyes pierced her. "It would change a lot of things, wouldn't it?"

"What the Sorceress is doing is wrong. She murdered my father."

"What if your father was the enemy? He kept many secrets from you." Desmond tilted his head, eyeing her.

"He wasn't the enemy."

"Then who is?"

She twisted her brother's ring around her forefinger. "Why are you talking so strange?"

"Maybe it's this place." He gestured at the stalactites hanging from the ceiling like hundreds of daggers. "Maybe it's almost losing you. I don't want to keep any secrets from you." His gaze settled back on her. "I would think you'd feel the same way."

"I have no more secrets." The rocky wall jabbed her back.

Liam padded closer with her ears back. Ayianna rested her free hand on Liam's forehead, trying to reassure her. She was fine. Desmond wouldn't do anything stupid. Not with Vian and Eloith so close.

Desmond arched an eyebrow and lifted her hand, pressing his thumb into her palm harder as if he could force her to comply. "In that case, come away with me. Now. The quest doesn't need us. You, me, Vian—"

"What? No." Ayianna squirmed in his grip. "Let me go."

"No." Desmond kissed her, his breath hot against her cheek.

Ayianna kicked his shin and shoved him away. "I said no."

"How dare you." He hopped away. "You belong to me. You signed the contract. We're legally bound."

"No." She ground her teeth. "I can't. I won't."

He snorted. "You can't mean that."

"What? That a woman would deny you?" she asked. "You're so full of yourself, you can't see—"

He grabbed her wrist. Liam snarled and leapt between them. Desmond yanked his dagger free, but Liam retreated and bared her teeth.

"Easy, Liam." Ayianna put her hand on Liam's neck, but kept her glare on Desmond, who paced along the water's edge. "Put away your dagger. She is only protecting me."

"Protecting you, huh?" He faced her. "Well, if your mutt isn't careful, you'll be sorry."

"Good girl, Liam." Ayianna rubbed the wolf's ears.

He slid the dagger into its sheath and strode toward her. "Where did you get that?"

"What?"

He grabbed her hand. "Did Kael give you this ring?"

Ayianna clenched her fist and tried to jerk free, but he dug his fingers into hers, prying them open. She brought up her other hand to hit him, but he blocked it and bent her fingers backward.

Liam snapped at his leg but ripped his pants instead.

"Call her off." Desmond bent her fingers farther.

Ayianna yelped. "*You* stop!"

Desmond's grabbed her neck, and she screamed.

"Liam, stop!"

Liam growled and retreated, but kept her head low, her teeth bared.

Desmond pried open her fist, twisted the silver ring off, and released her. "You dirty, little trull."

"How dare you! It's my brother's."

He smirked. "And I wonder where you got it from. You and Kael have a little tryst down here in the valley?"

"Give it back."

"No." Desmond pocketed the ring. "Maybe you'll think twice the next time you decide to talk back to me."

Ayianna gritted her teeth. Fiery anger surged through her and erupted. She could not, would not, contain it any longer. She leapt at Desmond, pounding him with her fists. But he shoved her away and backhanded her across the cheek. She fell against the stones.

Stabs of pain shot through her back, her vision blurred, and her cheek stung. On top of it all, her neck wound throbbed. She blinked and took short breaths. The sound of fabric tearing wrenched her back to the present.

Liam ripped Desmond's sleeve off. Blood darkened the shredded remains of his tunic and smeared across his forearm. Desmond punched Liam's muzzle with his other hand. Liam recoiled, snarling, and seized his leg. Desmond yanked his dagger from its sheath and plunged it toward Liam, but Liam dodged it and prepared to lunge again.

"Liam!" Ayianna grasped her and hauled her away.

Desmond leaned against the wall, breathing heavily. "Don't you ever do that again, or I will kill your mutt."

Disgust flooded her—choked her. She glared at him. "No. You have no right."

He laughed. "You are mine. You signed the contract." He pulled the folded parchment from his pouch and shook it out. "Or did you forget?"

The scrawling of her name mocked her. Fool, she had been, but no more. She jerked the certificate away from him, tore it in half, and threw it back at him. "I will never marry you."

A wave of heat burned Kael's face. The faint glow of the orbs did not penetrate the vast ocean of darkness stretching forever before him. An eerie moan floated on a breeze, bringing with it a rank, dusty smell. His skin prickled as the hair on the back of his neck and arms raised despite the warmth of the room.

"The whole mountain must be hollow," Jaeger whispered behind him.

"Through a maze of dark and stone, hangs the silver pinecone." Kael inched closer.

"Wait." Tariq's hand held him back. "Something is not right."

"It's the only way." Kael took a deep breath.

"But where is the tree?"

Kael shrugged. "Somewhere in the maze of dark and stone."

"Perhaps we should have your sphere of light. We could get it and come back."

"We don't have time." Kael stared into the darkness and stepped forward, but the floor gave way to a black abyss. Was he supposed to step out in faith? He took another step.

The air inside grew hotter, and a gust of wind blasted him. A stench of rotten eggs lingered. The ground heaved as if the mountain would vomit its smelly contents. Kael lost his balance and slid through the doorway. He gripped the edge of the stone and scrambled for a foothold but found none.

Tariq rushed toward him, but the ground shook again, knocking him off his feet. The orbs rained down upon them and rolled through the opening.

Kael clung to the edge, dodging the falling orbs. Jaeger appeared. He grasped Kael's forearms, bracing his feet against the stone doorway, and pulled.

Kael glanced behind him. The glowing orbs fell for miles. There was no maze, no pine tree, just a large empty cavity ending in a fiery soup of molten rock and flames. The spheres crashed against a stone ledge protruding from the side of the cavern. One exploded, filling the cavern with a brilliant light.

Kael tried to blink away his sudden blindness. The ground shook again and tilted. The heavy door trembled and began grinding shut. Jaeger hauled Kael inside the small room just before the door rumbled closed.

Darkness shrouded the room again as the tremors died down. Kael closed his eyes. How could he have been so foolish? The sound of rushing wind filled the room. Cold, white flames, brighter than the sun, erupted from the ceiling and spiraled down to the floor. The tunneling inferno dissolved into two fiery forms like giants.

"Son of Aiden." They spoke in union, their voices like thunder. "You and your companions are not prepared to enter. The Holy One has preserved your life, for if an unready hand touches the Versuch Pine Tree, his life will be sucked away."

Kael shielded his eyes. "Who are you?"

"We are servants of the Holy One, guardians of the silver tree. Go, before the cavern floods." Their crystalline bodies faded, and the flames dissolved into the dark.

"Vait!" Jaeger scrambled to his feet. "How are ve to prepare?"

"Finish the task that has been set before you," the wind whispered.

The room fell silent. Kael lay in the darkness. He had failed yet again. Everything he had put his hand to, he had failed. Let the water drown him, let the fires take him. He was done. Done with it all.

"Kael?" Tariq stood nearby. "The water is rising."

18

"YOU THINK IT'S as easy as that?" Desmond's eyes narrowed and shifted his weight to his right foot. Tatters of his left pant leg swung forward and revealed a scarred boot where Liam's teeth had scored the leather. "It doesn't have to be this way. You could come willingly, but no. I don't even know why I bother with you."

Ayianna pulled Liam closer. "Why do you? Surely, someone like you could have any other girl he wants. Look at how many of those girls back in my village wanted you. Why didn't you go after them? Huh? Why me? A half-breed in your eyes. Tell me why?"

"Because I'm a man of my word." He dabbed at the bleeding scratches, his pants leg hanging in shreds. "If I break my vows, what good am I? Besides, where would that leave you? Nobody wants a cursed wife."

As if he cared. Ayianna shivered. His words seeped into her heart, poisoning her just like the harpy lord's kiss. The torn fragments of the betrothal contract lay at Desmond's feet. Broken. Like her. Would she ever feel whole again? Guilt snaked through her and seized her heart. What had she done? What would become of her? Her mother? Her knees buckled, and she braced herself against the stone wall. *Osaryn, what have I done?*

"Where is that vial? Shouldn't you be trying to fix this mess?" Desmond jerked his arm up. Angry lines of red cut into his skin and oozed blood.

No. She could not, would not, force herself to live a lie. She straightened. "It's on the other side."

"Maybe Vian has a fire going already." He started climbing the rocks, but the ground shuddered. "What was that?"

The golden glow blinked out and darkness settled in the cavern once more, except for the faint light filtering through the hole Vian had made. The surface of the water trembled.

A shiver raced down Ayianna's spine. She glanced up at Desmond. "Your scratches can wait. The others might need help."

The cavern shook again. Stone and debris rained down from the ceiling. Ayianna lost her footing and fell backward into the pool. She kicked to the surface and wiped the water from her eyes, coughing, but a current tugged her down. She kicked against it and tried to reach for the edge. "Desmond!"

He hesitated; his face shrouded in shadows. Then he turned, scrambled up the rest of the way, and disappeared through the opening.

The water swirled, lower and lower, sucking Ayianna with it.

"You can feel sorry for yourself later." Jaeger grabbed Kael by the arm and yanked him to his feet.

"I wasn't." Kael jerked his arm free.

Tariq gripped his shoulder. "You're too hard on yourself."

Kael bristled and shrugged off Tariq's hand. "What do you know about me?"

"It's written all over your face, your actions, and the dithzamielis took advantage of it. They went for you first."

"All right, already." Kael strode away, his boots smacking across the wet floor.

"Ve vaited too long," Jaeger said. "Some light vould be helpful."

Kael frowned. "*Yetakoith taheza.*"

The light glowed again. The golden cavern was the same, except now water sloshed at his ankles.

"Maybe you can tell the vater to cease." Jaeger strode to the edge of the pool and dove in, but after a few moments he resurfaced. "The current is strong. Ve cannot swim against it, but if I had something to grasp, I could pull us out of here."

"I don't doubt your strength," Tariq said. "But this is water we're talking about, and maybe not even natural water."

"Do you have any better suggestions?" Jaeger said.

The water lapped at Kael's knees. He tried to think of words he could use. It wasn't like he had the gifting of the guardians yet. He couldn't channel power, unless the power already existed in the object. He scanned the ceiling. Maybe the room could show him the way out.

"*Praeza elel . . .*" he faltered.

"Say something." Jaeger gestured with his hands and then propped them on his hips.

"*Viko a ith lu koiso uza.*" Kael blurted out and glanced around the room. Nothing happened. The water swirled around his chest now. He pushed toward the half-moon pool and dove down, but the currents pushed him back. He resurfaced.

"I'm afraid we'll have to wait." Tariq rubbed the back of his head.

"For vhat?"

"The cavern to flood, the current to stop, then we can swim through." Tariq shrugged. "Not a problem, right?"

Ayianna clung to an outcropping of stone above the pool. A whirlpool had formed, pulling debris into its vortex. More water gushed beneath her, flowing from the waterfall on the other side. Her grip slipped. She scrambled to regain her grasp.

"Ayianna!"

She glanced up. Vian's face hovered above her, peering through the hole he had made earlier. He swung a knotted rope down to her, hitting her in the head.

"Sorry about that." He grimaced. "Grab on."

She tried to reach for it, but as soon as she let go, she slid toward the swirling waters below. She grasped the ledge tighter. "I can't!"

"You have to. There's no other way." He swung the rope again.

Ayianna eyed the vortex. What happened to Kael and the others? Was it too late to help them? She glanced up at Vian. "How much rope you have?"

"Enough, why?"

"I need all the rope you have." Ayianna took a deep breath and forced the words out before she changed her mind. "I'm going under."

"No, it's too risky."

"We don't have a choice."

Vian frowned. "Fine, give me a moment. I have to anchor it." He disappeared.

Her hands slipped again. What was she thinking? What if she couldn't find them? No, she had to try. For Kael. She owed him.

Vian reappeared. "Yank it twice when you're ready." He swung the rope toward her again.

Ayianna took a deep breath and lunged for the knotted end. Grasping the rope, she sailed through the air and plunged into the vortex. The current dragged her through the hole, scraping her knuckles against the stone. Then she was rising, higher, but the rope stopped short.

Instead of darkness, golden light blurred through the waters. Her lungs cried for air. She tugged on the rope, but it wouldn't budge.

Finally, she let go and kicked hard. Her head broke from the water quicker than she expected and hit the ceiling of a cavern. She gasped. The pain blurred her vision. She slid back under, rubbing her scalp, and resurfaced much slower.

"Ayianna?" Kael's eyes widened and then narrowed, his face hardening. The water lapped at his chin, and his head grazed the polished dome ceiling. How much longer did they have until the cavern was completely flooded? He inched toward her, his hand against the stone. "What are you doing here? What happened to your face?"

"I've brought a rope. Vian anchored it." She kicked to keep afloat, but the momentum slammed her head into the ceiling again. She gritted her teeth.

A smile softened his frown, but the water now lapped at his mouth, and he had to angle his head back. In a few moments, the cavern would be submerged. Then what?

Jaeger bobbed in the water next to him, a grin splitting his bearded face. "Ve are going to live! You all grab the rope and I vill pull us." And without another word, he disappeared beneath the surface.

"What are we waiting for?" Tariq asked. "Let's go."

Ayianna took a deep breath and ducked under, keeping near the stone wall. Something scratched her arm. The rope. She grasped it and jerked it twice. It started moving. Down they went, under the rock, but as they neared the edge of the stone, the rope pulled taut, scraping her fingers. She let go and pushed through to the other side. The current had ceased.

She surfaced and wiped the water from her face. Jaeger stood above the pool, hauling the rope into a pile. Liam paced behind him. She smiled. Everything was going to be all right. She swam to the edge where Vian's outstretched hand waited for her.

"You're one crazy lady," he said as he helped her out of the water. "But thank Vituko, it worked!" He turned to the others. "Let's go dry off. Desmond has a fire going."

Vian scrambled up the rocks and through the hole. The others followed except Kael. He picked up the torn certificate and squatted beside Ayianna. "You did it, then?"

The glow of her victory faded. She clenched her jaw and looked away. Was she ashamed to admit it? Where was her relief? Liam nuzzled her, and she scratched her ears. Why couldn't he talk about something else? Like, how she just saved his life?

"Don't let false guilt steal your peace or try to dictate your life. I don't know what fool lies he's been telling you, but I hope you'll see them for what they are. If it's about your mother—I've already told you—I will help you find her. And don't worry about what will happen after this is all over with. We hardly know what the world will look like, but I'll make sure you and your mother are taken care of."

Of course, he would, as if she were some kind of horse or something. She drew Liam closer and stroked her neck. "You speak as if you could stop the stars in their tracks." *And what happens if you can't?* She wanted to scream at him.

"I speak what I intend." Kael shifted to his knees. "If my strength fails me, so be it, but it won't be because I lacked the heart."

"All because of your vow to my brother, right?" She plucked a stone from the ground and tossed it into the pool. The water level was slowly returning to normal.

"Yes—and no." He stood and extended his hand to her. "We would have been family, and those kinds of pledges don't end."

Family. The sooner her heart came to terms with the fact he would never love her, the better off she would be. And what of her curse? Would his vow to her brother be strong enough for him to kill her if it came to that?

She looked up at him. "Be careful what you—"

"What happened?" His eyes narrowed, and he crumpled the paper.

Ayianna felt her cheek gingerly. The ache of Desmond's hand against her face lingered. Had it bruised?

"Where's your brother's ring?"

Ayianna dropped her hands into her lap. It was only silver threads—nothing to die over. Perhaps if she kept telling herself that, she'd believe it eventually.

Kael lifted her chin, forcing her to look at him. "Did he hit you?"

How could she answer him? Would Kael try to fight him? Desmond was bigger and an expert swordsman. The last thing the quest needed was more conflict. She pulled away. "I fell when the ground shook."

Kael's face hardened and any warmth that might have been there turned to ice. "Lying will not help you."

"And what would the truth do?" She drew her knees to her chest and hugged them.

"The truth would release you." Kael threw the crumpled parchment at her feet and climbed out of the cavern.

19

AYIANNA HUDDLED BEFORE the fire. The flames danced along the logs and branches, crackling and hissing. The waterfall hummed beyond their campsite. Liam lay next to her, her head resting in Ayianna's lap. She scratched the wolf's furry ears.

Kael knelt on the other side of the fire as he recounted what happened inside the golden cavern. Vian sat to her right, then Desmond. Tariq flipped the fur coats sprawled out to dry on the branches. To her left stood Eloith, his arms crossed, his feet planted in a soldier's stance. He'd been scouting, looking for another entrance, but had found none. Ayianna glanced around. Jathil was missing. Again. Perhaps she had run off this time for good. Why had she returned in the first place if she had only intended on leaving them again?

"That's it, then?" Vian asked.

Kael shrugged, but his eyes betrayed him. Something in that cavern stripped away their hardness. He was drowning in defeat. Was he still suffering from the hag's attack? He rubbed his scar. "We weren't ready."

"All this trouble for nothing?" Desmond rolled his eyes. "This is unbelievable." His gaze shifted to Tariq. "Some guide you turned out to be."

"Stop it." Kael plucked a branch from the ground. "None of us knew this would happen."

"So, what do we do now?" Vian folded his arms and leaned his elbows on his knees. His frizzy mass of red curls flopped forward, and he blew them out of his eyes.

"The men of flames said to finish the task." Jaeger crossed his legs in front of him. "Vhat does that mean?"

Kael snapped the branch in half. "Our task is to find the ingredients for the Dwalu Tonic and return before the Sorceress marches to war."

"I vould like to go on vith you. I can be of assistance. All I ask is for you to take me to my father vhen ve are finished." He fingered the rope of braided hair looped to his belt. "I have a message for him."

Kael fed the broken branch into the fire. "The trek will take us to the land of giants, to the seas of the merfolk, and back here again. You may join us, but we won't return to the plains until spring. If we are lucky."

"I am not in a hurry." Jaeger scratched his chin and pulled his fingers through his beard. "Are you planning on traveling through the jungle? The rainy season is near. You might have to svim through it."

"Our hope is to find the Keyon River and be far from the jungle when the rains hit." Kael peeled the bark off a twig. "If we had known our access to the silver pinecone would be denied, we wouldn't have gone this way."

"What did the Ruwachs, the fiery beings—as you called them—look like?" Eloith asked.

Kael dropped his hands in his lap and shook his head. "They shone like the sun. They had bodies of crystal and white fire—burning yet cold. Their voices were like thunder. And then they were gone."

"What I would give to see the servants of the Holy One." Eloith closed his eyes. "The memories are but vapor to me, like the haze in the morning which is gone in the sun. I cannot recall the Ruwachs."

The silence settled over them. Ayianna stroked Liam's fur. For a while no one spoke, and her thoughts drifted. She didn't want to make sense of what happened that day. It was all too fresh in her mind. She needed time to process.

Liam lifted her head. Ayianna scanned the area. What had caught the wolf's interest? A large white cat with black spots and fluffy tail padded out of the darkness. Ayianna smiled.

Desmond leapt to his feet. "What in the abyss?"

The white fur faded as Jathil's human form appeared. She strode up to the fire, adjusting her leather tunic. "So, what did I miss?"

Vian groaned and rubbed his face. "Too much to retell, really.

"Where've you been?" Desmond asked.

Jathil frowned and wiped her hands on her pants. "I've been looking for an exit out of this death trap, and I found one." She lifted her hand and gestured behind her. "The tunnel goes all the way to the other side, exiting near the boundaries of Arashel."

"At least ve have some good news." Jaeger pushed up from the ground.

"Good news for you, maybe, but I prefer to stay as far as I can from Arashel."

Jaeger smiled. "You vorry I vill turn you in for the revard?"

"I don't worry—I plan." Jathil's eyes narrowed. "And if I catch a whim of treachery, I will relieve you of your head."

"Vell then, it is a good thing that I have no intentions of taking you to Arashel." Jaeger stretched his arms above his head. "Ve should get some rest, if ve vant to move out in the morning."

Jathil reclined next to Kael. "Did you get the pinecone?"

"No." Kael continued staring into the fire.

"Why not?"

"We aren't prepared to touch the tree." Tariq stretched and stifled a yawn. "I think Jaeger has the right idea, I'm going to sleep, if I can."

"Me too." Vian straightened and stalked off toward his bedroll.

"I cannot sleep, so I will scout for the dragon." Eloith soared into the air and disappeared.

Desmond stood. Finally, he was leaving. Ayianna shifted her legs and dug her fingers into Liam's fur. Hopefully, Kael would not challenge him, and they all could get some sleep.

"What happened to your arm?" Kael asked.

Ayianna held her breath. With all the commotion earlier, she had forgotten to take care of his arm. Maybe he'd learn his lesson.

Desmond glanced down at the blood-stained rips in his tunic. The skin had been cleaned and the gashes healed. He had used the kulin. Dread crawled over her and sank into her gut. How much had he used?

He shrugged. "I fell." Then he strode away into the darkness.

Ayianna continued stroking Liam's fur. She could feel Kael watching her, and she dared to meet his gaze. The fire danced in his gray eyes but did not mask his anger.

"What happened to his arm?"

Ayianna averted her eyes. Why couldn't she tell him? Jathil leaned back on her arms and stared at the dark sky above. Of course, she was listening to their conversation. Ayianna's face burned. It wasn't her fault, so why did she feel the shame? She shook her head. "He said he fell."

"A likely story." His voice was quiet, but sharp, cutting her like a knife.

What did he want her to say? He had to know what happened when people stood against Desmond. Ayianna buried her fingers in Liam's thick fur. What could he do anyway? It wasn't like he could remove Desmond from the quest. He could just follow them. Wouldn't it be better if they could see him out in the open instead of him lurking in the shadows?

"You should sleep. Tomorrow will come quickly enough." He grabbed his bedroll and disappeared into the darkness away from the others.

The crackling fire and the hum of the waterfall filled the silence. Despite the weariness gripping her body, Ayianna refused to give into sleep.

Jathil crossed her legs and leaned forward. "Aren't you tired?"

"Not yet." Ayianna pulled her legs out from under Liam's head and crossed them as well. Liam yawned in response and rested her muzzle on her paws, but her ears were up, listening. Ayianna glanced around "Are you planning on continuing with us?"

Jathil shrugged. "It's not like I have a choice."

"You could always go home."

Jathil snorted. She slid a dagger from her boot and inspected it.

"Why not?"

"Because then I would have to pay for my crimes." Jathil threw the dagger into the dirt and picked it back up.

Ayianna's hands stilled. She hadn't expected Jathil to be so straightforward. "Who are you? The captain recognized you."

She frowned and threw the dagger again. "A lot of good that did."

"Tirza Jathil of Arashel?"

"I am no longer that person." She shifted her legs and plucked the dagger from the dirt.

She was getting nowhere, so Ayianna changed the subject. "Why did you leave us?"

"I came back, didn't I?"

"Why?"

She threw the dagger harder this time. "You ask a lot of questions, Dragonslayer." Jathil grabbed the dagger and slid it back into her boot. "I was scouting the area for dwarf patrols. You all might trust Jaeger, but you're not the one with a large sum of gold on your head."

"Will you tell me what happened?"

Jathil stood and strode over to the white bear rug Tariq had stretched out to dry. She ran her hands over it, inspecting it.

"Did you kill the bear?"

Jathil shook her head. "It's late. We should sleep. Once we cross beyond the waterfall, we will have more than just dragons and dwarf patrols to worry about." She ducked through the trees, her human form blurring into the white leopard, and she slunk off into the darkness.

Jathil could handle herself in any situation. She didn't need the protection of a male or the acceptance of a community. Free, but alone. Was that what Ayianna wanted? Perhaps Jathil's freedom came at a cost she wasn't willing to pay.

The mist remained, hovering above the valley, clinging to the trees. The waterfall rumbled, calling her to sleep. Still, she resisted.

The fire sputtered. She stared into the flames, and her thoughts turned to Desmond. She had told him no. The cage that held her had cracked. The rest of their journey would be different. He wouldn't dare touch her again. If he did, Liam would get him. She smiled and stroked Liam's head.

Tomorrow, they'd be on their way to the underwater city of the Kaleki, then the land of the giants. She didn't want to think of the possible dangers. Tonight, she wanted to relive her small victory. One step at a time. That's how all journeys were finished. She'd return and rescue her mother. Kael had promised. Ayianna curled up next to Liam, nuzzling her soft fur, the warmth of the fire lulling her to sleep.

Desmond watched Ayianna sleep. *I will destroy you.* His fingers rested on the dragon pendant hanging around his neck, his mind returning to the task at hand.

He pulled the small stone Semine had given him from his pocket. It looked like an ordinary stone, dull and lifeless, but the Sorceress claimed it would reveal remnants of the Tóas Dikon. If Ayianna knew anything of the dagger of Raemoja, she wouldn't tell him now. He would use the stone soon, but he would have to wait until everyone fell asleep. He smiled, a plan forming in his mind.

Desmond looked to the misty sky, waiting. A large black crow fluttered down to him. He stroked the bird's head and whispered words into its ears. Then off it flew. Desmond's desire intensified. How fair was it for the crow to return to the Sorceress and not him? His time would come soon enough. He stepped out of the shadows.

"You think you are clever, Desmond."

Desmond whirled around and unsheathed his sword. He scanned the trees for the spy.

Eloith floated into view, his eyes glittering in the fading light.

"What are you doing—trying to scare me?" Desmond said. "I thought you were scouting for the dragon."

"I am."

"Good." Desmond sheathed his sword and adjusted his belt. He turned to his bedroll. "Well, if you don't mind, I will be getting some rest. Some of us need to sleep."

"I have seen people treat their donkeys better than the way you treat her."

Desmond frowned. "Ayianna is mine, and it is none of your concern how I treat her."

"You are not yet married."

"That can be remedied."

"Betrothal contracts can be broken."

Desmond glared at him. Eloith must not have seen Ayianna tear up the contract. But what was a piece of paper when the Sorceress had other plans for her?

"I will be watching you. If you lay a hand on her again, you will be sorry." Eloith flew away.

"No," murmured Desmond. "It is *you* who will be sorry."

PART TWO

20

"LIAM?" AYIANNA SHOVED through the jungle ferns. Despite several hours of sun still left above, only a few rays of light flickered through the gaps in the leaves. Shadows shifted and played on her imagination. Was that Liam? Or something else?

"Liam?" Her voice caught in her throat. Ferns rustled next to her, and she jumped.

"Easy there." Desmond came out from behind a tree.

"What are you doing here?"

"I am trying to help you find your cur of a wolf. If you had tied her up like I suggested, she wouldn't be lost."

Ayianna faced him, placing her hands on her hips. "Whatever happened to 'she can take care of herself'?"

"That was before we were traipsing through the jungles of Rimanga. She's not used to this environment."

"And now you care?" Ayianna turned away. Frustration gnawed at her composure. Who was Desmond trying to fool?

A gray blur burst through the ferns and crashed into Ayianna. Ayianna stumbled backward, swallowing a scream. Liam panted and wagged her tail in greeting. Her curved lips and sparkling eyes made her appear as if she was laughing.

Ayianna grabbed her in a big hug. "You shouldn't go running off like that, especially this close to evening."

"You should tie her up." Desmond ran his hands through his scraggly blond hair. It had grown longer since they left the mountains behind. A beard and a layer of grime hid his handsome face and that suited Ayianna just fine.

Ayianna led the way back to camp and found Tariq sprinkling a powdery substance on the ground from a pouch. He had explained its necessity to keep away what the natives called the dudzuchi klhordan, a large, nocturnal ape-like creature. She hadn't seen any so far. Maybe it was working.

Tariq looked up at their approach. His black curls bounced around his bronze face as he moved. He smiled. "You found her."

Ayianna nodded and sat down at the edge of the campsite.

Jathil arrayed kindling and branches in a pyramid. She had remained aloof since their descent into the jungles. What was bothering her now? Did she think the dwarf captain would want his gold and come after her? But how would he even find her? The dwarves weren't known for their great tracking skills. Perhaps it was the heat.

"You'll be sorry." Desmond hounded her footsteps. "Your pet will meet her end out here."

She leaned into Liam's shoulder. Why was Desmond so anxious to tie Liam up now? As if he cared.

"Ayianna." Tariq put away his pouch. "Desmond is right. It would be best for Liam, especially at night."

Ayianna lifted her head and ran her hand through Liam's fur. Restricting Liam was the last thing she wanted to do. A wolf could take care of herself. But now Tariq sided with Desmond, and that was a first.

Tariq stood and brushed off his knees. "Don't forget to reapply the salve in the evenings, or you'll risk what the natives call the xaduira fever." He tugged his hammock from his pouch and shook it out.

Ayianna dug in her knapsack for Tariq's jar of oily salve and smeared the cinnamon-lemony scented oil over her face, arms, and legs. She'd have to prepare her hammock as well.

Sleeping on the ground was highly discouraged. Not that she was complaining. She would never know if creepy crawlies were feasting on her flesh until it was too late. She shuddered and rubbed the oil in quicker.

Eloith fluttered down from his lofty post and placed his hand on her shoulder. "It is for the best. Liam can hold her ground most of the time, but, here in the jungles, predators become prey. What seems harmless becomes deadly, and what is thought deadly is not."

"Like in Inganno."

"Perhaps, but do not worry. You have Tariq and me. We know the secrets of the jungle."

Ayianna smiled and placed her jar back into her knapsack. With Tariq and Eloith watching over them, they would be safe for now. The Sorceress's dragon couldn't find them with so many trees sheltering them, and the dwarves would never venture so far into the jungle. Hopefully.

Eloith leaned forward and whispered, "And I do not think Kael would let any harm befall you or Liam."

Ayianna's gaze snapped to his, her face burning. Eloith grinned and flew back to his look-out post. Ayianna glanced around the campsite. Had they heard him?

Jathil struck the flint, sending sparks into the pile of wood. Desmond lay stretched out in his hammock, his arms behind his head, his eyes closed. Tariq shook out his blanket. Why did it feel like everyone was staring at her?

Vian and Jaeger broke from the shadows, straining under armfuls of wood.

"You would not believe how hard it is to find dry wood in a jungle." Vian dumped his load next to Tariq. He stretched his arms over his head and groaned.

"It is a jungle. It is supposed to be vet." Jaeger chuckled and piled his logs into a neat stack.

"Yeah, but it's still the dry season. For a little while."

"You do not know how to find the dry vood, my young prince. Is Kael back vith supper? I hope he has better hunting than yesterday."

"Ho!" Tariq jumped to his feet. "Speaking of supper . . ."

Ayianna turned as Kael strolled into camp hoisting a gutted lizard the size of a dog. He hung his bow from a gnarled tree wart.

"Jaeger, can you prepare a spit?" Kael flung a rope over a low-hanging tree branch and hoisted the lizard. He wielded his hunting knife with ease and precision as he carved it into pieces. Even in the mundane or disgusting tasks, he moved with grace.

A fleeting desire to be more elven twisted in Ayianna's heart. The elf folk were much more dignified than she would ever be. As a child, she had admired them, wanting to prove she could be just like them. And then her father uprooted them to live among her mother's people. The rules had changed then, and her future among the elves had been lost. She turned her gaze back to Jathil and her attempt to light the wood on fire. Sparks fell, but quickly fizzled out.

"That's not supper." Vian covered his mouth with his hand. His pale skin seemed even whiter.

Kael plopped a hind leg on the top of the other meat. "It's no different than what you ate back in Bonzapur."

"That was different." Vian scooted to Jaeger's side, who was chopping a spindly branch into a spear. "It was cooked."

"Well, that is my intention."

"Not if we can't get this fire to light." Jathil struck the flint harder.

"We have to." Tariq knelt next to her and scraped his knife across a log's outer layer. "Or our clothes will rot."

"Lovely." Vian gagged.

"You are not going to be sick on me—eh, no-beard?" Jaeger slapped the prince on the back.

Vian raised his brows and folded his arms. "I have a beard."

"That is not a beard. This is a beard." Jaeger pulled at his beard's long red curls. "Vhat you have is fuzz."

Hours later, Desmond peered out from the fire's warm glow. Evening had overtaken the jungle, and the nocturnal creatures had wakened. He couldn't see them, but he could hear them—slithering, screeching, clicking, padded footsteps swishing through the ferns all around him.

His watch would end soon. He took a deep breath and let it out slowly through his nose. He glanced at the others.

Kael lay with his back toward him. He could be awake, but after such a hearty meal, Desmond doubted it. Tariq and Vian had talked later than usual about the geography of the jungle, but now they too slept along with everyone else. Yet he waited. Caution never failed a man, but he was tired of wasting time.

He had waited long enough. He dug the polished stone from his pocket and tiptoed over to Ayianna. Liam lifted her head, her eyes following his every move. Desmond sucked in his breath but continued. He was only patrolling their campsite, right? Making sure no one suffered any harm from the jungle creatures.

Ayianna slept in her hammock beneath her cloak. He told himself he had no remorse as he held the stone above her. He waited. Nothing. Doubt formed in his mind. Maybe Semine was mistaken.

Desmond bent down and moved the stone along her body toward her head. This time the stone flickered and then blazed to life—so the Sorceress was right.

Ayianna shifted in her sleep.

Desmond froze, holding his breath. The stone's glow grew in its intensity as his hand drew closer to her head. Her dark hair shimmered beneath its slowly pulsating light. Like always, she wore it twisted into a braid and wrapped in a leather binding— nothing unusual. None of this made any sense. Then he caught sight of the knapsack under her head. Of course, the dagger had to be hiding in there.

A sharp metallic point pricked Desmond's neck. He exhaled through his teeth and looked up.

"What are you doing?" Eloith asked.

"None of your business, pesky fairy." Desmond straightened and slipped the stone into his pocket. "I'm only making sure my betrothed is resting well. And what about you? Why aren't you asleep like the rest?"

"I have the second watch."

"Well, it's about time." Desmond yawned. He put another log on the fire and unrolled his blanket. "Don't let the jungles spook you."

Eloith frowned. "I do not spook easily."

"Suit yourself." Desmond stretched out in his hammock and closed his eyes, shutting out the fairy's icy glare. He would find out what was in Ayianna's knapsack, but first he had to get rid of Eloith.

21

AYIANNA PLOPPED HER knapsack and bedroll down and unbuckled her sword belt, letting it fall atop her belongings. When would the jungle end? She glanced at the rough-hewn rope in her hand. Three days of Liam straining against the makeshift leash had rubbed her skin raw with its wiry fibers. Ayianna sighed and tied the wolf to a tree limb. Liam looked up at her and whined.

"It's for your own good. We will be out of the jungle soon, and then you can run wild and free again." Ayianna patted the wolf's head and scratched behind her ears.

Above, Eloith darted through the large, moss-covered limbs, dodging the vines as he went. He landed near Tariq. Catching his breath, the fairy spoke in a hushed tone, gesturing with his hands.

Ayianna moved closer, but a hand on her shoulder restrained her.

"Now, you wouldn't be trying to eavesdrop, would you?"

"What do you want, Desmond?" Ayianna shook his hand free and stepped back. Did he not understand what no meant?

Desmond frowned. "Is that how you talk to your future husband?"

"There is no contract anymore, Desmond. The betrothal's over. When will you accept that?"

"It isn't over until I say it is." His eyes narrowed and he leaned closer. "Or did you forget that I hold your very life in the palm of my hand? One word and the rest of the world will kill you. Harpy." He pushed the words out through his teeth. "And Kael can't save you this time."

The ugly truth marched against her like an army, accusing her, condemning her, but she couldn't, wouldn't surrender. She took a deep breath. "I've got wood to gather before nightfall."

Keeping the camp in sight, she gathered dead branches and the dried vines that hung stiffly from the trees. She paused, inhaling the rich scent of dirt and vegetation. She couldn't breathe in enough air to calm her nerves.

"Don't walk away from me when I am talking to you." Desmond plowed through the ferns behind her.

"Well, the night isn't waiting for you." Ayianna wrenched a woody vine free from a tree limb. Bits and pieces of bark and decaying debris rained down upon her. She blinked away the dirt and shook her head. Her skin crawled, aching for a bath.

"Let me give you a hand there. It looks like you could use one." His voice was louder than normal. He grabbed the branches from her hands. "You're not still angry with me for . . . you know . . . back up there in the mountains. I mean, it was only a misunderstanding."

Ayianna whirled around. "Only a misunderstanding? You hit me."

"Hardly. If I had wanted to hit you, you would have known it." Desmond snorted. "I was merely blocking your assault on me."

She stared.

Desmond shifted the branches under his arm. "I'm only looking out for what's best for you."

"And you would know?" Ayianna clenched her jaw. The anger festered in her heart like an abscess. "Everyone knows what's best for me, but nobody has ever stopped to consider what I think."

"And where has that gotten you? A disgrace to your family. How could a miserable peasant girl like yourself know what you want when your whole life has been a lie?"

Ayianna opened her mouth, but words failed her. She turned away and pressed through the ferns.

Desmond followed, his footsteps heavy and clumsy behind her. "Your mother and father loved you very much, Ayianna. Things would have been different if all this hadn't taken place. Just like any other village girl, you would've been rushing to consummate the—"

"What?" She spun around. "You! Just because all those other women would have . . ." She shook her head. "No, I had dreams, but you killed them."

Desmond flung the branches aside. "We've already discussed this. You had no future in Zurial."

"You're wrong. My grandfather was an Esusamor elf, a very prominent elf at that."

"Which only makes you a half-breed like Kael."

"Are you so jealous of Kael that you must resort to name-calling like an insolent child?"

Anger clouded Desmond's face. "Kael could never love you. He would be repulsed if he knew what the curse would do to you if you didn't have that vial of healing water from the fishwoman."

She clenched her fist. If only she had something to throw at him, something to thrash his words into oblivion. Why did he torment her so?

"I saw the thing that bit you and what you will become. It's really only a matter of time, isn't it?" Desmond grabbed her arm and rubbed the gold bangle against her wrist. "Unfortunately, I am a man of my word." He smirked. "Unless of course, something should happen to you."

He jerked her closer and grabbed her neck, his fingers squeezing her old wound. Pain erupted and sent sparks through her body. He pressed his chin against her temple and whispered. "It could be so different, Ayianna. Come with me willingly. Or I will take what is mine. All of it."

Her stomach twisted. She turned her face away, his breath hot on her skin.

Desmond squeezed her neck again, and she gasped. "If you deny me, you will force me to tell the others about your curse. We wouldn't want a harpy on the loose, now would we? They might decide you're not worth the risk. What then?"

He released her, and Ayianna stumbled back.

"You are unbearable!" She scooped up the branches and took off in the direction of the camp. The truth haunted her, flayed her, exposing her. No one would risk a harpy on the loose. She'd be better off dead.

"The choice is yours." His deep-throated laugh rumbled behind her.

She shoved through the leafy ferns. She could never be willing. She'd die first, but what good would she be if she was unable to rescue her mother? Was there no way out? If she lost the kulin, she would be doomed. They would kill her.

She halted. Where was the camp? She turned. In every direction, ferns blanketed the ground, strips of vines hung from moss covered-tree trunks. The day faded like a dying flame and darkness consumed the jungle.

"Kael? Tariq?" Ayianna glanced around. Her vision swam with inky blackness. Where was the campfire? "Desmond?" No answer. Where had he gone so quickly? She clenched her jaw. He probably had distracted her on purpose.

She rushed forward, searching the shadows for her companions. She tripped and crashed into a solid surface that could only be a tree trunk. The branches flew from her hands as she fell. Crawling to her feet, she chided herself for going so far from the camp.

A tree groaned as if a great weight leaned against it. Ayianna held her breath and scanned the shadows.

Two large, fiery orbs blinked in the canopy above her. The creature drew a raspy breath.

Ayianna's heart pounded against her ribs. She had to break the terror clutching her limbs and flee, but her legs refused to move.

The groan continued until a loud crack shook the jungle. The vibrations tingled through her body and sparked something in her brain—run!

Her legs wobbled as she bolted. She swung her arms, probing the darkness. The trees seemed to reach for her, to block her escape as slender branches slapped her face and tore at her clothes.

Several more glowing orbs appeared, their fiery light casting an eerie glow on the jungle's vegetation.

Ayianna's foot caught and she stumbled. Rolling to the ground, she reached for her brother's dagger and prepared to fight.

Ape-like faces took shape in the shadows. Their breath whistled through sharp, ivory teeth. Long, willowy arms hung from muscular shoulders down to their knees, their skin black and smooth—the dudzuchi klhordans. They quietly hooted and hummed to each other as they surrounded her.

22

THE FIRESTEEL AND flint clanged one last time as Kael bent over and blew lightly on the glowing ember. The kindling ignited and cherry flames lapped at the wood. He sat back on his heels and returned the steel and flint to his belt.

Tariq had finished marking the camp's perimeter and had started preparing dinner: some odd-looking fruit with a spiny peel, mushrooms, and green fuzzy leaves. They hadn't had meat in several days, but he'd try again later. Maybe he would get lucky.

"Why have you been so quiet lately?" Jathil sat beside him.

"I might ask you the same." Kael eyed the highlander.

She picked up a branch and stuck it into the growing fire. "What's an elf like you doing on a quest like this?"

An elf like what? He held no pretenses. Saeed had given him the responsibility of finding the cure to the Sorceress's curse. He did what needed to be done. But if tragedy hadn't driven him away from Zurial, would he have chosen this path? Or would he have taken his place as one of the elven lords like his father had intended? He turned one of the logs over and scraped the lichen from it. "I was sent."

"Sent?" Jathil raised an eyebrow.

"The guardians." He added the log to the flames. The fire sparked in protest and then wrapped its consuming warmth around the newest addition, its heat burning his face. He sat back.

Jathil snorted. "The guardians have outgrown their usefulness."

"People will never outgrow their need for the guardians—they just forget." Kael stared into the flames, allowing the warmth to draw him away. His sorrow had desiccated into an arid hollow where his heart had been. He was determined to accomplish the mission or die trying. That was all that mattered. He plucked another log and added it to the fire. "If the guardians stand alone, they will fail; and if they fail, we all fail."

Jathil rolled the staff in her hands, the flames reflecting in her silvery eyes. "Perhaps you are right."

"Why do dislike the guardians so?"

She shrugged. "Lazar was always stirring up trouble with my father, and then he—I don't know—he got involved in something he shouldn't have. It's complicated. My mother, on the other hand, welcomed him with open arms."

"So your grudge is a personal one."

"Depends on how you look at it."

"Seven years is a long time to be holding bitterness in your heart." He rubbed the scar over his eyebrow. As if he should talk. But he wasn't bitter. He had made a vow, and he would make sure he upheld it.

Jathil straightened. "I never said that is why I left Arashel. Besides, I'm not bitter."

"Maybe not." He added another log to the fire. "Just don't let your personal issues dismiss the entire Guardian Circle on the account of one guardian."

She opened her mouth, but Vian yelped from the other side of the camp. Kael started and unsheathed his sword. The young prince shrieked and danced about the camp, rubbing his arms and chest like a man swarming with fire ants.

"What is it?" Alarm rang in Tariq's voice. "Did you forget to apply the balm this morning?"

Kael eased toward Vian and scanned the trees, but no wild creature waited to pounce on them. No giant spider crawled about. Maybe the prince was just imagining things. He kicked at a rotting log, and a green and black boa slithered out. He slid the flat of his blade beneath the snake and hoisted it in the air.

Vian ceased his erratic dance and calmed down with a final shudder. "S-s-s-snake."

"No—dinner." Kael dropped the snake to the ground and pinned its head with his sword. The snake's body writhed in a final attempt to escape, and then went limp. Kael took out his hunting knife, slit the skin, and proceeded to gut it.

Liam howled. She pulled and pawed against the rope.

Kael's blood turned to ice. Where was Ayianna? How could he not notice her absence? Desmond and Eloith were gone as well. He reached out into the darkened jungle and sought Ayianna's presence. Terror slammed into him. Kael wiped his hands on his pants and grabbed his sword.

"What is it, Kael?" Tariq asked.

"Ayianna is in trouble."

"The klhordan!" Tariq unsheathed his sword. "Eloith told me they had been hunting us."

"And when were you going to tell us?" Kael swung his quiver of arrows over his back.

"Tonight, once Eloith had confirmed it." Tariq picked up his shield. "The arrows are useless against these beasts. Only a dwarven blade can penetrate their hide."

He slammed his quiver down and the arrows spilled out. "Then we shouldn't have let Ayianna gather wood by herself."

"Desmond was with her."

"Desmond—" Kael's throat constricted. He shoved the anger back down. He had to remain calm and focused. Without knowing where she was, he'd lose precious time. He couldn't run pell-mell out into the jungle. But he might.

Kael sought Ayianna's presence again. Liam snarled and twisted against the rope, breaking free. She lunged into the trees. Kael chased after her.

Behind him, Tariq yelled, "Stay here in case Ayianna returns."

A klhordan charged her. Ayianna raised her brother's dagger and stabbed it. Pain exploded in her hand and swept up her arm like a thousand needles puncturing her skin. She fell back, dropping the weapon. Its blade had melted into a tiny lump at its handle. She reached for her sword but found the sheath empty.

"Ayianna!" Eloith dove out of the sky, brandishing a sword twice as long as he was. Her sword.

He sliced the klhordan's throat, and its body slumped to the ground. The other klhordans hooted and shrieked, ducking back into the shadows.

"Eloith!" Ayianna darted toward the fairy. "How did—"

"No time for questions." Eloith scanned the trees. "It will not take long for the klhordans to regroup. We must get back to camp."

But just as Eloith finished, the klhordans reappeared. Eloith pressed Ayianna's sword into her hand and unsheathed his own. He charged them as though he were a lion instead of a fairy the size of a cat.

Encouraged by the fairy's boldness, Ayianna gripped the ivory hilt and rushed forward, hacking away at their slender bodies. No pain riddled her arms this time as the blade struck the klhordans. With each blow, chunks of gray matter splattered her clothes and hair. Ayianna wiped the slime from her face and nearly choked on the smell.

"Ayianna!" Eloith swept down beside her. "There are too many. You must flee."

"No, Eloith, I won't leave you." Ayianna ducked as the klhordan's sharp claws swiped the air above her.

"Do not worry about me. I can distract them until you are safe." Eloith whirled around and soared into the air, lopping an arm off at the elbow as he went. The creature stumbled backward, roaring in pain. It rebounded and slashed at the fairy, but Eloith dove out of its way.

She had to run, but where? A klhordan bore down upon her, and Ayianna raised her sword. The creature's long arms reached for her, but she swung, and its hands flopped to the ground. Bracing herself, Ayianna pivoted, driving the blade into the klhordan's waist. Its arm stubs pounded against her, spraying her face with hot blood. She yanked the sword free, and the klhordan collapsed.

"Ayianna!"

The klhordan scattered and retreated into the shadows. Eloith fluttered spastically, trying to stay afloat. To her horror, he crashed into the ground in a crumbled pile, his wings broken and torn.

Ayianna rushed to his side and dropped next to him. A dagger protruded from his back. Her mind spun. The klhordan didn't use weapons. Who then? She yanked the blade free and tossed it aside. She turned Eloith as gently as she could and picked him up in her arms. The fairy's pale face contorted in pain.

"Leave me. I will depart—I have earned my rest." He coughed and closed his watery eyes. "I will return home."

"Eloith . . . no." Ayianna's throat knotted.

The klhordan emerged from the shadows. Ayianna glanced up, certain of death, but they halted. They twisted their necks and surveyed the area as they exchanged soft hoots. Lifting their heads, they sniffed the air. One of them howled. Its shrill cry scraped Ayianna's ears and nerves. Then it attacked.

Ayianna fumbled with her sword, determined not to let go of Eloith. She slashed at the klhordan. Her blade sank into its target, but without the strength of both hands, the sword slipped through her fingers.

She lurched forward and shielded Eloith from the oncoming attack, fearing the worst. She groped for a weapon, a stick maybe, anything to fight with, but to no avail. She caught sight of her sword gleaming a few feet away.

Suddenly, a blur of silver sailed through the air and collided with the klhordan. Liam! The wolf tore into the creature with her fangs and claws. The klhordan swept Liam aside as if she were a pillow.

Leaving Eloith behind, Ayianna struggled to her feet and grasped her sword. A dank stench saturated the jungle, burning her nose.

Kael and Tariq exploded through the ferns and crashed into the klhordans. Ayianna's courage bolstered. She fought harder, but never strayed far from Eloith's side. The shadows surged with klhordan. Shrieks and howls of death pierced the air, but their numbers never waned. How many were there?

A klhordan knocked the sword from her hands. She dodged another blow and scrambled backward.

"Fall back!" Tariq yelled over the clamor.

Ayianna bent to pick up Eloith, but the fairy was gone. "Eloith!"

Kael leapt between Ayianna and an oncoming klhordan. With one blow, Kael split the creature in half.

A whine shattered Ayianna's soul—Liam. And for a moment her heart stopped. To the right, a klhordan held Liam up, its sharp claws digging into the wolf's blood-splattered fur.

Ayianna screamed and lunged for the klhordan, but Kael restrained her. She twisted against him and pummeled him with her fists. How could he do this to her?

She wrenched free from Kael and charged. She had no sword, but fury drove her on. She would tear the klhordan with her bare hands. The creature grasped Liam with its other arm and buried its sharp fangs into the wolf's belly.

Ayianna's knees buckled. She felt Kael's arm seize her waist, whirling her around as he cut down the klhordan. Blind with anger, Ayianna tore at Kael, but he held her tightly, pulling her away.

She shrieked. "No, not Liam!"

23

KAEL DRAGGED AYIANNA back to camp, his heart breaking for her. He wanted to wipe the tears from her face and tell her it was all a bad dream. To kill Desmond for leaving her in the jungle alone. Her blows against his chest hammered his failures deeper. Desmond should never have been allowed on the quest. For once, Saeed had been wrong.

He crossed the edge of the makeshift perimeter and glanced into the shadows. The klhordans hadn't followed them.

Tariq appeared and helped ease Ayianna down. Tears coursed down her filthy face and mingled with blood. She collapsed into a fit of sobs.

"What happened?" Vian rubbed the hilt of his sword as he peered out into the jungle.

"We will be safe. The klhordan won't come near the camp." Tariq squatted next to Ayianna and gently probed her bleeding wounds. "Someone boil some water."

Jathil grabbed the tin they would have cooked supper in and set about getting hot water while Jaeger stoked the fire.

Desmond crouched at the edge of the perimeter and rummaged through Ayianna's belongings.

Kael's fury exploded. He grabbed Desmond by his jerkin, hauled him to his feet, and punched him in the face. His hand stung from the blow, but the pain felt good.

Desmond stumbled back; his blue eyes livid. "You want to fight, do you?"

Desmond swung, but Kael dodged the loose punch. Channeling his anger into his fists, Kael plowed into Desmond, knocking him to the ground. He lunged forward, but a hand on his shoulder held him back.

"Calm down." Tariq's grip tightened.

Kael inhaled and pushed his anger out with his breath. Reason crept back into his senses, and he lowered his arms.

"Stand up, Desmond," Tariq said. "I have a mind to beat you myself, but violence won't solve our problems."

"Some think otherwise." Desmond staggered to his feet. He touched his face and glared at Kael.

"Why did you leave Ayianna by herself?" Tariq's words were measured and heavy like a butcher quartering meat with precision.

Desmond shrugged. "She did the leaving."

"So you'll pass the blame till it suits you, is that it?" Kael asked through clenched teeth. "Does it not concern you that she was almost killed?"

"Well, it obviously concerns you."

Kael stared at him. He couldn't believe the man. Twisting his words and actions to befuddle him and escape judgment. Holding a conversation with this brute was like holding a slippery fish bent on jumping back into the sea. "Release her from your bonds. You don't love her."

Desmond smiled and straightened his jerkin. "What do you know about love, half-breed?

"You know nothing of me." Kael clenched his fists. The desire to bash Desmond's face nearly overwhelmed him, but he remained still. Out of the corner of his eyes, he noticed Jathil had moved Ayianna near the fire.

"I know more than you would like." Desmond cracked his knuckles and glared at Kael.

Tariq held up his hand. "Enough."

"No." Kael pushed Tariq's hand away. "We've gone too long with this liar and thief among us."

"Such unfounded accusations." Desmond raised his hands and looked at Vian as if he would speak up for him.

"Where is Teron's ring?"

"What?" Desmond cocked his head. "What are you talking about?"

In one swift movement, Kael slid next to Desmond and jerked his hand up for all to see. A glint of silver circled his fifth finger. Desmond twisted his hand from Kael's grip.

"Don't think I didn't notice," Kael said.

"Nor I." Desmond's eyes flashed as he rounded on Ayianna and grabbed her by the hair. Ayianna screamed as he wrenched her up. "Is that what you want, a half-breed for a husband?" He threw her at Kael's feet. "May she kill you while you sleep."

Kael attacked. Fist after fist. The dam broke, and all his anger and bitterness flooded his senses, blinding him. He would kill him. But hands grasped him and hauled him away.

Kael's chest heaved as his lungs fought for air.

Desmond lay on the ground, barely moving. His face trickled with blood from a split lip and a bruised cheek.

As he calmed down, Kael noticed the throbbing of his own body—punches he hadn't seen coming, hadn't been aware of until now. He glanced down at his knuckles, the skin cracked and bleeding.

"On my honor and my oath to Teron," Kael pushed the words out. "You will not lay another hand on Ayianna, or I will kill you."

The others stared—not at Kael, but at Desmond—their faces barely masking their disgust. Desmond yanked the ring off and threw it at Ayianna's crumpled body. He glanced at Vian, but the prince shook his head. Desmond crawled to his hammock, gathered his belongings, and disappeared into the darkness.

24

"AYIANNA."

A voice pulled Ayianna from her ethereal state of slumber and into a world of sorrow. She lay, unmoving. Her strength, like her tears, was spent. Grief had seared her emotions as if her heart had been ripped from her chest. Somehow, she had managed to fall asleep, and she didn't want to wake up.

"Ayianna." The voice spoke again, and a hand gently shook her.

She pried her sticky lashes open and looked up. Kael's face hung over her, his brow wet with sweat. The jungle remained dark, and morning still seemed a long way off.

"What is it?" Her voice scratched over her dry throat. She blinked to clear her vision, her eyes raw and irritated. Her face felt swollen, and the back of her head throbbed. At least she was alive.

Kael hesitated, his gray eyes boring into hers. "Follow me . . . before the others wake."

Ayianna grasped Kael's outstretched hand, and he helped her to her feet. Her world tilted. She closed her eyes against the dizziness and leaned into Kael.

"Are you all right?"

Ayianna straightened. "Just stood up too fast, that's all."

Kael studied her for a moment. Apparently satisfied, he turned and disappeared into the forest.

Stiff and sore, Ayianna followed Kael away from camp. The frightening images of the klhordans raced through her mind, and she halted. She reached for her sword, but she had left it back in camp. "Is it safe?"

"Yes but brace yourself." Kael parted some ferns and stepped through them.

The stagnant air reeked of dead flesh. Ayianna covered her nose with the edge of her sleeve and suppressed the urge to vomit. She pressed on, but trepidation slowed her steps. What was Kael up to? Why would he take her back? Reliving yesterday's nightmare was the last thing she wanted to do.

The leafy ferns gave way to the scene of the attack. Mangled bodies of klhordans lay in heaps. White bones protruded from clumps of torn flesh. Bile seared her raw throat as Ayianna turned away and vomited.

Kael placed his hand on her shoulder.

Ayianna shrugged his hand off and wiped her mouth on the back of her sleeve. She glanced at his somber face. "We could have saved her."

Kael clenched his jaw and looked away.

Ayianna's throat tightened. The memory of the klhordan flashed in her mind. Liam's whine lingered in her ears. She shuddered, but then swelled with anger. "Why did you bring me here?"

"I thought that . . . " Kael rubbed his scar and glanced away. "You'd prefer a proper resting place for Liam." He turned and led her deeper into the jungle to a small mound of overturned dirt.

Ayianna stared at the narrow pile of fresh soil beneath a large tree. The elvish rune for the letter *L* had been carved into the smooth tree trunk. A fresh wave of tears moistened her eyes. Her grief reawakened, but a new feeling emerged. A deep sense of appreciation surged through her. But Kael had prevented her from saving Liam. How could she forgive him?

Ayianna frowned. "The grave is so small."

"I found only a few patches of fur and the rope."

"That's all?" A spark lit in Ayianna's soul. "Maybe she survived!"

He slowly shook his head, and the spark snuffed out. How could she be so foolish to think otherwise? He handed her a knife. Dirt encrusted his hands and jagged fingernails. Had he dug the grave with his bare hands? "I found Teron's dagger."

"My brother's dagger was destroyed when I stabbed a klhordan." Ayianna rubbed her arm, remembering the awful tingling sensation. "That's the dagger that killed Eloith."

Kael turned the weapon over in his hand. "Klhordan don't carry daggers."

"But who . . ." Ayianna felt the blood drain from her face. "Does that mean we are being followed? Maybe the Sorceress . . ."

Kael shook his head, his face grim. "Eloith would have noticed and alerted us."

Then realization hit Ayianna. She had left Desmond in the jungle, only to find him in the camp after the attack. Could he have killed Eloith? A chill crept down her spine as she peered into the jungle, the shadows fading as dawn approached. Desmond had taken his belongings and left last night, but where did he go? Was he watching her right now?

"We should return soon," Kael said. "Tariq will want to put as much distance as possible between us and the klhordans. They might come back."

Ayianna nodded. She faced the small grave. Liam's final resting place. So far from all that was familiar, from home—a place that didn't exist anymore, but that hadn't mattered with

Liam at her side. Would she ever feel at home again? The ache in her heart overwhelmed her, and she sank to her knees. A fresh wave of tears splashed down her raw cheeks. She hunched over and wept.

Nothing. She had nothing. Her father, gone. Her brother, gone. And now Liam. Her only constant in the chaos around her. Gone. Her soul screamed within her. *Why?*

Kael knelt next to her and wrapped an arm around her shoulder. She curled into him, wishing the void would swallow her whole.

After a time, Ayianna stood and dried her face. She gazed at the letter *L* carved into the tree. Something was missing. Liam hadn't been the only one who had tried to protect her. She took the dagger and carved the elvish letter *E* into the tree.

25

AYIANNA STEADIED HER footing along the limber branch as she attempted to peer through the leafy canopy. The sun blazed high overhead, blinding her for a moment. Hot air suffocated her and sent a stream of sweat trickling down her forehead and neck. She shifted. Her damp tunic stuck to her back beneath the weight of her braid. Since entering the jungle, she had been tempted more than once to cut her hair.

Once her eyes adjusted to the light, Ayianna looked around. Thick vegetation stretched for miles in each direction like a sea of mottled green. Behind her, the dark mountains of Kha Vaaro rose from the jungle floor and disappeared into the gray-blue sky. Its snowcapped peaks were lost in a haze. *Like my soul.*

The days had passed in quiet drudgery. No one spoke much after Desmond left, but Ayianna relished the solitude the silence gave her. She remained apart from the others and kept her hands busy gathering firewood or fruit or clipping lianas to glean what water they could.

Questions and doubt lingered like ash after a fire. Would Desmond come back? Where would he go? How could he just walk off into the jungle? An odd mix of relief, guilt, and doubt churned in her heart. It would suffocate her if she continued to dwell on it.

"Well?" Tariq called from below, breaking her reverie.

"No river." Ayianna plucked at the lianas twisting around the tree's trunk, reluctant to join the others and feel their questioning eyes. With no sign of the river, all they could do was keep traveling west with the hopes of not being too far north or south when they arrived at the Sea of Pavinai.

Then an idea occurred to her and, with a sliver of excitement tingling through her body, she gripped the vines and began her careful descent.

"We've been walking for days with no sign of the river." Vian pulled a boot off and shook it.

Ayianna let go of the last branch and dropped to the ground. She looked around, allowing her eyes to adjust to the dimness.

Kael and Jaeger reclined against the gnarled roots of a nearby tree. Jaeger puffed on a clay pipe and blew smoke out of his large, hooked nose, giving his red-blond moustache the appearance of being on fire. Kael's eyes were closed, and his arms were crossed. His face harsh, his jaw clenched. Even feigning sleep, he appeared to be cross. Kael opened his eyes and looked up as if sensing her gaze.

Ayianna turned away.

Jathil paced the clearing. Her eyes glimmered as she walked under a stray ray of light, reminding Ayianna how different the Haruzo were. Jathil threw her hands in the air. "We can't just sit here."

"And we can't risk walking in circles. We must wait for the sun to set." Tariq sat cross-legged on a large moss-covered stone. He wielded a knife, carving something out of wood. He seemed relaxed, and not one ounce of worry marred his countenance.

Ayianna crossed her arms. "How are you at peace in such discouraging circumstances?"

Tariq lowered his hands and looked up at her. "Because I know that I am not in control."

"And that helps how?"

"Ah-ha, good question." Tariq uncrossed his legs and leaned forward. "You see, among the Haruzo, we call him, Parzanah or Parzan—"

"Not all Haruzo," Jathil retorted. "My father says a true Haruzo has no god."

"Do you believe that?"

Jathil shrugged and paced away.

"Everyone has a god. It's just a question of who they serve . . . the Nuja, Raezana, themselves, or they serve the One-With-Many-Names. The guardians call him Vituko, the Shadow God. The Esusamor Elves call him—"

"Dreyu Osaryn." Kael sat up.

"Yes, yes." Tariq's smile lit his face. "It is recorded in the Ruyelems, Trygg's vision of the great halls of Zohar, and the twelve thrones of the Chai, and of Arius, the keeper of the silver cords and the flaming gold bowls."

Ayianna paused. *Chai.* There was that word again. The woman from Durqa had used it, but it had sounded like another foreign god to invoke or appease like the Nuja, not something associated with Zohar. "What is the Chai?"

Tariq cocked his head, studying her. His eyes shimmered like Jathil's, but his were kind and inviting. "I'm not sure how to describe them. I guess you could say they are the essence of Vituko, yet his servants. It is said that Karasi, the Sacred Pearl, is one of the Chai, but she has never claimed it, nor denied it. Back to your question, I do not fear in life or in death, because my name is inscribed upon a silver cord whose length is maintained in Zohar."

Ayianna sat for a moment, her mind trying to wrap itself around what Tariq just said. Her father had served the elven god, Osaryn. She hadn't thought much of it until they left Zurial, and her mother returned to the worship and requirements of the Nuja, the divine quartet of the plains people. Ayianna had to admit she preferred the elven god, Osaryn.

"Does everyone have a silver cord?" Ayianna grabbed her knapsack and rummaged through its contents.

"Yes."

"Interesting," she said, but her mind was elsewhere. She pushed aside the leather cuirass and dug deeper. Where was her flute? Wait, where was her hair pin? Had she lost it? Her heart sank and anger twisted her gut. How could she have been so clumsy! Her mother's precious handiwork, her father's last gift gone.

"If we keep the mountains behind us, couldn't we continue walking east?" Jathil paced back toward them.

"Theoretically." Tariq settled back on the stone and crossed his legs again. "But the Kha Vaaro Range curves around, and we could end up walking north. We'll just have to wait for the sun to begin its descent, which will only be another hour or two. Besides, it'll give us a nice break from the heat."

"Right, just as long as the clouds don't decide to move in on us." Vian stood and stretched. "We will never make it out of the jungle at this rate."

"Don't be so pessimistic." Tariq turned the wood in his hands and carved a chunk from it.

Vian grumbled something in return and stalked away.

Ayianna pulled out the small wooden flute the Durquian woman had given her so long ago. It seemed like years since that fateful day. Had it been only a few months or so since her father was killed? She ran her thumb over the delicate carvings in the wood and glanced up. "I have an idea that I think could help us find the river."

Vian faced her and put his hands on his hips. "And how is that going to help us?"

"Ah, yes, your dryad flute." Tariq leaned closer to her, inspecting the flute. "How did you come across such a rare instrument?"

Ayianna hesitated. "A woman from Durqa gave it to me."

Vian snorted and crossed his arms. "If you can trust a criminal. It's probably bewitched or something. The dryad in the Forest of Inganno thought as much."

"A mystery indeed." Tariq went back to whittling. "Don't be too hasty in your judgment, Vian."

"We could ask a dryad where the river is." Ayianna held up the small flute, so that the others could see it.

Jaeger raised a bushy eyebrow and slid the pipe from his mouth. "Vhy vould they help us?"

"Well, as a flute bearer, I am considered a friend to all dryads."

"Except the ones in the Forest of Inganno." Kael rested his arms on his knees. "So that was why the dryad was so interested in your flute."

"I should probably be alone when I blow on the flute, or he might not show up."

"He? How do you know it will be a he?" Jathil asked.

"Because dryads are male whereas the hamadryads are females, which we learned so well in Inganno."

"We can't leave you completely alone," Kael said.

"I will go with her." Jathil straightened her shoulders and added, "In feline form."

Everyone agreed, and Ayianna and Jathil trekked away from the others. After a few strides out, Ayianna faced Jathil, but froze. Would she ever get used to seeing a snow leopard in Jathil's place? The cat sat on her haunches and turned her icy gray eyes on Ayianna.

Stop staring and blow the flute already. Jathil's voice projected into Ayianna's thoughts. *It is unbearably hot!*

Ayianna brought the flute to her lips, but her eyes never left the regal cat. A soft note lifted and hung in the humid air. Ayianna and the snow leopard waited. Time slipped by like the beads of sweat slipping down Ayianna's back, and all Ayianna could think about was Jathil and her thick fur. Did snow leopards perspire?

She blew several other notes, and the haunting melody mingled with the cries and chirps of birds, bugs, and whatever else might roam the green vegetation beyond them. She shifted her feet. Maybe they should go.

Before she found her voice, a slender dryad shimmered out of a tree trunk. He had smooth, green skin and broad leaves sprouting from his head. He stared at them with abnormally large eyes.

"A flute bearer is quite unheard of in our jungle." The dryad's voice poured from his mouth like a breeze ruffling through leaves. "What brings you here?"

Ayianna told him about the Sorceress, the curse on the plains people, and how the Guardian Circle had sent them on a journey to find its cure. After explaining the importance of their mission, she asked him, "If you please, we need your help in finding the Keyon River. Will you help us?"

"Perhaps."

The snow leopard growled but didn't move.

The dryad turned to the large cat, his hands on his wooden hips. "You do not scare me."

Tell him, my claws could use a good scratch. To emphasize her point, Jathil stretched and fanned out her sharp claws. Then she began to knead the ground in front of her as Ayianna relayed the message to the dryad. His body seemed to wane for a moment as if he might disappear, but he pressed his lips together.

"It was merely a statement. I can go only so far as my tree will let me. Other dryads will have to help. Tell your friends they can come out, and we will go." The slender dryad pivoted and darted away. He looked back, his lips cracking in a mischievous grin. "But you will have to keep up."

26

SIX DRYADS AND three days later, Ayianna and the others were hiking along a tributary the dryads had insisted would take them to the mighty Keyon River. The atmosphere seemed lighter to Ayianna, despite the coils of grief that bound her heart. Everyone grieved Eloith's and Liam's death, but Desmond's absence made the grief more bearable. Even Prince Vian appeared more at ease, speaking freely with Tariq and Kael.

And they were making progress.

According to the last dryad, they would reach the shores of the Keyon in five days. In five days, they would be free of the jungle and closer to finishing their quest. The rush of the small river beside them cheered them on. Ayianna straightened her shoulders and hiked with greater confidence.

She inhaled, filling her lungs with the earthy smells of damp dirt and natural decay. Flat, white toadstools grew like stair steps along the remains of a fallen tree trunk. Woody vines climbed trees and disappeared into the canopy. Spindly ferns splayed over the riverbank. A chorus of frogs croaked somewhere nearby, and every once in a while, came the cry of the jungle's famed Yazzuro Blue—a large, bright blue-and-orange parrot with a wingspan of six feet.

Heeding Tariq's warning, Ayianna didn't get too close to the river. Its brown, murky waters could hide potentially dangerous animals such as a giant anaconda or the gloru'bor—a small, wingless dragon, who would love to feast on careless people's flesh.

Tariq and Vian walked ahead, engrossed in a conversation about kingdoms and social obligations. Lagging behind Ayianna, Jaeger and Jathil discussed the finer points of the Rahzac Treaty between the Northern Haruzos and the Stozic Dwarves.

At the sight of Jaeger, a pang of pity hit her. He seemed to struggle the most with the humid air and thick ferns. He had tied his hair back and braided his beard to keep cool. Still, a sheen of sweat bathed the sinewy muscles sculpting his arms and stomach beneath his vest. He had long since discarded his wool tunic.

Kael slipped through the ferns ahead as he scouted the area and searched for possible food options. Every so often he would pause and glance back, but not once would he catch her eye. He seemed distracted, or he was absorbed in his duties. Either way, he avoided her gaze.

By midday, Ayianna's stomach twisted with hunger, and the others had lapsed into silence. They wouldn't stop until evening, and hopefully Kael would find something other than the furry fruit and toadstools they had been munching on, most reluctantly.

Jathil fell into step with Ayianna. "Are you all right?"

"As well as I could be, I guess." Ayianna glanced to her left.

Jathil punched the ground with her staff as she walked. The hilts of her twin blades protruded from the pack strapped to her back. She had removed the long sleeves of her tunic and strode barefoot, her leather pants folded to her knees.

"Well, don't isolate yourself."

"Like you do?"

Jathil lifted her chin. "I did not choose to live in isolation because of grief. But I know what it's like to mourn in the absence of others. You, on the other hand, are surrounded by friends who have tasted the bitterness and sorrow that death brings."

Ayianna's throat constricted. "What sorrow lingers in your heart?"

"It's an old ache of things that could have been." Jathil shook her head. "The others tell me you have been through much, but we can't help you if you don't share it with us."

"What is there to share? You all know everything already. My father and brother are dead, my mother has been kidnapped, and two faithful friends are dead. How will sharing that help anything?"

"It does." Jathil stepped around a thick batch of ferns. "My mother would say that unspoken feelings will destroy you."

"You press me to share, yet you have lived alone out in the middle of nowhere and have been reluctant to share anything about yourself. Why?"

"Lessons learned." Jathil smiled, but sadness tainted her expression. "There are other ways to release feelings, but you are among people who care about you. You might not realize it, but you are hurting them by pushing them away as if you blame them for Liam's and Eloith's death."

Ayianna focused on the ground before her, keeping the river at a safe distance to the right. Why did her words have to hurt? Why did she have to be right? More truth to rip away the flimsy veils she tried to hide behind. Sorrow's gaping void threatened to overwhelm her, and with it, the torment of tears and endless heartache. No. She couldn't. Not now.

She exhaled the rising emotions and plodded on in silence until she could finally breathe again without the threat of tears. "So what happened? Why are you no longer Tirza of Arashel, but Jathil on the run?"

"Oh, it was years ago." Jathil ducked under a low-hanging branch and rubbed her ears. "Not much of a story really. I found the man I was to marry with another woman, so I left."

"That's it? You just left? That doesn't sound like you. I would have expected you to try to kill him or make him hurt."

"I did."

"Oh." Ayianna nearly tripped but managed to catch herself before she fell. "Is that why the king is offering a reward for your return?"

Jathil shrugged. "I didn't kill him, but there's no telling what lies he's told my father."

"Your father? Is he a friend of the king?"

"No." Jathil half-chuckled. "He is the king."

A princess? With her wild black and white hair, turned up pants, and sleeveless tunic, Jathil did not look like royalty. But then, what did a Haruzo princess look like? Surely, the northern race would wear more clothes than their cousins in Bonzapur. Still, she expected someone a little more refined.

Ayianna stepped over a root. "So back in the dungeons, the dwarves . . . your name . . . they knew you."

"I had thought I could barter for our release, but I was wrong."

Ayianna tried to watch where she was going, but her gaze kept returning to Jathil.

"Stop looking at me like that."

"Sorry." Ayianna averted her eyes. "But you're a princess. Why—"

"It doesn't matter anymore. I am no longer that person. What is done is done. I can never go back." Jathil scanned the jungle. "Do you hear that?"

Ayianna paused. "Hear what?"

"Whistling."

Ayianna shook her head.

"Keep moving, ladies." Jaeger trudged past them.

Ayianna followed slowly, not wanting to get too close to the dwarf and risk Jathil changing the subject. "Why don't you return?"

"I would lose my right hand or my head, depending on the accusations."

"Oh." Ayianna pushed aside some ferns. What kind of brutal rules did Arashel impose? "So . . . are you guilty?"

"I—no." Jathil stabbed the ground with her staff. "Maybe. I don't know what he accused me of to make my father turn against me."

"Will you tell—?"

"Hold on—who is whistling?" asked Jathil. "Whoever it is needs to stop. It's giving me a headache."

"I do not know vhat you are talking about," Jaeger grunted through his thick moustache. "I hear no vhistling."

Ayianna shrugged. She didn't hear anything either.

"Wait." Tariq halted and tilted his head. "I hear it, too."

"Maybe it's the birds." Vian scanned the sky and rubbed the back of his neck.

"Birds don't whistle like this." Jathil rubbed her ears. "Let's just get out of here."

Farther down the riverbank, Kael perched atop a broken tree stump and pivoted, his gaze taking in the landscape. He dropped to the ground and jogged back toward them. "We are not alone."

"Is it the klhordan?" Ayianna gripped her sword. A mixture of anger and fear surged through her.

Tariq's eye widened. "Run."

Ayianna and the others stared at him. "What?" they asked in unison.

"Whatever happens, keep to the river!" Tariq urged as he darted away.

Ayianna scrambled after him, followed by Vian and Kael.

"Vhat are ve running from?" Jaeger jogged behind, doing his best to keep up.

"The natives!"

"The what?" Vian stumbled over a log but caught his balance and kept going. "I've never—there's no such thing!"

Ayianna didn't bother to argue but focused on darting between the trees.

Soon shrill cries filled the jungle as gusts of wind swooshed around and through the ferns. What kind of beings swept through the ferns like wind?

Ayianna pushed herself to run faster, but she soon lost sight of the others and the river. A sharp pain exploded in her neck. Her legs stiffened, and she collapsed into darkness.

27

WARMTH POOLED IN Kael's veins as he oozed in and out of consciousness. He lingered in the sweet embrace of slumber, wishing he could sleep forever. A strange warning throbbed in his head, and he struggled to open his eyes.

As Kael's vision grew accustomed to the darkness, a wall of wooden slats blurred into focus. It pierced a thatched roof above them. Flashes of light flickered through the slats as shadows stalked past. Somewhere drums boomed a syncopated rhythm and added to his headache.

A soft groan sounded nearby, bringing his attention to the other inhabitants of the small hut. Jaeger and Vian lay in a heap next to him, but another person, probably Tariq, huddled against the wall in the darkness. Kael saw no sign of Jathil or Ayianna.

Jaeger sat up and rubbed the back of his neck. "Vhere the *vamsr* are ve?"

"Good question." Kael stretched his legs and arms. Their captors hadn't seen it necessary to tie them up. *Why?* Kael closed his eyes and pushed his senses beyond the slatted walls.

He encountered a mass of unfamiliar minds, well-ordered, but savage. The natives, Tariq had called them. A tumult of excitement vibrated from them.

Kael crawled closer to the wall and peered between the slats. He blinked to clear his vision. He couldn't have really seen what he had seen. Miniature humans? They were short like dwarves, but had human proportions, like fairies with no wings.

Wearing tuffs of dried grass and feathers, the natives danced around a roaring fire. Blue and orange feathers swayed above their heads as they shook colorful gourds. They rattled with each step as they bounced to the rhythm.

"Tariq?" Kael noticed the tall wooden spikes surrounding the area. "What did you mean, natives? I thought all the races of Nälu had been accounted for. But . . . this? What had you called them in Bonzapur?"

A low chuckle erupted from the darkened corner and grew into a humorless laugh. "Well, well . . . I can't believe this. What luck!"

Desmond.

Kael clenched his fist against the urge to punch him. The last thing he needed was to waste his energy and strength. "Didn't get far, did you?"

"Oh, I'm farther ahead than you think." Desmond broke out laughing again.

"Desmond?" Vian sat up and peered into the corner. "Is that really you?"

"Vhat about these circumstances strike you as humorous?" Jaeger rubbed the side of his neck and rolled his shoulders.

"Never mind him." Kael swallowed the snide remarks rising in his throat and felt for his hunting knife. The natives had confiscated that as well. He walked the perimeter of the hut, testing the wooden slats. "We could easily break through, but our stealth would be compromised, and right now, stealth and surprise are our only weapons."

"Right." Vian, still unsteady on his feet, stumbled to the side and looked through the slats. "But once we free ourselves, we wouldn't know where to find our weapons or the others."

"Ve vill just have to take that chance, no?" Jaeger stood and brushed his pants.

"Vian's right. We should—"

"Hey, look, look." Vian motioned for the others. "The little people are leaving. This might be our chance—wait . . . this can't be good."

Kael rushed over to Vian's side and looked into the clearing. His stomach soured at the sight of a green lizard the size of a horse—a gloru'bor. About twenty natives struggled to match the reptile's strength as they tied it between two stakes.

The gloru'bor hissed and snapped at the natives as it clawed the dirt. It shook its leathery red mane and leapt, but the stakes held firm, and the lizard toppled back to the ground. Plumes of dust hung in the air as it thrashed against the ropes. Its eyes swiveled in their sockets.

Under other circumstances, Kael might have felt sorry for it. Until it bared its jagged teeth and shot a cloud of mucus from its nose. The mucus hit one of the natives and the man screamed. He scrambled to wipe it off, but he got too close to the lizard.

The gloru'bor snatched the man and ate him whole. The others fled.

The drums started up again, and a loud cheer erupted from the sky. High above the spiked wall, hundreds of pale faces peered into the arena, enraptured with the gloru'bor. The spiked walls, the wingless dragon, and hundreds of spectators. The hut was a cage.

He jumped back. "We must get out of here—now! Jaeger, can you break through the opposite wall?"

Jaeger grunted and stuck out his hairy chest. "Can I? Vhat kind of question is that? I can break through stone valls, if I vanted to."

But Jaeger didn't have a chance to test his might against the wooden slats. The cage pitched violently to the side and jerked up off the ground. Slowly, it tilted.

Kael scrambled to grab hold of the edge, and a splinter plunged beneath a fingernail. His hand exploded in pain. He let go and tumbled into the arena with the others.

Kael scanned the arena. Who would make the first move? Silence greeted them. Even the lizard had stilled, one eye on them, the other cocked upward. Above the walls, faces leered down at them. Perhaps they were wondering the same thing. Would the gloru'bor attack first? But thick ropes still bound his neck and legs. Was it strong enough to snap them?

Pain pulsed through Kael's hands and fingers. More slivers had managed to lodge into his skin from his stupidity. How was he supposed to fight a giant lizard with such petty distractions? Maybe they could find a weakness in the walls or scale one. What were slivers when lives were at stake?

The gloru'bor shrieked. Kael's attention snapped back to the lizard. A native had been lowered into the arena and was slicing through the ropes.

"Kael, what do we do?" Vian's face blanched and his eyes widened.

Kael inhaled deeply and shoved the fear aside. He had to think. Flames flickered in a trench down the center of the arena. At least they could use that to their advantage, couldn't they? But they needed a strategy of some kind. He blew the air out through his nose. "Don't panic."

"I'm not panicking!" The prince flung his arms up and crossed them across his chest.

"You're pathetic, Vian." Desmond shook his head, his matted hair flopping against his bruised face. A silver pendant hung from his hand. He lifted it to his mouth and blew.

Vian turned on Desmond, his eyes narrowing, but Kael grasped Vian's shoulder. "Run for it. Keep the fire between the lizard and us."

The little man slashed through the last rope, and the gloru'bor spun, its tail thumping against one of the stakes. It leapt and snapped at the native being pulled to safety. The arena erupted into cheers. *Well, so much for kinship.*

Kael dashed away from the lizard and scanned the scarred walls for a point of entry or a weakness. Enormous tree trunks formed the walls, their tops sharpened to a point, stabbing the sky like spears. Deep grooves and dark stains revealed years of abuse and no defects. He glanced over his shoulder for the gloru'bor, but it had disappeared. Where had it—

The lizard landed in front of Kael and scuttled toward him on its hind feet. Its feathery mane rippled wildly around its head. It snapped at Kael, but Kael stumbled backward and rolled out of the way. The lizard's nose hit the ground and it hissed.

"Over here, you beast!" Vian shouted as Kael scrambled to his feet.

The gloru'bor spun toward the voice, and its tail slammed into Kael's stomach, sending him flying. Kael hit the wall in a daze, gasping for air.

Jaeger ran to his side and pulled him to his feet. Kael winced as Jaeger jarred his fingernail, and together they rushed to save Vian.

28

LOUD CHEERS AND applause erupted, sending Ayianna to her feet and into a nearby fern. Her heart pounded in her throat. Her head buzzed and felt twice its size. She steadied herself and looked around. Evening had settled on the jungle, but a glow reflected off the broad leaves of the surrounding trees. She tried to remember what had happened, but her muddled brain refused to cooperate.

A large white leopard sprang from the trees. Ayianna leapt back, making her head hurt even worse. The leopard only yawned and turned its silver eyes on the fiery glow emanating from the other side of a large wooden wall.

"Jathil?"

Keep your voice down.

"What happened?" Ayianna breathed. She rubbed her temples, hoping the buzzing would go away. "Where are we? Where are the others?"

You've been out cold most of the day. Tariq and I escaped the poisoned arrows and were able to rescue you. But the natives captured the others.

A furor of applause and cheers rose above the wall again. Ayianna glanced at Jathil.

Jaeger, Kael, and Vian are fighting a gloru'bor beyond that wall.

"A what?" Ayianna exclaimed, and Jathil knocked her over with her massive leopard's paw. Ayianna opened her mouth to protest, but one look at the leopard's icy glare lodged the words in her throat. Instead, she stood and straightened her clothes.

"So," Ayianna whispered, "What's the plan?"

Tariq's going to create a distraction, you're going to kill the gloru'bor, and—

"What!" Ayianna hissed, trying to keep her voice low.

You have the noqui stones. Tariq is . . . let's say he's preparing a tree for you. Are you feeling up to climbing?

"You're funny." Ayianna massaged her neck, and a flood of sparks rippled through her body. She had forgotten about her wound. She stretched her body, loosening her tight muscles. Could she use a sling in a tree? A feat she hadn't tried before.

The air swished above her head, and Ayianna ducked. A large black jaguar dropped to the ground effortlessly and slinked toward her, its shiny coat glimmering from the glow. Tawny eyes blinked at her.

It is time.

"Tariq?" Ayianna's voice wavered.

The big cat bowed its head. *I have secured a tree for you. I'll take you there. Jathil, their belongings are located at the southern wall in a ground hut. I think a fire would be a most efficient distraction.* The jaguar winked. *But be careful. The natives would love nothing more than a nice snow leopard pelt to add to their collection.*

Ayianna thought she saw the leopard flinch, but Jathil raised her head. *Or a glossy black coat such as yours.*

You forget, Jaguar pelts are common among the natives.

Jathil snarled and shook her head before slipping away into the thick vegetation. Ayianna turned her attention to the black jaguar in front of her.

Follow me.

The jaguar crept through the ferns, and Ayianna did her best to follow quietly. It didn't help that she couldn't see well and was constantly tripping over lumps of soil, tree roots, and holes. She tightened her grip on her sword and focused on breathing.

Reaching the tree, Ayianna found several dead bodies scattered on the jungle floor. They looked human, like miniature adults, no bigger than children.

The jaguar sat on his haunches and nodded.

Ayianna looked for her first foothold and discovered a ladder built from vines and tree limbs. She looked back at Tariq, but he had already disappeared.

Fear permeated her, but Ayianna wasted no time in scaling the ladder. She reached a platform woven from reeds and hoisted herself atop. Looking down, she sucked in her breath.

In the arena, four men scattered as a giant green and red lizard vaulted over a bonfire.

Ayianna slipped a noqui stone from the pouch on her belt. The small marble-like stone was cold and heavy in her palms. If only the lizard would come closer, she could just throw it at him like she did with the dragon. She prepared her sling and scanned the area. What would Tariq's cue look like?

Then her stomach clenched as she recognized the fourth man.

Desmond.

He skirted the edges of the arena, keeping opposite of the gloru'bor. He held something in his mouth.

She scanned the surrounding area and saw similar trees with platforms filled with the natives absorbed in the fight below. Many carried spears and banged them against the top of the wall, creating a peculiar rhythm.

Flames leapt in the distance. The sign. She whirled the sling and released the stone with a snap. It sailed into the arena and fell into the fire.

The gloru'bor darted forward, chasing Kael and Vian. Its tail slapped the ground and knocked Jaeger on his back.

Ayianna flung another stone. It sailed right past the lizard. What if she missed again and hit her friends? Her heart hammered against her ribs. She couldn't do it. Not so far away and in a tree; the angles were all wrong. She couldn't waste any more stones. They were half-gone already. What would she do when they ran out? The crowd burst forth in another cheer, and Ayianna's attention returned to the arena.

The gloru'bor lunged for Kael, its claws catching him across the shoulder and chest. The force of the blow sent Kael flying into the wooden wall where he collapsed on the ground.

The lizard snapped its mouth and dove for Kael but was brought up short. Jaeger had grasped the creature's tail and was pulling it away.

Ayianna gasped. She tucked the sling in her belt and grabbed the nearest vine. Wrapping its corded fibers around her arm, she jumped over the platform. For a moment, she swung forward, and then she dropped. Her stomach floated into her throat, but the vine caught. She slammed against the wall, the fibers snapping, and she fell into the arena.

Ayianna rolled to her feet and ran toward the lizard. It was still too far away for her to throw it by hand. Instead, she whirled the sling above her head, counting its rotations.

The gloru'bor spun and snapped at Jaeger. Then its fringed head turned, and its beady eyes focused on her. The fringe sprung open like a mast at sea, shuddering in the wind. It bared its teeth and hissed.

She inhaled and blew the air out through her nose, trying to calm her racing heart. The horse-sized, swamp lizard was nothing compared to the dragon she had killed, right? Except maybe quicker.

The gloru'bor charged, dragging Jaeger behind. It ran upright, hissing and barring its slimy teeth at her.

Ayianna tried to reclaim the momentum of the sling, but the stone released prematurely and hit the fence. She grabbed for her pouch, but the stones slipped through her trembling fingers.

The gloru'bor shrieked. Its hot breath billowed toward her. A gurgling sound rumbled in its throat.

Ayianna dove to the side just as the lizard spat. A glob of saliva splashed against the dirt and wood, sizzling, eating a hole in the wood.

Still, it rushed her. Two more strides and it would be on top of her.

She seized another stone and flung it at the gloru'bor. A ripple of white washed over it, turning its scales into salt. The lizard collapsed, and a spray of salt crystals showered her.

It was gone.

The arena erupted. The natives pounded their spears and yelled at each other, but none dared to crawl over the wall. Yet.

Ayianna raced to Kael, reaching for her velvet bag containing the kulin. Would she have enough for him? He lay against the wall, eyes closed. Dirt and soot smeared his face and sweat drenched his hair. Blood soaked his shirt. Ayianna held her breath as she knelt beside him.

"Kael?" She peeled back the shredded tunic. She gently prodded his skin, and a fresh wave of blood gushed from the wounds. She gagged.

Kael grunted, and his eyes flew open. "Don't be sticking your filthy fingers in there."

"You have more to worry about than filthy fingers." Ayianna clenched her teeth against the other words rising to her tongue. A verbal lashing was the last thing he needed.

She tugged the velvet bag free of her side pouch. Something wasn't right. Her stomach sank. The bag was too light. She tore it open. Nothing. "It can't be. It's gone!"

"Ayianna!" Vian and Jaeger came running up to them. "Come on. Time to go."

"Up we go, Kael." Vian grabbed him under the arms and helped him to his feet.

Kael grimaced but steadied himself.

A loud roar thundered above them, and Ayianna glanced up just in time to see a dragon's yellow underbelly glide over the arena. The natives cheered. Some screamed as the dragon landed in the arena, knocking their spiked wall down as if it were nothing more than dried reeds.

Imps poured from its back and scampered toward the natives. The jungle broke into chaos. The dragon had crushed more than half of the arena's wall. The other half burned. The natives and imps were locked in combat.

Ayianna leapt up. "How did they find us?"

"Never mind how they found us." Vian wrapped his arm around Kael's waist. "Let's go while they're distracted."

Her answer came soon enough as Desmond crawled atop the dragon. Anger flooded her. She grabbed a noqui stone and hurled it toward him, but the stone fell short. Too far. She should have known better. She loaded her sling and lunged forward, but a hand grabbed her other arm.

"Are you mad?" Jaeger swung her around. "Ve go, now!"

A black jaguar leapt over the flaming wall and bounded toward them. *Hurry! To the river. Jathil is waiting for us there.* He sprang to the right and rushed across the broken wall into the jungle.

Ayianna clenched her jaw and raced after the others to freedom, but the image of Desmond straddling the dragon's neck burned in her mind. Traitor. Hatred surged through her. For Eloith. Liam. Her father and brother. For all the lies.

Next time, she'd kill him.

29

"STOP MOVING." AYIANNA forced the words out through clenched teeth. She tightened her grip on Kael's hand and grasped the splinter sticking out from under his nail for the third time. She closed her eyes and swallowed the wad of nerves stuck in her throat. Taking a deep breath, Ayianna yanked as hard as she could, hoping this time the splinter would come out.

Kael jerked his hand away, and Ayianna held up the large sliver of wood. Victory was hers. But her excitement was short-lived.

With eyes closed, Kael slumped against the tree's exposed roots, breathing heavily. Despite the dried scabs that had formed overnight, the slashes across his chest oozed blood. The wounds should have been taken care of last night, but Tariq wouldn't risk it. They had waded down river until morning's gray haze filtered through the canopy above. Thankfully, the tributary was only knee deep. Then Tariq ordered them out to attend to their wounds, even risking their whereabouts with a fire.

"The water's ready." Vian set Tariq's tin on the ground next to Ayianna. He looked over his shoulder. "The dwarf won't let me help him clean his cuts."

Ayianna followed his gaze and saw Jaeger trying to wash the backside of his shoulder. His hairy chest was matted with dried blood. "Maybe I should have a look, Jaeger, you're covered in blood."

"Not my blood." Jaeger glared at her. "It is the filthy gloru'bor's, that is vhat it is. Kael's injured vorse than I. Tend to him and leave me alone."

"You don't have to be so ornery." Vian stood. "And if I remember correctly, we didn't leave a mark on that beast. So it *is* your blood."

"Leave him alone," Kael said.

"Well, if he comes down with *lavi aezar*, it's not my fault." Vian strode away. "I'm going to get more firewood. Tariq and Jathil will be back soon, and hopefully they'll have found some food. I'm so hungry I could eat a . . . a gloru'bor."

Ayianna squeezed the cloth and dribbled the hot water into Kael's cuts. She worked in silence as she swabbed away both the dried and fresh blood. The work kept her tears at bay, but not her relentless thoughts and fears.

If Desmond hadn't taken the vial of kulin, she would've been able to heal Kael's wounds. Would Tariq's *maeta* paste be enough? The red, swollen flesh screamed no. How could Desmond do this? Did he want them to fail? For her to turn into a harpy? Him, the dragon—traitor!

"Take it easy." Kael clenched his teeth and leaned against the tree, refusing to lie down.

Ayianna mumbled an apology as she gently dabbed the wound dry.

"Are you all right?" Kael asked as Ayianna packed crushed *maeta* leaves into his wounds.

"I'm fine." Ayianna winced at the sharpness of her own words. She hated responding to Kael like that. It wasn't his fault Desmond stole the vial of healing water. What else had he taken? "Do you think the natives will come after us?"

"Doubtful. They had their hands full with those imps and a dragon."

"What about the imps?"

"Hopefully, the river washed away our scent."

She wanted to believe him, but she couldn't push Desmond riding the dragon from her mind. The bitter smell of the crushed leaves burned her nose. She pressed the rest of the leafy paste into the wounds.

"Are you almost done? My back is getting stiff."

Ayianna wiped her hands on her pants and grabbed the rag. "Almost, just need to wrap it now."

"Don't you have that vial from Nerissa?"

Ayianna took a deep breath and twisted the rag in her hands. "Desmond took it."

Kael cursed and moved to stand, but Ayianna pushed him back against the tree.

"Quit moving or you will reopen your cuts, and then you'll bleed to death."

Kael settled back against the tree and closed his eyes. "Well, that's convenient."

Ayianna dipped the rag back into the water and rinsed the blood from it. She felt the trembling begin somewhere deep inside of her and ripple outward. She handed the rag back to Kael. "Here, hold this against the leaves so they don't all fall out and we have to start over. I need to make bandages."

Kael did as he was told. Ayianna pulled out the spare outfit the queen of Bonzapur had given her and began to rip it into strips using the tip of her sword. *If Desmond hadn't taken the vial, I wouldn't have to be doing this right now, Kael wouldn't be bleeding, and I wouldn't be dying!*

"Ayianna?"

Her attention snapped to the present. She glanced down at the strips of cloth and the blade in her hands. Fresh blood swelled across her forefinger.

Foolishness! She examined her finger. A minor cut. How could she be so clumsy? She clasped her hands together, but the trembling didn't stop.

"Are you certain you're all right?"

"I told you, I'm fine." Ayianna turned away. She finished tearing her clothes into strips and began wrapping them around Kael's chest and shoulder. She fumbled with the fabric, and Kael seized her hand.

"You're shaking." Concern flooded his eyes. "Are you injured?"

Ayianna averted her gaze and shook her head. She struggled with the tumultuous emotions raging within her. She tried to pull away, but Kael held her firm. The truth squirmed inside of her, desperate to be freed. She looked at Kael, searching his eyes.

He would be repulsed! There is nothing left for you. You are cursed! Who could love you? Desmond's voice shot arrows through her heart. She faltered. "I—we need the kulin—the merfolk's healing waters."

"Why are you worried about Desmond taking your vial?" Kael arched his eyebrows. "People have lived without magic potions and talismans healing and protecting them."

"No, you don't understand." Ayianna took a deep breath to steady her voice. "If I don't have the kulin, my . . . I will . . . don't you see? I'm cursed. Whatever happened in Nganjo, has cursed me for the rest of my life."

His face grew rigid, and his eyes were guarded. "What do you mean?"

Ayianna looked away and gritted her teeth. "Nerissa said my wound will never heal. It will reopen without the healing waters, and I . . . I could . . ." He didn't need to know what she might become, did he? Maybe it would be easier for him to kill her when she did change. No. No more secrets. "I could become a harpy.

She pulled her hand away and stood. "Desmond knew, and by taking the kulin he has condemned me."

Kael straightened and threw his bloodied, torn shirt aside. "Why didn't you say something sooner?"

"I didn't know he had taken it until now."

"That's not what I meant." Kael climbed to his feet and tugged his vest over his makeshift bandages. He belted on his sword. "When was the last time you took the kulin?"

"In the mountains." Ayianna shoved the rising panic deeper into her gut. "I'm supposed to take the kulin every three months."

Kael rubbed his face with his hands and retied his dark hair. "That has to be well over a month ago, maybe two. It doesn't give us much time."

Kael grabbed the tin of water and dumped it on Jaeger. The dwarf sputtered and yelped as the water disappeared into his wiry hair.

"Vhat did you do that for?" Jaeger mopped at his hairy chest.

"You're taking too long," Kael replied. "You better let Vian help you, or we're going to leave you behind."

Ayianna went over and tried to assist the dwarf, but he wouldn't have any of it. Instead, he dried himself and hobbled after Kael. "Vhat bit your backside all of sudden?"

Kael glanced at Ayianna, and for a second Ayianna was afraid he was going to tell the dwarf. "We're breaking camp. We'll find the others on our way."

30

NERISSA PEERED OUT from the shadows. The winter sun faded from the sky, but within the walls of Badara the world seemed darker, colder. More so than the many winters she had spent at Dagmar studying to be a guardian. Not that the cold affected Nerissa as much as it did her companions.

Bawdy music drifted through Badara's streets and alleyways as the city's inhabitants celebrated Blood Month, the festival where the plains people butchered much of their livestock in order to make it through winter. Nerissa shuddered. Why anyone would live so far north and in such conditions puzzled her.

Most of the plains were white with snow, but within Badara's walls most of it had turned to filthy slush. A woman's squeal echoed against the stone buildings as she darted through the streets with a giddy drunk in quick pursuit. Laughter ensued once the man caught up to his quarry, and Nerissa glanced away as they disappeared into one of the buildings, groping each other.

"How much more of this are we going to have to watch?" Nerissa tightened the heavy cloak around her shoulders and tried to squelch the revulsion rising in her throat.

"The beheading will not take place until morning." Darin, the half-giant, sat on a large wooden crate, his legs stretched across the alleyway. His head rested against the building; his good eye closed. The other hid behind a leather patch. A fur-lined hat kept his bald head warm, and a wool cloak covered his shoulders.

"We are not waiting for morning, are we?" Hadrian limped over to Darin and slumped against the wall. The dwarf had spent the last hour pacing the small alleyway.

"We wait for dark," Darin replied without opening his eye. "You need to relax, or you will draw attention to us."

Hadrian grunted and pulled his hood over his head. "Well, I cannot take much more of this. I am going to have a look around."

"Keep your eyes open and your head down."

"No, I am going to walk around with them closed." Hadrian stomped away muttering under his breath. "And if my head was any closer to the ground then I would step on it."

When Hadrian disappeared, Nerissa turned to Darin. "Why did Saeed choose Hadrian for this job?"

"He trusts the dwarf, and I suspect he wishes to prove Hadrian's loyalty to the Guardian Circle." Darin uncrossed his long legs and drew his knees up. "Hadrian might be cantankerous, but his allegiance belongs to Saeed and the Circle."

"Then who is it, Darin?" Nerissa asked. "First, Zajur, then the attack on the plains and the journey to Kvazkhun? Someone is leaking information to the enemy."

"Hadrian would not betray his own people."

Nerissa pressed her back against the brick wall. "A traitor does not care who he betrays. Once a traitor, always a traitor."

"Hadrian did not betray Elothryn thirty some years ago as everyone assumes."

"No, but then nobody knows who did."

"Nerissa, if we cannot trust each other, our mission will fail. Do you think to challenge Saeed in his decision?"

Nerissa sighed and shook her head. Darin was right. Saeed had not once led them astray. Still, she couldn't shake the feeling that somehow Derk might have information pertaining to their mission. Even if only Darin, Hadrian, and she had been entrusted with its importance. If Saeed trusted Hadrian, then Nerissa would do no less. They would rescue King Valdamar, and Derk would be none the wiser until morning.

"Nerissa?"

She looked at Darin. His blue eye was bright and piercing.

"It is time. You know what you need to do."

Nerissa nodded. A wiggling mass of worms exploded in her stomach. Pulling her hood over her face, Nerissa glided through the shadows until she reached the open courtyard. She halted as a group of bickering women strode by, debating the new color of Badara's banner.

From there, she could see the large pillars guarding Badara's great cistern. Elaborate aqueducts carried water from outside into the cistern and distributed it to different parts of the city. This would be their element of surprise.

Once their chatter faded, she darted through the pillars to the heavy door and pulled out the key Saeed had given her. She unlocked the massive door and pushed her shoulder into its polished surface. The door groaned in response. She slipped into the darkness and shoved the door shut behind her.

Nerissa waited. The musty smell of wet stone engulfed her, and the worms in her stomach vanished. She sighed. She felt for the railing and found it, the iron cold against the palms of her hands. She inched along until she came to the edge of the stone floor. She could almost taste the water now. A shiver of longing tickled her skin. How long had it been since she felt the watery kiss of the sea?

Nerissa stripped down to her swimming robe and slid into the frigid waters. A surge of excitement flooded through her as her body transformed. She took a breath, and the slits on her neck opened as a rush of cold water pushed through her gills. Soon her land legs disappeared into an ebony-green tail. She flexed her muscles, and the tail propelled her through the waters with ease. She closed her eyes and for a moment enjoyed the embrace of the water, even if it was a little stale.

She sought the rear aqueduct. It would take her to the back of the castle where Darin would be waiting. It didn't take her long, and soon she reached the end of her watery journey. She lingered for a moment, but a warning sounded in her head.

She heaved herself out of the water and onto the cold, dry stone. Her first gasp of air burned her lungs as the gills sealed shut. She tried to muffle the coughs that shook her body. Dragging her tail out of the water, Nerissa rubbed her hands along its smooth scales. She gritted her teeth as her tail burned. She refrained from cursing old age and thanked Vituko for still being able to walk the land as a guardian.

She closed her eyes and hunched over her tail. She focused on breathing as her muscles cramped, and spasms of pain shot through her body.

After what seemed liked hours, Nerissa sat up and stretched. She was getting too old for this. Soon her legs would fail to transform, but she refused to be confined to land for the rest of her life. She had to speak to Saeed. It was time for her to retire.

Guardians never retire, Saeed's voice echoed in her head. *They die.*

And she would die a merwoman beneath her beloved waters.

Nerissa left the cistern behind and darted down a corridor to the right. Sliding her hand along the wall, she sought the secret passage. Frost covered the stones and sapped the warmth from her hands and feet. Finally, she stood in front of a stone wall, shivering. She felt the edges of the faded triangle and pressed it. The stone beneath her hand sank into the wall, and a hidden door opened.

Darin ducked in, and the wall ground shut. Nerissa shuddered, hoping no one else had heard the noise.

"How was the swim?" Darin asked.

"Too short," Nerissa replied.

A smile softened his face. "Isn't it always? Your part is done here. Go to Hadrian and wait for me there. I will go the rest of the way alone."

Nerissa snorted. "I think not. What does Saeed always say? Two fare better than those who go it alone."

"And three even better, I know. If you insist but stay out of sight in case something goes wrong."

Darin took off down the dark corridor. His soft, padded steps were the only sound, but even that seemed loud in Nerissa's ears. She picked up her pace to keep up, but it was no use. His strides were longer, and she fell farther behind.

The closer they came to the dungeons, the warmer the air grew and the worse the stench became. The shadows faded into the glow of fiery torches mounted along the walls.

Then the corridor was empty. Where had he gone?

Footsteps vibrated through the stones. She halted. The air shivered with voices. Nerissa darted down the hallway. She had to warn him.

"Darin!" she whispered as she caught sight of the half-giant slinking into a darkened doorway. He faced her. His eyebrows furrowed, and his one good eye begged her for silence.

Nerissa slipped next to him. "Someone is coming!"

"I can elude a couple of guards."

"But what if it is not a couple of guards?"

Darin glanced up the corridor and returned his attention to Nerissa. "Only you, Hadrian, and I know of this mission. We are safe. Besides, it is too late to turn back now. You wait here, and if anything happens, warn Hadrian and get out."

Nerissa glared at him, but the half-giant turned and disappeared down the corridor. She gritted her teeth and waited. The silence seemed to stretch on forever. Did he make it? She could shield herself, but she didn't dare use the Yenzo Tanil and risk being discovered.

Akonamalihi . . . please Vituko. She breathed a silent prayer for Darin's safety. The sensory filament along her skin trembled. Something—or someone was moving. If it was Darin, he hadn't gotten as far as she had hoped.

A commotion broke out down the hall, sending shock waves into Nerissa's sensitive receptors. She held her breath.

"You?" Darin's voice ricocheted off the corridor's walls. "How could you? Saeed trusted you!"

"Where's the merwoman?" a rough voice asked.

Nerissa froze. Her heart pounded in her ears. The corridor was silent. Who was speaking? Had Hadrian betrayed them?

"You three, lock him up," the voice continued. "The rest of you find that merwoman, or I will hang you from the gallows. By the power of Raezana, we will have the king's head tomorrow. That will send a message loud and clear to the foolish guardians."

Nerissa's mind raced. The guards would be prowling the halls soon, and her chances of returning to the cistern would be lost. She had to retreat, to think. How was she going to rescue Darin and the king?

Darin's voice rang in her head, "*Warn Hadrian.*" But he had betrayed them. It had to be him. Wasn't that his voice? But what if she was wrong? Maybe he was still outside watching for the guards. She had to make sure.

Every moment she wasted, the guards drew closer. She took one last look up the corridor and dashed back to the cistern. Slipping beneath the surface, the cold rush of icy water engulfed her, and her panic subsided. Sparks of excitement flew over her legs as they melded together into her ebony tail.

Nerissa shot through the water, careful to miss the great pillars bracing the cistern's ceiling. It wouldn't be long before they searched the aqueducts. Moments later she resurfaced and grabbed her heavy robe. She rubbed vigorously to dry her scales. Seconds felt like hours. She tried to breathe through the pain, but the fiery sensation overwhelmed her. She doubled over, gasping for air.

Once her land legs had formed, Nerissa threw her robe on and darted to the entrance. She took a deep breath and inched the door open.

She scanned the area. Hadrian was nowhere to be found. Her heart sank. Could Saeed be so wrong? A band of guards marched toward her. Nerissa pushed the door shut and locked it. She gritted her teeth.

The dwarf had betrayed them.

31

BENEATH THE WATERY depths of the cistern, Nerissa hid. She ran through various scenarios in her head, still unable to decide what to do next. She lay in the dark waters against the inner wall, not daring to move until she was sure the guards had lost interest and looked elsewhere. As cold as it was, she was certain no one would try to look for her in the water. Most likely guards had already been posted at the two entrances, blocking her exit.

She shivered. The frigid water drained the warmth from her body. She would have to get out soon. Fighting sleepiness, she recounted the different aqueducts leading into the cistern. She could use any one of them to escape and abort the mission, but she refused. She would not leave Darin behind.

Vibrations shook Nerissa awake. She sat up, disoriented. How could she have fallen asleep? What had awakened her? The water remained calm, but shock waves continued to break against her feathery fins lining her back and arms. The tremors from above could mean only one thing—marching soldiers.

Nerissa unfurled her tail and found numbness had gripped the edges of her fins. She couldn't wait any longer, or she wouldn't be able to swim. She clutched the swollen satchel, stuffed with her robe and sealed shut, and slid along the bottom of the cistern.

Reaching the inner entrance, Nerissa waited below the waters. She felt nothing. Had the place been deserted? How long had she slept? Her heart quickened. *Am I too late?*

She lifted herself onto the cold stone walkway and hauled her tail out of the water. With her limbs numb, she moved slower. Bending over her tail, she closed her eyes and braced for the painful transformation. Fire seared up her tail and burned along her spine. She trembled. The pain increased, made worse by the cold temperature.

Shaking, she opened her satchel and pulled out her heavy cloak. She was going to have to warm up before anything else. She rubbed her arms and legs dry; the friction melted the numbness in her fingers and toes. She paused at the arched entrance. Sensing nothing, she darted down the corridor to the dungeons.

Nerissa held her hands near a torch and contemplated her next move. She tried to remember the layout of the dungeons, but her memory was sluggish. She stood outside its only entrance and peered inside. The place was too quiet. The guards and the prisoners were missing. Her stomach sank.

A loud grunt broke the silence, and the groaning of metal bars echoed down the corridor. She slipped into the shadows and drew closer to the sound. Torches lit the room in front of her. Iron-barred cells lined the wall, all of them empty and brown with rust. Something moved in the last cell. A person leaned into the bars. The groaning rang out through the dungeons again.

Nerissa glanced around. Where were the guards? Wouldn't they hear the noise? She inched her way toward the lone prisoner, and as she neared his cell, she gasped.

"Hadrian?"

The dwarf turned his face to her. Dried blood clung to his beard and face. His right cheek was cracked and purple, and his left eye was nearly swollen shut.

"But I thought . . . how did you—what happened?" She knelt by the cell. The stone floor bit her knees and the cold leeched what little warmth she had regained. She slid out her kulin and dribbled the contents over his cheek.

"The guards were waiting for me when I arrived. I was ambushed."

"But who?" She slid the vial back in her satchel.

He shook his head. "What took you so long?" He pushed against the weakening bar and with a final cry of protest, it gave way. "Would you stop gawking at me and give me a hand?"

"What do you expect me to do, you brute?" Nerissa cocked her head. "I cannot bend iron."

Hadrian pushed his stout body through the warped bars. "Grab my hand and pull!"

Nerissa stood and did as she was told, and the dwarf became lodged between the bars. She pulled harder.

"Pull, pull, PULL!" The dwarf squirmed to be free.

"If-you-would-just-stop-talking." Nerissa paused to catch her breath.

"This is humiliating." Hadrian sighed. Suddenly, he slipped forward and tumbled onto the ground, free of the bars.

"Where are the others?" Nerissa helped him to his feet.

"Off to the beheading. Where've you been all night?" Hadrian ran down the hall, peering into different rooms.

Nerissa took off after him. "You expected me to take on all the guards? Where are you going?"

"In here." Hadrian slipped into a room, and Nerissa followed.

Armor and weapons lined the walls and sat in heaps along the floor. Hadrian inspected the various weapons, selecting a few. He scooped up some clothes and dumped them at Nerissa's feet.

"Put on these clothes and armor."

"I do not wear pants." Nerissa shuddered at the thought.

"You will today. The beheading will be happening soon. You will dress like a solider, infiltrate the ranks, and find Darin and the king. Once you've found them, I will create a distraction or something."

"You could sneak around better than I can."

"They will recognize me. You can blend in better." Hadrian paused as he picked up a crossbow and swung it over his shoulder. "Just keep your head covered and your dragon whistle at the ready."

Nerissa glanced at the pile of soiled clothes and grimaced.

A ram's horn blared throughout Badara, and Nerissa's heart skipped a beat. She pressed through the sleepy crowd as they made their way toward the outer bailey. She peered through her leather helmet, hoping no one would notice a spindly, old merwoman. Or the white braids tucked beneath her armor.

The people yawned and stumbled into each other. Why would anyone want to watch a public execution? Especially so early in the morning after celebrating all night? Pursuing desires without restraint had a cost. How did they like their new-found liberty now?

But what she saw reflected in their eyes ate at her heart. Resentment, despondency, hopelessness. She saw the Sorceress's curse. She quickened her step, searching the crowd for signs of Darin and the king.

This had better work! Nerissa gritted her teeth. No matter which way she moved the woolen tunic scratched at her sensitive skin. Its musty body odor clung to her and burned her nose. If her borrowed armor and clothes did not convince others she was a soldier, then at least the smell would keep them away from her.

Breaking through the crowd, she finally came upon the procession. Darin stood atop a wagon, gagged, hands bound, and tied down. Valdamar slumped to the side, his pale face gaunt and his red hair disheveled. The wagon bumped over the cobbled street, and Darin struggled to keep his balance.

Nerissa pulled her leather necklace out from under her clothes and placed the round shell between her lips. She scanned the city's walls for a sign of Hadrian. Her heart pounded, the pulse thrumming in her head, pumping fire through her veins. She inhaled the foul, winter air and forced her nerves to calm, her face to cool. She'd have to free the prisoners without detection and signal Hadrian when she was ready. Timing was everything. She did not need rampant emotions or uncontained energy to misguide her.

She prepared to leap aboard the wagon, but a group of women broke from the crowd and approached the slow-moving wagon. Their heads covered in the traditional colorful veils, they danced along the wagon and began to taunt the prisoners.

"What do you think now, Valdamar?" One of the women leapt atop the wagon and tore off her veil. She shook out her blond hair and sneered. "We are free to do as we please. And it pleases us greatly to see your head roll across the ground."

A loud cheer rang out from among the crowd. Several women threw their head scarves at the wagon and cursed the king and the guardians. A few tightened the veils around their heads and withdrew into the throng of people.

"Long-live Raezana!" The words rang out and echoed off the walls.

Horns resounded throughout the city, and the procession stopped. The crowd stilled. A flurry of whispers rushed among them.

A guard approached the wagon and shoved the leering woman down. Nerissa followed him and tucked the shell into her cheek, hoping her helmet hid the leather necklace. Keeping her head down, she nodded to the other guard and jerked Darin aside. Did he know it was her? She tried to catch his gaze, but she didn't dare lift her face. She slid the dagger from her belt and sliced through the ropes binding the prisoners to the wagon. Next, their hands.

A lone horn sounded, and Nerissa glanced up. The crowd parted, their faces peering up at the top of the bailey. A carriage constructed from the bones of a dragon creaked to a stop. Derk sat within as if it were a throne. Nerissa bristled. How dare he disgrace such a noble creature! The bones had to be from one of the stolen hatchlings so long ago. She vowed to flay Derk and build a privy with his bones.

She turned her attention to the task at hand. She maneuvered the shell back between her lips and blew. No noise sounded, but a few dogs howled in response. She cut Darin's wrists free.

"I should have known it was you, cold as your hands are," Darin said after he had removed the gag from his mouth.

"You try spending a night at the bottom of the cistern in the middle of winter."

Whistling of arrows sliced through the air. The guard next to her fell. Nerissa spat the shell from her mouth and sliced through the king's bindings.

Horns blasted, and the crowd erupted into chaos. Some tried to flee, but others surged forward to see what was happening.

More arrows hissed through the air and found more targets. Nerissa helped King Valdamar to his feet, but he was too weak to fight.

Soldiers charged them. Darin swiped a sword from a fallen guard and plowed into them.

Another soldier rushed toward her. Nerissa unsheathed her blade and swung. The clang of metal stung her ears. She gritted her teeth and blocked another attack. The blow sent sparks through her arm. She recoiled, slipping a sea-star from her belt, and flung it at the guard's throat. The man gagged and collapsed.

A loud screech rent the air and cries of horror rippled through the crowd. A bright green dragon soared above the city. Nerissa grasped the shell around her neck and blew long and hard. The great reptile looped around and headed toward her.

"*Polehi luwe'kiwo. Kolihi ahi maewa lukoko!*" Nerissa shouted, and the dragon belched flames.

The guards fell back into the crowd. Voices bellowed for order, but guards and people alike rushed over each other to get out of the way.

The dragon swept down and landed. He shook his head and wings as a volley of arrows whistled through the air. *Hadrian had better not hit my dragon!* Nerissa leapt atop the dragon's back and pulled Valdamar into the saddle with her.

"Go, Nerissa, before Derk launches his dragons." Darin scrambled behind her and grabbed the king's shoulders.

"How dare he use dragons!" Nerissa bound the king to the saddle and strapped herself into her seat. "But no, his dragons are not here, or this would never work. Hold on! *Lukohi, lukohi!*"

The dragon's enormous leathery wings rose high around them. Nerissa tightened her grip. With great force, the dragon dropped his wings and leapt into the sky. Nerissa and her companions were jerked backward and then forward, but soon leveled out as they gradually climbed higher into the sky.

"We did it!" Darin shouted into the wind. "Wait—where's Hadrian?"

Nerissa pointed. The dwarf scurried along the top of the southern wall. She urged the dragon lower.

Darin slipped from the saddle and onto the dragon's feet. Moments later, he reappeared with a furious dwarf.

"Tie me down! Tie me down!" Hadrian screamed, clinging to Darin.

Nerissa tried to relax, but her skin cried for relief. She yanked the leather helmet off and shook out her white hair. "Where to?"

"Talem." Darin's face hardened. "We must get there before Unai."

Unai?

Nerissa dipped her head against the dragon's cool scales and urged her mount to hurry. They had to warn Saeed.

32

NEVIN SAEED SAT in the deserted council room and studied the map of Nälu, his mind taxed from the planning and debating he had done earlier. He questioned the Alliance's strategies and the strength of its small army, but he knew they were only buying time so Kael could return with the Dwalu Tonic before they marched against Badara.

Yes, that is the plan. Let the enemy think we have hidden ourselves in Kvazkhun, lure them out, and from the south we shall attack. Yet all will fail without the tonic.

Saeed slid his fingers over his braided beard. *What irony that the future of the world should rest on such a few.*

"Oh, Vituko." He sighed and closed his eyes. "How will we ever win this battle? To ask this of me in the vigor of my youth, I could have led a great army to your victory. Instead, I sit here like a moldy garment, unfit to clothe the poorest wretch."

Silence answered his prayer. Saeed opened his eyes and stood. Peace evaded his soul. He glanced out the window. The sun had set, painting the small city of Talem in cold shadows. A few plumes of smoke curled into the sky as the remaining guards and families stoked their hearths against the onslaught of winter. Saeed shivered.

On the other side of the room, the long, thick curtains rustled as if the wind blew them, but the window was closed. Something scraped across the floor. Perhaps a dog or a child left behind? But no one had brought either to the meeting. Or maybe it was a rat. Saeed sought the intruder with his mind but found nothing. Strange. Even animals would give off energy.

He inched closer until he reached the bend in the auditorium where the steps led to the podium below and the rows of chairs wrapped around the room. Just beyond the chairs' covered backs, a shadow shifted along the wall.

Saeed stepped forward and the shadow froze. The hair on his forearms lifted. He should flee, but instead, he drew closer.

The shadows gave way to a woman. She cowered against the wall and rocked back and forth, clinging to her knees. Tufts of gray hair swayed loosely around her wrinkled face. The rest crawled down her back in a tangled mass of knots and clumps.

"Madam?" Saeed inched closer not wanting to startle her.

The woman paused from her rocking and turned; her eyes glazed white. Streaks of swollen bloodied flesh etched her pasty white face. She lifted her arm, and the skin drooped off the bone. Her hands trembled as she pointed a finger at him, its nail unusually long.

"Have you come to torment me too?" The woman's voice rattled with phlegm. "I have it not!"

"I have not come to torment you, nor take anything from you. I have come to help you." Saeed knelt near her. How had they missed one of the cursed? Pity and compassion coursed through him, but anger took root and raged into fury. Could not the Sorceress see what happened when the free will was twisted and coerced?

"Help? Ha!" the woman whispered. "No one can help me. Hope flees from me like chaff in the wind. It is over."

"It has only begun."

"I have failed."

248

"No—"

"You do not understand." The woman wailed. "The great Vituko will punish me—destroy me." Her face contorted with anger and pain. She raised her hands toward her face.

Saeed moved to restrain her, but he was too late.

The woman shrieked as she tore into her flesh with her fingernails. Blood seeped from the wounds, black against her pale skin. She hissed at him. "It's what I deserve."

Why did he argue with her? The Twammurt Curse bound the inhabitants of the plains like a boa constricted its prey. Reason and rationality ceased in their despair and inner turmoil. Leora would have to administer the sleeping charm for her own good.

"I am neither friend nor foe, but a guardian charged with the protection of Nälu. Tell me your name so that I may help you." Saeed patted her hand.

She shook her head. "I am Madam of Arlyn of Zurial. There is no help for me."

Saeed froze. Arlyn? The Arlyn, son of Elothryn. Ayianna's father—her mother? "You know where the dagger is . . . that means—

"Is that all you people ever care about—that blasted dagger?" The old woman trembled. "My family—destroyed, all because of this dagger."

Saeed recoiled. Why was she here? Had she escaped her kidnappers? Or were they here, watching him? He scanned the council room and reached out with his senses. Why couldn't he sense them? He turned back to the woman. "Your fury is justified, but it is misdirected."

"And where else should I direct it? At Vituko, the shadowy bringer of bad tidings? Are you not the High Guardian of the Guardian Circle charged with the protection of Nälu? Where is your protection now?"

"If the dagger falls into the hands of the Sorceress—"

"Semine!" The woman gasped, and her body convulsed. She attempted to claw her face again, but Saeed grabbed her arms. "Semine is—no!" The woman's wrinkled face contorted in pain. "I will not—the Sorceress is . . . my . . . master." She doubled over, screaming, her body going limp.

"It is too late," she whispered. "In the halls where north meets south, you will find Trygg locked forever in battle."

Trygg—Morning Star—locked in battle. What had Ayianna said? The star locked in stone. Little did she know the message her father had given her! Still she hadn't said anything about halls or battles.

He tugged at the braids in his beard. Halls, north meets south? Talem? Of course. He scrambled to his feet. The dagger was hidden here in Talem, but where was the traitor? Had he already discovered it?

As the sun dipped below the horizon, the air grew colder, the room darker. Nothing seemed out of place. Then his gaze rested on the platform at the bottom of the auditorium. At its center, a large, ornate table sat. Just minutes ago, he and the generals had leaned on it, pouring over a map. A sculpted battle scene wrapped around its base to where Trygg fought with the shield of the Chai. All chiseled out of stone.

Should I? The prize of finding it first called to him. He could use it as bait or throw it down a well somewhere. Maybe hide it in the dragon lairs of Ganya, or he could just leave it and hope no one else would discover it.

But where was the dagger? Was it hidden beneath the table? Or in some secret place within it? Saeed stepped closer to the podium and hesitated. He didn't want to touch it. He had seen the death it had created, the blood it had spilt. It repulsed him. He wanted nothing to do with the blade that killed his brother.

But with knowledge came responsibility. *And with age comes even more knowledge and even more responsibility. How lovely! The weight of the world rests on my shoulders. Thanks,*

Vituko. Nevertheless, he would accept his plight however the Shadow God deemed fit to give.

The battle is not yours.

Saeed paused. The words poured through him like a cold glass of water, and with it came peace. Saeed repeated the words to himself, enjoying their sound on his lips. "Of course, how could I be so thick-headed? My apologies, Vituko."

A door creaked and swished open. Saeed closed his eyes. He had lingered too long. He turned to face the traitor.

"Nevin Saeed, you're here late." Unai stepped into the council room. A red silk robe replaced his usual gray one. A black and gold sash circled his large midsection, and the ends hung halfway to the ground. A nervous smile parted his jowls. "The meeting was over hours ago, and you've let the fire go."

Saeed had no words to volley. The cold ache of realization seeped through him. Behind Unai, Ayianna's mother slid along the wall like an injured dog, disappearing into the shadows and heavy curtains on the far side of the room.

"Something bothering you, old friend?" Unai waltzed around the room, picking up discarded books and papers as if that had been his intention all along.

"The corrupt shall be snared by the labor of his hands."

Unai dropped the books and straightened; his fake smile gone. "So have you come to spar with words alone, my friend?"

"Why, Unai?" Saeed held his gaze. "The path you've chosen leads only to destruction. You know this. You've taught this. How could you choose it?"

Unai shook his head. "What makes you so certain that Vituko is right and Raezana is wrong?"

"The evidence is in the life lived."

"Is it? No one really knows until the end, do they?" Unai folded his arms atop his rotund belly. "However, there is no doubt Raezana will win. She has more power than some shadowy figure hiding in the mountains of Zohar. You can see it, feel it."

"Tainted power brings death. Lies, Unai, all of it is lies. You of all people should know that."

Fire danced in Unai's eyes as a wicked smile crossed his lips. "Today you shall see the power of the Goddess Raezana."

Saeed drew his sword. He would fight, but he would not kill. How could he? Unai. Guardian. Friend. So many years— centuries—they had served together. Was it all for naught?

"How long have you lived a lie?"

"Long enough." Unai unsheathed his own sword and held it up. "So Vituko sends you alone and powerless to meet the great power of Raezana?"

How could he have been so blind? But matters of life and death had no time for hurt feelings. Saeed shoved them aside and leveled his blade. He fought not for himself, but for Vituko and all of Nälu. "I am never alone."

"Keep telling yourself that, but we shall see the truth of it. Vituko has no power to save you now."

"If death be his choice . . . " Saeed tightened his grip on the sword despite the tremor in his hands. "Then so be it."

Unai raised his sword above his head and charged. Bracing himself, Saeed repelled Unai's aim. The clash of blades echoed through the council room. Unai whirled around, and Saeed sidestepped and deflected another blow. Give and take, the deadly dance of blades had begun.

"Give up, old elf." Unai retreated to the first row of chairs and wiped the sweat from his brow. "You're no match for the Tóas Dikon." An orange ball of flames exploded from Unai's hands.

"*Voart!*" Saeed brought his fists together, creating an instant barrier between him and the blast. The shield shimmered, consuming the flames, and then dissolved.

"Is that the best you can do?" Unai threw a chair at Saeed, but Saeed dodged it. The chair crashed against the podium. Unai strolled toward him, flicking his sword back and forth. "Your god can't even give you power to fight back."

"The Yenzo Tanil are gifts to create, not destroy; to help, not hurt. I want nothing to do with powers of the Underworld."

Unai swung. Saeed blocked him and brought his blade down upon Unai's, but his aim was off, and he pitched forward into the chairs. He tried to regain his balance, but Unai was upon him, his sword slashing across his back. Fiery pain ripped through his shoulder. Saeed hit the floor. He grasped a chair and thrust it between them.

Unai's blade sank into the wood. He cursed and slammed the chair into the others, sending them flying.

Saeed crawled to the second row and heaved up from the ground, his shoulder burning. He faced Unai and hoisted his sword. His joints creaked and his muscles protested. He was too old for this. What was Vituko thinking?

Unai yanked his sword free and kicked the chair aside. "The Tóas can set you free, Saeed."

"There is no freedom in lies."

Saeed ducked as Unai slashed the air with his sword. He straightened and brought his sword up with all his might, shattering the other blade. The clang of metal reverberated throughout the room. The impact shot sparks up his arm and into his teeth.

Unai stumbled backward and caught his balance on the podium behind him. He muttered something in Táchil, and the swords hanging on the wall above him sailed through the air.

"*Voart!*" Saeed slammed his fist together, and the blades melted. The hilts clattered to the floor. Saeed advanced. He had to gain the upper edge, or he'd lose more than his life. He raised his sword. For Nälu. For his brother.

Unai lifted his round face to him—a face of a friend. Saeed froze. *I can't do this . . .*

Unai uttered something, and Saeed prepared to block the curse, but Unai flashed a knife instead.

Saeed leapt back. He heard Unai's foul words as a great force slammed into him and flung him across the room.

Saeed hit the wall and slid to the floor. Battered and unsteady, he crawled to the last row of chairs and pulled himself up.

Unai brandished his dagger and lunged toward him.

Saeed felt sluggish, his limbs heavy. He barely managed to block Unai's thrust. He shook his head to clear his thoughts. *Darin should be here soon. Focus . . .*

Unai moved forward, waving the curvy blade in the air. Raw hatred and anger burned in his eyes—so different now. How had he failed to notice his friend's transformation?

Saeed locked blades with Unai and shoved him backward.

Unai sidestepped. "*Wisil thikolt!*"

Unai's broken sword flew overhead and landed in his outstretched hand. He brought the remaining blade down, crashing into Saeed's.

Saeed stumbled. Unai spun, and Saeed attempted to block him, but Unai's other hand thrust upward.

A blade plunged into Saeed's stomach. Pain seared his midsection and rippled outward. He fell to his knees and grasped the dagger's hilt. Hot blood trickled over his hands. He tried to pull, but the hilt slipped through his trembling fingers. Saeed looked up at Unai. "Why?"

"I have nothing more to say to you." Unai clenched his jaw and kicked Saeed in the stomach.

Sparks exploded on the edges of Saeed's vision. He collapsed. The cold stone floor welcomed him and calmed the fire in his bruised skin. Somewhere above him Unai lingered, and for the first time Saeed could sense him. Unai loathed him.

Saeed curled against the pain and hate. *Leave me be and let me die in peace.*

But Unai gripped his shoulder and flung him over.

Saeed's body trembled as shadows consumed his vision. Above him, light glinted from a broken blade, and then the shards pierced his chest.

33

NERISSA RUSHED AFTER Darin through the corridors of Talem. Landing a dragon in the middle of the courtyard would take some explaining, but right now she didn't have time. She could only hope they weren't too late.

She burst through the heavy doors and froze. Splotches of black soot scorched the walls where pieces of smoldering tapestries hung. Chairs had been smashed and scattered about the room. Acrid smoke stung her nose and burned the back of her throat. She covered her mouth with her hand. She remained calm, but within she screamed.

Darin stepped over the debris and descended the steps toward the podium where the ornate table lay on its side.

Nerissa shoved aside the broken chairs and charred papers. Could her heart sink no further? They had failed. To hope now, she would be a fool.

Whimpering snapped Nerissa's attention to a bulge in the curtains. Dread crawled along her spine. Was Unai still here? Did he have an accomplice? She unsheathed her sword and drew back the curtains. A woman huddled in a ball, crying. Her matted hair hid her face.

"Hello?" Nerissa touched the woman's shoulder. "Who are you?"

The woman shuddered. "Kill me now and end my misery."

"I cannot." Nerissa bent down and brushed the hair aside. Red, swollen scratches covered the woman's face. "Have you seen Saeed?"

"It's too late . . . too late." The woman groaned. "The dagger is gone. I have failed."

Dagger? Could this be Ayianna's mother? Nerissa stomach sank. She had to be—Unai had succeeded. "Where—"

"No!" Darin's voice thundered throughout the council room.

Nerissa straightened. Darin stood in the lower level where the table should have been. She followed his gaze to the bottom of the stairs. A body lay sprawled, a broken sword protruding from its chest.

Her knees buckled, and she staggered back against the wall. No! It had to be someone else. Not Saeed. She stumbled down the steps.

"Saeed?" Nerissa knelt and touched his cheek. Cold. Saeed's amber eyes stared at the ceiling, their thoughtful glow absent. Dried blood splattered his face and clothes. *Oh, Vituko, what purpose does Saeed's death have in all this? Could you not have spared your faithful servant?*

Darin bent forward and touched his head to Saeed's shoulder. He straightened, forcing composure, despite the tears flowing down his cheeks. He reached over, brushed Saeed's eyes closed, and sat back.

"Who will lead us, Saeed?" He rubbed his bald head and adjusted the eye-patch, now wet.

Footsteps echoed off the corridor outside. Moments later, a gruff voice bellowed, "What happened in here?"

"We were too late, Hadrian." Darin stood. "Unai got here before we could."

"No." Hadrian shook his head. "Please don't—" But he stopped short, then growled. He grabbed the leg of an upturned chair and flung it across the room. It crashed into the wall and splintered. He huffed down to where Darin stood. "I'll kill him. I'll kill that no-good dog."

Darin placed his hand on Hadrian's shoulder and squeezed. Hadrian groaned as he dropped to his knees. The dwarf's shoulders shook between loud sobs. His cries broke the heavy silence shrouding the auditorium.

Nerissa draped an arm over Hadrian's back and closed her eyes. The pain crushed her and squeezed her chest. She forced herself to breathe slowly. How could they go on without Saeed? If she hadn't fallen asleep, maybe they would have been able to stop Unai. Unai—the traitor. She doubled over and shrieked. The sound tore through her throat, burning her gills, and bounced off the walls. *K'mahi, k'mahi, Akonamalihi? Why, Vituko?*

They mourned in silence, broken only by Hadrian's loud sobs.

Finally, Darin stood. "Where is Valdamar?"

Hadrian straightened. "We should have left him in the dungeons. Badara would have been better off."

"We will not talk like that." Darin untied his cloak and tossed it on a few chairs left standing. "We will finish what Saeed started."

Hadrian grunted and blew his nose on a handkerchief. "He went down to the kitchen."

"Nerissa . . ." Darin gripped her shoulder. "See to the king, so that we may build a pyre."

She nodded but did not rise from Saeed's side.

"But what about the others? Surely, they should be here." Hadrian glared up at Darin, his beard soaked with tears.

"We don't have time. As soon as the enemy knows Saeed is dead, they will strike, and we must be ready to fight."

"No!" Hadrian punched his fist into his palm. "It is not right by the Circle or by Saeed."

"We have no choice."

"We always have a choice." He kicked a chair, sending its splintered remains against the others, and paced the podium where the table should have been.

"And all choices have consequences." Darin charged up the steps, back the way they had come. "We will give Saeed what we can, but our priority here is stopping Semine."

"You heartless giant." Hadrian dropped his fists and trudged after him. "But I'd rather dig a hole than a pyre."

Nerissa slowly rose to her feet and made herself obey. Ayianna's mother needed her. The king needed her. Her duty was to the living, even if her heart was dying.

"Ridiculous!" Hadrian paced in front of the kitchen's hearth.

The fire had long since faded to embers, but no one moved to throw another log on it. Nerissa preferred the shadows. She could hide in their silent embrace. Perhaps the others thought so too. A large kettle hung to the side half full of onion broth. She had scoured the cellars but had found nothing else to add to it.

She shook her head. A guardian learned to endure the ridiculous and much more, but Saeed's death would be the end of them. Nerissa breathed a silent prayer and lit an oil lamp, casting the kitchen in muted light.

She returned to the table. Three bowls of broth remained untouched, hers included, but she wasn't about to eat while she still wore the itchy, smelly garments from the dungeons. As soon as the others leave, she would bathe and wash the stench and itchiness away. What she really needed was a swim. A river, a pond even. Anything to cleanse the filth from her and ease the ache in her bones and her heart. Maybe she would wake up from this nightmare, and Saeed would still be alive.

Hadrian continued pacing and muttering to himself. Darin sat on the steps leading out of the kitchen, his elbows on his knees, his head resting in his hands. Anguish squeezed the room into a painful silence.

Except for the king.

Valdamar hunched over a bowl of broth at the far end of the table. He slurped the last of it, his hands no longer shaking. His pale face had regained color. His eyes were bright and alert. He would be fine, given a little time. But his indifference to Saeed's death galled her. Even if they hadn't been on speaking terms for years, he should have been at least concerned about the impact it would have. What did he think now that they had rescued him? If he was grateful, he wasn't showing it.

Perhaps his hatred had to do with the influence of the Nuja priests. Or was this a more personal matter? Saeed had been close to Valdamar's foreign mistress and had hidden away his illegitimate son. Did Valdamar know his child lived? A death, perceived or otherwise, could make a person turn against another.

At the back of the kitchen, Ayianna's mother groaned in her sleep. She had refused to eat and had sobbed herself into a stupor. Nerissa placed the vial of kulin in her satchel. Why couldn't her beloved waters free the plains people from the curse—or bring Saeed back? At least it could heal, and, by morning, the scratches and infections on the woman's face would be gone. But the state of her soul was another matter. The guardians had not yet come across someone so afflicted by the curse. Were they too late?

Hadrian grunted and faced Darin. "The others should be here."

"We feel the same way you do." Darin stood and stretched, his arms nearly brushing the ceiling of the stairwell. "But the matter is settled."

Hadrian kicked the wooden table, and it jumped, rattling the plates and spilling their untouched broth. Valdamar shot him a glare, and then downed a pint of ale.

Nerissa placed a hand on Hadrian's shoulder. "We will do what we can to honor Saeed, but we need to consider what our next move should be."

"Aye." Darin straightened. "First, we must inform the others. I suggest, Hadrian, you take Ayianna's mother to Kvazkhun, make sure everything is secure, and inform Leora. Unai knew of our plans; he will be watching."

"Why don't we use the stones to communicate?" Hadrian asked.

Darin gripped the stone pendent hanging from his neck and tucked it in his shirt. "Unai has one. I will not risk him intercepting our messages."

Valdamar thumped his bowl down. "What news do you have of my son?"

"He is fine." Hadrian plucked at the seams of his sleeves.

Darin cleared his throat. "Your Majesty, Prince Vian is on the quest for the Dwalu Tonic that will set your people free from this curse."

"Speaking of which." Hadrian crossed his arms "Saeed was going to meet Kael in Praetan, I think. Should we have them go to Kvazkhun, instead?"

Darin shook his head. "I don't know. There is no telling what Unai knows of our plans. We need a new strategy."

"Kael and the others should be reaching Ganya soon." Nerissa shifted on the bench again, the rough fabric scraping her legs and arms. "I could intercept them. If the timing is right, they could return with the Royal Aviation Force."

"What if you're wrong?" Darin asked.

"Three months have passed since we have received word from Kael. They should already be in Ganya, if not, then at the Great Falls." Nerissa shrugged. "If their journey has tarried, I could look for them. They would not be hard for my dragon to find."

Darin shook his head. "The quest was a fool's hope, Nerissa. We must prepare for battle with or without Kael."

"You're wrong." Nerissa lifted her chin. "Saeed believed otherwise, and I will stand by his decision."

"Wait, who is this Kael?" Valdamar straightened. "And why is my son on the other side of the world? He should be here."

Nerissa raised her hand. "Your son joined the quest to save your people. He trusted Saeed and the guardians to save you. And we did."

The king slammed his fists down. "He is the heir to the throne. He should be here. I must find him."

"Your Majesty." Darin squared his shoulders and strode toward the king. "While you were languishing in the dungeons, the rest of the world has been preparing for battle. The Alliance has reunited to help you. Your people need you here. Your son will find us."

Valdamar narrowed his eyes and worked his jaw. "Much has transpired then. Who is leading the Alliance?"

"The kings and generals who stand united for Nälu. The nations of Praetan, Zurial, Bonzapur, Kvazkhun, and Stratuvec stand with you. They will convene in Praetan within the week. You and I will join them as quickly as we can. They must know what has happened here." He glanced over at Nerissa. "You will go to Zurial and warn Eldwyn."

"But what about—"

"Our first and foremost duty is to Nälu and the Alliance."

"You are not the next High Guardian, Darin." Hadrian growled. "What makes you think you can order us around like this?"

Darin threw his hands up in the air. "We do not have time for this. I am not the High Guardian, but I am still in charge of this mission. We shall meet with the others and decide then who will lead us, but mark my words, dwarf, if the enemy catches wind of any division, it will be a glorious day for them."

"Fine, but I will wait for Kael in Kvazkhun," Hadrian said. "Saeed knew that the battle would be lost without Kael and the tonic. A fool's hope, it may be, but it is our only hope."

Nerissa stood and pulled her satchel over her shoulder. "I will do as you say, for I see wisdom in your words. I will go see Eldwyn, but I am needed in Ganya. I have a few projects . . ." Nerissa's voice wavered, but she regained her composure and continued. "Projects that Saeed had asked me to oversee. I will be expected to accompany the Royal Aviation Force to Zurial. If Kael and the others are there, I will have them join me. We will check in with Hadrian in Kvazkhun to administer the tonic."

"That settles it." Hadrian grunted and limped to the door.

Nerissa pressed her fingertips to her lips. "May Vituko go with you." She nodded at Darin and strolled toward the scullery room. First, she needed a bath and a change of clothes. As she closed the door behind her, Darin's words followed her.

"Best rest, your Majesty, Praetan will be at least a three-day ride."

"I've done enough resting," Valdamar replied. "We leave now."

34

BACK IN GWYDION, Semine stood in the darkness of her own dungeons, observing her prisoner. If she could call her that. The Sacred Pearl lay in a pile of filthy straw. It grew dimmer with each passing day, but the spirit inside refused to die, refused to speak. For centuries, Karasi remained dormant. No new prophecies, no teachings, no words of wisdom—nothing but cold silence. Everyone suspected she had died or was dying. But Semine knew better.

The Perimeter remained steadfast, guarding the Abyss and binding the Goddess Raezana to the Underworld. Somehow Karasi was linked to the power of the Perimeter. If she died, the barrier between the worlds would crumble. But Semine wasn't going to wait for Karasi to die. She would kill the king's son, open the portal, and free the goddess from the Underworld once and for all.

The cold gleam of the pearl mocked her. How many times had Semine taunted it, smashed it, thrown it? No matter what she tried, she could not wake Karasi or force her to speak.

But once the altar flowed with blood again, she'd speak. She'd scream and weep. And there was nothing she could do to stop Semine.

She gathered her robe and kicked the pearl. It rolled across the stone floor and came to a rest against the wall. "I will destroy you."

"No, you won't." A muffled voice drifted through the dungeons. "You cannot, stop!"

Semine held her breath. Had Karasi spoken? She inched closer to the pearl, willing it to speak again. What triumph she could claim over the guardians! She had roused the sleeping spirit and made her speak. Her! The Sorceress they rejected. Surely, the guardians had lost their way and that was why Karasi was silent.

"Speak, Karasi. Why do you hold your tongue?"

Nothing.

"Perhaps I will cut your tongue out for you."

"Return at once, or you will be punished," the voice cried out again.

Semine straightened. "Return to what? Vituko?" She laughed, her own voice bouncing around the cell.

The door swung open, and a bright, fiery light exploded into the room, blinding Semine. For one small moment, fear flooded her, and doubt crashed into her wall of unbelief. Had Vituko decided to intervene now? Was Karasi calling the Ruwachs?

She straightened and forced steel into her voice. "Who disturbs me?"

"Are you daft?" the voice asked again, and then a servant appeared next to the fire and shoved it aside, revealing Derk's face.

"Forgive me, Mistress." Her servant bowed. "He would not listen. He insisted he had to see you right away and wouldn't wait."

Semine clenched her teeth and took a deep breath. Anger fought her disappointment. It had been only a servant she had heard. Yet her anger won. She had been made a fool! "Out!"

The servant fled, but Derk lingered. He had never feared her like the others had. Perhaps he saw remnants of what she once was, what she could have been. He had been her closest friend, but now? She was high priestess of Raezana. She had no time for divided loyalties.

"We need to talk." He flicked the torch back and forth, scanning the cell. "What are you doing down here anyway?"

"You couldn't wait?" She ushered him out of the cell, but before closing the door behind her, she glanced back at the silent pearl. If Karasi refused to speak, she was as good as dead. No one wanted to listen to her anymore anyway. Semine slammed the door shut and rushed up the stairs, Derk close behind her.

Back in her study, Semine plucked the scrolls from her desk and shoved them into their slots between the shelves. "So, what was so important that you couldn't wait?"

"Valdamar is gone. The plan didn't work." Derk crossed his arms and leaned against the door frame. His dark hair had grayed considerably since the last time she had seen him. "Saeed sent the dwarf, the merwoman, and the half-giant to rescue him." He cocked his head. "They had a dragon!"

Semine returned to her desk and shifted the parchments onto a pile, the ink long since dry. She glanced up. "How do you know it didn't work?"

His frown grew deeper. "Were we not trying to bring Valdamar's son out in the open?"

She shrugged. "Vian is on the other side of the world right now."

"And when were you going to tell me this?" Derk straightened and strode to the window. "Now with Valdamar free, he can rally his people and lead an army against us."

"The plains people are no longer his to control. They are yours."

"Have you seen them lately? The people grow rowdier and more unmanageable by the day. It's as if the curse has removed all restraint, and they have no respect for authority."

How simple could he be? Anger burned, but was it her own? Or Raezana's? Semine grabbed his shoulder and spun him around. "You are their restraint. You are the source of the curse. If you cannot learn to control them, then you are worthless to Raezana and will be replaced."

Derk stepped back and raised his hands. "Calm down, Semine. I can handle the plains people. I was only saying—"

"Well, if it isn't my two favorite people." A voice floated into the room.

Hate flooded Derk's eyes, and he turned back toward the window, away from the newcomer.

Semine didn't have to see the speaker to recognize the voice of her old mentor. She faced him. His round face sagged, and his hair was nearly gone. The years hadn't been easy on him. Or was the mantle of a double-crossing guardian too much for him? She crossed her arms. "What is it, Unai? It had better be good."

"Oh, it is." Gloating filled his voice and face as if he had won the affection of Raezana herself. He held up a blade. "I have the dagger."

And he had. Semine rushed to his side and plucked it from his hands. For so long she had searched for this blade! The ancient bronze glinted in the afternoon light. Its angular blade had turned a mottled green and was beyond dull. She turned it over, and a black hole glared back at her.

Raezana shrieked within her. *The stone! The eye of death! Where is the stone?*

Semine raised her gaze to Unai's. "Where is the rest of it?"

"This . . . this is all that was there."

Semine shrieked this time. She slammed the dagger onto her desk and pulled at her hair. All this time, and yet she was still found lacking. Where was the stone? She pressed on her temples as if she could draw up the events so long ago. "Elothryn hid the dagger. He must have removed the stone somehow." She paced her study.

The imps had not found any trace of the stone nor the dagger on him when she had found him. What had he done with the stone? Semine stopped. "Elothryn's son had to have had it. That's why we were lead to him and his family, yet they did not have the dagger." She clenched her teeth. "Ayianna. She must have the stone."

"And where is she?" Derk turned away from the window.

"Believe it or not, she is with Prince Vian on their silly little quest." Semine tugged a small chest down from a shelf, placed it on the table, and opened it. Inside, the uisol stone drank in the fading light of the late afternoon sun. She plucked the stone from its cushion. "If you'll excuse me, I have work to do."

"Oh, but there's more." Unai smiled, but his eyes held no mirth. "Saeed is dead."

Semine halted. Raezana's glee flooded her senses, and for a moment, Semine allowed the goddess's emotions to become hers. Then they faded, leaving a hollowed emptiness in its wake.

The news should have delighted her. Raezana's greatest enemy in all of Nälu was gone. The Guardian Circle would be in shambles. The Alliance would be without its central leadership. Without Saeed, who would influence the nations against Raezana? Saeed's death could prove to be a fatal blow to the Alliance. She should be rejoicing, but all she could see were the kind, amber eyes of an old elf who had taken in an orphan so many years ago.

Raezana's glee turned to anger, and Semine banished those memories. She nodded toward Unai. "You have proved yourself worthy. Raezana will reward you richly . . . in due time." She glanced back at Derk. His eyes were shadowed, but she wasn't going to waste time trying to read him. "Prepare your army. We will march to war at the first sign of spring."

She brushed past Unai and descended into the temple.

The evening worshippers had already gathered beyond the thick curtains separating them from the inner sanctuary. Their monotone chants and sweetly spiced incense laced the air and marked the end of Blood Month.

Semine stepped over the channel of oil circling the basin of dark water. The last known portal to the Underworld. Soon, she'd have the dagger and the prince, and she would open the portal. Together, she and Raezana would rip the fabric separating the worlds and unleash the dead from their grave. There would be no more death, except for those who opposed her.

The surface of the dark water thrummed with the chants, but otherwise remained still. Semine knelt at the edge of the basin and slipped the uisol stone into the water, silent rings rippled to the edge. She took a knife and slid it across her skin. Blood welled up, black against white in the shadows. She scraped the back of the blade across her arm and swirled it in the basin. And then she chanted.

"*Kozan, Koletu, Aenlu, Ninol. Thöm uisol thil, sram za sil, shoza isür thil.*"

A glow blossomed in the depths of the small pool and grew brighter until it flooded the room and nearly blinded her.

"Seek Eye, toward the west, beyond the shifting sands of Zriab, beyond the mountains of Ta'vazi. Seek Ayianna, the daughter of Arlyn."

The glow dimmed. Images of golden sand dunes fled beneath the water's surface. White peaked mountains rose and then disappeared into the lush green of the Rimanga Jungle. But still the Eye roved west until the green faded into the gray of the swamps. Trees emerged from the haze, perched on spindly roots, the water well below its normal level. The Eye dove deeper until a girl blurred into view.

Ayianna stumbled through the swamp, trying to keep up with the others. Next to her a dwarf had an even harder time, since his knees barely cleared the mud. Ahead of her, a dark-skinned Haruzo glided with ease over the swamps, followed by a Northern Haruzo, and the red-haired prince. Kael hiked with determined steps but kept glancing back at Ayianna and the dwarf. Where was Desmond? Shouldn't he have sabotaged the quest by now? These bumbling pests were the last thing she had wanted to find.

"Eye, show me Desmond!"

The vision swam backward until a dragon's form filled the basin. Desmond sat in the saddle. His blond hair matted and his face bruised, but determination hardened his gaze. A dozen or so imps clung to the saddle. What had happened to others? There should have been at least fifty or more. He would need reinforcements, and she would send them. She squinted. "Eye, let me see Desmond and Ayianna."

The dragon grew smaller until miles and miles separated the two of them. Desmond pursued them, but Ayianna and the others might make it to the falls before he could reach them. She couldn't risk losing them to the merfolk. She had to slow them down.

The exposed roots and the dry river basin beyond the swamp sparked an idea. The wet season would come early, and with a vengeance unseen before.

PART
THREE

35

DAYS HAD TURNED into weeks, weeks into a month, or so Kael figured. There was no moon or sun to mark the passing of days. Time ceased to exist in the bogs and mires of the Thi'taiso Swamps. Kael sloshed through the warm mud. Despite the dry season, the ground was still very much wet. It was a concentrated wetness, which made the mud more viscous and their progress less than desirable. His weary companions hadn't said much about their hurried state, nor the silence of the swamp.

Ayianna picked her way through the mud, jumping from one weed patch to another. She seemed slower, weaker, or was he imagining it? Did she feel the effects of the curse already? The image of Lord Nach flashed before him, and Kael was back in Nganjo, watching the lord of the harpies pull his blood-stained mouth from Ayianna's neck.

Kael clenched his jaw and pushed harder through the swamp, burying the guilt and condemnation deeper. He tried to think about something else. He stretched his injured shoulder and a spasm of pain shot through his body. His anger flared.

If I ever see Desmond again, I'll kill him!

From the beginning, Kael had hated him, but Saeed had cautioned him, and Kael gave him a chance. A chance the no-good cur should never have had! Still, there had been no proof of treason. Until now. And on a dragon, no less. Not once had he sensed the enemy on him. Actually, he hadn't been able to sense Desmond's presence at all. That should have been a warning. How had Desmond deceived them all?

Well, all except Eloith. Why hadn't he listened to Eloith? The pain in his shoulder throbbed, and he gritted his teeth. Despite the time that passed, his wound still hadn't healed as well as it should have. Of course, it didn't help that he kept reopening it. The *maeta* leaves had better keep the infections at bay. The last thing he wanted was to die in the swamps from a lizard's scratch.

But it would be easier.

Would it? His pace slowed. To be released from his burdens, his failures. None of it really mattered, did it? The hope of Nälu rested on the tonic, not him. He could die, and the rest of the world could continue striving without him.

Wait—what was he thinking? Was he an elf without honor? No. He would accomplish the task set before him—or die trying. But he would not welcome death until it was his time.

"Take care where you're placing your feet," Tariq said.

Kael turned to see Jaeger struggling to keep up. The dwarf's stout form had him wading knee-deep in mud. Kael and the others had assisted him several times already, much to the dwarf's chagrin.

"Swamps have a manner of deadening your senses," Tariq continued, "and giving you a false impression of security."

"Security?" Vian faced Tariq. He raised his eyebrows, and with his matted red curls and shaggy beard, he could have passed for a crazed swamp man. "We are wading through muddy waters, hoping to avoid snakes and whatever else this dejected place harbors. And to think that Badara wanted to expand its western borders."

Tariq halted and leaned on his walking stick. "The lands of Bonzapur stretch westward from the Kha Vaaro Mountains to the farthest edge of the Rimanga Jungle. Arashel claims the north. I do believe everything in between resides with the dwarves and Saryhemor elves. Where had you planned on expanding your little empire?"

"Really, Tariq." Jathil sauntered up to them and placed her hands on her hips. "How could you even be concerned? Humans would die of disease before they could even establish a settlement."

"You misunderstand me." Vian rubbed his face and arms as if to test the effectiveness of Tariq's salve. "We were only considering the western coast, where our ships could make berth and carry on trade with the Pauden and Kaleki without having to go through Zurial every time—the import tax is heavy enough without having to pay rent too yet. Why should Zurial have the monopoly on shipping and trade? A western port would be closer to Ganya and Moruya, and then Bonzapur and Arashel could ship through there instead."

"And you don't think Bonzapur has thought of this?" Tariq shot a glance at Kael. "Not that we have a problem with how the elves have been operating in Zurial. It's cumbersome being landlocked." He returned his attention to Vian. "Why would we let the humans open a port on our land? We would have just opened our own, but the port would be too vulnerable to pirate raids, not to mention the western edge is mostly cliffs. Besides, it is easier for us to ship through Zurial than to cross mountains and jungles and deal with the natives."

Kael tightened his grip on his bow. "Gentlemen, could we discuss politics another time?"

"Vhat is your hurry?" Jaeger leaned against a tree, his shoulders sagging.

Kael frowned. "Aside from the fact that the rest of Nälu is counting on us to return and free the plains people, we are nearing the end of the dry season. I would hate to be caught in these swamps when the rains finally do come."

"You have a point." Tariq shook his head. "I apologize. We should at least continue walking while we talk. These swamps take on a whole new dimension during the wet seasons."

"What do you mean?" Ayianna asked, her face tense and pale as if the dreariness of the swamp had seeped into her skin.

Kael didn't know what to expect, but he remained alert. Would it be like Nganjo all over again? Would the black spidery veins sweep over her body and finally kill her? Or would he wake up one morning and discover her gone—changed to a hideous bat-like woman who wanted nothing more than to claw his eyes out? He shuddered and banished the image from his mind. If they were too late, would he be able to end her misery? His stomach twisted.

Tariq eyed the gray haze above. "If the rains catch us in the swamps, we will be swimming out of here, rather than walking."

"Oh, that's a comforting thought." Vian rolled his eyes and schlepped away. One by one the others followed him, but Kael lingered.

He glanced around, seeking other life forms or disturbances. Nothing, except unremitting dreariness. Tall trees stretched up from the mud, perched atop their exposed roots. He moved away. He didn't want to be around when the rains came. A distant caw of a bird broke the slurping and smacking of their footsteps. What kind of wretched creature would call such a dreary place home?

"Help!" A voice broke Kael's reverie and pierced his heart. He plowed through the mud toward the voice. Where was Ayianna? Had the transformation begun? He tightened his grip on his dagger.

He caught up to the others.

"Vian, don't move!" Tariq hauled Ayianna away from Vian.

"I'm not!" Vian snapped back. "I can't."

"What's going on?" Kael asked, but Tariq grabbed his arm and yanked him backward.

Beyond Tariq, Vian stood up to his knees in mud, slowly sinking deeper.

"Well, as you can see, Vian was so clever to discover a sinkhole." Jathil's bright silver eyes were fixed on Vian, her hands planted on her hips.

Kael moved forward, but Tariq restrained him. "Careful, we don't know how big that hole is, and we don't want to be fishing anybody else out."

"Don't just stand their gawking at me," Vian cried. "Hurry up!"

"Vian, relax," Jathil said. "If you squirm, you will only sink faster."

He snorted. "You try and relax as you sink to your death."

"So overdramatic." Kael tore the rope from his belt. The mud was up to Vian's waist now. Kael reached his arm over his head to throw the end of the rope to Vian, but Tariq stopped him.

"It would be better to make a loop than rely on him to hold it." Tariq took the rope and tied a loop at the end. He whirled it in a circle above his head until it hummed, and then he let go. The loop sailed past Vian and plopped in the mud beyond his reach.

"You missed." Vian flung his arms and slapped the mud. "I can't believe you missed!"

"Shut up, Vian," Kael said as Tariq tried again and missed.

The prince sank to his armpits. "It's getting hard to breathe."

"Stop panicking," Jathil said. "Keep your arms above your head."

Tariq pulled the rope quickly and prepared to launch it for the third time.

"You can do this, Tariq." Kael pushed the air out of his lungs with a silent prayer.

The rope hummed in the air again, but this time it hit Vian's outstretched hand. "Now, put it under your arms!" Tariq handed the end of the rope to Jathil.

Vian did as he was told, and once the rope was secured, Tariq tugged it tight. "All right, everyone, pull!"

Kael and the others grabbed the rope. Not waiting for Jaeger to join them, Kael leaned into the pull with the others, and his wound reopened. Again. He grimaced as warmth seeped beneath the bandages and leaked down his side. When would he learn?

"Move aside." Jaeger sloshed through the watery mess and shoved Kael away. "You don't need to be pulling." Jaeger wrapped the rope around his waist and arm and heaved.

Kael bit back an angry tirade and resorted to watching. No, he couldn't just watch. He grabbed Jaeger's ax from the dwarf's pack and hacked a large limb from the closest tree he could find. He flung it across the mud in front of Vian. Kael clenched his jaw. The effort brought more pain to his shoulder.

Vian grasped for the limb as the others strained against the rope. The mud groaned and slurped, refusing to let go of him. Then it released him with a loud smack, and everyone flew backward. Vian plopped face first in the mud.

"Keep pulling!" Tariq shouted. "Vian, lie flat and use the limb to keep from sinking."

Vian hauled himself atop the limb, coughing and spitting out mud as they dragged him to safety.

"The limb was a good idea." Tariq wiped what mud he could off his pants.

"Right." Jaeger scowled at Kael. "Next time, do not grab my veapon vithout permission."

"Hopefully, there won't be a next time." Kael helped Jathil to her feet.

"Can we get much dirtier?" Ayianna sat in the mud with a look of surrender on her face.

"At least you weren't dunked in the mud." Vian stood and shook himself, flinging mud everywhere. Kael shielded his face, but Ayianna wasn't so lucky.

"Vian!" She scooped up a handful of mud and threw it at the prince. He ducked and the lump of mud hit Jathil in the neck. Jathil gasped and sloshed mud back at Ayianna, spraying Kael as well.

Kael smiled and flung a pile of mud back at Jathil. Soon mud was flying everywhere, and everyone was laughing. For a moment, the tension had dissolved, and Kael enjoyed the delight in Ayianna's voice.

Hours later, the motely band of travelers found themselves on a flat, sunbaked plain. To the north and south, the ground rose and bore slender trees. A dirty river snaked down the middle and stretched toward the western horizon.

"We found it." Ayianna sank to her knees. They were close, so close to reaching the healing waters and finding the roots. She smiled. Hope felt good.

"What's wrong with you?" Jathil squatted next to her. "Have you been applying your balm? We wouldn't want to have to drag you all the way to Ganya because you got xaduira fever." Jathil's eyes twinkled, and her lip curled up into a half smile, nevertheless the words pierced Ayianna's heart.

"No, I'm fine—just tired."

"Last one in eats dragon dung!" Vian crowed as he ran toward the river, stripping off his muddied clothes.

"Should we tell him about the snakes?" Tariq asked.

Kael shook his head. "He needs a bath."

"We all do." Jathil stood and placed her hands on her hips. "Let's not ruin the moment."

"Then vhat are ve vaiting for?" Jaeger took off for the river. "I am not eating dragon dung."

Ayianna stood and tried to run, but the jar of each step burned deep in her joints. She resigned to walking, hoping no one noticed, but Kael did. He always did.

He paused at the edge of the river and waited for her. "Are you all right?"

"I'm fine." She ignored the throbbing pain in her neck. He raised an eyebrow. Ayianna dug her foot into the dirt. "I'm a little tired."

"Can I see it?"

Ayianna didn't have to ask what he meant. She lifted her hair and showed him her neck. Kael touched the skin around the wound, and shockwaves exploded through her body. Her vision blurred. For a moment, she thought she would fall, but Kael's arm steadied her.

"It has reawakened, then?" Kael's eyes were hard. Was he repulsed?

Ayianna swallowed and looked away. "I don't know . . . maybe. I'm sure I'll feel better after a bath, and I eat some food and get some sleep."

"Of course." Kael removed his shirt. A dark red stain seeped through the bandage across his shoulder and chest.

"I don't think you should go in that water," Ayianna said. "Your wound has reopened again, and it could get infected."

"Then let's hope Tariq has some more *maeta* leaves, because my skin is crawling, and I stink." Kael touched his bandaged chest gingerly. "Are you coming in, or am I going to have to drag you in?"

Ayianna smiled. "Last one in eats dragon dung."

36

TWO DAYS LATER, Kael hiked along the river. His wounds had been cleaned and rewrapped, he had a belly full of fish, and he no longer stank. For the first time since entering the jungle, he had slept hard. He should have felt refreshed, but he didn't.

Instead, a feeling of unease gripped his soul like a snapping turtle and refused to let go. The river valley should have had more vegetation than the endless sand and patches of mud stretching far into the distance where the brown met green as trees waved above the ground. Downstream, a grove of large trees towered unusually high above the sand and narrow stream. But what did he know? He'd never been this far west before.

But Tariq had. He strode ahead of everyone, his long strides easily maintaining his lead. Kael jogged to catch up to him, passing Jathil and Vian. He glanced over his shoulder. Ayianna and Jaeger fell farther and farther behind. They would never find shelter for the evening at this pace. Shouldn't Ayianna feel the urge for haste? Unless the curse grew stronger.

Guilt stabbed him and Kael slowed. His questions could wait. First, he'd check on Ayianna. Still, the agitation in his soul escalated. What bothered him? Was there a presence beyond his vision watching them? He didn't sense anything, but that didn't mean someone couldn't be spying on them. Veiling one's presence wasn't unheard of or forbidden.

Like Desmond. He could still be out there, following them, and Kael would never know it. How could Desmond, a mere human, hide his presence? Unless someone was doing it for him—like the Sorceress. Was he working for her? If he were only after the dagger, then why would he follow them now? Surely, he knew that Ayianna did not have it. What more could he want?

Kael shoved the growing anger aside and tried to refocus his senses. He couldn't risk tainting them with emotion. Or had he already? Maybe his apprehension stemmed from Ayianna's curse and their less-than-desirable progress.

The weather didn't help his unease. Dark, sculpted clouds loomed in the sky. Yesterday, he had watched them build and blot out the western horizon, but now not a speck of blue could be seen. The river flowed sluggishly past him as if it ached for the rain to come and refresh its dirty waters. Hopefully, they'd find cover before the rains came.

Perhaps the contrast of the jungle's thick vegetation and the river basin's empty terrain disturbed him. If the enemy still hunted them, they'd certainly see them now. But did they? The small natives were nothing but ants against the dragon and all those imps. No doubt Desmond had escaped with them, but where did he go? The open landscape left little for hiding places.

No, it was more than just being exposed. He squatted and ran his fingers over the ground. The smooth clay broke into patches, their edges curving up—like a massive, dehydrated mud puddle. In the distance, a crack of thunder rumbled, sending a chill down his spine.

"Tariq," Kael called out. "We are standing in the riverbed."

Tariq faced him. "That can't be right." He jogged toward Kael, but stopped, and his eyes widened. "No, oh, no." He clasped his hands over his head and pivoted to the north, then the south. "Oh, this is bad."

"I thought you came this way. Didn't you know?" Kael's throat tightened. How could Tariq not know? He shoved the anger aside. Where could they go? If it started to rain, they'd drown.

"I—it was at the beginning of the dry season. I didn't think about the river being dried up. I thought we were farther upstream."

"Never mind that now. We need to get out of here before it starts raining."

Tariq jerked his thumb in the direction of the distant trees. "That must be the riverbank over there." He glanced back toward the jungle. "The rain has already started, near the edge of the mountains. There's no telling how long it's been coming down nor when its impact will reach us."

"We won't make it to the banks in time." Kael scanned the area again. How big was this river? The turbulent clouds grew darker by the moment. He took a deep breath and pushed it through his nose. Where would they go?

Tariq shook his head, backing up. "We have to try. Or maybe those trees there, it could be an island." He pointed downstream to the trees towering over the sand and river.

He jogged downstream and Kael joined him. The others followed, quickening their pace. Ahead, the grove of trees sat atop an elevated land mass—an island? The trees along the edges perched on their exposed, spindly roots and revealed the true level of the river.

A splat of rain hit Kael's forehead. He turned to warn the others, but his words caught in his throat. On the horizon, a wall of rain obscured the jungles and mountains and raced toward them. It broke up the flaky ground, kicking up dust before consuming it. A rush of wet wind pummeled his face, and then the rain swept over him.

"To the trees!" Tariq hollered. "Run!"

"Vhat is all this fuss about rain?" Jaeger jogged after him. "A little rain never hurt anyone."

Tariq sprinted ahead. "We are not talking about a little rain. We are talking about torrential downpour, flooding."

And as Tariq spoke, the clouds burst open and released oceans of rain. Kael yelled to the others, but a thunderclap swallowed his words. The weight of the water bore down on his head and shoulders. He shielded his eyes and sought his companions. They ran toward him and Tariq. Vian passed him, but Ayianna slipped. Before he could move, Jathil yanked her from the ground and pushed her onward. She darted after Tariq and Jaeger followed. They would make it.

Kael took off for the trees, sloshing through inches of water already pooling on the ground. The downpour pummeled his back and drove him forward. By the time he reached the trees, the inches covered his foot. He scaled the exposed roots, ignoring the ache in his shoulder, until he had landed upon the island's embankment. Jathil and Tariq scrambled past to higher ground. Vian came next scampering up behind him and joining Tariq.

The sky rumbled again, but this time the grumbling grew louder and continued. He whirled around. A mountain of water surged toward them. Where had that come from? Where was Ayianna? Jaeger? They had been right behind him.

Ayianna raced across the river basin just ahead of Jaeger. The water was gaining on them. He gritted his teeth. How could he have been so foolish? He tried to climb back down, but the roots had grown slippery. He couldn't risk it. He grabbed the rope from his belt and anchored it to a large tree trunk. The rumbling had now turned into a loud roar as if a hundred dragons were descending upon them. He didn't dare take his eyes off them.

Ayianna neared the roots beneath him and leapt to catch hold. Her hands slipped, but she managed to lodge her arm between the crisscrossing roots. It held. Kael tried to reach her, but he was too high up. He stole a glance at the oncoming wall of water, growing ever nearer to Jaeger.

Kael slid down his rope to a lower position among the roots and threw Ayianna the end of the rope. She grabbed it and twisted it around her forearm, but instead of climbing up, she waited. Jaeger huffed toward them, the flood roaring ever closer. Ayianna reached out and grabbed his hand.

Kael pulled against their weight, his shoulder screaming. Above him, Tariq and Vian grasped the rope and heaved, but they couldn't budge them.

Kael held tight and stretched his other arm out for Ayianna's hand. Not close enough. He strained harder.

"Brace yourselves!" Tariq hollered.

A huge wave slammed into the trees, nearly tearing Kael off the roots and banging his body against them. Spasms of pain shot through his shoulder, dulling the ache where he hit the tree. He coughed and spat water out.

"Jaeger!"

The rain muffled Ayianna's screams, and then they were gone. Kael quickly lunged down the rope. Where was Ayianna? The rope pulled taut, and Ayianna's head surfaced above the water. She sputtered. "Kael! He's gone! He's gone!"

Kael towed her closer to the roots. He fought the rising waters as they pushed and tugged at him. He locked his leg around a root and reached for Ayianna's outstretched hand. Blood covered her arm where the rope had gouged her skin. His hand slipped from hers, and instead, he grabbed her around the waist.

With the help of Tariq, they climbed back to the base of the tree. Kael held Ayianna close. Her body trembled, and he could feel the grief and guilt raging through her.

"Farther in, there is land. We can rest there." Jathil joined them. Her eyes darted to Ayianna's arm. "Where's Jaeger?"

"The water—he might have grabbed a root or something. We have to check." Kael set Ayianna down.

Vian grabbed his arm. "Attend to Ayianna, we will go." He joined Tariq and Jathil as they darted down the island's shore.

Kael jerked his rope free and looped it together. He should have been the one looking for Jaeger. The dwarf couldn't have gone far. He could have grabbed a root and held on—he was a dwarf after all. Kael's shoulder throbbed. No doubt, he had reopened the gash again. Would it ever heal?

He squatted next to Ayianna. She huddled over her injured arm, her eyes closed. Blood dripped from the cuts circling her forearm. They needed to be cleaned and wrapped, but how was he going to do that without a fire? Hopefully, Tariq had more *maeta* leaves.

Jathil was the first to return.

He looked up, but she shook her head, and his heart sank. "Tariq and Vian are still looking. But we found shelter." Jathil's gaze drifted to Ayianna.

Kael wrapped his arm around Ayianna's waist, but she pushed him away. "I can walk."

He stepped back and dropped his arms at his side. The gesture shouldn't have hurt. She was angry at herself. A feeling he knew all too well. She crawled to her feet, hugging her arm to her chest. She stumbled after Jathil, and Kael followed closely, ready to catch her if she fell.

The cave's opening sat beneath the roots of a tree where part of the land had collapsed at one time. Kael stooped through the spidery roots and into darkness, but at least it was dry. He dug out his sphere. The ceiling was just tall enough for them to walk without bumping their head. Pieces of driftwood and bones littered the sides of the cave. Or was it a burrow?

Kael squeezed the water from his hair. "We need a fire."

"Right, good luck with that." Jathil ducked back out of the cave.

Ayianna stepped away from the opening and crumpled into a heap. Blood smeared her skin and face. Rivulets of red dribbled down her arm, mixing with water and staining her clothes.

He threw his bow and quiver aside and unbuckled his sword belt. What should he do first? Stop the bleeding, and then he could tend to a fire until Tariq returned. She needed the crushed *maeta* leaves. He pulled his soaked shirt over his head and wrung it as dry as he could. Ripping the sleeves off, he knelt next to Ayianna. She glanced up at him and then away as he grabbed her arm and began wiping the blood. She flinched.

He worked in silence, wrapping the wounds tightly and providing pressure with his hands. A breeze blew through the cave's entrance and carried with it the smell of worms, fish, and wet dirt. The thick rock walls muffled the roar of the rain.

He looked up at Ayianna, feeling helpless, and he hated feeling helpless. Tears streaked down her cheeks, the only visible sign of the volatile mix of grief, guilt, and anger frothing inside of her. He reached up and brushed the tears from her face.

What do I say, Osaryn? Kael took a deep breath. He knew all too well the feelings coursing through her. "It's not your fault."

"How can you say that?" Her dark eyes pleaded with him as if wishing what he said were true, or wishing he'd shut up. She looked away. "If I could have held on tighter, longer . . . I felt his fingers slipping." She shook her head. "Then he was gone."

Kael opened his mouth to argue with her, but no words came. The image of Rysa flashed in his mind right before the waves of the sea had whisked her away. He had tried to save her, but he too had failed. He touched the scar on his temple and frowned. *Where is the great Shadow God when you need him?*

Huh, Osaryn? We serve you, abide by your decrees, and what has it gotten us?

"Kael!" Vian's voice jarred him. "We found him!"

Kael jumped to his feet as Tariq and Vian exploded through the cave's entrance, hauling Jaeger between them.

"You-you're alive!" Ayianna sprang from the ground and grasped Jaeger by the shoulders.

"Of course, I am alive." He grunted, but a wide grin broke through his moustache. "It vould take more than a blasted flood to kill me."

Kael smiled and slapped Jaeger's back. "Good to see the water hasn't affected your bloated sense of self, or your humor."

"Bah!" Jaeger burst into a fit of coughs. "Vhat is a d'arf, if he loses his humor, eh?"

"Or his bloated sense of self." Jathil snorted and smacked his shoulder.

"Are you injured?" Kael eyed him.

"No, just tired from fighting the current." Jaeger backed up against the stone wall and sat down. "I—uh—I just need to rest a bit, and then I vill be back to normal soon enough."

Kael nodded and turned to Vian and Tariq. "We need a fire and crushed *maeta* leaves, if you have any more left."

Tariq opened his pack and dug out the tin. "It's almost gone, but there might just be enough for Ayianna's arm." His gaze shifted to Kael's shoulder. "How about you?"

"Never mind me." Kael took the tin from Tariq.

"I'll get the fire going." Vian started gathering driftwood.

"Right, prince, I'd like to see you try." Jathil joined him, and Jaeger's hoarse laughter filled the cave.

Kael sighed. Perhaps Osaryn was listening after all. He glanced about for Ayianna. She had settled against the wall near the opening, her eyes closed, her skin a faint green. His stomach twisted.

Please, let us make it to Ganya in time!

37

AYIANNA SLUMPED AGAINST the cave's wall. The rain had lessened but continued to fall. She cradled her arm in her lap and embraced the pain pulsating beneath the tight makeshift bandages. Still, the throbbing of the cursed wound vied for attention. She closed her eyes. The curse was winning, and Kael knew it.

Footsteps announced Jathil's approach. Kael had insisted she stay behind with Ayianna, despite the highlander's protest.

"The cave goes way back." Jathil sat next to Ayianna and laid her staff on the ground.

Ayianna glanced over at her. "Did you find more wood?"

"Some, but I did find this." She handed Ayianna a strip of some sort of material. It was translucent like the thin vellum her father had used to copy intricate designs from old scrolls. She rubbed it between her fingers. The texture was bumpy and waxy.

"It's snakeskin."

Ayianna arched her brows and handed it back to Jathil. "Will it burn?"

"Don't know, but I only cut a piece off. This thing is huge. I followed it about twenty feet in and decided I didn't want to meet it in the dark of its home."

"Do you think it's still here?"

"If it isn't, it might be soon with the wet season upon us."

"That's a lovely thought." Ayianna gazed outside. The rain had turned to a drizzle, and a damp breeze blew in through the cave's entrance. She shivered. "Will this rain ever give up?"

"Not likely. We're still too close to the jungle. If we're lucky we might see a little sun each day, once the initial storm blows over. When we reach the cliffs, we will have plenty of sun."

"So, I take it we'll be hiking in the rain?"

"Yes."

Ayianna watched the light rain swirl with the wind. She sat in silence for a while, wishing she could fall asleep.

"So how are you holding up?"

Was it that obvious? Ayianna looked at her. Her bright silver eyes shimmered in the meeting of light and dark. Concern flickered in their depths. Ayianna's stomach clenched. "I'm just tired."

"Right." Jathil drew her knees up and rested her arms around them. "I can spot a lie when I see one."

"What do you expect?" Ayianna leaned away and cocked her head. *I am not like you. I am weak and I am cursed. What more do you want from me?* She took a deep breath and pushed it out through her nose. "I *am* tired. We've been hiking for months across deserts, mountains, and jungles. I've lost everyone and everything I hold dear. How do you think I am holding up?"

"If you don't snap out of this self-pity, loathing, feeling all sorry for yourself, then you're not going to overcome this curse." Jathil threw her hands into the air. "I tell you, you and Kael both."

"Curse?" Ayianna straightened. "What do you know about my curse?"

"I . . ." Jathil averted her eyes. "Kael told me."

"He what?"

"He told everyone . . . last night, while you were sleeping."

"The-the pig! How could he?" Ayianna fell back against the wall, tears stinging her eyes. "Why?"

Jathil moved closer. "Calm down. Tariq confronted him last night about his erratic behavior of late, and Kael told us about the urgency of getting you to the fountain of healing waters."

"And what did he say if we don't make it?" she demanded. "That I would turn into some hideous creature and kill everyone?"

"No-o-o." Jathil's eyes narrowed. "He said that you'd die if you didn't get there in time."

Ayianna buried her face in her knees. So, he hadn't told them that part. What comfort she might have received from that eluded her. Why'd she have to say that? Would Jathil think less of her now? She felt Jathil's hand on her shoulder as Jathil pulled her close.

"Did you think you couldn't trust us with this? Doesn't the Thar'ryn say something about sharing burdens, two manage better than one?"

"I thought you didn't believe in the Shadow God."

"I didn't say I didn't, but the point here is that you do."

Did she? Ayianna leaned into Jathil's side. The pain dulled her mind. She was too tired to think about grandiose ideas like the Shadow God, the Book of Thar'ryn, and the Sacred Pearl. Things her father embraced, but her mother had turned her back on. She had always accepted her father's teachings. They had seemed true at the time, but what about now?

The Sorceress had plunged her world into chaos. For what? A corrupted dagger that could give mortals immortality. Wasn't that what Saeed had said? Her father had known but kept it secret. Yet, he had taught her and her brother about Osaryn, the

Shadow God of the guardians. It was all connected, but how? If only she had paid more attention to her father's teachings.

Her arm throbbed, but it was nothing compared to the fire burning in her veins. Where was the numbness that had enveloped her body before? Had the transformation begun? Tears stung her eyes and pressure built inside her skull. *Osaryn, is this it then? Am I to die cursed?*

Ayianna straightened and wrapped her arms around her waist. "If we don't make it to Ganya in time, will you kill me?"

Jathil's brows jerked up. "No."

"Someone has to."

"Kael will make sure you make it."

"But if we don't and I turn into a harpy, I need to know . . ." The words stuck in her throat, and she swallowed back the rise of tears. Why couldn't she be strong like Jathil and not feel sorry for herself? A damp breeze pushed through the opening of the cave and brushed across her face. She plucked at the bindings on her arm and added, "Just in case Kael can't."

"If it comes to that." Jathil leaned back, placed one ankle atop the other, and crossed her arms. "I have seen the way Kael looks at you. There is raw love in the depths of his eyes. He will do what he needs to, no matter what."

Ayianna shook her head. "He's only fulfilling an oath he made to my brother."

"People are obligated to fulfill oaths, not fall in love." A sad smile crossed Jathil's lips. "Just give him some time."

"For what?"

"He'll recognize the love he has for you."

"Wait a minute—this is coming from someone who rejects the very notion of marriage and love, and now you are trying to tell me otherwise?"

Jathil grabbed her staff from the ground and slid her hand along the polished wood. "I saw love like this once, and I'm telling you, don't cast it aside."

"Your betrothed?"

"We don't betroth one to another." Jathil shifted again and placed her left ankle atop the other.

Ayianna kept her eyes on the worn toe of her boots, waiting, hoping she'd continued, but the silence lengthened.

"In Arashel," Jathil finally said, "we have traditions I don't expect you to understand. A princess does not choose her mate, but the games do. A game to the death. In the final round, two remained. One who I had desired to win until I saw him for who he really was. And another who showed me what true love really could be. I didn't recognize it right away, but it had been in his eyes, his actions. He respected me." Jathil rolled the staff between her fingers. "That is the look I see in Kael's eyes."

Could Ayianna believe her? Should she? But the words had already wormed their way into her soul and taken root.

"So, what happened to him?"

"Mathani killed him." Jathil dropped the end of her staff on the ground and the sound ricocheted around them. "And now Mathani waits for me to return so he may seize me and the throne. That is why I cannot go back to Arashel."

"But your father, surely, he would listen to you."

"The charges remain. I may have been wrongly accused of killing a man—it's complicated—but my actions caused a tavern to burn. That offence alone would demand I lose my right hand." Jathil lifted her hand and turned it over. "A maimed bride is still a king's bride. Mathani could still impose the punishments for my crimes and demand the throne. I will not give it to him." Jathil clenched her fist and dropped it over her heart.

The entrance to the cave exploded with activity as the men burst inside, spraying water everywhere. Ayianna scrambled out of the way and mopped the rain from her face. The men tore off their cloaks and shook them out near the entrance.

"It's the only way." Tariq ran his fingers through his dark curls.

"It's absurd, that's what it is." Vian stomped his feet and tossed his cloak to the side.

"What are you talking about?" Ayianna's gaze darted from one person to the next, lingering on Kael.

He was somber and his jaw set. He had removed the bandages from his chest. Red, swollen whelps, where the gloru'bor had scratched him, stretched from his shoulder to the edge of his ribs. It had healed somewhat, but she didn't think they were supposed to be that red.

"What did you all find out?"

"We are smack dab in the middle of a giant river." Vian placed his hands on his head. "Can you believe our luck?"

"We knew that." Tariq rummaged through his pack. "We're going to have to build a raft to get off this island."

Ayianna took a deep breath. "How long do you think that will take?"

"A day." Kael removed a ball of sinew from his pack and pulled on a loose string, testing its strength. "If we get started right now." He looked up at her. "How's your arm?"

Or did he really mean the curse? "Well enough," she said. "I think I can help with something."

Kael paused. "If you ladies can gather vines, we'll need plenty to bind the wood together."

"How about snakeskin?" Jathil winked at Ayianna and held up the piece she had cut.

Vian choked out a laugh. "Funny, but no."

"Too fragile." Kael eyed the skin. "Where'd you get that?"

"I wasn't serious." Jathil jerked her thumb toward the back of the cave. "There's plenty, if you could find a use for it. Hopefully, we will be long gone before it returns."

"Well, what are we waiting for?" Vian sidestepped Jathil and made his way toward the entrance.

"We only have one axe—Jaeger's." Tariq shoved a dagger back into its sheath and hung it from his belt. "But while he's chopping down the wood, we will remove any branches or knots. We'll work as quickly as we can." He plopped his pack against the wall and ducked out of the cave.

Ayianna cringed. Hopefully, the dryads would forgive them.

"At least it's warm out." Vian followed Tariq outside.

She shivered. It didn't feel warm to her.

38

THE SLENDER VINE slipped over the smooth trees as Kael laced it through the logs and tied it as tight as he could. He wiped the water from his face and grabbed another vine, his sinew long since gone. Hopefully, he wouldn't have to restring his bow for a while.

"Here are some more vines." Ayianna and Jathil dumped their armloads of green twisting vines at his side.

"Hey, I need some." Vian glanced up from his work. Droplets of rain slid off his red curls and disappeared into a full beard framing his jaw. With his beard and curls all bushy and grown out, he looked a lot like Tariq. And maybe he even seemed more mature, if Kael could believe that.

Jathil scooped up a handful of the vines and took them over to Vian. "How's it coming?"

"Slow." Vian stretched his arms over his head and sighed. "Once evening is upon us, we are going to have to stop."

"I've got my sphere," Kael interjected. "It will give us enough light to continue."

Vian groaned and yanked one of the vines from the pile.

"How much bigger does the raft need to be?" Jathil strode along the ten logs lined up between Kael and Vian.

"We're making two." Kael tightened the vine knot before picking up another vine.

"Two?"

"It'll be easier that way."

"How so?"

"Trust me, it will." Kael straightened. His back and shoulder burned, which added to the distraction of his stomach's grumbling.

"No need to get ornery about it." Jathil planted her hands on her hips. "I was only wondering. What do you want us to do now?"

"Go check on Tariq and Jaeger. They're on the other side."

"I'll go." Jathil grabbed a bundle of the vines. "I'm certain Ayianna would like to discuss some things with you."

Ayianna stood wide-eyed for a moment as a faint color crept into her cheeks. "Um, what do you want me to do?" She dropped to her knees in the dirt next to him. Her long braid fell forward and smacked his arm. She pushed it back and picked up a vine, studying the making of the raft in front of her.

"What was that all about?" Kael pushed the vine under the wood.

"Well, I—we've been talking." Ayianna pushed against the log as he secured it. "You told everyone about the curse."

Kael glanced up. She didn't look at him as she untangled the vines. Her movements were jerky and slow. He finished tying the knot. "Are you angry with me?"

"I was, but I understand why you did it." She looked at him. The sparkle in her eyes was gone. "I want to thank you for . . ." She turned away, and her movement exposed the festering wound on her neck. "For everything. My brother must have been proud to call you his friend, and I'm sure he'd see that you've done the best you could and release you from your oath."

He reached over and grabbed her arm. "Don't. I'll not have you talking like this. We're leaving as soon as we're finished, and we're going to reach Ganya in time."

Ayianna shook her head. "I feel it. First it burned, the pain . . . but the cold is coming. There's no telling how much time I have left. I just want—"

"Stop talking like that." Kael's heart jumped into his throat. "You'll be fine. We're almost finished. Look, we only need a few more logs, and then we'll be off. Traveling by river will be a lot quicker than hiking."

Ayianna nodded. She looked up into the sky. "It's getting dark."

"Of course, evening is near."

But not that near. Even the low-hanging clouds could not mask the slow decline of the midafternoon sun that much. Was this the start of her demise?

Kael clenched his jaw and slipped another vine between the logs. "Why don't you bring me the sphere?"

"Sure, anything I can do to help." Ayianna stood and brushed off her knees. "Then I'll check on Tariq and the others."

She disappeared into the mist, and Kael felt a splatter of rain on his face. He looked up. *Please no more rain.* Distant thunder answered his plea.

"How much time do you think she has?" Vian asked.

The clouds burst open for the hundredth time and poured out their warm tears, drenching Kael as he tried to tie another knot.

He frowned at the prince. "Not much."

39

"TIME TO GO!" Tariq hollered from outside the cave. "The rafts are ready and waiting for our departure."

Kael buckled his sword belt on. He shouldn't need it, but he didn't want to chance knocking it into the waters. The sphere's light lit the dirt and rock walls. Twisted roots protruded like fingers of the dead grasping for their next victim.

"Jathil, Ayianna, time to wake up." Vian nudged Jathil's leg with his foot.

Jathil sprung from the ground. The next moment, the edge of her knife pressed against his throat.

"Whoa!" Vian stumbled back and raised his hands.

She recoiled. "Don't wake me like that again."

"Right. I like to keep my head attached, thank you very much." Vian rubbed his neck and tried to pull his fingers through the matted curls frizzing around his face.

Jathil shoved the knife back into her belt and stretched for a moment. "What time is it?"

"Early dawn," Vian said. "The rafts are loaded. You're riding with Kael and Ayianna, and I'm riding with Tariq and Jaeger."

"Great." Jathil scooped up her belongings. "A horrid dip in the river is all I need."

Tariq ducked in and grabbed his pack. He scanned the cave, his eyes bright and his jaw set. He was more awake than anyone else, considering they had worked long into the night. "Ready?"

Kael nodded. Except Ayianna had yet to wake. Fear's icy grip clutched his chest, but he thrust it aside. He had to focus and be prepared to do what needed to be done. But could he? How could Osaryn ask this of him? He took a deep breath and bent down next to her.

"Ayianna?" He grabbed her shoulder and turned her toward him.

Wisps of green webbing tainted her skin. Dread crept over him. It was Nganjo all over again, but this time there would be no Darin to save them. He clenched his jaw. No, they still had time. Unless the harpy lord's venom worked quicker this time. He touched her forehead. She was burning up.

"Ayianna, can you hear me?"

She moaned and her eyelids fluttered. "Kael?"

Tariq crouched next to him. He checked her pulse and opened her eyes. "She's running a fever. We must hurry. Jathil, you'll need to keep her cool with water from the river." He handed Jathil a piece of Kael's old tunic.

Kael lifted Ayianna from the ground and shoved the rising panic deeper into his gut. Her head lolled to the side, and he shifted her until her cheek rested against his chest, her skin hot. He looked at Vian. "Get the blankets and lay them atop the raft."

Vian nodded and dashed out of the cave.

Kael followed, carefully ducking through the dangling roots at the cave's entrance and making his way down to the riverbank.

Vian shook out the blankets and folded them to create a cushion. He stepped aside, concern etched across his face and eyes, but he didn't say anything.

Kael positioned Ayianna atop the blankets, the raft bobbing haphazardly in the water. The wood and vines had better hold together, at least until they reached the falls. After that, they'd have to figure out something different. He grabbed the pole to shove off, but Tariq's hand was on his.

"Wait, we need to pray for her."

"We don't have time for this."

"When will you let go of the bitterness?" Tariq stepped aboard the raft, and it rocked back and forth. He placed his hands on Ayianna's head and prayed. Kael clenched his jaw. *Forgive me, Osaryn, I shouldn't be angry, but I am. I'm angry with me, with you, the whole world.* Kael sighed and blinked tears from his eyes. *I can't keep doing this.*

Then let it go and trust me.

Kael started. *Let what go?*

Everything . . . including her.

Tariq gripped Kael's shoulder and stepped onto the shore.

Kael steadied the raft, placed the pole into the riverbank, and shoved off. He glanced over at Ayianna.

Jathil stooped over her like a mother hen, holding a cloak above her face as the sky blessed them with another bout of rain.

The distant bank sped past. How far had they gone? The clouds had thinned and perhaps the faintest of blue rimmed the western horizon where the water met the sky. The other raft raced on ahead. Vian and Jaeger lay sleeping while Tariq sat with the pole across his lap.

"Don't you think we should move a little closer to the riverbank?" Kael hollered.

Tariq turned around. "We'll risk crashing into rocks. We'll have to wait till we're much closer to the falls."

"How close is too close?" Jathil glanced up at Kael and shifted her legs under her. "We won't be able to pull away from the current if we get too close."

"That's what concerns me." Kael took a deep breath and blew the air threw his nose. "How's she doing?"

Jathil laid her hand across Ayianna's forehead. "Her skin is cold and clammy now."

"Keep talking to her. Maybe that will help."

"I've run out of things to say. Why don't you talk to her? I'm sure she'd much rather hear your voice than mine."

"Me? What would I say?"

"I'm sure you could think of something. Like . . . I don't know—about her family, Zurial, your feelings for her." Jathil's silver eyes bore into him.

He had to deny it, but the words stuck in his throat. He didn't, couldn't. He had made a vow. Surely, Osaryn held him to it. He had not made it rashly. Temporary feelings were the last thing he needed. And even if he had feelings, he would deny them. He was going to be a guardian or die in his service to Nälu. He tore his gaze from hers. "You're mistaken."

"Why don't we trade places for a while? My legs are near cramping." Jathil stretched her arms above her head.

"And risk tipping the raft? I don't think so."

"I'm sure we could manage. Besides you don't want to be all stiff-legged when it comes to swimming."

"Hopefully it won't come to that."

"Ha, not if Tariq has his way." Jathil stood, balancing with ease on the bobbing raft. "Come on."

Kael hesitated. It was the last place he wanted to be. Or was it? He had to be strong, in case they were too late. Ready to end her misery. No, he wouldn't think like that! But he had to. It was his responsibility, his fault. How could she ever forgive him? Her still form beckoned him. He needed to comfort her. But how?

He hated being conflicted. But the burning in his shoulders and lower back persuaded him to take the offer. He handed the pole over to Jathil and inched toward Ayianna as Jathil made her way to the back of the raft.

He brushed Ayianna's cheek with his finger. *I do not have feelings for her, at least not the way she meant it. More like a sister. Really . . .*

He reached out to touch her mind, afraid of what he might find. Had the transformation already begun? At first, he found only layers and layers of numbed grief and death. He pushed his thoughts deeper. He could encourage her with his thoughts, his willpower—elves had done it before. He could will her to live.

Use your heart.

Kael flinched. *My heart? The most troubling and afflicted thing that would lead someone astray. She doesn't need that.*

It does not have to be like that.

Since when did you start talking to me?

I have always spoken. You have not always listened.

Kael took a deep breath. He didn't want to open his heart. He had locked it away for a reason. But if it would save her . . . *Forgive me, Osaryn. Help me let go.*

He took Ayianna's hand in his. So lifeless and cold . . . He closed his eyes and focused his attention on her. He saw her in his mind's eye. Her dark hair flowed around the green dress she wore at the Bonzapur's wedding feast. Her shy smile and sparkle in her eye drew him in. They had danced. He couldn't, shouldn't. But a kaleidoscope of feelings erupted within him and poured through him and into Ayianna.

He sought her soul, delving deeper into her unconscious form. He could feel the scathing poison searing through her veins. Still, he pushed deeper, seeking where the curse had yet to touch, and there he found the slightest glimmer of hope. He fought the urge to cry and begged her to live.

"Kael!"

The voice jolted him and jerked him away. No, he wanted to stay longer, to keep the connection, but it slipped like water through his fingers.

"Kael!" Jathil hit him with the pole. "The falls! Move it!"

"What?" An ominous rumble thundered in his ears, but he couldn't tear his gaze from Ayianna. Spidery lines of green masked her neck and stretched to her face. He would lose her by evening if they didn't make it to Ganya. They didn't have time to descend a cliff. *Osaryn, please!*

"We're nearing the falls. What were you doing anyway?"

"Praying." Kael straightened, but Ayianna's hand wouldn't let him go.

"Ayianna?"

If they made it to the banks, they'd still have to find a way down to the sea. They wouldn't make it. Time was against them. The falls grew closer and louder. Her eyelids fluttered and her mouth moved.

Kael leaned forward.

"Kael . . . shell . . . use   shell . . ." Ayianna whispered. "Nerissa said . . . use shell."

"What do you mean? What shell?" Kael shook her gently, but she only mumbled the same phrase. "Jathil, do you know anything about a shell?"

"I don't know, but you better get over here and start pushing us to shore. Can't you hear the falls?"

Of course, he heard the falls. He wasn't deaf. He pried her hand from his and grabbed Ayianna's knapsack, looking for a shell of some sort.

"What are you doing back there?" Tariq's voice hollered above the growing roar of the falls. "You're going to go over the falls!"

Kael kept digging until he found a shell. He held it up.

Jathil frowned. "What are you going to do with that?"

"Tell Tariq we're going over."

"Are you serious?"

Kael put the shell to his lips and blew, long and hard. The eerie moan rose above him but was swallowed up by the rushing water. He blew a couple of more times. Each time the raft sped closer to the falls.

Ahead the river broke away, and the blue sky stretched beyond. In the distance, a shadowy island protruded from the sea like a giant turtle. That couldn't be Ganya, could it? Or was that Moruya? He knelt and scooped Ayianna into his arms.

She clung to him, her nails digging into his skin. At least, he hoped they were her nails.

"Are you insane?" Jathil screamed as she scrambled to secure her belongings.

"It's the only way." Kael balanced on the raft and prepared to jump.

"You know cats don't like water!"

He glanced at Jathil. "She's dying."

"Okay, maybe I can deal with a little water." Jathil stood next to him and took a deep breath.

A shadow swept over him, bringing a blast of wind with it.

"Dragon!" Tariq cried out.

The beast circled above and dove toward them. Where did he come from? No. Desmond would not win. They'd jump before the dragon reached them. They had to.

Kael dropped Ayianna's legs and crushed her against his chest, her skin ice next to his, but her heart raced. She was dead weight. If she hit the water wrong, she'd die. Would he be able to hold her tight enough against the impact?

"Keep your legs straight, feet first!" Kael hollered.

Could Tariq and Vian hear him? They stood, their faces to the sky, watching the dragon descend on them.

"We can do this," he whispered. *Please Osaryn!*

Ahead, the other raft approached the falls, and then they were gone.

A sick feeling hit his stomach. What if he were wrong? He brought the shell to his lips and continued to blow. Would the merfolk even hear the shell?

The dragon swooped toward them, but the edge was upon them.

He clasped Ayianna and jumped.

The dragon's scaly foot collided with them, jarring Ayianna from his arms. No! He scrambled to regain his grip, but the talons enclosed around her, plucking her out of the air, and away from him.

Down, he plummeted, the air tearing away his breath.

White mist billowed upward and swallowed Jathil. Tariq and Vian were gone. The mist filled his vision, and he braced for impact.

He slammed into the sea feet first. The froth of bubbles and water engulfed him. The falls pummeled him, shoving him down. He kicked but could not propel himself.

Something gripped him around the waist and wrenched him deeper. He groped for what held him—a thick, slimy appendage. The thing was no merfolk!

To what death had he condemned his friends?

He struck it, but it only tightened its grip. Blurred shadows surrounded him and jostled something over his face and into his mouth. Salt water gushed over his tongue.

He choked. He shook his head and tried to spit the object from his mouth but couldn't. His lungs burned, begging for release. Was this how it would end? *Osaryn!*

More appendages probed him. He thrashed and squirmed, but it was no use. Strong bindings tightened around his body and hauled him backward. The current flowed over him and clawed through his hair.

His lungs screamed. Death beckoned him like a warm blanket on a wintery night, dulling the edges of his mind. Failure or not, he had done his best. There was nothing but to surrender.

He relaxed and released his breath. But instead of salt water, damp air rushed into his lungs.

40

KAEL JERKED AWAKE, his heart pounding in his ears. Pale blue light flooded his eyes, and a warm cushion hugged his back and legs. Where was he? What happened? He took a deep breath and blew it out through his nose. He'd have to calm his heart, or he wouldn't be able to hear anything.

Slowly his senses returned to him, and he began to process what had happened. The flood, the river, the raft . . . they had gone over the falls . . . the dragon! Ayianna!

He leapt from the squishy cot. The floor was smooth and cool to his feet. He glanced down. His clothes had been replaced with a silver skirt of sorts that hung just above his knees. A light painted the small room blue, but he couldn't see its source. A gentle swishing hum seemed to come from without. He touched the walls, and they shimmered and wavered. He searched for a door but found none.

"You're awake."

Kael spun around and recoiled at the sight of Tariq's bodiless head floating against the wall. Tariq smiled and pushed the rest of his body into the room.

"What the . . ." Kael hesitated. "Are we dead?"

Tariq laughed, and the room vibrated with the sound of his voice. "No, these are the lower levels of the infirmary. We're in Ganya. We made it, Kael. We made it!" Tariq grasped him in a hug and shook him.

"Ayianna?"

"She is fine."

"How? What happened? The dragon . . ." Kael rubbed his arms as if he could erase the memory.

Tariq's grin widened. "It was Nerissa's dragon. She had been searching for us and heard the horn—the shell."

Relief flooded Kael. The dragon—not Desmond's, but Nerissa's! How different everything could have been if only he had known.

"So, Ayianna is well?"

Tariq nodded.

"What about Jathil? And Jaeger and Vian?"

"Jaeger, as you know, is fine." Tariq squared his shoulders and raised his eyebrows, giving his best impression of the stocky dwarf. "It vould take more than a vaterfall to do me in."

Kael grinned and smacked Tariq's arm. "And what about Vian?"

"Well." Tariq's smile fell. "He broke his arm, but he'll be fine."

"Oh?" Kael cringed. How could he continue the quest with a broken arm?

"But with the healing waters and the merfolk's attention, he's on the mend." Tariq strode over to the side of the room as if looking at something. He faced Kael. "So . . . what do you think of our new attire?" He slapped his hip and smiled.

Kael shook his head. "I prefer my own, thank you. How's Jathil?'

"She's with Nevin Nerissa, waiting for us. Nerissa would like to meet with us as soon as possible."

"I'd like to see Ayianna first, and the others." Kael glanced down at his silver skirt. "Actually, I'd rather get dressed first."

"What? You don't like it?"

Kael snorted. "You might be comfortable walking around half-nude, but I am not."

"I can't help you there, but I can take you to see Ayianna. She was up in the infirmary with the others." Tariq slid his hand along the wall and pressed. "The trick is to remember which way you came in."

"What would happen otherwise?"

"Oh, you'd find yourself hundreds of feet underwater." Tariq pushed through the shimmering material and disappeared.

Kael touched the wall and slowly applied pressure. His hand went through. The strange material hugged his arm. He asserted more force, and the material washed over him like a cold bath. The next moment, he was staring into Tariq's smiling face.

"Refreshing, isn't it?"

"What is that?"

"Amazing, these Kaleki." Tariq led Kael down a corridor. "You could say it's a giant bubble of sorts."

"Are all the rooms like this?"

"No."

Kael halted as he realized he could see through the corridor's walls. He stared at the spiraling turrets of the underwater city. Muted light rippled over the stonework and sea life.

"Beautiful, isn't it?" Tariq whispered.

Kael nodded.

Mermen and merwomen swam in and out of its grand arched doorways, busy with whatever life the merfolk had underwater. Little merchildren played tag among the waving seaweed gardens. Schools of colorful fish flitted about in a hurry. Other larger creatures, like sea turtles, floated lazily past him without a glance in his direction. Everything undulated in a unique underwater dance. The quiet hum and flow were strangely calming. He relaxed and the tension in his shoulders eased.

Tariq took off down the corridor, his steps barely making a sound. Kael followed slowly, unable to look away until they reached a staircase carved out of stone. It swirled upward toward the surface. Kael passed several floors with corridors branching off like the one he had just left. The higher he climbed, the brighter the lighting became, the more his eyes hurt.

Kael emerged into the bright day, blinking and leaving behind the muted colors and peaceful hum. The afternoon sun blazed overhead. Before him, the upper level of the infirmary sprawled over an inlet. Tall pillars spiraled upward into dome-shaped buildings. The outlying ones featured wide windows open to the elements. Magnificent gardens with flowering trees and heady blooms lay to the left and to the right. The sea shimmered and pulsed with the breeze.

Tariq continued over a bridge leading to what appeared to be an inner courtyard. He spoke with a mermaid dressed in a short silver robe, and she shook her head. He faced Kael.

"She hasn't seen Ayianna, but Jaeger is in the courtyard. I'll go get Vian." Tariq plucked a quill, dipped it, and signed something. "We will meet Nerissa for lunch."

Kael nodded. He scanned the courtyard. At the sight of Jaeger perched on the edge of a stone railing, excitement coursed through him. He couldn't believe it. They had all survived. *Thank you, Osaryn!*

Kael strode around the ferns and flowering bushes. "Jaeger!"

Jaeger turned his head toward him, and a grin split his red-blond beard. He jumped down from the railing and grasped Kael in a hug. "It vould take more than a vaterfall, my friend."

"I know." Kael chuckled.

"Kvamiig is vatching out for us, he is." Jaeger rubbed his eyebrow. "Vhat do you call him? The Shadow God of the guardians? Osaryn, yes?"

Kael's throat tightened. Despite his failings, Osaryn was watching out for them. But it wasn't about him and what he could do, was it?

"Vhat are ve going to do next?"

"Get the healing water, then it's off to Moruya Island for the tree root. From there, we'll head back to Kha Vaaro Mountains for the silver pinecone. Do you still want to travel with us?"

Jaeger nodded and ran his fingers over the braid of blond hair attached to his belt. "I must find my father."

"If you don't mind me asking, why do you wear a braid on your belt?"

"It is my mother's." Jaeger plucked an end and lifted it.

"A good luck talisman?"

Jaeger snorted. "You do not know much about the Stozic d'arves, do you? Ve do not part so easily vith our hair. Shearing is punishment . . . cut locks, a broken covenant. But my mother, *dukv,* her story is something special, I tell you."

"Special indeed, since Hadrian is a guardian."

"*Dukv*, and this here braid is . . . *tahrl na sromic* . . . like a message for my father." Jaeger squared his shoulders. "I vill give it to my father vhen I see him."

Perhaps Kael didn't understand the significance of a braid of hair to dwarves, but he could not mistake the importance it carried to Jaeger, nor his father, once he received it. And what could he say in turn? Words seemed too trivial. Still, he clasped Jaeger's shoulder. "May it go well with you."

"Thank you." Jaeger brought his right fist over his heart. "So vhen are ve going to eat? I am famished."

"Soon." Kael smiled and dropped his hand. "Have you seen Ayianna?"

"She vas headed to the gardens the last time I saw her."

"Thanks. I'll be back."

"Bah, do not vorry about me none. Go see your pretty girl."

"She is not my girl."

Jaeger chuckled and climbed atop the stone railing again. "Vhatever you say. I vill be here, vaiting on Vian and Tariq, unless my need for food overcomes me."

But Kael was already over the bridge, Jaeger's words chasing him through the courtyard.

Rich, floral smells mingled with the fragrant trees and the salty sea air. The smooth path before him wound through strange plants with vibrant blooms. Twisting vines hung everywhere, dotted with tiny red star-shaped flowers. He turned a corner and halted.

Ayianna stood amidst purple flowering trees. Their limbs drooped and brushed the grass with their delicate blooms. Her silver robe flowed from her shoulders to her knees. A small belt pulled the fabric around her waist and accentuated her curves.

Kael's breath caught. A desire to run to her and hold her overwhelmed him. He took a deep breath.

Ayianna looked up, and a smile brightened her face. The golden glow of her skin had returned. The spidery webbing was gone. But best of all, the sparkle was back in her eyes.

Before he could respond, Ayianna was in his arms, hugging him. And for the first time in many years, peace filled the hollow ache in his soul. For a moment, all was well. If only he could bury himself in that quiet exchange, he would die fulfilled. The need to kiss her ignited within him. He quickly released her and stepped back.

Questions flitted across her eyes, and then her face flushed. She pulled at the robe's short hem. Her dark hair poured forward and hung loose to her waist. "Your scars have healed well, haven't they?"

"Ah—yeah, they have." Kael rolled his shoulder. Felt as good as new.

"Did you hear? Have you spoken with Nerissa yet? They've found my mother!" Ayianna's face glowed like the sun. "Hadrian is taking her to Kvazkhun where the dwarves will look after her."

"That is great news." Her smile was contagious. And why not? Things were looking up for once. He held out his arm. "Come on, the others are waiting for us."

Ayianna slid her hand into the crook of his elbow, and they walked back to the infirmary. Warmth blossomed in his chest. Was this what hope felt like? He couldn't hide the silly grin on his face if he tried. It felt good to have her near and well again.

41

KAEL AND AYIANNA followed the others to the Man'nohi Pwoka Inn. Mountains sculpted into spiraling turrets rose around him and disappeared into the waters below. The rocky island curved, creating a bay for the Kaleki's import and export docks, but the foreign ships didn't reach this far into the heart of the mountains. He stepped through the carved arches leading to the inn.

Merfolk dressed in silver robes and wraps reclined at tables, conversing in low, fluid tones. An elderly woman wobbled over to a table in the back, wearing nothing but a silver wrap around her hips. Kael averted his eyes. Where was Nerissa?

A merman strolled toward him. A well-formed ridge circled his head, much more defined than Nerissa's. He touched his fingers to his lips. "Can I help you?"

Tariq returned the greeting. "We are looking for Nevin Nerissa."

"Yes, she is waiting for you." The man motioned with his arm. "Please follow me."

Kael felt eyes scouring him and his companions, but he kept his own focused on the merman's green feathery fins lining his elbows, shoulders, and back.

He led them through archways and up a majestic, winding staircase to the third floor. Kael looked over the edge of the polished granite railing and saw the expanse of the inn below. How he had missed the fountain and gardens he didn't know.

"This way." The merman stood at the end of the corridor and swept a curtain made from tiny seashells aside. The little shells clinked against one another, revealing a doorway big enough for only one person.

Ayianna's hand slid from his arm as she strolled ahead of him. When he entered the room, a breeze brushed his face. Two of the walls were completely gone and the floor dropped off to the sea below with only a curled railing to keep them from falling to their deaths.

"Welcome to Ganya."

Nerissa brushed her fingers to her lips. Deep sorrow radiated from her, but her face revealed nothing. Her eyes, though, were dark like a gathering storm. Her white hair fell in braids past her waist. She wore the typical sleeveless robe he had seen most everyone else wearing. She stood next to a table full of platters. Jathil was there already, sitting by the open window.

"Come eat." Nerissa motioned toward the table. "We have much to discuss."

Kael chose one of the backless chairs away from the railing and sat down. What news did she bring? Why did she mourn? Maybe her grief had nothing to do with them or the news she brought. Not likely. He steeled himself to whatever it might be. Ayianna slid into the seat next to him. Did she sense Nerissa's feelings? She showed no signs if she had.

Vian sat to the right of Ayianna, and Tariq and Jaeger took spots across the table. A tantalizing aroma drifted from the silver dome in front of him. Kael hoped it tasted as good as it smelled.

Nerissa removed the lid from her platter. "The chef's specialty, boiled crab with kelp rolls courtesy of King Pekelo. Allow me to demonstrate the use of your utensils." She held up a pair of slender sticks and arranged them in her fingers. She plucked out a chunk of red and white meat and ate it. "Simple."

"Right." Vian tried to maneuver the sticks with his left hand, but they clattered to the table.

Kael slid the lid off his platter and picked up the ornate sticks next to his dish. He glanced over at Ayianna. She smiled and clicked her sticks together with her fingers. She seemed a natural. He positioned the utensils in his fingers and tried to grab a hunk of meat, but the sticks tumbled into the soup.

After the third time, Kael managed to finally pick up a piece of crab and ate it. The meat was sweet and rich, a perfect contrast, he soon found out, to the bitter kelp. Tariq and Jathil had already finished their bowls and now munched on kelp-wrapped rice and fish. Vian, on the other hand, lifted the sticks as if to throw them over the balcony. Instead, he stabbed a lump of crab and stuffed it into his mouth.

"I am relieved to have found you."

Kael looked up at Nerissa. Her eyes roved from one person to the next but lingered on Tariq before turning her attention to Kael. "How has your journey fared thus far?"

Water swished below, filling the silence. Kael wanted to ask her the same. He shifted in his seat and fiddled with his sticks. Where to begin? "It has been slow and difficult. We've lost Eloith and Desmond, but we've gained some new friends, Jaeger and Jathil."

"Now, Jathil told me how you all met." She cocked her head. "But how did you meet up with a dwarf?"

"Oh, you know, the usual." Vian stabbed another chuck of meat. "In the dungeons of Ta'vazi."

"What were you doing there?" She plucked a kelp roll with her sticks and popped it in her mouth.

"Yes, well, that . . ." Vian swirled the kelp around in his bowl. "We were fighting off some imps when the dwarves rescued us and then threw us in the dungeons. Luckily, Jaeger was sympathetic and helped us escape, even though he had put us there in the first place."

He dropped his sticks into this bowl. "This has been one insufferable journey. First, there were dragons and imps chasing us, oh yeah, no thanks to Jathil, who refused to believe us—we, I mean, Ayianna took down a dragon. Then there were these ghastly hags, the dwarf escapade, and not to forget our time with the jungle natives. I am not sure how Saeed could say the journey is greater than the destination. We'd been dodging the enemy and battling the elements and creatures only to discover we had a traitor in our midst."

"Ah, and that would be Desmond?"

Remorse brewed in Vian's eyes, but his jaw was set firm, determined. A mixture of anger and grief emanated from him. What did the prince think of Desmond now? He had been a close friend—the kind who would become a king's right-hand man. Had that been Desmond's goal all along? Until something better came along. The truth had to hurt.

Kael glanced at Ayianna. She held the sticks against the edge of the bowl. Her face a mask, but hurt, anger, and confusion churned from within her. He should have known, seen it coming.

"Have you found the ingredients?" Nerissa asked.

Kael's attention shifted to Nerissa. "No."

"What? All this time, and you are no closer to achieving the tonic than when you started out?"

"Knowledge must count for something." Tariq plopped one of the kelp-wrapped medallions in his mouth. "We know where the silver pinecone is and that we weren't ready to obtain it. The remaining ingredients are the *kulin maekoha* and the root of the famoruya tree. Their locations are not a mystery to us."

"We were wondering . . ." Kael laid the eating utensils down. "If you could take us to the birthing place of the kulin?"

Nerissa shook her head. "I cannot take you there. It is against the law for a foreigner to enter the sacred pools, but I can go. How much do you need?"

"We need at least a few gallons." Tariq propped his elbows on the table. "Carried back in new waterskins."

"I know how to carry the *kulin maekoha*."

"Of course." Tariq shifted in his seat. "I meant no disrespect."

Kael fingered the platter in front of him, tempted to just pick it up and drink the rest of it. Instead, he picked up the sticks again and propped them between his fingers and thumb. "Also, Ayianna needs a replacement for her vial."

"We have already taken care of that." Nerissa nodded at Ayianna. She turned her stormy eyes on Kael. "I will make arrangements for your transportation to Moruya Island."

"Thank you, Nevin Nerissa." Kael hesitated. Saeed had been easier to talk to. Why was he finding it so difficult to speak with her? "I was also wondering, once we got the roots, could someone transport us back to the mainland?"

"And what do you consider the mainland?"

"Well . . . Nälu. I don't think we could scale those cliffs, and we need to make it back to get the pinecone. If we could borrow a dragon, it would make the journey quicker and easier."

Nerissa tilted her head and leaned forward. "Have you ever ridden a dragon before?"

Kael preferred not to remember his first encounter with a dragon. Of course, clinging to a dragon's scaly foot while struggling with a thief wasn't the same thing as riding one. Still, he'd rather not face weeks in bug-infested jungles, narrow mountain trails, and a scorching desert again. How hard could it be? "No, but the journey back will take us three months or more."

"You do not know what you are requesting." Nerissa slid the eating utensils between her fingers, grabbed a wrapped

319

medallion, and ate it. When she finished, she said, "The dragons only know one tongue, Nihi. Do you know how to speak our tongue?"

Kael shook his head, but Tariq said, "I can, a little."

"They are smarter than a horse, stronger than twenty oxen, and more dangerous than any animal known to Nälu. Would you even know how to handle one?"

Kael clenched his jaw. The small spark of hope he had for a quicker journey darkened. But as Tariq had pointed out earlier, knowledge had to count for something. Perhaps the return trip could be quicker. They could avoid the jungle natives, the dwarves, the hags. He shuddered. Their icy touch still hadn't faded from his soul. But what about Vian? A broken arm would slow them down.

Nerissa sipped from her cup and set it down. "There are only ten or so full-grown males that could make such a distance, and they are preparing for battle. They will leave for Zurial soon. I doubt King Pekelo would allow one to be removed from his squadron."

"If the quest is so important to the success of the Alliance, then why not?"

"Because the king does not see the effect of the curse on the plains people. He thinks the Alliance will win with brute force alone, but there is much more at stake here than battles won or lost. He does not believe a curse could be so strong, to bind the people's will and make a nation turn against another. The Sorceress will use them until the curse destroys them—an entire nation will be wiped out. He will not believe until he sees what we have seen. But I will see what I can do."

She tucked a white braid behind her pointed ear. "I will speak with King Pekelo, but we do not have much time. In a few days, I will accompany them to Zurial, and then you will be on your own again."

"It shouldn't take us but a day to get the roots."

"You underestimate the famoruya tree. Two days minimum."

Kael nodded. He took a drink from the small goblet. The sweet elderberry wine warmed his insides, and he decided it best not to drink too much of that. He cleared his throat. "So how goes the Alliance and the other guardians? I take it Saeed has everyone planning for a war."

Nerissa took a deep breath and looked away. "Yes, we are planning to fight. Many nations have joined us, but a few remain aloof. I suppose I need not name names, for you can guess who."

"Arashel and Ta'vazi," Jathil said quietly, keeping her gaze on the plate before her.

"Yes, and the Pauden and the elves of Striisa Vaar, but that is not the worse of the news I harbor." Nerissa's eyes grew cloudy, and her jaw tightened. Kael leaned forward as she continued. "The Guardian Circle has decided for the moment we will not speak publicly about this yet." Nerissa took a deep breath. "But Nevin Saeed is dead."

"What?" Kael dropped his sticks. "He can't be."

"I do not lie."

Pressure built inside his head, his heart. He stood. "Not now . . . not when Nälu needs him. How could Vituko allow this?"

"Kael." Nerissa tilted her head. "Vituko does not take our choices away from us but rather directs the events and consequences about for his glory and our ultimate good. We must only trust him."

Trust? How can I, Osaryn? You tell me to trust. How am I to do that when you take everything away? Why didn't you just kill me at the falls? Kael took a deep breath and blew it out through his nose. His anger was misdirected. As if Osaryn snapped the silver chords of life himself. *Where is the hope you promised us, Osaryn? The world just keeps getting darker.*

"We will see Saeed again."

"A whole lot of good it does now."

"You have suffered much, Kael, son of Aiden, but Vituko is not done with you."

Kael's face burned. "So, what happened? Who killed him?"

"Unai has betrayed us."

Her words hit him in the chest. "A guardian, his friend?"

"From what we can gather, Saeed was trying to stop Unai from taking the dagger."

Kael slid back into his seat. "What do we do now?"

Nerissa straightened her shoulders. "Everything continues as planned." She pushed her plate aside. "Do you know why the enemy wants the dagger?"

"Yes." Vian swirled the slender sticks in his soup. "To release their so-called goddess from the Underworld."

"But to do that, they will need to sacrifice the marked one."

"Who is that?" Ayianna asked. "Do they have him or her yet?"

"They do not yet have him. A son, born to King Valdamar, chosen by the priestesses at his birth."

Vian's face blanched.

"Then ve have nothing to fear, eh, prince?" Jaeger grinned and slapped the prince on the back.

Vian cringed, favoring his right arm.

Nerissa set her sticks down next to her bowl. "Still, we plan to go to war. We must free the plains people from the curse and eliminate the Sorceress once and for all. So retrieve the ingredients as quickly as you can. Hadrian and I will meet you back in Kvazkhun and help you with the tonic."

"Oh, speaking of Hadrian." Vian leaned forward and was about to continue when Jaeger cleared his throat and kicked him under the table. "Ou—I mean—has he had any luck with Ta'vazi?"

Nerissa shook her head. "The old Alliance will never be again until the nine stones become one. We are not yet in the end times. Still, I would hate to see what will become of Nälu if the Sorceress succeeds."

Kael shuddered to think what that could entail. No doubt Nälu would return to the wicked tyranny of years past. He drained his goblet and felt a fire rage through him. "Is that all, Nevin Nerissa?"

She sighed and nodded.

Kael stood. "Then we must take our leave. We've much to do before tomorrow."

"Yes, I too. May Vituko give you grace and speed. You are our only hope. If you fail, we all fail."

"A darkened hope at that."

42

AYIANNA RUBBED HER toes in the velvet grass. The full moon shone bright over the sculpted peaks of Ganya. Moonlight danced on the waters and bathed the gardens in a silver glow.

The silhouettes of trees drooped and swayed. The rich floral scents drenched the salty breeze as fireflies flitted and sparkled among the closed blooms and glowing moonflowers. Ayianna breathed deeply. Her heart burst with gratitude. Though the journey was far from over, at least her mother was safe! *Thank you, Osaryn!*

"Ayianna?"

The evening couldn't have gotten any better. She turned around and smiled. Kael stood on the glowing pathway. He had changed back into pants and had donned a new shirt.

"Am I disturbing you?" he asked.

"No. I'm just sitting here, thinking, thankful to be alive."

His face clouded. "Aren't we all? Except Saeed."

"Oh." She hadn't meant to lessen Saeed's death. "I'm sorry."

"What are you sorry for? You haven't done anything wrong."

"Well . . ." Ayianna fumbled for a reply. "I'm sorry that you are hurting."

Kael looked out into the night sky.

Ayianna remained quiet, listening to the wind rustle the leaves and the waves lapping at the shoreline.

"I studied under Saeed for several years. He was always there for me, became like a father to me." Kael sighed. "He had asked me to join the Guardian Circle, but of course we hadn't planned on the attack at Dagmar or this quest." He grew quiet again.

Ayianna placed her hand on his arm. He shook his head. "But now, I don't know . . ."

"Well, right now, all we have to worry about is getting those ingredients," she said. "My father once told me that it was like walking in the dark with a small lamp to guide your feet. You can see your feet and the path and all the stuff around you, but you can't see your destination or even the next turn in the road."

The words meant for Kael pricked her heart. Here she was spouting off wisdom as if she knew what she was talking about, but she didn't. Otherwise, she wouldn't have been so fearful of her future. How did she not see it before?

Kael turned and studied her. "You're right. The Thar'ryn says just that, perhaps not so clearly as how your father explained. He served Osaryn, didn't he?"

Ayianna nodded.

"Do you believe in Osaryn?"

She hesitated. She had always been comparing, never really choosing . . . But a warmth of understanding bloomed within. She had already decided, hadn't she? "Yes."

"Really? I had thought you were a follower of the Nuja."

She shook her head. Of that she was for certain. "Mother is, though. I hope after all this is over, she will see the truth."

"Sometimes it is hard to see the truth, hard to believe when things go wrong."

Ayianna nodded.

They lapsed into silence. The waves splashed below them, a sign of the rising tide. Realizing she was still touching his arm, she dropped her hand and strolled toward a drooping tree. Its long limbs brushed the ground as the wind rolling off the bay swept through the garden. She turned back toward Kael.

"I need . . ." She paused. "I'd like to know what happened on the raft, when I was sick."

Kael's brow knitted together. "What do you mean?"

"Well . . ." Ayianna had hoped she wouldn't have to explain it. She leaned against the tree's smooth trunk. "I've never experienced anything like it before. Someone was speaking to me, I think. It was all so dark and numb. Then a bright light pierced the darkness."

Kael stood next to her and crossed his arms. "Maybe you were close to dying and were seeing the light of Zohar. Some say that happens."

"It wasn't just light. It was like an essence of a person . . . their soul maybe. It was like they were trying to communicate to me." Ayianna trailed off. She couldn't say it. What if she was wrong? "I thought maybe it had been you."

Kael leaned closer. "What did you hear?"

"I don't remember words, only feelings."

"What did you feel?" His gaze bore into hers, but she couldn't read him.

She looked away. Had she really felt it? Why couldn't she just say it? "They were strong feelings. Pure, pleading . . . they—"

Kael touched her cheek and turned her face back toward him. Ayianna's breath caught. His eyes reflected those feelings.

His fingers trembled as he slid them under her chin and brought his lips to meet hers.

The kiss sent fire through Ayianna. His arm slipped around her waist and pulled her closer. His heart pounded beneath her fingertips. Energy flowed from him and washed over her. She was back on the raft again, the feelings deeper, more powerful, singing a song with all of creation. Right then, she knew. She would live or die for him. Then his hand slid to her neck.

Searing pain shocked Ayianna out of the euphoria.

Kael released her and stumbled back. Had she screamed?

"I'm sorry." He turned and rubbed his face. "I . . . we should . . . tomorrow comes early."

Then he was gone.

Ayianna sank to the ground and hugged her knees. Her senses returned and her face grew hot. Thousands of questions spilled from her mind, but the warmth of his lips lingered. She squeezed her eyes shut.

Stupid curse.

43

KAEL HALTED AT the top of the stone stairs. Two dragons the size of houses crouched on the cobbled half-circle. Emerald scales streaked with yellow covered the larger of the two and faded into an ivory underbelly. It curved its neck around to inspect the bundles Nerissa was securing to its saddle. It snorted and arched the scarlet crest lining its neck and head. The smaller dragon was a mottled brown and yellow, and its smooth, serpentine head lacked a crest. It scratched at the stones, its claws bigger than Kael's arms.

His stomach twisted into an even tighter knot. Why had he thought this would be a good idea? He took a deep breath and approached Nerissa. She turned around and touched her lips in greeting.

"Did you sleep well?"

"Fine, thank you." Kael stifled a yawn and handed her his bag so she could secure it with the rest of their meager luggage. She didn't need to know the truth or what a fool he had been. He glanced around. "Where is everyone?"

"Finishing the morning meal. Have you not eaten?"

"Don't know if I could." He eyed the dragons again. The green one swung its head around and ogled him with a purple-marbled eye. He stepped back.

"Are you reconsidering your request for dragon transport?"

"No." He crossed his arms. The dragons weren't the cause of his lack of appetite nor his lack of sleep. "Are these the ones we'll use for our journey?"

Nerissa shook her head and scratched the brown dragon's chin. "Her name is Kolua, one of the brood females. She will not be going to Zurial with me. Neither will he." She pointed to the other dragon. "He's too old. We call him Oko, short for *okowo lekikae,* meaning 'old man of the sea'. They will transport you to Moruya, but they cannot journey beyond that."

Kolua turned her neck, so that Nerissa's scratching reached near the top of her head.

"How will we get to Kha Vaaro?"

"King Pekelo has spared one dragon of his fleet. Ol'wa Maewali is getting outfitted for the journey and will join you on the island. Had you gone to breakfast, you might have met Kaemon, his *lekli'wan.* In the common tongue, you could call him rider, master, but *lekli'wan* means more than that. It is a partnership, a friend."

Nerissa tipped her head. "There are shovels and axes for your work. I would suggest scouting the island's eastern shores for a cave of sorts. Less digging for you, and the Pauden hardly ever go there. You should find no trouble."

Kael nodded. "We definitely don't need any more trouble. And the kulin?"

"Already secured in one of Kolua's saddle bags."

Voices and footsteps drifted up to him, and he turned around. Tariq and Jathil bounded up the steps, taking two at a time. Jaeger was close behind, although a bit red in the face. Vian came slower as he and Ayianna chatted. An onslaught of mixed emotions surged through him.

Why did he have to kiss her? He hadn't meant to. Perhaps it had been the elderberry wine and the news of Saeed's death. He had been drowning in sorrow, and for one moment, he had wanted her words to be true. Such emotion had poured from her and washed over him. He had wanted to embrace it, her. But he couldn't. That chapter in his life was over. He had allowed himself to be vulnerable, but not again.

They reached the top, and a chorus of good mornings rang out. Kael returned them, though the morning was anything but good. He avoided eye contact with Ayianna. Still, he could sense her questions. He closed himself off to her and blocked his senses.

Kael chose Oko after Nerissa buckled Ayianna and Jathil into the saddle on Kolua. He climbed up the knotted rope and tied himself to the saddle as tight as he could.

Tariq scaled the dragon's side and sat down behind him. Jaeger scrambled up next and settled into the saddle behind Tariq.

"Ugh, I hope I do not regret this," Jaeger mumbled under his breath.

A hand squeezed Kael's shoulder. "Everything all right?" Tariq asked.

"I'm fine."

"And the sun is the moon, elf." Jaeger grunted. "Ve have crossed half of Nälu together. Ve can tell vhen you are not fine."

Kael peered over his shoulder. "Just because we travel together, does not entitle any of you to my personal affairs."

"Unless your affairs are disturbing everyone else." Tariq tied the rope around his waist. "When you want to discuss it, we're here, but there's no need for you to—"

"I think you should remain behind." Nerissa's interruption brought Kael relief. She boosted Vian up as he pulled himself into the saddle with his good hand.

"I won't hear of it," Vian said. "I can do this."

330

"It is not a question of whether you can or not, but a question of whether you should." Nerissa touched his shoulder. "A broken arm will—"

"I've already made up my mind. You can't persuade me otherwise."

"I see." Nerissa tied Vian into the saddle. "Well, if Moruya Island proves no trouble for you, then have my blessing, but if it does, I want you to return to Ganya. I can make arrangements for you to sail to Zurial with the next ship."

"Thank you kindly, but I will be fine." Vian gave her his most promising smile, and she slid down from the dragon's back.

Kael hoped Vian was right. The Kaleki's healers could work miracles, and his arm would mend sooner than he would otherwise, but maybe the prince should stay behind. He'd only slow things down.

Two thin men strolled toward them. They didn't wear the customary silver wraps Kael had seen around Ganya, instead they wore dark green leather pants laced up the side with brown fringe. Why hadn't he been given pants to wear rather than those scanty wrap-skirts?

Nerissa touched her lips and turned back to Kael and his companions. "These are the *lekli-wans*, they will take you to Moruya and then—"

"Nerissa!" An elderly woman's wrinkled face appeared at the edge of the stone stairway. She paused to catch her breath and then jogged up the rest of the way to the top. She stood, heaving, her breasts jiggling against her navel. Despite the length of white hair falling to her waist, it did not hide her bare chest.

Kael averted his eyes, his face burning. One of the dragon masters drew near his dragon. He mounted with ease and strapped himself in the front. The merman's seat was a good two feet away—too exposed for his liking.

"What is the meaning of this?" The elderly woman finally caught her breath. "The king said . . . I was to find you. But what do I find? You are not to leave until the full moon, and here, I am told, you are at the launching stone. And not a word of it to your family—this is outrageous."

"Nela." Nerissa sighed and turned toward the woman. "I am not leaving today."

"Oh . . ." Nela looked around at the others. "I apologize. You are always coming and going, and then gone for so long. You are not getting any younger, my dear, and we begin to wonder if we will see you again."

Nerissa shook her head. "I will see you tonight for the evening meal. I have work to do."

"Of course, of course." Nela nodded. "But the king wants to see you right away. Something about the aviation squad and a stray dragon sighting. He's not in the most patient mood right now, so you best hurry."

"Thank you." Nerissa turned back to Kael and his companions. "And that is my great niece."

Kael couldn't think of what to say. He really wanted to forget what he saw. He ran his fingers over the leather ridge separating the dragon master from the passengers.

"Um . . ." Vian cleared his throat.

Kael closed his eyes. *Don't go there, Vian, don't go there . . .*

"I was wondering, if you don't mind telling us, why she doesn't wear a robe like everyone else."

Nerissa shrugged. "She is of the older generation, still clinging to traditions."

"Great niece?" Ayianna twisted around in the saddle. "How can that be? She looks older than you."

"The guardian's mantle prolongs life so that we may fulfil our duties properly."

"Yet you are fully clothed. If you don't mind me asking, why the difference?" And Vian had to continue. Did he know no shame?

"I have learned to embrace life and cultures beyond my own. And as trade grew between our nations over the years, most of the Kaleki have grown sensitive to what other cultures deem appropriate. Others, like my niece, prefer the old ways. Now where was I?" Nerissa stepped back as her gaze swept over them. "The masters will drop you off, and Maewali should arrive tomorrow. If you need anything, you have Ayianna's horn." She nodded toward the other dragon. "Oh, and for takeoff, you'll want to lean forward."

Kael swallowed. "Thank you, Nerissa. We shall see you in Kvazkhun in three weeks or less, if all goes well."

She nodded. "May Akonamalihi protect you and guide you." She brought her fingertips to her lips, turned, and disappeared down the steps.

The merman in front of Kael leaned forward. "*Na-koa!*"

The dragon beneath him lurched and stretched out his wings. The claws ground against the stones as they inched closer to the end of the cobblestone half-circle.

Kael glanced over and saw the sparkling green seas far below. He tightened his jaw and closed his eyes.

The dragon jumped.

A garbled yell escaped his throat, and Kael was glad he hadn't eaten that morning as his stomach wedged itself between his ears. The wind pummeled his face, and he gasped for air. A hand on his back shoved him down.

Kael buried his face into the saddle ridge and drew in long, deep breaths. But his heart continued to race. He needed air. Ground. His head was going to explode, he just knew it. Soon the downward plunge leveled off and the pressure elevated, but he wasn't about to lift his head anytime soon. The smell of well-polished leather and the salty tang of the sea filled his nose and relaxed him.

"Look, Kael," Tariq said behind him. "Or you'll miss it."

Kael opened his eyes and slowly straightened. White-capped waves stretched out miles below and around. It didn't seem so bad now. It was like sailing but without the constant bobbing of the ship, just the periodic plunge of the wings propelling them forward.

He shifted in the leather saddle. His bindings held him snug, boosting his confidence. The wind whipped through his hair, and a sense of exhilaration swept through him.

The other dragon sailed next to them. Jathil had her arms out and her face shone with pure joy. Ayianna sat behind Jathil, her eyes closed. A contented smile crossed her lips. Vian, on the other hand, grasped the saddle with his good hand, his face tinged green.

Then Kolua soared to the right and spiraled down toward the sea. Screams floated up from their descent, but then the dragon leveled out and skimmed the waters below.

"Showoff." The wind ripped the dragon master's words past him, and Kael hoped he wouldn't try to outdo that dive.

By midday, a fuzzy shadow rose from the flat seascape—Moruya Island. The waters sped by, and the trees grew larger. The dragons descended. Kael's stomach swam up to his throat, and he gripped the saddle. Were they supposed to lean forward again?

With a mighty thud and jerking, the dragon landed and folded his wings. Kael took a deep breath. He definitely preferred sailing.

Massive red-brown trees towered above him, the girth of the trunk larger than the dragons they rode. Their deep green canopies blotted out the afternoon sun. A blanket of ferns covered the ground and stretched to the rocky eastern shore. Across the sea, the mainland's great cliffs loomed in the distance. The immense expanse of the Keyon River poured over the edge and into the waters below. *How did we survive that?*

"It is safe to dismount," the dragon master said, but he didn't move from his seat.

Kael unbuckled his bindings and tried to climb down using the knotted rope, but his legs refused to support him. He slid off the dragon and landed in a heap on the ground.

"Don't ride much, do you?" Ayianna stood above him. She offered him her hand, but he brushed it aside.

"Not dragons, that's certain." He stood and turned around to untie their packs. He couldn't endure her luring, questioning dark eyes. He clenched his jaw. Why couldn't he have kept his feelings in check? He pulled his pack free, threw it on the ground, and took a deep breath. It wasn't her fault he blundered. At least, he could be more civil. He turned to her, but she had already left.

44

THE WAVES ROLLED into the rocky shore and pooled in holes, leaving behind an assortment of marine life and bugs. Ayianna picked her way over the rounded pebbles and avoided the crabs skittering across the ground. She lifted the hem of the dress the merfolk had given her. The silver layers wrapped across her chest and were gathered by a large triangular belt. It was simple enough, but how she longed for the pants from Bonzapur! The merfolk didn't believe in pants, unless of course, one was a dragon rider-master-whatever they were called.

Ahead, a wall of dirt and roots stretched to the top where the ground evened out and the great trees made their homes. But here, perhaps in the recesses of the tangled roots and clumps of dirt, she would find an opening that would lead them to the famoruya tree's famed roots. Of course, they could always start digging from the top.

Ayianna moved forward and peered into the dark crevices, hoping for a larger entrance. She'd have to hurry if they wanted to start extracting the roots before the tide came in. *I hope the others are having better luck than I am . . .*

"How's it going down there?"

Ayianna started.

Jathil's smiling face hung over the edge of the cliff. "Did I scare you?"

"A little." She took a deep breath and blew it through her nose. "I haven't found anything here."

Jathil leapt from the cliff and landed next to her, still wearing the same leather tunic and pants—just cleaned. How had she managed to keep her own clothes? "Well, you can stop searching, Vian found something farther up the shore. We're going to eat and then probably split into shifts, depending on how it goes."

Ayianna followed Jathil back up to the campsite. The men were already eating and had pulled out the shovels and axes.

"The tide will rise in a few hours," Tariq said through a mouthful of stringy kelp. He chewed some more and then swallowed. "Kael, Jaeger, and I will go down first, make sure everything is safe, and figure out where to start digging. The rest of you will see about setting up shelter for tonight."

Ayianna nodded. At least she wouldn't have to be working with Kael. He sat apart from the others and slid a whetting stone across the blade of an axe. The sharp ring was absorbed by the trees and plant life surrounding them.

She turned away and dug in her knapsack for the kelp roll Nerissa had prepared for them. Kelp, salty fish, and some unknown sea vegetable all rolled up into a compact meal. Ayianna took a bite. Not too bad. The tangle of bitter kelp, a nutty sweetness, and salted fish mingled well together.

The meal was soon finished, and Tariq, Jaeger, and Kael headed for the shoreline, leaving Ayianna and the others to figure out some kind of shelter for the evening.

"We should split up and see what we can find." Vian craned his neck to look at the leafy canopy above. His red curls hung at his jawline and blended into his red-gold beard. He had refused to cut it. It made him appear older, tougher, and more dignified, like a prince should be. What would his father say? Desmond had certainly disapproved of the beard. Maybe that explained why Vian wore it now. Or maybe it was the influence of Jaeger's full beard.

Vian strolled over to a famoruya tree and placed his hand on its ridged trunk, its base so big it could have housed a letinili. The first time she had seen one of the famed elephant-like creatures of the Pauden, she had stood amazed atop the third-floor balcony as it had passed beneath her. Kael had been there. A friend unknown then, but now . . .

"I don't think we should go too far," Jathil said. "We don't need to be running into any of the Pauden."

Ayianna nodded her agreement, but her thoughts returned to Kael. The feel of his hands in her hair, his lips on hers . . . Her stomach flip-flopped as a wave of sparks shot through her insides. She jumped to her feet. "Well, what are we waiting for?"

"You." Jathil cocked her head and studied her for a moment. "Are you feeling well?"

"Yes," Ayianna said rather too quickly. "I was just thinking, that's all . . . about the shelter. We don't want to cut anything down."

"No, I have a tent of sorts from Nerissa, but we need to find someplace to hang it between a few trees far enough apart."

"I don't see the big deal of setting up a shelter when we are only going to be here for two days." Vian faced Jathil. "It's not like we haven't slept out under the stars before."

Jathil shrugged. "If you want to sleep out under the stars, we won't stop you."

"No, no, that's quite all right. I wouldn't mind a little cover from the elements. Besides, it looks like it might rain." He lifted his chin toward the coastline.

Ayianna turned around and frowned. Deep purple clouds loomed on the western horizon. "Let's hope the tent is waterproof."

"I'm checking out the northern shores." Vian turned to leave. "I'll let you know if I find anything."

Jathil waved him off and started in the opposite direction. Ayianna hesitated, and then followed her.

The sun slid behind the dark, amassing clouds, casting the island and sea into purple and red-gold hues. Ayianna and Jathil moved the last bit of their belongings into the makeshift shelter.

The tent stretched between three smaller trees, and its front hung open like sails waiting to be secured. Wooden spikes anchored the walls into the ground, strengthening the flimsy material. Hopefully, it would keep them dry in the oncoming storm. Hearing voices, Ayianna glanced up. Tariq, Jaeger, and Kael emerged from the lengthening shadows, trudging through the waist-deep ferns.

"Did you find it?" she asked.

"Yes." Tariq dropped his axe next to his bag. "But the tide came in before we could actually start chopping away."

"Oh, I hope the dryads don't mind." Ayianna paused. "I wonder what the dryads of the famoruya look like."

"Probably big and red, just like their trees." Kael entered the tent and looked around. He rubbed the edge of the tent's side. "Nice work. Where's Vian?"

"Somewhere out that way." Jathil pointed. "Had to relieve himself. Though, he's been gone an awful long time. Perhaps we should go look for him."

"He'll be fine." Kael picked up his quiver and pulled out an arrow.

"What are you going to do?" Ayianna tried to read his face or sense his familiar aura, but all she met was coldness.

"Hunt."

"Probably best we didn't." Tariq sat down against the base of a tree. "Nerissa said no fires. We don't need the Pauden to get wind of the smoke."

Kael frowned and shoved his arrow back into the quiver. "Then, I guess I'll go for a walk." He strode away as if he couldn't leave camp quick enough. He dodged a tree and disappeared.

Ayianna wanted to follow him, but her feet wouldn't move. Last night had torn a vast rift between them, and her soul begged for resolution. Why was he behaving this way? Was it because he kissed her? Or did her curse repulse him? Had she done something wrong?

"Vhat has bitten his backside this time?" Jaeger dumped his gear at the edge of the tent.

"He's conflicted." Tariq uncorked his waterskin and took a drink. "Just give him some space."

"Who is conflicted?" Vian strolled up from behind the tent.

"Really, Vian?" Jathil threw her hands into the air. "You better not have relieved yourself anywhere near here."

Vian's face flushed behind his red-gold beard. "Pardon me. I will go where I well feel like it, thank you very much. And I'm not a fool. I did not relieve myself behind the tent. As if it was any of your business."

"It would be if you had."

Vian snorted and glanced around. "Where's Kael?"

"He went for a walk." Tariq stretched his legs out and leaned back. "We've got a bit of time before the storm reaches us, if you've a mind to join him. We won't be able to work on the roots until tomorrow morning."

"No, thank you." Vian sat down next to Tariq, favoring his injured arm. "I've done enough walking, and I don't think anyone should stray too far from camp. There's a big pile of ashes northeast of here. It looked old, but I didn't see anything else out of the ordinary."

"Or you didn't stay long enough to see anything else." Jathil squatted in front of Tariq and Vian. "Were there no footprints? Was there a path?"

Vian shifted. "I did not intend to be found out while I tried to snoop around. Besides, Nerissa said we should be fine."

Jaeger grunted. "I do not know much about the Pauden here, but if they are anything like the d'arves, they vill not like an odd band of travelers digging holes in their island." He leaned forward. "Especially, if they hold grudges—even I know the history of the Pauden. There is bad blood between them and the other races. Except, of course, the merfolk."

"I will go—we need to warn Kael." Ayianna stood and brushed off her dress.

"Don't everyone panic now." Vian hugged his arm to his chest. "The ashes were cold, days old. There's probably not a giant within miles of this place. The storm is what you should worry about. It will be here before you know it."

She pushed through the ferns toward the shoreline. She'd have a good view of the approaching storm, and no doubt she'd find him there. A desire to feel his touch, his lips again, surged through her. No. She would not think like that. She wanted, more than anything, for the barrier that had sprung up overnight to disappear.

She halted where the ferns gave way to long, wispy grass. Kael sat atop the embankment, his back toward her. In the distance, a flash of lightning forked across the purple sky. He wanted to be alone, but her questions drove her forward.

"Why are you here?" Kael asked as he continued to gaze out over the sea.

She stepped up to the ledge. The dark waters churned below, receding and advancing, lapping at the exposed rocks. "Vian spotted an old campsite, thought you should know before you go off wandering the island."

"Well, it is the land of the Pauden."

"And . . ." She inhaled the salty air and tasted the coming rain. "I need to talk to you."

He shrugged. "Have a seat."

Ayianna sat down next to him, making sure she didn't touch him despite the urge to do so. She hated the distance that had suddenly interrupted their friendship. She pulled her knees to her chin and stared at the darkening clouds drawing ever closer. Lightning spiked through them, turning the deep purples to lavender to white, revealing their swollen bellies.

Several times, Ayianna opened her mouth to speak, but the words escaped her. What was she even trying to say? That she missed him? That he awakened something inside of her so deep and alluring she couldn't understand it? That she loved him so much it hurt? And what of him? Did he love her?

Or she could be content to just sit there forever and watch the storm blow in.

"I . . ." Ayianna hesitated. "I don't know if I did something wrong, or if you're angry with me. If—"

"Angry?" He looked at her, his brows arched. His dark gray eyes searched hers.

"Well . . ." She swallowed the lump of nerves in her throat. "About last night?"

A flicker of tenderness crossed his eyes before he looked away and clenched his jaw. "I said I was sorry."

"But why?" Ayianna blurted out, then added, "I mean, you didn't do anything wrong."

He shook his head. "You wouldn't understand."

"I might if you'd try to explain." She touched his arm. "We've been through a lot together."

He stared out over the sea. "Can't deny that."

Had his countenance softened? She kicked her legs out over the waters below, the spray of the surf misting her skin. She twisted the grass between her fingers. "We've shared . . . stuff. And maybe I've not been open about it, but . . ."

Kael looked at her—begging her to stop or continue, she couldn't tell. She took a deep breath. The thunder rumbled in the distance.

"Perhaps we should go, before the storm hits," he said.

"No, not yet. I must tell you this because I don't want our friendship to be marred, and the memory of my brother tainted. If I'm wrong, forgive me. I just . . . I thought that . . ." Ayianna closed her mouth. Why was this so hard? "It's just that after last night, I knew . . ." She searched his eyes for something, anything, but they remained hard. She couldn't stop now. She shoved past the knot in her throat. "I knew that I would live or die for you."

A flash of lightning lit up Kael's eyes, and Ayianna barely heard the thunder. His fingers brushed the side of her face, melting her doubt away. His presence, his touch. It felt right. Not like Desmond's. "Ayianna, please . . ."

She leaned in and kissed him. A torrent of passion-tangled feelings exploded from him and poured over her. Something wasn't right, he was holding back. He broke from her embrace, but lingered, his forehead against hers. "No," he whispered and pulled away.

Ayianna recoiled. The tall grass rippled in waves as the wind picked up. A splat of rain hit her face as tears stung her eyes. What was she doing? *He must hate me.*

He looked at the oncoming storm and sighed. "I don't hate you."

"On the raft, I had thought—" A loud clap of thunder shook the sky and stole the words from her tongue. Kael's eyes were intense and unreadable.

"We should go back to camp." He clenched his jaw. "The others will be worried."

"No, you go."

"I'm not going to leave you here by yourself."

More rain splattered them. Soon the clouds would open and drown them. They really should return.

She gritted her teeth. How could she have been so stupid? But it wasn't entirely her fault, was it? He had kissed her. "Why did you do it? Why did you kiss me if it didn't mean anything to you?"

"I didn't say that."

"Then what are you saying?" Her throat closed. Did she really want to know?

"It's complicated."

Ayianna scrambled to her feet. "I—I'm sorry." Lightning crackled and the sky erupted. She fled back to camp, her tears mixing with the rain.

45

THE STORM CLEARED sometime in the night, but not the one brewing in Kael's soul. He rubbed his face and glanced at his sleeping companions. His eyes passed over Ayianna's still form, and a sharp spasm shot through him. What a fool he had become! A traitorous fool.

He was supposed to be on his way to becoming a guardian. How had his heart become so entangled in this young woman's life? It had been a vow. A vow to protect—like a sister, not to— no. He would not consider it. He picked up the tools and bag and headed out toward the eastern shores.

Dawn hid her face, and the world slumbered on, but not him. Not with Ayianna haunting his dreams, her dark eyes demanding truth. Why had he kissed her? He slid down the slope and into a foot of water. He took out his orb, lit it, and made his way to the small cave Vian had found.

Inside, he inhaled the rich smells of the dirt and sea and exhaled through his nose. The peace of early morning seeped through him and calmed his troubled mind. He set his glowing orb in the dirt and began digging.

With no sun to mark the passing of time, he lost himself in the rhythm, the crunch of metal against dirt, and the smell of wet earth. He dug harder and deeper, numbing the voices in his head.

"You're up early."

He started and glanced over his shoulder at Vian. The glow from the orb made the prince appear much paler than he was, as if he were an apparition bent on haunting him too. Why did he have to intrude on his work? Didn't he know manual labor prohibited conversing? Of course, he didn't. He was a prince.

Kael slammed the shovel into the tunnel's wall and lifted a load of dirt. He dumped it to the side, barely missing Vian's feet. "Everybody else up?"

"Yes, eating. Do the merfolk ever eat anything aside from fish?"

Kael smashed the shovel into the wall again, but this time it hit something. He quickly cleared away the dirt to reveal a hint of red root. "We've found it."

Vian scooted up closer and peered into the hole. "That's supposed to be the famed famoruya root?"

"You're only seeing a fraction of the whole." Kael brushed away more dirt. He went back to hacking away with the shovel until a good portion of the gnarled root lay bare.

"So did anything happen yesterday?"

Kael paused and looked over at Vian. "What do you mean, *happen*?"

"You know . . . with Ayianna?" Vian grinned. "I know the look when I see it."

Kael stuck the shovel into the ground and grabbed his axe. "I don't know what you're talking about."

"Come on," Vian said. "Everyone can see it."

He gripped the handle tighter, resolving not to hit Vian, and chopped the thick, red root with his axe. "I don't want to talk about it. If you can't make yourself useful, leave."

"I can be useful. I can hold the fragments of the root you're hacking to pieces." Vian picked up the bag lying by the orb and shook it open with one hand. "Hopefully, your hacking isn't going to taint the root in any way."

He jerked the blade free and struck the root again, his hand smarting from each impact. "Maybe you should've stayed behind in Ganya."

"She is a lovely young woman," Vian said.

"Who is?"

"Ayianna."

Kael hacked the root harder. Maybe if he ignored him, he'd go away.

"And I'm not speaking just about her wonderful attributes, and how she'd make a good wife some day for a man who deserved her." Vian paused. "And maybe I'd like to get to know her a little more myself, if she is available, you know. Those merfolk robes could get a man a dreaming. She—"

Kael lunged for Vian, grabbed him by the throat, and slammed him against the dirt wall.

"The arm! Watch the arm!" Vian squirmed, cradling his splinted, wrapped arm. "Watch the arm."

Kael exhaled heavily. "Don't."

Vian's face broke into a grin. "I knew it. You love her."

Kael released him. He picked up the axe and severed the root. Would he ever get rid of him?

"What's your problem?" Vian rubbed his throat.

"Right now? It's you."

"You're only upset because I'm right." Vian scooped up the piece of root and shoved it into the bag. "You love her."

"No, I don't."

"Then stop playing with her heart."

"What do you know about these things?"

"I know I don't go around kissing women I don't love."

"How do you . . ." Kael shook his head. "You would never understand. I don't . . . I can't love her." He looked over at Vian and froze. Behind the prince stood Ayianna and Tariq. The hurt in her eyes pierced him like a barbed spear.

"Your morning meal." She dumped the contents of her hands into the dirt and left.

Kael closed his eyes and sighed. "I told you I didn't want to talk about this."

"You don't deserve her." Vian tossed the bag of roots to Tariq and disappeared after Ayianna.

Kael slammed the axe into the exposed root. "You're right. I don't."

"Parzanah didn't create us to harbor bitterness." Tariq stepped closer. "It'll destroy you."

Kael clenched his teeth and continued hacking at the exposed root. "It keeps me focused."

"You're lying to yourself."

"What's going on?" Kael jerked the axe free, and a piece of the root fell away. "First Vian, and now you." He scooped up the splintered wood and tossed it to Tariq.

Tariq shoved it into the bag. "That's what we'd like to know. What's going on with you?"

"I don't know." Kael slammed the axe into the dirt. He had tried to stay focused. He didn't love her, did he? No, that chapter in his life was closed. Osaryn hadn't seen the need to keep Rysa and Braedon alive. Why should he think a second time would be any different? He was going to be a guardian or die trying. At least that was what Saeed would have wanted, right? Why did everything have to be so complicated?

"Whatever you got going on between you and Osaryn, you need to work it out, but stop wallowing in self-pity and think for once how your actions are affecting everyone else."

Kael clenched his jaw and threw the axe down. The truth seared his soul. Fool. He closed his eyes. When would the tormenting stop?

"You need to make amends."

Kael wiped the sweat from his forehead with the back of his sleeve. "I know."

46

AYIANNA SCRAMBLED UP the steep slope of the shoreline. It was over. Out of his own mouth, he had denied it. He wouldn't, couldn't. Didn't he say as much back in the mountains? Why had she ever thought differently? Jathil. She had encouraged it, hadn't she? His kiss hadn't helped either. If only she could scrub her heart and mind clean of it all. Perhaps then it wouldn't hurt so sharply.

Her legs bore her to the camp, but that was the last place she wanted to be. She took a deep breath and tried to settle her emotions. Jathil and Jaeger did not need to know about it. She could act as if nothing ever happened, right?

"Ayianna!" Vian cried after her.

No. The last person she wanted to see—well, second to last. But her feet slowed, and she turned toward him.

He jogged up to her and brushed his red curls from his face. "I didn't mean to hurt you. I was only goading Kael on, so that he would wake up and see the truth."

"Well, he certainly made the truth plain enough, didn't he?" Ayianna crossed her arms and headed back to camp, slower.

Vian strolled next to her. "Kael is a boar's behind, and if he can't get over himself, then he doesn't deserve you."

She faced him. "No one deserves a harpy-cursed wife." The coldness of her words hit her like an icy river. What did life hold for her now?

A red flush tinged Vian's cheeks. "That's not what I meant."

"But it's the truth." She turned away.

"No." Vian grabbed her shoulder with his good hand and spun her around. "You can choose to let this curse ruin your life or you can choose to overcome it."

"What do you know about curses?"

"More than you think." He lowered his voice. "I know what it's like to listen to people whispering behind your back for things you have no control over. My mother died in childbirth. My father spurned me. Rumors of being the marked one, destined to die beneath the blade of a Nuja priestess, followed me throughout my childhood. My friend betrayed me. I know what it's like when the world turns against you, and you're all alone." He tightened his grip on her shoulder. "Everyone bears curses, some are just easier to hide."

Ayianna's throat constricted. Had she been so consumed with her own troubles and heartache that she had overlooked his? How selfish she had been! "I—I'm sorry."

"Listen,"—Vian released her shoulder—"I don't know how this journey will end, but you have friends who will see you through. If we fail, Vituko will not, so don't go basing any more decisions on your curse. All right?"

She nodded. And for the first time in a long while, a spark of hope burned in her soul. It did not depend on her family and their choices, or Desmond's false promises, or even the feelings she had for Kael. No matter what happened, she would never truly be alone. Curse or no curse.

"Well, now that that's out of the way." Vian straightened his shoulders. "We should prepare to welcome that mer-dragon-master-rider-person—Kaemon. He should be here this morning, and then it's off to Kha Vaaro and our journey will be finished."

"Right." Ayianna's mind snapped to the present. "So, we should start packing." She continued back to camp with a lighter heart than she thought possible.

A large branch cracked, and Vian grabbed Ayianna's arm. Ayianna held her breath. What could have made such a noise? They had not seen any animals on this side of the island, nor would Jathil and Jaeger make such a ruckus. Or had she exaggerated the sound?

From behind the massive trunks of the red famoruya trees stepped a giant.

47

THE GIANT SLID a knife from his belt. "Who are you and what are you doing here?" His voice rumbled like a herd of stampeding cattle. He stood twice as tall as Ayianna and had a round face the size of millstone beneath a shaggy cap of greasy dark locks. His teeth could have easily ground their bones into flour.

Not that giants ate people. Although, a few bard's tales suggested otherwise, Ayianna did not want to find out. She stepped back but bumped into Vian.

"Well, this just keeps getting better and better." Vian pulled Ayianna behind him and lifted his chin. "I am Prince Vian of Badara, and we are here by permission of the Peha of the Kaleki. We seek—"

"Shut your blowhole."

Vian stepped forward. "Excuse me, but I was answering—"

"And I've decided I don't like you." The giant sneered. "Don't do anything fast like, or you and your girl will be skewered."

"She's not my girl—not that I wouldn't mind. Not the skewered part, the girl part—I mean, oh, never mind." Vian clenched his jaw as his face burned red.

The giant rubbed the back of his hand under his hooked nose. "What do you think we should do with them, eh, Boril?"

Four more giants stalked out from behind the trees and flanked the first. All five wore similar dark shorts and sleeveless tunics.

"Well." The smallest of the five leaned on his staff. "The proper thing to do would be to interrogate them, and if they're found lacking, which most trespassers are, we should take them to the elders."

"I didn't ask you." He waved his knife in the air. "This is Boril's hunt, not yours. And if I'd had my way, you wouldn't be here."

He shrugged and stepped aside. He swished the staff through the grass, shoved it into the ground, and leaned on it again. "Whatever you say, Lonket, but the chieftess will not be happy if you take matters into your own hands—again."

"That old woman is not fit to rule us." A wicked grin cracked Lonket's face. "Well, Boril?"

A giant with a blond braid twisting over his shoulder lifted his chin and smirked. Boril. "I think we need to teach them a thing or two about trespassing."

"I doubt your fathers would approve." The smallest one raised his eyebrows as if he could persuade them by facial expressions alone. Or he was bored. Why couldn't one of the other larger giants be more sympathetic to their presence? "Besides, you're wasting time. Boril needs to return with the peacock by the full moon, or he will fail."

"We have time enough," Boril snorted and eyed Ayianna and Vian. "I think we should gather all of them and leave them as examples on the coast."

"And risk jeopardizing the rebellion? The merfolk could retaliate." Grizzly brown hair swirled atop the scalp of the fifth giant, and dark bags hung under his eyes. Was he the oldest? "But the best lessons do not end in death, do they?"

A shiver crawled down Ayianna's spine. The sun burned the remnants of the morning as it inched higher in the sky. What chance did they have against five giants? Should she try to run for Tariq and Kael? Or make for the camp?

"Trespassers are better dead," Lonket said. "We can bury their bones and no Kaleki would know the difference. And,"—his eyes cut to the smaller giant, before returning to the grizzly giant—"Korgal tells me that the two of their companions are the feline-folks. I wouldn't mind a new pillow, would you Domin?"

Domin shook his head. "What are we waiting for?"

Vian straightened. "Aren't you going to let us talk?"

"I don't see why it would matter." Lonket turned his beady eyes on him. "It didn't matter to the rest of you when you enslaved us and destroyed our homes."

"I . . . I cannot answer for what my ancestors did and did not do. That was a long time ago. Why do you still hold on to it?"

"You didn't have to relocate and learn a new life." Lonket clenched his fist and raised it. "Forever to be feared and hated."

"And you think your actions now are helping you?" Vian cocked his head. "Would you cross Nevin Darin?"

Lonket growled. "Darin has no friends here."

"Would you destroy the years of peace Darin has fought for you?"

"Words don't win battles." He aimed his blade at Vian's neck, and Ayianna cringed. "We will bring back the glory of the Pauden, and all the nations will tremble once again."

"If the Sorceress succeeds in destroying Nälu, you will never regain your former glory. You will go back to being slaves." Why did Vian have to keep talking? "As I recall the Alliance freed you from your bonds of slavery. If they are no more, who will free you then?"

"Bah!" Lonket waved his knife closer to Vian and Ayianna. "Boril and Domin, go get the others. We shall mete out a proper reprimand before lunch."

"I don't think so." Jathil launched herself from a tree and slammed her staff across Lonket's forehead.

Ayianna stumbled backward as Jaeger plowed into Domin's legs. The giant lost his balance and crashed to the ground.

Jaeger shoved a pair of sword belts into her hands. Hers and Vian's.

"You can't be serious?" She passed Vian his belt and slid her sword from hers. How did one fight a giant? Could they outrun them?

"Not to kill. They are only younglings." Jaeger shifted his own belt, fingered the braid of hair hanging from it, and untied a thick rope. He whistled and Jathil leapt to his side.

"This isn't going to end well." Vian hoisted his sword awkwardly in his left hand. "I'm right-handed!" He tried to swing, but Lonket staggered forward and knocked the blade from Vian's hands. Vian stumbled backward and scooped up his sword.

Boril charged, but Jaeger and Jathil rushed him. Just before reaching him, Jaeger and Jathil separated and jerked a rope taut between two trees. Boril flipped and collided with a tree. The large trunk hardly trembled from the impact.

Korgal leaned on his staff, his gaze following Jathil and Jaeger. He was the only giant with a weapon, aside from Lonket's hunting knife. If he started swinging, they'd have no chance. Whose side was he on anyway?

Ayianna twisted the hilt in her hands. If only she had her stones and sling! But Jaeger had said not to kill. What could she do? Jaeger and Jathil regrouped and sprang after Domin, but Lonket snagged Jaeger by the hair.

"Tear him limb from limb!" Domin snatched Jaeger from Lonket. "You will pay for this."

"Put me down, you over-grown pup." Jaeger punched Domin's thigh. Domin's knee buckled. He roared and shook Jaeger.

Vian attacked, but Domin swung Jaeger into Vian and the sword bit into Jaeger's arm. Vian yelped and toppled to the ground.

Jathil raced toward the nearest tree, scaled it, and somersaulted in the air. She landed atop Domin's shoulders. She wrapped her legs around his neck and yanked his hair.

Domin released Jaeger and pummeled her. His aim at first sloppy, but then his fist slammed into her side. Jathil jerked and her face blanched.

No! Ayianna charged, but Domin wrenched Jathil from his neck and flung her aside. Ayianna swung her sword as hard as she could, and the blade sank into the giant's leg.

Domin grasped her neck. Pain shot through her body, her vision blurred, and the sword fell from her hand.

"Enough." Lonket held Jathil, his knife at her neck.

Jaeger halted, his chest heaving, and threw down his axe. "Ve do not vant any trouble."

"Well, it is a little too late for that, now, isn't it?" Lonket said.

A roar shook the air as a shadow slid over them. Domin released Ayianna and scrambled behind a tree.

Ayianna collapsed and tried to blink the stars from her eyes. Had Kaemon arrived?

A bright orange and yellow dragon plunged toward them. The girth of his neck rivaled the giant famoruya tree trunks. Two ivory horns the size of a person curved from his temple and swirled upward. He slammed into the ground, and the earth trembled. He folded his wings and crouched low.

Kaemon leapt from the saddle, spun in the air, and landed on his feet. He wore leather trousers, arm bracers, and a vest. None of his inked circles could be seen, except for those across his left cheek. Quite a contrast from the silver wrap he had worn at breakfast back in Ganya. His black plaited hair hung down his back, and green feathery fins lined his muscular arms.

"What is the meaning of this?" He scanned the scene until his gaze rested on Lonket. "You—explain."

"Me—we—they are trespassing!"

Kaemon's eyes narrowed. "Is there a law against visitors? Does the chieftess not welcome guests?"

"The chieftess has grown soft." Lonket crossed his arms.

"Do you disrespect her authority?"

Lonket lowered his gaze. "No, sir."

"I will have to report your behavior to her." He growled and threw his hands up in the air. "I do not have time to deal with wayward kids."

"We aren't kids." Lonket nodded toward the giant sitting on the ground and rubbing his forehead. "Boril has come of age, and we are on the hunt."

"Then be on your way, and if I see you all again, I will roast your backsides."

Lonket glanced at the others and nodded. The giants got to their feet and disappeared into the trees.

Kaemon turned his glare on Ayianna. "I trust you have the roots by now."

"We're making progress." She rubbed the back of her neck and stood.

Jathil held her side and limped over toward them. "Well, aren't we glad to see you."

"Are you all right?" Ayianna reached for her arm, but Jathil pulled away.

"I'm fine—just a bit of bruising."

"We should take a look." Kaemon touched her shoulder, but Jathil recoiled and snatched his wrist.

"Thank you, but I'm fine." She released him and jerked her thumb toward Jaeger. "Although, he could use some attention."

Jaeger turned his arm to reveal a bloody gash across his bicep. "Just a scratch." He blew out his mustache. "It vould take more than—"

"We know!" Vian hugged his arm to himself as he tried to untwist his sling. "You're slowly convincing us you're invincible."

"Here." Ayianna untangled the fabric and smoothed it over his shoulder.

Vian shifted his arm into the sling. "Thanks."

Kaemon poured a good amount of the healing waters into Jaeger's wound. "Give it some time, and it should be good as new tomorrow morning."

"Sorry about the sword and all, Jaeger." Vian picked his up and sheathed it. "I hadn't meant to flay you."

"Bah, it vas not your fault." Jaeger pursed his lips while Kaemon wrapped the wound with a silver gauze. "Luckily, ve have the healing vaters vith us, eh? Ve are no match for an enemy vithout."

"The waters cannot heal every wound." Kaemon clucked his tongue. "Once we leave the sea behind, we will have a limited supply, so I suggest you all be more careful."

"Right." Vian snorted. "As if we wanted to slice each other to pieces for the fun of it."

Kaemon's head snapped up. "Pardon me?"

Vian raised his hands. "I was jesting."

Kaemon stood and wiped his hands on his pants. "I will check on the progress of these roots. We may yet leave before sundown." He glanced up at the sky. "Has any of you seen anything out of the ordinary? A stray dragon, perhaps?"

48

BY THE TIME the others returned with the root, Ayianna, Jathil, and Jaeger had taken down the tent and packed up the remaining supplies.

Tension hung in the air, and nobody made any attempt to break the awkward silence. What had transpired with them? Ayianna avoided Kael and rummaged through her bag as if she were checking its contents. Again.

"Vian and Kaemon told us about the giants." Tariq finally broke the silence as he swung the bag of roots off his shoulder and dropped to his knees next to his pack. "Are you all right?

"We are fine." Jathil leaned on her staff, and her eyes shifted to Kaemon. "These giants had no regard for their chieftess and spoke of rebelling. We can't leave until we notify her, or we risk undoing the work of the guardians."

"*Hi-aeke*." Kaemon planted his fists on his hips. "I will go. Are you ready to leave?"

"Ve must refill our vaterskins." Jaeger plucked a waterskin from the pile. "Then ve vill be ready."

Kaemon nodded. "Go inland to the north, and you will find a stream. I will show you. Maewali will remain here for you to secure your belongings while I speak with the chieftess."

"Won't you need your dragon?" Jathil flinched, and her hand moved to her side where the giant had hit her.

"I intend to relay secrets, not announce them. I will swim, the Pauden are not far."

"We will be ready when you return." Jathil slid to the ground.

"Are you okay?" Ayianna knelt beside her. "Did the giant break your ribs?"

"No. Just bruised, tired, and winded." Jathil leaned against the base of the tree and closed her eyes.

Kaemon pulled out a vial much like the one Ayanna carried and uncorked it. "Here, drink this. It will help speed the healing."

Jathil eyed his proffered hand as if he held poison.

"By the stone's blood, Jathil!" Jaeger crossed his arms. "If you do not drink vhat he is giving you, I vill sit on you and pour it down your own throat, I vill."

"It's probably the same thing the merfolk gave me to help my arm." Vian lifted his splintered arm. "It's feeling better, despite a certain elf's temper."

"You shouldn't be here." Kael scooped up his sword belt. "This journey is no place for a broken arm."

Ayianna cringed. Why did Kael have to be such a jerk?

"Pardon me?" Vian straightened.

"We've already discussed this." Jathil accepted the vial, took a drink, and handed it back to Kaemon. "We are not splitting up."

"No, Jathil, he is right." Vian sighed and touched his injured arm. "I could not even hold my own against the giants. I will return to Ganya and go with Nerissa."

"Too late." Kaemon slid the vial back into a pouch at his side. "Nerissa left earlier than planned, and I will not fly out of my way to Ganya. I must rejoin my squadron as quickly as possible." He unslung a shell from his neck. "But you may call

Oko, he will come for you and bring you back to Ganya. The next ship to deport leaves in two days."

Vian took the shell. "Thank you." He faced Kael. "Set my stuff aside. I will not be joining you."

Ayianna scrambled to her feet. "No, Vian."

"It's all right." He forced a smile and shrugged. "My father will need me as quickly as possible, and I'll enjoy the ship much better than this boar's company."

She glared at Kael, but the hurt and humiliation nearly overwhelmed her anger. She averted her eyes and jerked her bag from the others. "As I recall, this journey is no place for a woman either. I will go with—"

"You will not!" Jathil grasped her hand. "We are a team."

"Vell, you all sort this out. Merman here vill alert the chieftess, and I vill go for the vater." Jaeger scooped up half of the waterskins.

"I'll help you, Jaeger." Ayianna grabbed the rest of the waterskins.

"Don't be foolish." Kael buckled on his belt. "You two will never be able to carry all those skins back full of water."

"Are you underestimating my strength, elf?" Jaeger lifted his bushy eyebrows and blew out his moustache. "I have never—ve vill just see about that. Right, Ayianna?"

"Come, I will show you the river." Kaemon strode away from camp. "Let us be done with this island. We have a war to win."

"Nice one." Jathil glared at Kael and Vian. "It would be best not to anger the merman with the dragon and our only transportation off this island."

Jaeger snorted and jogged after Kaemon. Tariq and Kael grabbed several of the packs and headed toward the dragon. Jathil rested against the tree, her eyes closed, her jaw clenched.

Ayianna twisted the waterskins. How could they split up? It wasn't right.

Vian pulled his gear aside and attempted to buckle on his sword belt. No, he couldn't go alone. Ayianna had made the right decision. Kael didn't need her. The quest didn't need her. She could go now, be reunited with her mom, and be done with it all.

Kaemon and Jaeger slipped farther away, and Ayianna dashed after them. The sooner they left, the sooner she could be reunited with her mother.

49

KAEMON'S BLACK TAIL slid into the water, and then he was gone as he shot up stream to warn the chieftess. Jaeger and Ayianna worked in silence as they filled each waterskin, corked it, and set it aside.

"You know, Kael is right." Jaeger set the last waterskin down. "Ve vill not be able to carry all these skins back by ourselves."

Ayianna plucked three from the pile. They were heavier together and awkward. The skins wriggled and waggled, and she dumped them back on the ground.

"But he is an elf, not a d'arf." Jaeger scanned the riverbank and touched the braided loop of hair hanging from his belt. "I just need a good-sized branch."

"Why do you wear a braid of hair on your belt?" Ayianna sought the pocket of her dress for her mother's talisman, but she had long lost it. Not that she needed it, but she would have welcomed anything at this point that reminded her of home and simpler times.

Jaeger grabbed a branch twice the size of him and dragged it near the waterskins. "It is a long story. A story of love and loss, but also of hope. Maybe I vill have the time to tell you on our trip back to Kha Vaaro."

"But I won't be going with you."

"Oh, that is right. Kael and his poor manners." Jaeger began tying the waterskins to the branch, and Ayianna helped him. "Are you certain of your decision?"

Ayianna took a deep breath and knotted the leather binding. "Vian can't make the trip alone in his condition. He'll need someone to help him."

"*Du, du,* that is the truth." Jaeger shrugged. "But just the two of you vould not be good, if something should happen."

"We'd be on a ship, with merfolk, and others. What could possibly go wrong?" Ayianna tied the last waterskin.

"Pirates, for one." He bent down and lifted the branch of hanging waterskins to his shoulders. "Kael has Tariq and Jathil, and now Kaemon. *Du,* they could complete the quest vithout me. Perhaps I shall join you and Vian. Three are better than one, no?"

Ayianna grinned. "I would love to have you, and I'm sure Vian wouldn't mind."

"Need a hand with those?" Kael's voice sent a dagger into her heart.

"I can manage." Jaeger turned slowly, the waterskins swaying, and strode back toward camp.

Ayianna started after him, but Kael grabbed her arm. "Wait."

The hurt and humiliation burned hotter, welling in her chest and stinging her eyes. She glared at the wrinkled bark of the tree next to her and refused to cry. Hadn't she shed enough tears over men, elf or not?

"Ayianna." His voice was strained. "I didn't mean to—"

"But you did." She bit back the angry tirade building on her tongue.

"When my wife died, I chose a path away from . . . companionship. The death of my son and sister reaffirmed it."

If he didn't stop, the ache would suffocate her. "Does your path still lead to the Guardian Circle?"

"I . . ." He released her arm. "I don't know."

She glanced up at his charcoal gray eyes. They held the same crushing hurt from the night she had fled Dagmar, and he and Saeed had found her. It tore at her heart. And now Saeed was gone too. An abyss of emptiness swallowed her, and she averted her eyes, blinking back the tears.

"But I was arid and dead like the desert—you-you've made me feel again."

Her breath caught and her gaze snapped to his. Did he—was he?

"When I'm with you, the world is right." He shook his head. "But I've failed so many times."

"You act as if you're the only one to fail. We all fail, but you forget that you succeed far more than you fail."

He lifted his hand as if to stop her. "I *will* fail."

"Then we will fail together." She touched her fingertips to his. "Fear of failure will only rob you of your life. I should know."

He clenched his jaw and pressed his palm into hers.

She swallowed. "Love is more powerful than fear."

"Will you forgive me?"

The hurt and humiliation fled, stealing away the dams holding back the tears. A new feeling emerged and swallowed up the ache in her heart. It echoed the song in the garden and the raw emotion from the raft. She nodded.

Kael embraced her, and she buried her face in his chest. A flood of emotion mirroring her own surged from him, and she was back in the gardens. This time he held nothing back.

A dragon's roar rent the air.

"Is that Maewali?" Kael pulled away.

"Maybe he's angry that Kaemon left?" Ayianna wrapped her arms around her middle. What would they do with an irate dragon? They couldn't calm him. Maybe they should hide.

A louder, sharper shriek pierced her ears. A second dragon? What was going on? Jaeger's battle cry shook her.

"Come on."

Ayianna raced after Kael, beyond their empty campsite toward the coastline. The others should have been loading Maewali with their belongings. Shouts rang out and a smell most foul drifted on the air.

Imps.

They reached the edge of the trees to find their companions fighting a horde of imps and a handful of men. Where had they come from? In the sky, an enormous black dragon wrestled Maewali, but they were losing height. They plowed into the earth and the ground shuddered. With claws and teeth, the dragons fought, carving a path of destruction along the coastline and into the trees.

Ayianna reached for her sword, but Kael placed a hand on her shoulder. "There is only one way to take down a dragon."

The noqui stones.

"Make your aim true."

She nodded and started for her bag, but he grabbed her arm. His eyes clouded, his jaw clenched. He pulled her close and kissed her. A rush of quiet joy and perfect peace surrounded her. She had found home again, but fear flitted at the edges of her soul. The shrieks and clanging blades tore at her resolve. Still, he lingered, his forehead on hers.

"May Osaryn protect you," he whispered. And then he was gone, rushing into the throng of imps.

If only she could savor the moment! Why did it have to be like this? Ayianna darted back to their pile of belongings, although considerably smaller, and searched for her pack, but couldn't find it. Had they already secured it to Maewali?

She sought the orange dragon. Maewali corkscrewed through the sky, but the black one closed in on it. The black one was bigger and stronger, but Maewali was quicker. If she didn't find the stones soon, Maewali would be defeated.

Ayianna dropped to her knees and threw the bags and bundles aside. Where was her pack?

"Looking for this?" Desmond stood near the edge of the cliff with her bag in his hand. "Or were you looking for this?"

He held up the bag of Noqui stones. "I couldn't let you deprive me of my transportation." He flung them into the sea behind him.

No! Ayianna clutched the hilt of her sword and refrained from charging him. How badly she desired to! But she was no match for him. "What do you want?"

"The Sorceress needs her sacrifice and wouldn't mind a harpy pet to call her own."

So now the Sorceress knew of her curse, but Ayianna would die first rather than be an instrument of evil. "No one commands the harpies but the harpy lord."

"Semine will take her chance." He stepped closer. "Bring me Vian and surrender, and I will let the others go."

Tariq, Kael, and Jaeger battled the imps and men farther down the shoreline. She could not see Vian or Jathil. What should she do? She couldn't fight him. But the others could! She could run, lure him closer to them, and together, they could gain the upper hand.

She turned her glare to Desmond. "Never." And she fled toward the trees.

50

WHERE WERE VIAN and Jathil? Ayianna darted into the trees and zigzagged between the trunks. Was Desmond following? She didn't dare check yet. She rounded one tree and skidded to a stop.

Kaemon charged toward her. "What is the meaning of this? Who commands the black dragon?"

"Desmond. He's with the Sorceress. And wants to take Vian to be sacrificed."

Kaemon's eyes darkened. He reached for a slender shell and brought it to his lips. No sound fell on Ayianna's ears, except the roaring of the dragons, clash of blades, and the screeching of the imps. He strode toward the melee, scooped up the large branch with which Jaeger had carried the waterskins, and whittled a sharp point.

Maewali swerved away from the black dragon and dove for Kaemon. Orange and yellow scales hung from his neck, and blood oozed where the other dragon's teeth had punctured him. The whoosh of wind from his wings blasted Ayianna, but he didn't land. Instead, Kaemon had scaled a tree and leapt atop the dragon's back.

"Today, you will die, cursed brother." Kaemon angled the branch like a spear as Maewali soared back into the sky, and he was lost from view.

She scanned the trees and coastline. Where had Desmond gone? Had he followed her?

"Ayianna!" Vian's voice hailed her from above.

She glanced up. There, the prince of Badara perched in the boughs of the largest tree in Nälu and waved at her. "What are you—how did you get up there?"

"Maewali stuck me up here. I guess he figured I'd be no good."

Ayianna scanned the area again. "Desmond is here, and he wants to take you back to be sacrificed."

"Lovely."

"Where's Jathil?" Ayianna unsheathed her sword and paced between the trees, circling Vian's spot.

"How should I know?"

"You're up in a tree, you dolt!"

"Watching it only makes me want to join the fight more. Hold on." Vian shifted between the boughs. "She's at the edge of the tree line, probably trying to keep them from finding me."

Ayianna darted through the ferns and out into the open. Kael and Tariq fought to her left, swords clashing. Five men surrounded them. Closer to the shore, Jaeger plowed through a group of imps. To her right, Jathil battled three men and several imps, but she lacked her normal flexibility and speed.

Could Ayianna remember how to fight? She hadn't practiced like she should have. She hoisted her sword in front of her and advanced on the smelly imps. She could at least take them down. They didn't have swords, and they were smaller than her.

And they had killed her brother.

She swung her blade into an imp's side, and it screeched. A chill raced down her neck and spine, but she jerked her sword free and prepared to swing again.

"Aim for their necks!" Jathil blocked an assault with her double blades. "Less restriction, quicker kill."

The distraction cost her. The imp charged, but Ayianna brought her sword up. It impaled itself.

"That works too." Jathil spun and kicked an imp that was getting too close.

The imp fell backward, and Ayianna slammed her sword down on its neck, decapitating it. She averted her eyes, refusing to even think about it. Only that one was down, and two more to go. If she kept moving, she wouldn't think, wouldn't feel. She braced herself, charged, and slashed the first one's throat and caught the second one on the rebound.

One of the men lumbered toward her, his eyes glazed. Blood dribbled down his face from an open gash across his forehead. He swung, but Jathil's blade blocked him. She counterattacked with her other blade, catching the man in the side. He stumbled back, but another one replaced him. He stood a head taller, and his shoulders were twice the size of the other one. Had Ayianna seen him before? He charged forward, his sword raised.

"You're out of your league here." Jathil flashed in front of Ayianna and brought her blades down. A clash of metal rang in Ayianna's ears, and she inched back. "Something is not right about these men."

Jathil's blade came down on the man's sword arm, severing his wrist, and the sword fell. He seized it with his other hand and kept swinging, his strokes sloppy and jerky.

"Their eyes are lifeless. And they're immune to pain. They don't even speak." Jathil snapped the sword from his hand and flung it into the ground.

Ayianna stumbled back. The memory of the blacksmith shop sped through her mind. The blacksmith! He had helped them clean up Kael's arm. She had seen him in the tunnels beneath the Inganno Forest, bound and weeping. What had happened to him? Why was he fighting against them? "Stop!"

But Jathil's blades whistled through the air, slashing across the man's throat. He slumped to his knees and fell forward.

"No! I knew him! He was a blacksmith in Badara."

Jathil shoved Ayianna aside and took off one of the other men's legs. He collapsed.

"They are trying to kill us." Jathil spun around and kicked the third man, who was sneaking up behind her, in the gut. "And you are going to get us killed."

Shadows flashed across the shoreline, and a burst of flame swept overhead. Maewali spiraled downward, snapped its wings open and soared into the sky again. The black dragon crashed into him, throwing Maewali into the trees. A thunderous crack reverberated, and a tree half the size of the grand famoruyas pitched toward Ayianna and Jathil.

Ayianna scrambled upright and slammed into Jathil, but she wasn't quick enough. The tree smashed into the ground, and the branches tore at her face, clothes, and body. Pain shot through her, and she lay still.

How badly had she injured herself? Where was Jathil? She wiggled her toes, fingers, and then shifted her legs and arms. Nothing was broken, but fiery darts shot through her skin and body.

"Ayianna?" Jathil's voice sounded to her left. "Are you hurt?

"Not bad, I don't think." Ayianna wrestled through the branches toward the voice and stumbled out of the tree's canopy. "You?"

"Just a few scratches."

"Where's the—"

Behind Jathil, the third man lurched toward them with a splintered branch protruding from his stomach, his sword ready to strike. To his left crawled the maimed man. Somehow the tree had missed him.

Jathil spun, blades swinging. Ayianna scooted backward into the ferns, but the maimed one continued creeping toward her with no regard to his bloody stump of a leg. His eyes were glazed, much like the others, but his intentions were clear.

She gripped her sword. She should swing for his neck. End it now. But she couldn't. Ayianna scrambled farther back and hit the base of a tree. He was upon her, sword raised. She rolled to the side as the blade hissed past her face. She sprang to her feet and brought her sword down on his shoulder. The bones crunched and he collapsed.

She turned and vomited. Tremors shook her limbs and tears slid unchecked. She had killed him. She had to. He would have killed her instead. But no amount of convincing could erase the guilt flooding her soul. She grabbed her sword and stood, albeit wobbly.

Jathil joined Jaeger, and they slashed into the last group of the imps. Kael and Tariq were down to two men now. What should she do? Jathil was right, she was out of her league here. Without the noqui stones, she would cause more harm than good.

Where was Desmond?

A belch of fire tore through the sky. Maewali ducked, swooped low, and shot into the air. Kaemon stood, brandishing his spear still. The black dragon gave pursuit, but Kaemon leapt, shoving the spear into the black dragon's eye. It shrieked and snapped its teeth at Kaemon, but he was already gone, falling toward the ground. Maewali dove and caught him.

Ayianna almost cheered.

The black dragon plunged toward Maewali and slammed him into the ground. Maewali's nose hit the dirt, and he tumbled.

Kaemon! Maewali's body slid across the shoreline toward Jathil and Jaeger.

"No!" Ayianna sprinted toward them. "Jaeger, Jathil! Get out of there!"

Maewali roared. He scrambled to right himself. His leathery wings, broken and torn, dragged behind him. But the black dragon was on him, chomping down on his neck and shaking him.

Jaeger and Jathil raced inland, but they were too slow. The black dragon hurtled Maewali aside, flinging dirt into the air. Maewali rolled ever closer to them, but the other dragon slammed into him, and he plowed into the dirt.

Jaeger disappeared, but Jathil was thrown high from the impact. The black dragon leapt atop Maewali, stretched his wings, and roared.

"No!" Ayianna rushed forward, but an arm grabbed her and swung her around and into an embrace. Kael. She clung to him, trying to keep the tears inside.

"Now what?" Tariq's voice was next to her.

Ayianna pulled out of Kael's embrace. "We have to check."

"Wait."

"But—"

"And you're just going to rush out there and take on that blasted beast?"

"Yes." She stilled. "No."

"What happened to the noqui stones?"

Her stomach clenched. "Desmond dumped them into the sea."

Kael raised his sword. "Where is that coward?"

"Patience." Tariq squeezed Kael's shoulder. "Let's find the others first."

The black dragon shook its head and waltzed to the shade of the trees, probably toward Desmond.

Ayianna, Kael, and Tariq rushed over to Maewali and the upturned dirt. How would they ever find their friends? Tears burned in Ayianna's eyes, but she brushed them aside. She'd not think of their end. They circled the dragon.

"Kael, keep Ayianna over there. She does not need to see this." Tariq's voice lifted over the dragon's broken and bleeding body.

"Jaeger?" Kael asked.

Ayianna bit her sleeve. No. no. no. Not Jaeger. He had to find his father. He couldn't die. She scanned the shoreline for Jathil. *Please let her be alive!*

"Kaemon, too," Tariq said.

"Hey, half-breed!"

Ayianna and Kael spun around.

Desmond stood at the edge of the tree line, clutching Jathil in his arms and a dagger at her throat. Behind him, a man held Vian in the same manner. The betrayal, the lies, the hurt crashed into her like waves in a storm. How could he?

"Give me Ayianna," Desmond said. "Or I will kill all of you."

"Never."

Desmond pressed the dagger harder against Jathil's neck, and Jathil whimpered.

"Stop!" Ayianna cried. Deep down understanding mushroomed into horror, and she knew what she had to do. *Oh, Osaryn, there has to be another way!* She grasped Kael's hand. "We can't let him—I must."

"No." Kael's anger and fear billowed over her like smoke from a raging forest fire. He clenched his jaw, his eyes hard. He faced Desmond. "Take me. Kill me. I'm sure you'd enjoy that much more."

"I would at that. Unfortunately, you don't have harpy poison running through your veins."

Ayianna squeezed Kael's hand. "Listen, if they want me to turn, they won't kill me."

"I can't." Kael tugged her closer. Would he allow Desmond to kill Jathil, instead? Didn't he see there was no other way?

The black dragon lumbered toward them.

"One word, and he will destroy you." Desmond pushed forward, dragging Jathil with him, the blade biting into her neck.

Ayianna could save them—buy them more time. The quest had to be successful, or all of Nälu would fail. If only she had been pure elf, perhaps she could have opened her soul to Kael and reassure him. But could he not see? She had to do this.

Jathil's whimper startled her. They didn't have time to argue. She clenched his hand. But could she go through with it? She swallowed and forced her tongue to move. "You have three months. Get the pinecone and find us before they sacrifice Vian."

Kael's gaze bore into hers. A fiery rage engulfed her, pleading for another way. She slid her fingers from his and faced Desmond. She clenched her fists and inhaled deeply. She would not look back.

"No harm will come to them." Ayianna shoved the words out. "Or I will rip your heart out."

Desmond smirked. "As if you could trust my word."

"No, but you can trust mine."

He shrugged. "I think I've done enough harm already. I doubt they will be getting off this island anytime soon."

"Release Jathil."

"Drop your sword first."

Ayianna threw the sword aside and strode toward him. If he gave any hint of treason, she'd claw his eyes out. But Desmond released Jathil, and she collapsed, curling into a ball slowly, and didn't move again. As soon as Ayianna was close enough, Desmond snatched her hair and spun her against him, his blade against her throat.

The dragon stomped toward them and crouched low. Even so, he towered above, his girth like two of the massive trees.

Desmond shoved Ayianna toward the dragon, and she scrambled up the rope ladder to the saddle. Desmond followed. He secured her to the saddle and then himself behind her. When he had finished, he returned the blade to her throat. As if he needed it. The dragon would have killed anyone attempting to rescue her.

The man flipped Vian over his shoulder and climbed up behind Desmond.

"Kael!" Vian flung the shell that Kaemon had given him. "*Oko vi . . . Oko vi rohryn!*"

Oko, be here. What did he mean? Oko—the old dragon! Vian's ride back to Ganya. A spark of excitement shot through her. The quest would go on!

"You speak elvish?" Desmond's voice snarled into Ayianna's ear. Was he asking her or Vian?

"Not as well as I would like," Vian said. "Something I plan to change."

51

THE BLACK DRAGON stretched its wings and lurched forward.

Kael raced toward it. He pushed himself until his knees nearly buckled. The dragon leapt into the sky, and Kael lunged for its foot but missed. He tumbled down the slope and into the waves below.

He resurfaced, cursing. A hand grabbed his shoulder, hauling him back toward the shore. He spun around, his fist ready to strike.

"Take it easy." Tariq's face was scratched and bloodied.

He shoved Tariq's hand away and splashed toward the shoreline. He clamped his mouth shut on the fiery words burning on his tongue. They raged against Desmond, Saeed, Ayianna, but most of all, Osaryn. How could he? How could he do this to him again? Why couldn't he have remained heartless and cold for the rest of his life? Would the Shadow God continue to torment him?

His footsteps took him to Maewali. And to Kaemon and Jaeger. Kaemon's body had been crushed just a few yards away from the dragon. He would have been a great addition to the quest. Not like Desmond. What would the merking say?

Closer in, Kael halted. Jaeger lay in the sand, his neck twisted. Of all the things the dwarf could have died from . . . He didn't have to join their quest, and now he would never meet his father.

Grief overwhelmed Kael, and his knees buckled. He knelt by Jaeger's side.

Tariq's panther form draped a paw over Jaeger's face, dipping his large muzzle in a feline bow.

Kael closed his eyes. It was all too much. First his family, then Teron, Eloith, Liam, Saeed. The anguish burned deep, his chest aching. *And now this.*

Kael opened his eyes, and his gaze landed on the braid of hair on Jaeger's belt—his mother's. Whatever significance it held to Jaeger; Hadrian would understand. Kael slid the braid free and placed it in his pouch. "We will give him a proper dwarven burial." He stood. "How long until Oko gets here?"

Tariq shook his feline head and loped over to where Jathil lay. Kael joined him. Jathil remained in her fetal position and groaned at Tariq's paw touching her. He licked the blood from her arm, and she shifted.

"Stop that." Her breathing came in short gasps.

"Did you break something?" Kael asked. "Can you move?"

"Hurts to move, breathe. Nothing broken, I don't think."

Tariq withdrew and changed back into his human form. He pressed along Jathil's spine, but when his fingers touched the lower left side of her ribs, she yelped.

"I'm sorry, but I have to see if you've a broken rib or merely cracked it." He continued touching her back, and she grunted in response. "It's not loose. I don't think it's broken."

Kael straightened and placed his hands on his head. How could they continue like this? If Jathil had a cracked rib, she'd be unable to do anything for weeks, months. What were they going to do?

Evening would be upon them soon. The last thing he wanted was to stay one more night on the island, but what if the merfolk didn't come until tomorrow? He took a breath and shoved the panic deeper.

"Tariq, we must prepare to spend the night, but be ready to leave in a moment's notice." Kael strode over to their scattered belongings and picked up a shovel. At least he could give Jaeger and Kaemon a proper burial.

"What do you mean you can't give chase?" Kael glared at Oko's dragon master. Evening had descended, and the remains of Maewali and Kaemon burned bright against the night sky. Jaeger, instead, lay beneath layers of rock and dirt.

"Kolua is a brood female, she won't go farther than a day's ride from her eggs. Oko is too old to make such a journey."

Kael stood and paced through the ferns. "This is ridiculous. We have to—where's Nerissa? Are there no dragons capable of flight?"

The older dragon master shook his head, his gray ponytail brushing the sides of his slender face. "Nerissa has left for Zurial, and with her, the rest of the dragons."

Of course. He knew that. Kael gritted his teeth and stared at the rising cliffs in the distance. The mist from the falls rose into the starlit sky. The moon's pale face frowned upon them like a disappointed headmaster. He faced the dragon master. "How is Jathil? Will we be able to leave tonight?"

"I'll be fine, Kael." Jathil strode up to him, her hand on her side. "The merfolk have done what they can. It's now up to nature to run its course."

Kael frowned. "Don't you think you should return to Ganya?"

"Arashel is my home." Her silver eyes glinted in the flames. Not unlike their first encounter with her. "It is time I face my past."

Kael turned back to the dragon master. "How far can you get us into the Kha Vaaro Mountains?"

"Not in the mountains, the air is too thin for Oko, but we can get you near Arashel."

"Fine, when can we leave?"

"Be still." The dragon master raised his hands and cocked his head. "The dragons need their rest."

Kael kicked the branches he had gathered earlier. He felt a hand on his shoulder. Tariq. He cringed. Why couldn't he maintain his composure better? It wasn't the dragon master's fault. He couldn't fight against nature and win. He rubbed his face with his hands.

"Forgive us," Tariq said. "How long will Oko need to rest? So that we may prepare for our departure."

"Several hours."

Kael groaned. He shrugged Tariq's hand off and stalked away. He heard Tariq apologizing for his behavior which only made him cringe more. If he weren't careful, he'd disgrace the name of elves. The merfolk would think they were all uptight, self-centered, and unable to function under pressure. Whoever heard of an elf losing his self-control?

He made his way to the western shoreline where he and Ayianna watched the storm roll in the other night. He sat down and buried his face in his knees. His words, his actions ate at him. He took a deep breath and blew the air through his nose. He couldn't endure the tangled emotions and thoughts constricting his heart.

Tariq squatted next to him. The essence of peace emanating from Tariq was comforting—much like Saeed—and also annoying. How could he have peace at a time like this?

He lifted his face and rested his arms on his knees. What would he give for peace like that? Or to see Saeed again.

The moon's watery reflection trembled on the waves. "We have to save her. We have to."

"I know, and Vian too."

"Yes." He eyed Tariq. "We have only three months to get the silver pinecone and make it to Gwydion before she turns into a harpy. And probably less than that to save Vian."

"We have to give the ingredients to the Guardian Circle first."

"There's not enough time." Kael shook his head. "I can't go with you. I must go after Ayianna and Vian."

"We'll save them . . . together." Tariq squeezed his shoulder. "Let us pray for their protection and swiftness in the rest of our journey."

Prayer? The last thing Kael wanted to do was pray. He closed his eyes. *Osaryn, where are you? Why didn't you stop this? I can't do this anymore. My soul is dying.*

Do I not love her more than you? This battle is mine. Let go.

Tariq prayed in his native tongue, and the walls Kael had built around his heart quaked. A tear slid down his cheek. He struggled to remain composed, fighting . . . fighting what? Finally, he let go, and the walls burst open. A flood of memories, fears, and failings poured forth. He released it all. And with the emptying of such came peace and hope.

As long as he had breath in him, he would fight.

The journey was not over.

Acknowledgements

Writing is a lonely endeavor, but the journey to bringing a story to the world takes a village or three.

A huge thanks to James, my better half, for his constant support and belief in me and my writing.

To my first critique group, Kassy, Mike, Kymberly, Chris, and Kristen, who saw this story rewritten chapter by chapter. Thank you for teaching this newbie so much!

To the SCALAWAGS! For a safe place to share ideas, questions, and encourage each other. Thank you Robert Mullin and K. M. Carroll for taking the time to read and offer your feedback on this story!

To Rosalie Valentine, you are a dazzling ray of light amid the storms of writing. Thank you for your feedback and being a blessing!

To my editor, Nadine Brandes. I could not have brought this story to where it is now without you. I am forever grateful for you, your friendship, and ninja editing skills.

A special thank you to Ralene Burke for helping me keep my sanity and sift through the herculean task of bringing Darkened Hope to print. As my proofreader, I appreciate your keen eye for details. You rock!

To Lori and Jennifer, my personal publicists. To Rachael for beta reading and sharing your thoughts with me.

And to my Nälu Warriors, you all rock. Thank you for your support!

To God, for without you, I would not be here on this journey where I am living life balanced between reality and dreams.

And to my dear readers and fellow adventurers. Thank you. A hundred times thank you! May you enjoy the next installment of Ayianna's journey.

ABOUT THE AUTHOR

Writing as J. L. Mbewe, Jennette is an author, artist, mother, and wife, but not always in that order. Born and raised in Minnesota, she now braves the heat of Texas, but pines for the Northern Lights and the lakes of home every autumn. She loves trying to capture the abstract and make it concrete. She is currently living her second childhood with a wonderful husband and two precious children, who don't seem to mind her eclectic collections of rocks, shells, and swords, among other things. Here, between reality and dreams, she is busily creating worlds inhabited by all sorts of fantasy creatures and characters, all questing about and discovering true love amid lots of peril. She has two short stories published in *The Clockwork Dragon* anthology, and four short stories set in the world of Nälu. Her debut novel, *Secrets Kept*, was nominated for the 2014 Clive Staples Award.

Stay up-to-date with all things Nälu and her journey as a writer mama at JLMbewe.com.

WHAT TO READ NEXT . . .

The sorceress has Ayianna and Vian, but Kael
and his companions must finish their quest
before they attempt a rescue mission. Except,
they are running out of time. The Curse Bound
are waking and the nations march to war. The
battle for Nälu has begun.

CHAPTER ONE

FOOTSTEPS SLID ACROSS the cobbled stone behind Jathil as she slipped from the shadows to the darkened stairwell. Seven years had passed since she'd crept down these stairs. This part of the keep should have been abandoned.

Instincts sent her hands to the double blades hanging over her shoulder. Whoever followed her would die a quick, silent death.

No. No more blood will be spilt. She lowered her hands. Years of living as an exile had hardened her.

Jathil eyed the narrow stairway that led to her old room. Her chest tightened. Memories threatened to overwhelm her, but she couldn't give into them now. She had to remain focused. Afterward, she could cling to her mother and weep, but for now she had to live long enough to reach her father.

Maybe she should have listened to Kael. He had insisted their group enter Arashel properly and pretend they were returning her for the reward. But no. Her people, her father, had to know she had returned willingly to face her crimes. She would endure whatever punishment her father demanded in the hopes of aiding the quest and saving her friends.

Ayianna's disheveled form flashed in her mind's eye. Her dress soiled and torn, blood and dirt smudging her face. A scene of destruction all around her—the giant trees splintered, the ground tore up and littered with bodies of imps and men alike. Desmond had commanded the sorceress's dragon and held their lives in his hand.

Jathil flinched. She could still feel the crushing pain of her injured rib, the sting of the blade at her neck, and the humiliation of being so helpless. Ayianna had surrendered in order to save her friends. In order to save Jathil. Resolve burned in Jathil's gut. She would do what she had to do to rescue her friends. Even if that meant returning home to face her father, the king of Arashel.

He would be able to provide them with his fastest horses and enough supplies to cross the desert. Even if he didn't forgive her, she'd make certain Tariq and Kael would at least receive the bounty on her head. Then they could purchase whatever their journey demanded.

Hopefully, it wouldn't come to that.

Two shadows skimmed over the stones toward her hiding place, passing through the shards of moonlight cutting across the corridor. Her staff would be awkward, her blades quicker, but she couldn't risk adding another death to the growing list of crimes against her.

Jathil sniffed the air. Their scents were familiar, and her fear dissolved into anger.

She unsheathed one of her blades. As they slipped into the stairwell, she sprang and pressed the blade against the chest of the first one.

"Fools." She shoved the word through her clenched teeth. "I told you to stay behind."

Tariq's dark skin, curly hair, and beard blended into the shadows, but his amber eyes glimmered in the dim light. He leaned away from the blade. "We will not let you do this alone."

"But you could be caught for trespassing." Jathil lowered her arm and sheathed her blade. "Do you know what Arashel does to trespassers?"

Tariq nodded.

Kael stood behind him, blinking his eyes. The elf wouldn't be able to see anything in such darkness.

"Why didn't you leave Kael with our belongings?" Jathil frowned. "It's not like an elf can sneak around like a Haruzo."

Kael's brow furrowed, causing the scar across his left brow to bulge. "I can take care of myself."

Jathil rubbed her right side, the rib aching at her touch. She sighed. "If something goes wrong, you will jeopardize the entire quest."

"But it won't." Tariq squeezed her shoulder. "Kael and I are here to make sure you get to your father safely. A father cannot deny his child, can he?"

"Right, and what about yours?" The words slipped out before Jathil could stop them.

"I never knew him." Tariq cocked his head. "But we aren't talking about a stranger who abandoned his wife and child. I have met your father. He is a great Haruzo. Misled, perhaps, to stand in opposition to the guardians."

"He is also a king with obligations to uphold the law." Jathil took a deep breath. "But I hope you're right."

Wasn't that what she was counting on? That the father she knew as a child lay somewhere beneath the cold, callous exterior. Still, he couldn't just overlook what she had done. If it meant aid for Kael and Tariq, then she could live without her hand—if her father let her live at all.

"Let's get this over with."

She bent over as white and black fur rushed over her body. She relished the tingling of her skin and the surge of power that ran through her. Her feline form would gain her stealth, speed, and a heightened awareness of her surroundings, but her splotchy fur would not blend well with the shadows. A risk she was willing to take.

She sprang up the stairwell leading to her old room, her padded paws silencing her footsteps. Her whiskers brushed on the icy stone walls and sent tremors along her spine. She swiveled her feline ears, straining to catch the slightest sound.

In a few moments, she would see the face of her father. Her mother. Oh, how she longed to embrace her! And what of Bremli? Surely her little brother was not so little anymore. Then there was Mathani.

The tremor in her heart grew. What kind of reception would she receive?

She flexed her claws and maintained her composure. She had come home to face her past, her crimes. Let the Shadow

God's will be done, for she was done fleeing and hiding. If he saw fit for her to die, then so be it. She whispered a prayer of protection over her companions. And that Ayianna and Prince Vian might yet live.

Musty, stale air and a flood of bittersweet memories greeted Jathil as she stepped into her old room. The stillness pressed against her ears, her heart growing heavier. Cobwebs hung from corners in the ceiling and clung to the large bed. Mold, like a layer of fur, covered the wood and covers. A dark hearth sat lifeless against the far wall. On the opposite side was her wardrobe, the large mirror, and plumb chair. All exactly how she had left it.

Except for the portrait of her father. It had been removed from her room, but she didn't care. The painter hadn't captured her father's love. And the last thing she needed was his stern expression to crush her already quivering resolve.

Jathil stretched into her human form once more, avoiding Tariq and Kael's stares. She swept the cobwebs from the wardrobe and opened it. Her dresses and royal robes remained inside. Splotches of mold had ruined the fine fabrics. Worthless now. Not that she would ever go back to that kind of life, but at least her parents could have given them away. Instead, they sat within her wardrobe, decaying with time.

On the other wall, a heavy door separated her from her parents. Any moment her mother would sweep inside in her fur-trimmed robe like she had done so many times before. All her royal clothes and duties set aside, she would be there to brush Jathil's hair and chat about life, her father, and the mess Jathil had made of things.

And what a mess it was! Jathil ran her fingers through her choppy, short hair. In that moment, no matter the battles she had fought or how independent she had become, the desire to rush to her mother shot through her.

No doubt, after so many years, her mother no longer came to her room. The guilt and sorrow pierced her. How her mother must have felt! Jathil vowed to make it up to her even if her father sentenced her to death. She took a deep breath and buried the desire deeper. She couldn't allow her emotions to interfere with her mission.

"You should be safe here." Scanning the room one last time, she pressed her hand against the door. On the other side, she would meet her judgment and everything she had been running from. She glanced back at Kael and Tariq. "My father's private chamber is on the other end. I will go first, but, if anything should go wrong, you must leave at once. No one should be in the servant's stairwell at this time of night, especially since there hasn't been a reason for a servant to attend to these chambers for the past seven years."

"Let us help you." Tariq crossed the room to her.

Jathil held up her hand. "My business is my own. The choices, the accusations, the crimes—I must answer for them. But you do not. Your priority is to the Alliance and getting the tonic's ingredients back to the plains before the sorceress marches to war."

"Or sacrifices Vian to the queen of the Underworld," Kael added. His long black hair spilled over his shoulders and hid his pointed ears. He had left his bow and quiver of arrows with their supplies, but his sword still hung at his hip.

Jathil squeezed his shoulder. Kael didn't have to say the rest. The ache in his heart went beyond Vian or the tonic.

"If we don't help you and you fail, we will either freeze to death or starve in the mountains. And if we survive long enough to make it to the desert?" Kael shook his head. "We need you to succeed more than you realize."

Jathil snorted, which shot pain through her side. She touched her ribs. The dull ache continued to throb. Heaviness threaded through her muscles as the events of the past few weeks caught up to her. No, the past few years. All the fighting. All the running and hiding. She needed rest.

"How are your ribs?" Tariq's voice yanked her out of her reverie.

"Better." She breathed in slowly and exhaled. "Still has a sting to it."

"No fighting." His gaze dropped to the staff in her hands.

"Of course." Jathil twisted the staff, unwilling to part with it. She dropped it on her bed and unbuckled her double blades from her back. She placed them next to the staff. Without weapons, the guards could not mistake her intentions. Besides, she had other ways to fight. She faced Tariq, feeling naked and vulnerable. "I am here to answer for my crimes, not add to it. It is you that I am worried about. I have a right to be here, you do not."

"We could have pretended to turn you over for the reward." Kael's hand rested on the hilt of his sword. He had better not try to take on the king's guards. He wouldn't stand a chance.

"Too late for that." Tariq frowned. "Just be careful."

"Promise me, you will leave and not look back." She searched their eyes, willing them to forsake her. Yet deep within, she could not deny the comfort their presence gave her. "We cannot let Ayianna and Vian down, nor the guardians and all of Nälu, on the account of me."

Tariq and Kael remained silent and avoided her gaze.

"Promise me."

Tariq nodded slowly.

She turned away, holding their faces in her mind's eye. She pushed against the door. It creaked loudly and grated against her fraying nerves.

An oil lamp lit the end of the corridor. Cobwebs hung in the corners and dirt gathered in the stone's crevices. She sniffed the air for the scent of others. Her father, mother. Servants. Guards. Everything smelled of cat, but nothing smelled fresh. Perhaps her parents had abandoned this side of the keep as well.

Jathil glanced back at Tariq and Kael. "Thank you . . . for everything."

Tariq frowned. "This isn't goodbye."

If only that were true.

Jathil slipped through the doorway and crept toward her father's chamber. She barred the onslaught of thoughts and memories threatening to drown her. She'd have time enough to deal with it later, especially if her father threw her into the dungeons.

Closer and closer, she inched. The thick wood door loomed larger and more foreboding with each step. The trembling started in her core and swept toward her extremities. She clutched her fingers into tight fights and drew a long steady breath. A few more feet.

A gleam of white, and Jathil froze. A snow leopard sprang from the shadows and into the dancing light. Then, in one swift movement, a man stood in its place and held a spear at her throat.

"Who are you, and what business do you have here?"

Jathil couldn't move, couldn't speak. How had she not sensed him?

"Answer me! Or I'll slit your throat for trespassing."

"I am Tirza Jathil." She forced the words out. "I have come to see my father."

"Of course, you are. Do you know how many imposters have been paraded around in front of the king to receive the reward over the years? And why would you be sneaking in? If you knew the crimes she was accused of, you would not be coming in on your own freewill."

"Can you not smell me?"

He barely sniffed at her. "You smell like a wild goat."

"Please. I need to see him—and my mother."

"The queen has been dead for the past three years."

Jathil gasped and sank back. "You lie!"

"Why would I?" He pushed the spear forward, but hesitation flickered in his eyes. "No one sees the king without his permission."

Jathil lunged forward, but the man jabbed the spear toward her. She somersaulted over it and slammed into the door.

"Father!" she cried and banged her fist on its polished wood.

The man grabbed her from behind and yanked her backward. "The king doesn't like to be disturbed."

A growl shook the evening. Jathil and the guard froze. A large man, who looked more like a lion, towered above them. He was older, much older than she had expected.

"What is the meaning of this?" he bellowed, his voice filling the small corridor.

The guard jerked her upright. The shaft of the spear pressed against her neck, crushing her airway. "I apologize, Your Majesty. Just an intruder."

Jathil shifted, easing the pressure on her neck, and cried out, "Father!"

The beast of a man looked down at her, and his face hardened. "I have no daughter."

THE
TALES
OF NÄLU

GO DEEPER
THE TALES OF NÄLU

Can a desert princess find love with a foreign king?

Johari lives in the shadow of her beautiful sister until a foreign king notices her, but in her haste to prove herself worthy of affection, she finds herself compromised and on a difficult journey to make things right.

—◦◦◦◦◦—

What if all you knew was a lie?

The teaching of the guardians has guided Semine's footsteps since her infancy. When her mentor shows up with information contrary to what she's been taught, she doubts her decision to follow in their footsteps. She must decide if there is life beyond what she has always known or embrace a new, mysterious path and reject the Guardians' legacy.

To what lengths would you go to save the world?

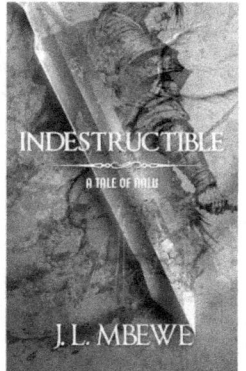

Elothryn keeps the darkest secret of Nälu: the cursed dagger of Raemoja. A weapon powerful enough to release the greatest evil from the underworld.

For generations, his family has lived without incident until now. The hunters have his scent and will stop at nothing to reclaim the dagger. Elothryn and his son flee, seeking help, but will they find it?

The hunt will choose her mate, but she will choose her destiny.

A hunt to the death will determine the mate of Princess Tirza Jathil and the future king of Arashel. When the Guardian Lazar shows up with two stones that could change the outcome of it all, Tirza must decide who to trust or risk losing more than she will ever know.